# Ruthless Obsession

# Ruthless Obsession

## A Silver Dingo Mystery

## When Family Is Involved - It's Personal

K.A. Hudson

Arrowsmith Publishing

A catalogue record for this book is available from the National Library of Australia

ISBN: 978-0-6452708-4-6 (Paperback)
ISBN: 978-0-6452708-5-3 (Ebook)

Printed & Channel Distribution: Lightning Source | Ingram (USA/UK/EUROPE/AUS)
Cover Designed—Laila Savolainen, Pickawoowoo Publishing Group
Publishing Consultants/Interior Design—Pickawoowoo Publishing Group
Arrowsmith Publishing: www.arrowsmithpublishing.com.au
About the author: https://kerriehudsonauthor.wixsite.com/website-1
For enquiries, write to: rights and permissions via publisher.

*To the men and women of the defence and police services, who daily put their lives on the line to protect the freedoms we all take for granted – Thank you.*

# 1

## Chapter One

The door slammed. My heart turned to stone.

Everything was grey. The walls, the ceiling, even the surrounding light. There were no windows and the air was filled with a stale musty tang that sat on my tongue like sandpaper. In one corner sat a stainless-steel toilet. In front of it the bare concrete floor was stained by fluids I didn't want to know about. The toilet gave a watery burp as an air bubble escaped the pipes. A shiver ran down my spine. This was my future.

On shaky legs I stumbled over to the concrete pallet opposite and collapsed onto the thin, blue-plastic mattress. The sour taste of fear and uncertainty churned around in my guts. To fight off the sensation, I curled into a tight ball, gripped my knees to my chest and swallowed hard against the bile scorching the back of my throat. A muscle spasm in my arm forced me to unknot my hands and roll onto my back. The abruptness of the movement threatened to set off a cramp in my calf. When I jerked my leg straight against the tension forming, I knocked the thin, grey wool blanket onto the grungy floor. Months of training kicked in. I leapt to my feet, picked the blanket up and folded it into a perfect rectangle before setting it parallel to the edge of the mattress. I took my time to ensure the space around its edges were of the same dimension. One did what one had to, to avoid giving the jailors a reason to punish.

*Dig deep, Faith. You've survived far worse. Life in this ugly jail cell should be easy for you.*

I was caught by surprise when a rib shaking sob escaped my clamped lips. It unlocked the nightmarish memories I'd valiantly held at bay all day. They flooded in and released a fearsome re-action. It started as a small jitterbug in my chest, radiated out and became a bone shaking tremor in all my limbs. My teeth joined the party and began to rattle as my whole body shook as though experiencing a force seven earthquake. In an attempt to get control, I threw myself onto the mattress, clamped my hands between my knees and squeezed. My injured arm and wrist throbbed in protest at the pressure I applied, but I managed to ignore the pain until the tremors waned enough for me to take some long, deep, calming breaths. When I felt I had some semblance of control I eased my grip and glanced down at the grubby bandage, that ran the full length of my left forearm, to check if I had done it any further damage. The once white cloth was stained with dried blood, but no fresh seepage wet its surface. Sucking in another large lungful of stale air, I reminded myself that along with black eyes, split lips, bruised ribs and mental anguish my arm was just another memento of the harsh life I'd been living, and the brutality that had come with it. A cold tentacle of bitterness merged itself around the icy lump centred in my chest. The frost there wasn't new. It was something I'd endured for long time. Lying on the cold bed, I cursed at my past stupidity. I should have heeded the warning in my gut when events started to go pear shape. Hindsight is a wonderful thing but offers no solace to the sufferer.

The toilet ceased it persistent burps, a quiet settled around me. The musty air hung like a heavy curtain as dull light dimmed the cell. Beyond the thick grey-rendered walls and locked metal door night approached. Not even a footstep disturbed the silence.

Alone in my prison, I ignored the cold rising from the uncomfortable slab beneath me and gave up the fight against the memories. The recollections crowded in, made themselves at home. I marvelled at the small unimportant incidents in life that determine the path a person's future will take.

My path to murder started when I forgot to set my alarm.

# 2

# Chapter Two

MC, my red Mini Cooper hatch, tore through the university car park at break-neck speed as I searched for a vacant parking bay. I love my car, with its jazzy black racing stripes and zippy little motor. I named her MC, short for megacycle, because I consider her one in a million. She was usually a reliable dream to drive, but today, MC, along with the universe, had ganged up on me.

My name is Faith Bergman, generally referred to by one and all as Burger. I'm a little on the short side, well a fair bit actually, but we won't go into that. I'm plump and resemble my nickname, something else I'm a touch sensitive about. My long, wavy brown hair is described by my cousin as, quote, 'chestnut with interesting copper highlights,' unquote. It lives in an untidy heap secured to the back of my head because it's an easy hairstyle to maintain. Easy is good as far as I'm concerned. I'm lazy when it comes to fashion. Depending on the season I live in shorts or tracksuit pants, oversized tees or sweatshirts. All are a cinch to wash, don't require the application of a hot iron and, most important, hides a multitude of sins as far as my figure is concerned. I hate to be rushed so refuse to indulge in anything that resembles excessive exercise.

This morning my way of doing things had backfired on me. It all started with Fleabag – my neighbour's tortoiseshell cat. She'd scratched and meowed with persistence at my bedroom window in a loud demand to be let in. The loathsome beast destroyed my delicious sleep and forced me to the surface of unwanted consciousness.

I cracked one gritty eye open to a dark gloomy room. 'Sheesh, what's a girl have to do to get some sleep around here.' I slipped a furtive hand out from under the covers, grappled around on the floor next to the bed until my fumbling fingers located one of my Oakley sneakers. I hurled it as hard as I could across the room in the general direction of where the cat had its face pressed against the glass pane. My shoe landed with a resounding thump on the window frame. Fleabag scarpered with a yowl of protest. With a grunt of satisfaction I snuggled back under my warm covers. Unfortunately, my treacherous brain was now wide awake and began to buzz with random thoughts, making delicious sleep an elusive commodity. Snuggling further down into the warmth of my bedding I decided to make the most of the opportunity to catch up on my social media. I slipped my glitzy pink phone case from under my pillow and glanced at the bold numbered time on its face.

'Bloody hell!' I screeched, as I bolted upright.

Somehow, I'd slept through my usual shower, breakfast and calmly leave for university time. When I checked the alarm, it was off. Chucking back the thick doona, I tumbled from my bed and received the second shock of the morning. It was bloody freezing in my room. I wanted to kick myself. Not only had I forgotten to set my phone alarm, I'd also missed flicking on the timer for the central heating. A few choice words slipped seamlessly from my lips as I scooped up a set of pre-worn clothes from my bedroom floor.

I was still shovelling my legs into my track pants as I descended the stairs. Unbalanced, I stumbled on the bottom step and fell flat on my face.

'Goddamn, evil universe,' I cursed.

Rolling onto my back I hiked my old, tatty track pants into place, sat up, bundled my sleep mussed mop into a pile on the back of my head and stabbed it into place with a chopstick hairclip. Vetoing the idea of a visit to the fridge for a tasty morsel of left-over lasagne, because I wouldn't stop at one bite, I lunged to my feet, snatched up my lecture notes and textbooks from the kitchen table and made a beeline for the shoe rack by the front door. Jamming my feet into a pair of old sneakers, I didn't bother tying the laces. They could wait. I flung open the front door to be greeted by a wet, stormy day, and a sodden furry bundle of fury. The angry tornado scurried between my legs, leaving a wet trail across the parquet floor, as she made a frantic dash across the living room and bolted up the stairs.

'Bloody hell, you scruffy, technicolour, flea pit! Why don't you go annoy everyone in your own home instead of haunting me?' I didn't have time to hunt the cat down to evict her from the premises, so I did the next best thing. I sucked in a large lungful of the crisp morning air and let rip. 'Stay off my bed or I'll wring your scrawny neck.'

I doubted Fleabag would listen, or obey, but at least I felt better for having laid down the law. Slamming the front door closed behind me, I pulled up the collar of my royal-blue and ash-grey UWA sweat-shirt, hunched my shoulders so my chin and ears sank deep into the material, and sprinted out into the downpour. MC usually resides behind a locked roller door in the comfort of a dry garage. Today she stood out in the cold, wet street in front of the townhouse. To make ends meet I was employed at a 24/7 café called, The Mariners. Most nights I worked shifts that didn't finish until the early hours of the morning. The previous night, cold and grumpy, I'd arrived home at 1 a.m. To avoid freezing my butt off while I opened and closed the garage's heavy roller door, when all I'd wanted was to be inside where it was warm, I'd opted to leave her parked at the kerb. I shook my fist at the icy rain as it hurled from the sky in giant blobs as I hastened over to MC. After two attempts and a broken fingernail, my wet fingers finally managed to reef open the car door. Soaked to the skin I dove behind the steering wheel. Frozen to the core I blew on my cold digits until they warmed enough to insert the key in the ignition. Anticipating the happy purr of MC's engine, my heart sank like a stone when all I got was a flaccid growl. Once again, I cursed the fates and a drained car battery. I took a deep breath, lifted my eyes up to the heavens and, with a silent prayer, turned the key again. This time MC gave a guttural grunt, shuddered and kicked sluggishly into life. I shoved the accelerator flat to the floor. She responded to the glut of fuel with a lethargic stutter. I kept my foot planted and shivered my way through the blast of frigid air that spewed from the air vents as I waited for satisfactory engine noises to be emitted from under MC's hood. The first hint she'd gotten over her sulk was a thin trickle of lukewarm air and a roar from the engine.

*Good enough.*

I jammed the gearstick at first gear. The transmission crunched in protest and refused to engage. Eyes shut I sucked in a lungful of air and counted to twenty. I had to slow down. My frantic state was only making matters worse. Taking control of myself I used a gentle hand and applied a small amount of pressure to the stick. The gear engaged with a satisfying click. Heaving a sigh of relief I tentatively lifted my foot from the clutch. MC rolled forward, gave a shudder, followed by a series of kangaroo hops.

'No baby!' I pleaded, as I slammed my foot down on the clutch and gunned the accelerator, 'don't stall. Please don't stall.'

The last thing I needed right then was for her to conk out right in the middle of the road because she may not start again. MC's rough motor noises smoothed. I sucked my bottom lip between my teeth, crossed my fingers and tried again. This time MC decided to behave by rolling down the street with a happy purr.

'Way to go girl!' I cried, planting my foot hard on the accelerator.

We took off at speed. Tires splashed up huge waves as they ran through giant rain puddles that had pooled on the bitumen. The wiper blades struggled to bat away the thick sheets of water that cascaded down the outside of the windscreen. It was hard to see but I still pushed the speed limit on the slippery roads, praying that any hidden speed cameras would be just as blinded by the heavy rain. As I turned onto Stirling Terrace and eased up for the turn into the University of WA's car park, MC gave a jerk and almost stalled.

I didn't appreciate my car's antics. 'Come on, you she-devil,' I yelled at her. 'Get a move on. We need to find you a place to park. You then have my permission to sulk.'

MC responded to my promise and the glut of fuel I fed her, with a surge of speed.

'Good girl,' I said, patting the steering wheel.

We circled around the packed parking bays, having no luck finding an empty spot. It seemed like every man and his dog in Albany had driven their car in that day, probably because of the bad weather.

'How rude! Well, if the campus can't provide enough parking, I'll just park in any available space I can find,' I informed MC, eying off a garden bed as a potential spot. Right at that moment my logical brain kicked in and began to argue with me. 'You do know that if you don't use, *'A designated and approved parking area'*, you'll cop a hefty fine from the rat-faced weasel, right?'

The rat-face weasel, or RFW as I sometimes called him, was Russ Johnson, the university's campus security guard. He's a scrawny, sharp featured bloke, with a black smudge moustache under a wedge-of-cheese shaped nose. RFW's face reminds me of those evil rats you see in cartoon movies. Hence the nickname. He's a smarmy, creep. I dislike him intensely. On my first day on campus, he sidled up to me and took up residence in my personal space. With a supercilious smile, he'd leant in close to introduce himself. Being the polite girl I was raised to be, I'd stepped back, given him a timid smile and held out my hand to take the parking permit he had clutched in his fist. Instead of just handing it over he'd clasped my fingers between both his sweaty palms and had given them an intimate squeeze. Uck! My sleaze-o-meter had registered off the charts, and I'd felt a strong urge to take a shower in bleach. After that he'd haunted my every foot-step on campus. When I parked, he would appear from nowhere and insist on walking me to my classroom. At the end of each lecture, I'd find him loitering in the corridor for one of our *special chats* - his term, not mine. Somewhere along the line, he'd gotten hold of my mobile telephone number and began to text me at all hours, wanting to know where I was, who I was with and what I was doing. It was downright scary. After some wise words and a not so gentle nudge from my cousin Chips, I found the courage to stand up to him and tell him if he didn't leave me alone, I'd report him to one of our campus councillors for harassment. After my threat, Russ had changed tack. Any indiscretion on my part resulted in him issuing me a hefty on-the-spot fine. It was like a red rag to a bull. I did everything to thumb my nose at him. As far as I was concerned it was all out war.

'I'll just have to give up Tim Tams and Maltesers for the next month to pay the parking ticket. A hard ask I know, to give up all that chocolate, but sometimes sacrifices must be made.' A brave vow on my part because I love my treats. I steered MC around three yellow safety bollards into a new row. 'No snacks are a better option than having to slog through the extra work Professor Murray will assign me if I'm late to his lecture.'

MC's response to me - she swished her wiper blades, cleared the sheeting rain on the windscreen long enough for me to spot a lone empty parking bay deep in the back of the lot. With a delighted grin I steered her rather crookedly into the space. I didn't bother to straighten her little red butt – no time. My heart pounded a mile a minute as I grabbed my books and lecture notes from the passenger seat and tumbled out of the door. With shoe laces whipping at my ankles and the soles sighing, I lumbered my heavy frame through the downpour and headed along the concrete footpath to the historical front entrance of the 1869 university building. The four-faced clock tower that sprouted from the building's roof, taunted me with a reminder of the lateness of the hour. My chest heaved as I blasted through the main doors. The soles of my wet shoes let out a loud squeak as they made contact with the ceramic floor tiles. I ignored the noise as I pelted along the main corridor. Rounding a corner into a new corridor, I slammed into something warm, solid and muscular, but was saved from landing in an indignant heap on my butt by two strong arms. They pulled me in close. My face snuggled into soft blue cotton that smelt deliciously of black pepper and patchouli. Too surprised to think I closed my eyes and breathed the scent deep into my being.

'Hmm, delicious,' I sighed.

A bark of laughter caused heat to flood my cheeks. Oh God, I'd spoken my thoughts out loud. Embarrassed I scurried backwards to stare up into a pair of silver-grey eyes, framed by long, thick, black lashes. They were crinkled in the corners by what I chose to interpret as amusement.

'I'm so sorry,' I gasped, as another wave of humiliation raised my blood pressure even further.

The amused young man's face seemed to hover way above me. Mind you everyone does seem to tower over me. I don't quite reach 155cm on a tall day. And before you ask, in the old language, that's around five foot. Anyway, his top lip lifted in a crooked smile and a very sexy dimple appeared in the corner of his mouth. My knees turned to unset jelly, and I had trouble standing.

'Don't be sorry, Sunflower,' he said, in a delicious bass tone. 'You've just made my day.'

I tried to form a coherent sentence. 'I...I...hi.'

'Hi, yourself.'

I let my gaze luxuriate up his very fit frame before hovering over his extremely handsome face, drinking in the kissable lips and a cute black curl of hair that formed a half-moon on his forehead. My brain ceased to work. My hormones kicked into high gear because he was so yum! He crooked an eyebrow and my stomach flipped. Butterflies fluttered and swirled as I wordlessly gazed upon him in fascination.

Waving his long slender fingers in front of my face, as if to break the spell I'd fallen under, the gorgeous man said, 'I hope I pass inspection.'

A fresh wave of heat rushed to my cheeks. They burnt like a red-hot incinerator. I snapped my mouth shut and swallowed. 'Y-y-yes...I mean...Oh crap. I'm sorry for crashing into you.'

'That's okay, my pleasure in fact. Having you throw yourself into my arms like that has made my day. My name is Ashley. Ashley Watson. You are?'

'Faith Bergman,' a male voice squawked down the hallway behind me. It was Russ Johnson. I'd recognise his nasal squeak anywhere. I turned. He tugged a notebook from his top pocket as he jack-booted his way towards us. 'I'm going to issue you a fine for running at breakneck speed in the hallway.'

'No way, come on. That's so unfair.'

Before I could argue further he started to prattle on about the safety of other students. I watched his moustache wriggle up and down, not really taking in the words he spoke, so bemused was I that he knew I'd been sprinting for a class. Russ stopped pontificating and waited for some sort of response from me. I was about to put into action my cousin's sage advice and turn my back on him when Ashley leant forward and ran his forefinger under the name tag pinned to Russ's blue chambray shirt.

'Mr Johnson, is it?'

Russ nodded and puffed out his chest. 'Campus Security.'

'Well, Mr Johnson, you must be mistaken. My friend isn't running down the corridor, she's standing here talking with me. I think you owe her an apology.'

Russ flushed.

'Hmm...yes, well. I'm watching you, young lady.' He shoved a finger in my face to emphasise his words and stalked away.

Amazed, I turned to stare after him. All I'd received was a lecture but no fine. Well, there was a bonus.

'Well, that was rude...ah, Faith, is it?' said Ashley.

Interest recaptured, I promptly forgot about the amazing sight of RFW being put in his place and feasted on the gorgeousness beside me. 'Yeah, but call me, Burger. Everyone does.'

'Burger?'

'Short for Bergman, plus I'm shaped a bit like a burger.' I stared down at my sodden, oversized clothes, pudgy figure and silently cursed the fact that I wasn't looking my best at that precise moment.

A hand landed with a thump on my shoulder, causing me to fumble the pile of books that were miraculously still cradled in my arms. A heavy text slid from my clasp and fell sharp corner down onto Ashley's foot. My face flamed again.

'Oh God,' I cried. 'I'm so sorry.'

The owner of the hand swung me around and breathed frantically in my face, 'Burger, your late! Where have you been?'

It was my cousin, Lucy 'Chips' Chippens. We live together and are both students at the Albany UWA campus. Chips is studying criminal law. In my opinion she is going to make a great lawyer. Besides being super smart, she can articulate a point with razor sharp precision. I, on the other hand, would make a terrible lawyer, mainly because I take everyone at face value, believe everything I'm told and can't argue a point, even if I know I'm right. My interests lay in the forensic side of things. I love to study physical evidence and puzzle out its meaning! My dream job would be reviewing cold cases and breathing new life into them.

Chips's words jolted me back into reality and the reason I had been rushing. I stared at her impish, elfin face, haloed by a crop of short, blue-black curls and gasped, 'Oh crap, Professor Murray's lecture! How late am I?'

'Ten minutes. Normally I'd suggest you slope off and get a sick note but you're in luck, the thunderstorm earlier knocked out the power. It's only just been restored. Class was delayed twenty minutes, to give the computers and servers time to reboot. That time's almost up. Come on, we need to hurry, before the professor arrives and notices we're not in our seats.'

She grasped my forearm and tugged me towards the lecture hall. Ashley placed a hand on my shoulder to halt my progress. I stared down at the *Crime and Justice – A guide to Criminology* textbook he held out and remembered his foot.

Before I could turn into a stuttering fool, again, he asked, 'Are you taking criminology with Professor Murray?'

I nodded. Chips gave a frantic tug on my arm. 'Yes, sorry we have to go...the Prof, well, he's a great teacher but rewards tardiness with extra work.'

Ashley followed us to the door. 'Mind if I tag along.'

'Come on!' growled Chips.

I nodded, giving him permission to join us and hurried after my cousin, leaving Ashley to follow in our wake. We made it to our seats just as Professor Murray entered the room. He ignored the assembled students and started fiddling with a laptop computer and overhead projector. While I flipped open my notes and textbooks, ready to focus on the class, I nudged Chips with my elbow and jerked a thumb at our new companion.

'This is Ashley Watson. Ashley this is my BCE, Chips.'

'BCE?' asked Ashley, his brows kicking together in a cute look of confusion.

'Best cousin ever,' I smiled.

'Hi ya, Ash. Welcome,' said Chips, giving him a finger wave.

'It's Ashley.'

'What?' Her nose wrinkled in puzzlement.

'My name is Ashley, not Ash,' he said. His voice was cold and his face expressionless.

Chips rolled her eyes at his correction and turned away from him. She flipped through her textbook and twirled her pen over her knuckles in a classic sign of irritation. A knot formed in my stomach. I don't know why, but I wanted these two to like each other.

I noticed Ashley was unencumbered by any books or writing implements, so I lifted my own notebook in an unspoken question.

He leant forward to breathe in my ear, 'I'm an author, doing research for my novel by sitting in on a few lectures.' Strange, I thought as I surreptitiously reached under the desk to tie my sodden shoelaces, I would have thought a writer would be prepared to take copious notes. My puzzlement was chased away when Ashley smiled down at me and whispered, 'Will you go out for coffee with me, Sunflower?'

Chips leant around behind me and growled, 'Her name's Burger, not Sunflower. Now shush. The professor's ready to start and you'll get us into trouble. I for one could do without any extra assignments.'

Ashley frowned. He opened his mouth but whatever he was going to say remained unspoken because the Professor began to speak.

'Criminology is the study of crime from a sociological perspective. Criminologists focus on the causes of crime and the social effect crime has on society. Throughout your career as a criminologist, you may travel the road for the development of effective policy aimed at the prevention of crimes in the future...'

# 3

## Chapter Three

'There was no need to be so rude to Ashley,' I said, as I fed my arms through the straps of the dull-grey work apron.

Once again Chips and I had won the Friday night roster raffle at the Mariners Cafe. First prize - the dreaded 9 p.m. to 3 a.m. shift. Just what a girl wanted to face after the previous night's late shift, the dramatic start to the morning and a full day of university lectures – not!

'Well, he was being a prat,' snarled Chips. With a firm hand she spun me around so she could jerk the apron strings tight around my waist. 'My name is Ashley, not Ash!' she parroted. 'What a snob. And who is he to come in and change your name.'

I sighed and chose to ignore her tantrum. Chips and I had been almost inseparable since birth. At the age of five we had taken a pinkie-swear to always love and look out for one another. Neither of us had faltered in that promise, although Chips could sometimes take it to extremes. I think her over-protectiveness stemmed from the time my parents died. Since that day, Chips had done everything within her power to ease the pain of my loss. To that end she still watches over me like a hawk in an attempt to stop me ever being hurt again. And that's one of the many reasons why I love her so much.

Chips was blessed with a willowy figure, crystal clear chartreuse-green eyes and the ability to look crisp and elegant, no matter what she wore, even the ugly washed-out work aprons our boss insisted we wear. I tied her apron strings around her svelte waist. 'Sign us in will you,' I said, giving her a gentle nudge towards the timesheet board with my hip as I made my way out to the service counter to relieve the guys who'd worked the previous shift.

I lifted my hand to wave farewell to the tall, lanky cook, Jim and his pimple-faced sidekick. Thirty-year-old Jim usually manned the kitchen grill, noon to 9 p.m. every day except Wednesdays. He never spoke much, which I put down to extreme shyness, but he always took the time to listen. Brad, the eighteen-year-old barista, on the other hand, was always eager for a chat and as they made their way out the door he was busy bending Jim's ear with a detailed description of the fun and frivolity he had planned for the rest of the evening.

After the door closed on Brad's babble I turned to my cousin and said, 'Chips, Ashley asked me out on a date.'

Her jaw fell open and she stared bug-eyed at me as if I were an alien. 'Wow that was fast. You only met each other a few minutes before class started.'

'What? Do you reckon it takes longer than that to want to take out an ugly frump like me?'

'No, Burger. You're not an ugly frump. Will you stop being so down on yourself.'

'Well, I am. Just look at me,' I said, pointing down at my waistline.

'You only need a little toning.'

'You know I hate to exercise.'

'Ahem.' A man's polite cough broke into our squabble.

I cut a glance to the other side of the service counter and saw a tall, lithe soldier who wore an Australian army slouch hat perch in the perfect position on his head. He held his back ramrod straight with his top lip stiff. A row of campaign ribbons pinned on the left side of his dress uniform lined up ruler straight with the white name tag pinned above his right breast pocket. It read Captain R. Lamb. The only incongruous image to the whole picture of gorgeous military elegance was the German Shepherd dog leaning affectionately against his leg. I smiled down at the panting, happy animal, then up at his master. The captain's eyes resembled tiger-eye gemstones, a golden hazel-brown with a silky lustre that a girl could drown in. Deep in my heart I felt a tiny glow of warmth.

'Steak sandwich, no onion or salad and a caramel milkshake, please,' he murmured.

I studied his face for a moment. Pain lines were etched at the corners of his eyes. I held back on the social chit chat I usually like to have with my customers and rang up the order on the till in uncustomary silence. Chips still hovered at my shoulder. Before she could say anything indiscreet or try to chat the guy up, I jerked my head towards the kitchen. 'You're on grill. A steak sanga, hold the salad and onion,' I barked.

She stalked off to prepare the order as I counted out the change for a fifty dollar note.

'I'm sorry,' I said, glancing down at the dog beside him. 'Pets aren't allowed in the dining room. But you can take your dog into the alfresco area. If you would like to take a seat outside, I'll bring your order out when it's ready.'

He gave me a short, sharp nod, clicked his tongue once and together the man and dog marched towards the glass swing doors that opened to the outside seating area. I caught Chips craning her neck through the service hatch, in an attempt to get a good look at the soldier's butt as he strode away. I followed suit and I must say she had the right idea because it was rather a nice view. I cocked an eyebrow at her. She gave a sheepish grin and withdrew from sight. As I whipped up the milkshake, I felt sorry for the young officer. The café was empty and warm. It seemed ludicrous he and the dog should have to sit out in the cold. But rules were rules. Nobody would thank me for bringing the health inspector down upon us by allowing them a seat at a booth inside, especially not the café's manager, Brian Zelinski.

Chips slid a white paper package across the stainless-steel counter towards me. With a cheeky grin, she dinged her little bell to tell me the order was ready, even though I was standing right there. I rolled my eyes at her. The tinkle of her fairy laugh followed me as I carried the food and drink outside. Winter was tenaciously making her presence known and it was a bitter evening. A misty vapour escaped my lips as I carefully set the captain's milkshake down in front of him on the table. With a murmur of thanks, he removed the straw and peeled away the plastic lid. After setting both items on the table, next to his slouch hat, he placed the milkshake container on the ground. The shepherd began to lap at the milk in glee. I studied the name engraved on the brown leather collar that hung around the dog's neck.

'May I pat Tennille, Captain Lamb?'

His head jerked up in surprise, like he hadn't realized I was still there. He stared at me for a full ten seconds, before allowing his glorious gaze to scour every inch of my face. Heat rose in my cheeks. Butterflies swirled in my belly. Embarrassed, I shuffled from foot to foot and wished I'd kept my mouth shut. To break the intensity of his gaze I gave a timid smile and took a step of retreat.

'Sure, you can pat her. Just don't crack any jokes about the Captain and Tennille. She's a tad sensitive.' His soft, deep, husky tone sent a delightful shiver up and down my spine but the reference in his comment puzzled me. What the hell did he mean by Captain and Tennille? I began to suspect he might have just come from the pub next door and that's why his words didn't make sense. I crinkled my nose to show my confusion.

'The Captain and Tennille, they sang, *Do that to me one more time!*'

I shook my head, still not getting it.

'*Love will keep us together*?'

Again, I indicated I was at a loss. The song titles were unknown to me. He arched a thick eyebrow. 'In the 1970's the duo of Captain and Tennille played keyboards for the Beach Boys. I hope you've heard of them?'

I gave a relieved smile. Finally, here was a name I recognized. 'Oh sure, my Uncle Alex is a big fan. He would amuse us on cold winters nights by pretending to surf in our lounge room to their music.'

The corner of his mouth twitched with the glimmer of a smile. 'After the Captain and Tennille left the Beach Boys, they got married and hit the recording studio in the hopes of starting a career for themselves.'

'And did they?'

'Did they ever! Fourteen billboard hot 100 hits, seven top ten songs and two number ones. Here, have a listen...' He stuck his hand in the pocket of his trousers as if to pull out some money. He didn't complete the action but instead glared through the glass window into the café dining area. 'Where's the juke box?' he asked.

'What's a juke box?'

'Oh God, it's all too much,' He scuffed his blunt fingers through the short black stubble on his scalp. He sounded quite upset.

'Are you okay?' I was confused as to why the absence of a juke box should cause such a reaction.

'I'm sorry...it's been kind of a rough day. Why don't you have a listen on U-tube when you get home, since the box is gone.'

I nodded and wondered if I would listen to the music as he suggested - probably not. I didn't really have time to surf the music sites, what with working late hours and struggling to squeeze in all my study.

The captain continued to stare inside the café. His gaze roamed the walls and the ugly metal framed booths. 'It seems all the auto-graphed album covers and photos that graced the walls of The Beach and Rock are gone as well,' he commented. A sad smile etched another line of pain at the corner of his eye. It hurt my heart.

'The cafe was renovated by the new management back in January. They also changed the name from *The Beach and Rock* to *The Mariners Café* and redecorated the inside to resemble a seaside village, hence the crass fishing net hanging from the ceiling and the ugly aqua paint on the walls,' I said. 'Not very appealing, is it?'

The captain sighed. 'Well, I guess everything changes or dies.'

The words had a forlorn ring to them. Not sure what to say in response, I bent to stroke Tennille's glossy sable coat. She lifted her milk covered muzzle from the milkshake cup and gave me a happy pant before applying her tongue in a noisy slurp around her muzzle to mop up the excess liquid. I fell in love with her.

'What a beautiful dog you have, Captain.'

'Call me, Ryan.' He gave a small proprietary smile as he watched my hand glide through Tennille's soft fur. The dog almost purred in pleasure. 'She likes you... ah?'

'Faith. I haven't seen you in here before, are you a local?'

'I used to be, before I joined the army. This was my Dad's place. We grew up here, my stepbrother Adam and I. We spent most of our teenage years hanging out, eating burgers and driving dad nuts with our music selection on the juke box that lived in that corner.'

Ryan pointed to the spot where a row of fridges held a vast array of sugary caffeine filled drinks. 'The Beach and Rock had a reputation for the best food in the state. Anytime a band came in after their gig at the pub next door, Dad would get them to autograph a copy of their album or sign one of the special plates he kept for such occasions. They were hung on the café's walls alongside the musical instrument memorabilia he'd collected in his youth. I wonder what happened to it all. Do you know?'

I shook my head. 'No, sorry, the cafe had already changed hands and the renovations finished when I started working here. I must say though, your décor sounds so much nicer than what we currently have.' I paused for a moment to stare at the bolted down metal furniture and soulless cheap wall decorations. 'There's a large picture, on the wall in the manager's office. It's of a man with tousled white hair and a happy grin. He's standing in front of a wall decorated with memorabilia just as you describe. Sound familiar?'

'That sounds a lot like my dad.'

'Why don't you ask your father what happened to all the music paraphernalia?'

'He's passed...today in fact.'

'Oh Ryan, I'm so sorry.' Sheesh, Burger way to go! Just shove a foot in your mouth why don't you. 'If you'd rather be alone with your grief...'

He waved an abrupt hand to cut off my words.

'No, it's fine. It's nice to talk.'

I heard the sigh of the door opening behind me and a man's husky voice cut across the open space. 'Here you are old chap. I should have known.'

The captain rose to his feet, a sad but welcoming smile on his face. He was at least 6ft 2in tall, but the thick soles of his highly polished boots added to his height. I felt tiny standing at his side. I spun around and studied the newcomer. He was a few centimetres shorter than Ryan, standing around 6 feet and wore a dark blue, Australian Air Force winter uniform. His chest was also covered in campaign ribbons. These boys had been busy.

'Hello, Chappie. You've missed saying goodbye. I'm afraid Dad's gone mate.'

The man called Chappie grabbed Ryan's out-thrust hand and pulled him into a man hug that involved a lot of back slapping. They stood like that for an age with Ryan's forehead against his blond friend's shoulder.

Eventually, Chappie spoke. 'I'm sorry I wasn't here sooner but a storm grounded me in Darwin. My flight to Perth arrived too late to make the Albany connection. I had to drive. I called but your phone was off.'

Ryan nodded. 'Hospital rules.'

'I went straight there. They told me about dad. I guessed you'd be here listening to the old jukebox and remembering.'

'It's gone.'

'What?'

'The juke box – it's gone! All Dad's stuff is gone.'

'No! How can *my guitar gently weep* without the box?'

The comment bought a small smile to Ryan's lips but confused me.

'Woof.'

'Hello, Tennille old girl. Are you keeping our songster out of trouble?' asked Chappie, giving the dog a scruff on the head. Tennille panted happily before giving another ruff as though answering the question. The newcomer glanced at me with sapphire blue eyes and cocked a blond eyebrow in an unasked question.

'This is Faith,' said Ryan. 'Faith meet Adam.'

'G'day, I'm Shanks's stepbrother,' he said, offering me his hand.

'Brother, mate, brother.'

Ryan's correction bought a dazzling smile to Adam's face.

I took his proffered hand as I queried the name. 'Shanks?'

'Yeah, Shanks as in lamb shank.'

I was startled when Adam suddenly burst into song.

'*The boss of my hood 'cause I'm back in my section...*'

'Give over, Chappie. Faith doesn't want to listen to you butcher *Onefour's – The Message*. God you'll be rapping Shanks and Shiv next.'

'I see you haven't lost your touch, bro. What about this one... *We share some history this town and I.*'

'I thought you could come up with something tougher than Cold Chisel, mate,' said Ryan, a small grin tugging at his lips.

I laughed. *Flame Trees* I knew. Evidently song lyrics was a game these two played with each other and Adam's banter seemed to have lifted some of the dark grief and depression hanging over them both.

'Can I get you anything, Adam?' I asked.

'Call me Chappie, everyone does.'

He watched Ryan feed the steak sandwich to Tennille and said, 'I hope your cook is as good as Dad was. Old Fuzzy made the best burgers in town.'

'Fuzzy?'

'Our nickname for Dad,' said Chappie.

The door behind him swished open.

'Burger,' barked Chips, as she stuck her head out the door and glared at us.

'Oh, yes please,' said Chappie, giving my cousin a look of admiration and the receiving end of his dazzling, even-toothed smile. 'Make it two. Unless you're going to join us...'

I burst out laughing. 'No...I'm Burger. It's my nickname.'

'Sorry flyboy, you'll have to chat up my girl some other time. Right now, she's needed. Come on, Burger, it's getting busy in here,' snapped Chips.

I took in my cousin's harassed look. 'Sorry, Chips, I'm on my way.'

'Chips, hey – crisp and delicious, hmm. Love it, it suits you. Hi, I'm Adam Best-Lamb,' he said holding out his hand to her.

'Lucy.'

I couldn't believe it! Chips had actually told him her real name. She never does that as she detests it. When their fingers touched a blush stole across her cheeks. I smirked at her.

'Come on, Burger,' she snarled in response, ducking her head to cover her obvious reaction. 'It's the start of grog sop. I need you at the counter.'

Startled, I took a quick peek at the time on the watch looped around my wrist and cursed. 'I have to go. The pub closes in half an hour. We are about to be swamped,' I said, as I turned and hurried towards the door. 'Your food will be ready in about ten minutes, okay. I don't know if Chips is as good a cook as your dad was, all I can say is she hasn't poisoned anyone yet.'

'Good enough,' said Chappie, not taking his gaze from my cousin's retreating figure as she stomped back into the kitchen. As I let go of the door to follow her, I heard Adam say, 'Oh God, Shanks, I think I'm in love.'

'Yeah, she is rather gorgeous...'

My heart sank at Ryan's words – of course both men would only have eyes for my beautiful cousin. She's certainly dazzling.

4

## Chapter Four

I faced the pubs flotsam. They were full of booze and hungry. Grog sop we call it.

The air in the café reeked of hot fat and stale beer. It hovered in a thick film overhead as customers exhaled the fumes from their evening of indulgence. Sweat beetled my brow. I had to run to keep up with the bevy of orders thrown at me by people intent on eating a belly full of alcohol absorbing carbs. The persistent ding of the kitchen bell gave testament to the hard work Chips put in, as she slogged her way through the orders. Packages of fish and chips, burgers and toasted sandwiches magically appeared on the stainless-steel shelf of the kitchen service hatch, accompanied by my cousin's muttered curses about pub closing time being a pain in the ass. I couldn't agree more. Two people were not enough staff to cope with this regular Friday night frenzy, but no matter how many times we'd asked, our manager, Brian Zelinski, the extra workers were never rostered on.

I glanced up from the milkshake mixer as four more men staggered into the café to join the long, crooked line of customers already waiting to be served. In loud voices the new arrivals conducted an argument about the legality of a goal scored in the soccer match that had been shown on the pub's big screen TV.

'Bloody refsss blind. The bastard was offside,' slurred one.

'Nah mate, youssss the blind one,' another replied.

'Sssays who?' asked the first.

'Me, you useless twat. And the piece of skirt you ignored all night.'

In response the first guy reached out to give his mate a hefty shove. To the amusement of his three sniggering mates he missed and staggered sideways. The group laughed uproariously and began to scuffle amongst themselves in an attempt to keep their companion off balance. Their antics caused a ruckus in the line as they bumped into the other customers in the queue. A murmur of protest went up.

'Watch it...'

'Settle down, ya mugs.'

'Fuck guys, stop shoving me around will ya. We came in for food didn't we?'

'Yeah, I'm fucking starving. What's the fucking hold up?' The red-head of the boisterous group barged past everyone and sprawled across the service counter. The ends of his long, greasy hair brushed the stainless surface as he shoved his ugly mug in my direction. A hot blast of beer fumes hit my face when he opened his mouth. 'Hello darling. How's about four burgers - and a kiss.'

'Way to go, Slugger.' The group hooted as they forged along behind giving a shove to anyone who stood in their path.

I ignored the drunk called Slugger and his mates as they ranged in a half-circle behind him, vying for my attention. Instead I concentrated on my current customer by holding out his food order and milkshake. Deep down I prayed we could get through grog sop, and everyone would leave before any trouble erupted.

My wrist was grabbed by tattooed fingers. 'Hey, don't ignore me, sweet cakes.'

Slugger yanked me towards him. I let out a squeal as chocolate milk, thick with ice-cream, upended and poured down my front. Icy cold it soaked through to my skin and left a brown splodge on my apron and the white skivvy I wore underneath. Amused, tattoo man bellowed with laughter. His mates pushed forward to get a better look. The murmurs of protest in the room rose to a roar. Someone threw a plastic bottle of coke at the group. It missed by a mile, whistled past my head, and with a loud splat, burst against the wall behind me. The soda exploded from the open neck of the bottle and sugary liquid sprayed the back of my hair and shirt. It was as though someone had ignited a keg of dynamite. The crowd erupted. Men began to push, shove and yell.

Mortified and frightened, I took the only action open to me. I sucked in a lungful of air and screeched, 'Get out - all of you. Right now! Or I'm calling the cops!'

It was a waste of breath. A fist flew. Suddenly the tussle got serious as the ruckus exploded into a full-blown brawl. I stood stunned, while milk dripped from the front of my apron onto my shoes and sugary soda glued tufts of hair to my face. I stared in despair as the food we'd worked so hard to make was thrown around the room, along with plastic table numbers, chair cushions and bunched fists. All I can say is thank god the bench seats and tables were bolted to the floor.

A tear leaked from the corner of my eye as I croaked out a whispered, 'Please stop.'

The last straw came when a sauce laden burger bun hit me full in the face. I began to sob. Suddenly, Chips appeared beside me with a fire extinguisher clutched in her fist. She held it ready to discharge over anyone who attempted to lay a hand on us. From the corner of my eye, I noticed the alfresco door swish open and into the fray strode Ryan and Adam. Without a word they grabbed the first brawling men they could lay their hands on by their collars and belts, and frog marched them out the door. After deftly depositing them on the footpath outside, they returned and repeated the process. Tennille trotted into the café and took up position in front of the counter. She barked and showed her teeth to anyone who came near us. The remaining men backed away from her. Tennille stalked them, forcing them into a hasty retreat. Suddenly the café was a quiet, empty mess with all the troublemakers outside in the car park looking ruffled and confused.

When the tattooed smartarse, named Slugger, made a beeline for the door, I heard Ryan say, 'Don't bother, mate. None of you will be coming back inside until you sober up and then only if you apologize with flowers to both Faith and Lucy. Now bugger off before the cops get here.'

Our military hero's folded their arms across their muscular chests and blocked the entrance. It was an intimidating sight. The drunk studied them for a moment, opened his mouth. He must have decided to err on the side of caution because without a word he swung around and joined his mates, who milled around looking sheepish.

'Sorry love,' sang out a middle-aged man who was one of our regulars. I nodded in his direction to confirm I'd heard him. He gave a small wave and shuffled away down the street. Others took the hint and followed. A few, aware of their shameful behaviour, also called out their apologies.

The fire extinguisher thudded to the floor with a resounding thump as Chips let go. She grabbed me by the shoulders. 'Are you alright, Burger?'

I studied the unshed tears that pooled in her eyes and pulled her into a fierce hug.

'I'm just dandy. What about you?'

'I'm banging girl! Gucci in fact,' was her muffled response. Her chest began to squirm against my cheek as I snuggled into her shirt. 'Yeew, you're all wet and sticky.'

I took a deep breath and loosened my grip on her. Chips tightened her hold around my waist, which gave me an inkling of how scared she'd been. Tennille poked her nose around the side of the counter and stared at us. I gently released Chips and gave my cousin's cheek a soft pat with my sticky fingers.

'Gucci?' I asked.

'Yep, top shelf my girl, top shelf.'

I rolled my eyes at the witticism.

Chips stared at me with a look of horror on her face.

'What...?' I asked, with a sniffle and peeled away a sticky strand of hair glued to my eyelid.

'You're a mess, Burger.' She grabbed a handful of serviettes and shoved them in my direction. I took them gently from her out-thrust fingers and used them to give my nose a lusty blow. Tennille whined. I squatted down and flung my arms around her neck.

'Thank you, Tennille. You were bloody awesome girl.'

The dog responded by running her raspy tongue up my cheek. She seemed to approve of the taste, so I let her enjoy the moment. Only when I was positive there could be no food left on my face, did I rise to my feet to survey the mess in the café. It was going to take a herculean effort to clean up.

Our saviours, Ryan and Adam, strode back inside with purpose.

'Are you girls alright?' asked Ryan. He didn't hesitate or pause to assess the disaster but stalked around the counter and halted in front of me. He studied my face for a moment before placing a gentle hand on my shoulder. It surprised me. I thought for sure he would have made a beeline for my gorgeous cousin.

I gazed up into his amazing eyes and sighed, 'Yeah, I suppose so. But now we have a huge mess to clean up and I just know we're going to get blamed for the trouble.'

Ryan's grip on my shoulder tightened and he began to draw me into a hug. Even with everything that had happened his uniform was still in immaculate condition. I didn't want to mess it up, so I stepped away from him. His right eyebrow twitched, and his hands dropped to his side. Before I could explain, Chips, who was snuggled in the comfort of Adam's arms, let rip with one of her rants.

'I told that bloody cheapskate something like this would happen.'

I flicked a surprised glance at her. 'Who?'

'Brian, of course! He's got to be the most useless bloody manager in the universe. Well, he can just bestir himself and drag his sorry butt down here right now to sort out the mess his penny pinching has caused.' She stepped out of the circle of Adam's arms and snatched the café's telephone handset from its cradle. She hit speed dial on the keypad. Her foot beat a rapid tattoo as she waited for Brian to answer. When he did she said with a deceptive sweet voice, 'Hello Brian, this is Lucy Chippens. There's been an incident at The Mariners. We need you here, pronto!'

She paused and mouthed to me that Brian was on a rant. Chips leant over and rested her cheek against my shoulder, raised her lashes and stared up at me with a frown. 'No, I'm not going to deal with it. As you so often remind me, I'm just the hired help.'

Brian who was well known for portentous pontificating must have launched into one of his pompous lectures because Chip's nose wrinkled, and she gave a dramatic eye roll. She held the phone away from her ear and began to examine her perfectly manicured nails. I could hear Ryan chuckle beside me.

When the tinny sound of Brian's voice paused, Chips winked at me and said, 'Ok, boss, it's your call, but just so you know, my first course of action will be to call the police!' She slammed down the receiver and stared at the watch on her wrist. 'Fifty bucks says he'll be here in five minutes.'

I snorted. There was no way I was taking her up on that bet. Chips has her ways.

I turned to Ryan and Adam. 'You guys better skedaddle. We don't want you or Tennille to get into any trouble on our behalf - especially with the military.'

'Bit late for that,' said Ryan and jerked a thumb towards the security camera dome above the counter.

I laughed. 'That won't be a problem. The domes are just for show. Brian's too cheap to pay for an actual security system.' I reached over and took a hold of his hand and gave his fingers a gentle squeeze. 'Thank you, Ryan and you too, Chappie. I don't know what we would have done without your help.'

Ryan gave the tip of my nose a soft flick with his forefinger. 'Anytime, Cutie,' he said.

I looked down at my milkshake sodden clothes; food encrusted legs; dumpy figure and shook my head. Two men in one day - life was nuts.

* * *

As predicted, Brian arrived five minutes later. A short, portly man, he barrelled through the door full of self-righteous importance.

'I'm a very busy man and can't be dashing down here every time you...what the hell?' He halted and stared around at the mess. 'What a disaster. I thought I could trust you girls to run the cafe but just look at this...' he spluttered, and lost the ability to speak for half a second. 'How useless are you? I have a good mind to dock your wages for clean-up costs and damages.'

I stood, my head bowed; taking all the abuse he threw our way. Not Chips. She refused to shoulder any blame.

With hands fisted on her waist, she snarled, 'It's not our fault, Brian. It's yours!'

His eyes popped in surprise. 'How do you figure that?'

'I told you something like this was going to happen. For weeks now I've...we've...' she flicked a forefinger between herself and me. 'We've been asking for extra staff to be rostered on to help with the pub closing time crush. The faster we serve those drunken heathens and push them out the door the less chance there is of this sort of thing happening.'

'And this is my fault, how?' asked Brian, jiggling the expensive watch looped around his wrist into a more comfortable position.

'You stonewalled the request.'

Brian began to splutter. 'Yes...well...why didn't you just deal?'

Chips cut him off. She was relentless. 'And just so you know. The next time, after calling the cops, I'm going to stand in the car park and let them wreck the joint.'

'There's no need to take that attitude.'

She ignored his quivering chin and bluster. 'And if you have the audacity to dock our meagre wage, I'll place a call to Fair Work Practices, the health inspector and the Albany Advertiser. The newspaper editor's a good friend of my father's.'

'Yes, yes...no need for that.' Brian didn't seem eager to call her bluff and back peddled on his earlier threat. 'I didn't really mean it. I was just angry about the mess. Look, I'll have a chat with Jim. Ask him to work Friday nights along with you girls from now on. Would that suit you?'

'It's a start,' said Chips folding her arms and glaring at him.

'Right,' said Brian. He rubbed his chubby, ring covered fingers together as if washing his hands of the whole incident. 'Well, don't stand there harping on about things you two. Times money you know. Let's get this place cleaned up.'

And by that he meant Chips and I. Brian's contribution was to empty the till and retire into the office.

\* \* \*

I crawled around on my hands and knees angry. My hair stuck out in stiff tufts and my toes itched abominably from wet socks. It was not the highlight on my evening but I had no spare clothes with me and Brian wouldn't let me go home to shower and change. Frustrated by his callousness I scrubbed a spot of sauce from the skirting board with the scouring brush and didn't care that I took off some of the ugly aqua paint as well. Serve Brian right if he had to pay to have the walls repainted.

The bell over the door chimed.

'We're closed,' called Chips, not bothering to turn around from the soda stain she was applying a wet cloth to.

'Delivery for Brian Zelenski.'

I studied the red-headed man with a broad Scottish accent. He wore an unfastened yellow reflective vest over a long sleeved, button-down khaki shirt. The gape of his vest revealed a Dash Deliveries logo emblazoned in purple thread above his shirt pocket. The man looked to be in his mid-thirties, was stocky, square faced and built like a boxer. Clutched in his hand were three padlocked, A4 sized, grey leather pouches. They resembled oversized pencil cases and were so bulky the zippers barely held them shut. I indicated towards the back of the store.

'He's out back in the office. Hang on a sec...' I raised my voice, 'Brian, someone to see you.'

Our boss daintily tip-toed his expensive leather shoes through the mess still waiting for the mop. He smiled when he saw the courier and crooked a finger for the guy to follow him.

'Come on in, Scotty. Office is this way.'

The courier craned his neck and checked out the cafe. 'Problems, Brian?' he asked, rolling his r's in that delightful way the Scots have when they speak.

'A couple of local yobos...full of soup. Ringleader was a redhead, with a West Coast Eagles logo tattooed on the back of his hand and the word *kill* emblazoned across his fingers. Know him?'

Scotty nodded. 'Sounds like Slugger Corvis. He's a cocky little prick. Works for the Huntsmen motorcycle gang as a low level mule.'

'Can you deal?'

'Sure, boss. I'll send Harley around to pay the Sergeant at Arms a visit. He'll make sure the gang members know this place is protected.'

'Good, the last thing we need is to draw any unwanted attention. Cub wouldn't like it...' The rest of the conversation was cut off as the men closed the office door.

Well, that was weird, I thought, as I staggered to my feet and set to work with the mop.

Ten minutes later, with his hands shoved deep into his trouser pockets and a jaunty whistle on his lips, Scotty sauntered back through the dining room. He winked at me before stepping out into the frigid night air, seemingly unaffected by the cold. I picked up the bucket of dirty water and lugged it towards the back door. When I was level with the office, I glanced in. Brian was busy counting notes from a large pile of cash stacked high on the desk. He secured a rubber band around the bundle in his hand and made a mark in a dark green ledger that was positioned by his elbow. Round-eyed

I watched as he rose from the chair and removed the impressive portrait of Fuzzy Lamb from the wall.

Well, wouldn't you know it, a wall safe!

Brian consulted some dates that had been circled on a one-page yearly calendar stuck to the back of the frame then ran his fingers over the safe's electronic keypad. He turned to reach for the money on the desk, and spotted me.

'You finished yet?' he growled. I shook my head. 'Well stop gawping and get on with it.'

I nodded and hastened to lug my heavy load out of the back door. As I sloshed the dirty water down the outside stormwater drain my snoopy brain went into overdrive. Where the hell had all that money had come from? It was winter and the Café couldn't have pulled in that much cash. We may be open 24 hours a day but often there were no customers between the hours of midnight and 6 a.m. Had the cash been in the leather satchels the Scottish courier delivered? If so it meant Brian had his fingers in more than one pie.

# 5

## Chapter Five

Chips bounced into my bedroom.

'Come on, lazy bones. Get up.'

I groaned, rolled over and threw my pillow at her.

'I don't see why I should. It took us ages to clean up last night. My back and knees ache like a bitch. As today is my first day off in weeks, I'll need a superb reason to emerge from my cocoon.'

'I've just gotten off the telephone with Adam. We're taking the boys out for lunch. I've booked us a table for one o'clock. That a good enough reason?'

I bolted upright.

'You've got thirty minutes to get ready before we pick them up in Kasam.'

Kasam is my cousin's car. Chips is a fast, erratic driver, who ducks and weaves through traffic oblivious to other road users. Being her passenger is not for the faint-hearted. Oh God, if Chips drove it was a test. Whenever she had a serious interest in a guy she'd insist on taking them for a drive and use their reactions to her behaviour behind the wheel to gauge their mettle. Most men failed.

'Are you trying to scare them off?' I gave my tangled mop a shove away from my eyes and stared at her in disbelief.

She wriggled her sculptured eyebrows. 'He's a pilot. If he can't take a little excitement in his life, he's in the wrong job.'

'Chips, please...'

My cousin leant forward, grabbed my foot through the duvet and gave it a wiggle. 'Come on, sluggard. Get out of bed. Time's a wasting.'

A stampede of emotions swirled around my belly. I was going to see the handsome soldier, Ryan again. The ache of my muscles was no longer a factor. I ignored their protest as I threw back my bed covers and leapt up. The room was toasty warm. Bless my thoughtful cousin, she'd put the central heating on. I sighed in gratitude.

'Pick me out an outfit to wear will you. You know I'm useless at that type of thing.'

'You're not useless, you just over complicate it.' She headed towards my small built-in wardrobe and flung open the door. 'Hmm...' With her head cocked to the left she stared at the limited choice hanging drunkenly on the hangers.

'Something comfortable and warm please, like you're wearing.' Chips had on a bell-sleeved, butter-yellow, ribbed turtleneck top. She'd married it with a plain black skirt that swirled softly around the butter-yellow tights encasing her calves. On her feet were the most gorgeous low-heeled, black leather boots. I stared at her in envy. 'You look stunning by the way. I especially love the boots.'

She flashed me a brilliant smile and waved me towards the shower, 'Go.'

Chips chuckled when I buzzed her cheek with a soft kiss as I passed.

Racing into the bathroom I tripped over Fleabag.

'Bloody cat, don't you have a home of your own?' I reached down, with gentle hands I picked her up to check she wasn't hurt. It wasn't her fault I was in such a flap. Fleabag's motor kicked in. She snuggled in and purred in a loud contented fashion. I gave her an affectionate tickle under the chin. She meowed for more, but as my time was limited I kissed the tip of her nose and set her down on the carpet outside the bathroom door.

I flicked the faucet to full blast, threw off the old, misshapen knee length shirt I slept in and smeared my face in a thick layer of moisturiser while I waited for the hot water to kick in. When the mirror began to fog I dove under the spray and let out a massive sigh of pleasure. Hot water cascaded over my hair and face, streamed down my body and tickled the tips of my toes as it ran away down the drain. I was in heaven. There's nothing better than a steaming hot shower. I managed to double shampoo, condition and scrub myself thoroughly with eucalyptus and the lemon-lime scented soap twice before the water turned tepid. Disappointed the hot water was gone I switched the shower off and wrapped myself in my soft fluffy robe to keep warm while I sorted out my sodden hair. After a vigorous rub with the towel I blasted it with the blow dryer. Maybe it was the result of being covered in sticky soft drink for hours the previous night. Today my wavy locks decided to behave and fell softly around my face and neck. The copper highlights glowed as if in excitement at the prospect of seeing Ryan again. After another application of face cream and a smear of mascara my face was as good as it was going to get. In a cloud of steam, I barrelled out of the bathroom, anxious to see what Chips had managed to come up with from my limited stock of clothes. On the bed lay a copper toned long-sleeved tee and a pair of moleskin trousers. Beside it was the teal Fair Isle knee-length knitted cardigan I'd bought on a whim the previous year but didn't wear, mainly because I didn't know what to match it with. A shoe box sat on the foot of the bed. Curious, I lifted the lid. Nestled in the confines of pale-pink tissue paper lay a pair of floral hand-embroidered, round toed, leather ankle boots that I'd been drooling over for twelve months.

'Surprise!' smirked Chips, strolling into the room with a self-satisfied grin on her lips. 'I bought the boots for you as a Christmas present, but this is more important.'

'Holy cow!' I screamed, bouncing up and down on my toes. 'They're for me?'

Chips nodded.

'Darling, I love you.' I flung my arms around her and rocked her from side to side. She squeezed me back before giving me a gentle push towards the clothes on the bed.

'Now, hurry up or we'll be late.' She took a quick glance at her phone. 'Five minutes, okay?'

I nodded and dove into my outfit.

I felt glamorous as we clambered into Kasam. For the umpteenth time I cast a glance down at my feet – the boots looked awesome.

'Where are we going?' I asked, wondering if I'd be able to eat with all the butterflies doing a mad dervish in my stomach.

'We're about to sample the cuisine at *Majuba*.'

My eyebrows rose in surprise. Majuba, a sophisticated bistro slash wine bar, was renowned for its delicious European food and excellent wine menu. The restaurant was very popular, especially with locals and reservations were hard to come by.

'I'm surprised you managed to get us a table on such short notice.'

'It was easy, cousin dear. The maître de, April, is my *Criminal Law and Ethic's* study buddy. As a favour she squeezed us in.'

'Cool. Though I hope it doesn't have too hefty a price tag. What made you choose Majuba?'

'Well, the restaurant has some fantastic online reviews. Thought we should check it out. I'd like to take Popsicle somewhere special next time he visits.'

Popsicle is the endearment my cousin uses for her father, my Uncle Alex.

'So, we're not trying to impress the guys then?' I fluttered my eyelashes and wedged my tongue in my cheek in amusement.

Chips gave me a cheeky smirk. 'Couldn't hurt...they did save our sorry butts.'

'Yes, they did.' I figured my credit card could take the hit because I would always be grateful to both Ryan and Chappie for their help the previous evening.

Chips planted her foot on the accelerator. I closed my eyes. I'd found it was the only way to cope with her driving. Complaints about speed only made her drive faster. It seemed like in no time at all we screeched to a halt in front of a cream, rendered brick house on one of Albany's most prestigious streets. I stared in amazement at the elegant three-storey building. It was flanked on the right by a single-story wing and had enough parking for a least seven cars. The whole building had been set forward on the front section of two acres of expertly manicured lawns and gardens. The flower beds were crowded with a riot of blushing blooms and laden fruit trees. It was a stunning property.

'I bet they have a fabulous view of Princess Royal Harbor from the upstairs balcony,' said Chips, as she craned her neck to take in all the house's features.

'I'm so glad Unk didn't know this was for sale when he bought our place.' I nodded to the heritage real-estate sign attached to the green wrought iron fence panel. 'You know what he's like.'

'Yeah, but Popsicle only wants the best for us.'

'I know, Chips, but can you imagine us rattling around in this monstrosity? We'd never find each other.'

A tinkle of laughter escaped her lips as she dug out her mobile phone from a tiny black leather Gucci clutch. I watched with interest as she hit speed dial.

'Out front, Flyboy,' she murmured and hung up.

I stared at her.

'What?'

'Speed dial...already!'

She winked and clambered from the driver's seat. I smirked to myself as I followed her from the car. Chappie's goose was so cooked!

The front door of the house was flung open. Chappie emerged dressed in a black suit, crisp white shirt and burgundy tie. He looked drop dead gorgeous. He eyed Chips from head to toe and electricity seemed to crackle between them.

She gave him a finger wave and jerked a thumb at Kasam. 'I'm driving.'

He dragged his gaze from hers, glanced at the car and his face broke out in an enormous grin. 'No way! Shanks, get out here, man,' he yelled. 'You gotta see this.'

He raced over to Kasam and ran a loving hand over the Subaru BRZ's bonnet. My top lip tilted in amusement. This was exactly the same reaction Chips had had the first time she'd met Kasam.

'What's first gear like?' he asked.

She winked at me and with a little rhythm in her voice said, 'It's alright.

'How does she handle in second?'

'I lean right.'

Chappie's head shot up, surprise written all over his face. Chips pointed to me and together we began to bop and sing, 'Third gear, hang on tight. Faster...' I couldn't do it anymore. I cracked up laughing.

'Beach Boys – *Little Honda* written by Brian Wilson - released in 1964 on their *All Summer Long* album,' breathed Adam in awe. 'You know lyrics?'

'Only the Beach Boys I'm afraid. My dad and his terrible dance steps were our cold winter's night entertainment when I grew up.' She went on to imitate some of the more ludicrous dance moves Uncle Alex had used while he balanced on a boogie board with music blaring from the stereo. I smiled at the happy memory.

Chappie erupted into laughter. 'I'd love to meet him, he sounds awesome.'

Chips flicked me a meaningful glance. Chappie was off to a good start in her books, because approval of her father was of extreme importance to my cousin.

Warmth began to tingle along my spine. I turned and my gaze was held by two golden orbs. Ryan gave me a crooked grin and my new boots nearly flew from my feet at the sensation it aroused in me. He too was dressed in a black suit and crisp white shirt. His teal tie matched my outfit. He looked devastating. I nearly melted into a puddle on the spot. To cover my reaction, I lifted my hand, in an imitation of my cousin, fluttered my fingers at him. In three rapid steps Ryan covered the distance between us and clasped my fingers in his warm grip.

'Hello Faith. You look beautiful.'

'Thank you. You too...handsome I mean,' I stuttered, and wished I had the courage to kiss him.

He leant forward. I took a hesitant step closer, mesmerised. An urgent out-cry from Chappie broke the spell. 'Shanks, you have to come see what Lucy drives.'

I sucked in my breath and clutched at Ryan's fingers. I cast a glance towards my cousin and waited for the explosion.

'What's wrong?' Ryan's whisper in my ear sent a flurry of goose bumps down my arms and spine.

'It's Chips...she hates...nobody ever...'

'What does she hate?'

'Nobody gets away with calling her Lucy, not even her father.'

To my surprise she didn't erupt. My cousin just smiled. My eyes widened in astonishment.

Ryan stared over at his stepbrother. Amusement lines creased the corners of his eyes. 'He's in trouble, isn't he?'

'Only if he passes the driving test,' I murmured. Ryan's brow lifted in a silent query. I gave him some sage advice. 'Just close your eyes. That's what I do.'

He squeezed my fingers in response to my pearls of wisdom.

Needless to say, both men, crammed together on the folding rear seat of the sports car, passed the test with open eyes and flying colours.

* * *

Seated in the restaurant, I peeked over the top of the menu at Ryan. 'What looks good to you?'

He gave me a cheeky grin. 'You!'

My cheeks ignited. I lifted my menu higher to cover the tell-tale stain. When my face cooled I gathered together enough courage to lower the menu and peer at my companion. Ryan was making a studious study of his menu with an amused grin on his face. He glanced up, caught me watching him and winked. My heart flipped.

'Can I order you a drink, Faith? We could share a bottle of wine, or would you prefer something else?'

'Would you call me Burger, I prefer it?' Ryan nodded. With a smile in his eyes he waited for me to answer him. 'No wine, thanks. I don't understand the whole rigmarole of matching food to wine. Can I have a beer? That seems to be acceptable with anything you eat,' I babbled, still unsettled by his obvious flirting. Something I wasn't good at.

'You can have anything you like, Burger. And just for the record, you don't need to believe all that guff about how only a refined palate can appreciate the nuances of certain wines with certain foods. I follow the philosophy, if you like it, drink it and eat whatever you want.'

Swamped by relief I grinned. I was never particular about what I ate or drank, or even in what order. Often I'd scoff a beer with a peanut butter sandwich for dinner and devour leftover lasagne with a glass of milk for breakfast. Gross, I know, but that's how I roll.

Ryan smiled at the waitress who hovered at his elbow waiting to take our order. I watched his gaze flick over the name tag pinned to her ample bosom then go straight back to her face. 'Two middies of *Fifty Lashes* thanks, April.' He nodded across the table to his step-brother and my cousin. 'What about you two?'

'A bottle of the Cullen Cabernet-Merlot, please.' A contented smile appeared on my cousin's lips when Chappie named her favourite local brand. He had just passed another test. April's lips twitched with her own seal of approval before she glided away with our order.

Ryan laid his work toughened fingers gently over the hand I'd rested on the table next to my cutlery. 'Tell me a little about yourself, Burger.'

'There's not much to tell really.' I was nervous at being the centre of his attention. 'I'm an only child. My parents were doctors.'

'Retired?'

'No, they've both passed.'

'I'm sorry,' he said. 'Was it a car accident?'

His question opened a locked door that allowed an unwanted memory to crash in. My eyes pooled with tears. Ryan squeezed my fingers. 'Sorry, Burger, I didn't mean to raise a painful subject. Just forget I even asked.'

'No, its fine,' I whispered. I knew I should talk about them. This was the perfect opportunity, because being in public I would need to keep a lid on my emotions. I flicked a glance across the table at Chips. She was in deep conversation with Chappie. 'My parents worked for *Doctors without Borders*,' I murmured. 'Mostly in Thailand. I travelled with them a few times, but it was dull and boring for me. I wasn't allowed to go out on my own. I spent long, lonely hours reading and watching crappy TV shows in the hotel room with a nanny, while they spent long, tiring days and late nights at hospitals or clinics. The year I turned eleven I jacked up, and announced I wasn't going with them anymore. My Uncle Alex went into bat for me and told Mum and Dad that I shouldn't have to waste my school holidays cooped up in a hotel room all day, every day. He was happy for me to stay with them while they went off and did their thing. Without much argument my folks agreed. I think they were secretly relieved not to have to worry about me being alone in a foreign country or having to alter their busy schedule to spend time with me.

Two days before my parents were due home, Chips and I evicted Unk...that's what I call my Uncle Alex...anyway...we banned him from watching his boring current affairs show on the kitchen TV and sent him off to his study to do some work, while we set about baking a welcome home cheesecake. Before I could switch off the panel of supercilious and opinionated talking heads supporting the Taliban's justification to suspend another round of peace talks, a yellow news ribbon threaded its way across the screen. It was one of those news flash thingies. It announced that a group called the Patani United Liberated Organisation (PULO) had detonated three car bombs.'

Ryan's warm gaze sharpened into something hard but he remained silent. I took a large gulp of beer in an attempt to ease the pain of the memory.

'Being young and not interested in the cruel antics of PULO, I flicked off the TV. Almost immediately the house phone rang. Chips breezed over to kill its insistent clamour and in a bright happy voice answered, "Hello, cheesecake chicks, name your poison." I snorted at her cheekiness and flicked some of the cheesecake mixture at her. "Alex Chippens, sure he's home...hang on a sec." She whisked the handset to the door of the kitchen and yelled at the top of her voice, "Popsicle – need you!" She scooped the blob of mixture from her cheek and gave it a seal of approval. "Yummo, Burger. That's delicious."

"I'm here, Lucy, what's up?" asked Uncle Alex.

"I wish you wouldn't call me that," she snarled at her father as she handed over the receiver. As always, Uncle Alex just smiled. He never takes a blind bit of notice when she demands he call her Chips.'

I gave a wistful smile as I visualized the two most important people in my life at that moment.

'Anyway, in that heartbeat the resemblance between them was so apparent. The only real difference, except for the obvious of course, is that Unk has round kissable cheeks and a small pot belly and Chips the high cheek bones and willowy figure she inherited from her mother. Sorry, I've digressed.'

'I can understand why. You love them both very much, don't you?' said Ryan.

'Yes, I do.' I gave him an uncomplicated smile. Warmth and affectionate friendship replaced some of my pain. 'Where was I? Oh yeah, Unk and the phone call. He kissed Chips on the tip of her nose and left the room as he spoke into the handset, "Hello this is Alex Chippens." There was a long silence from the other room before I heard him demand harshly, "You're certain?"

His tone surprised me. Unk never raises his voice, even when he's in court. Did I tell you that he's a lawyer - an extremely good one by all accounts?'

Ryan shook his head and didn't comment on my change of subject. He stared at me and waited to see if I would go on. I knew I was procrastinating as the next bit of my story was hard for me to put into words. The hand that covered mine squeezed gently. I took courage from it and continue with my tale.

'Chips and I began to chat about my mum and dad's return and the prospect of gifts, especially new clothes. At that moment Uncle Alex stepped into the room. He had large tears rolling down his cheeks. My heart stuttered and almost stopped when he gathered me into a tight hug and held me hard against his heart. "Faith my precious girl, I'm so sorry – terrorists have detonated a bomb at your parent's hotel. I'm afraid they are dead."'

Ryan whispered, 'That was 2012, right?'

The question surprised me. 'Yeah, it was. The 31st of March. It was my 11th birthday.'

He pulled his chair closer. I was enveloped in a delightful and sensuous aroma of woody spiced aftershave as he placed a comforting arm over my shoulders and drew me close.

'I was there!'

His words stunned me. I forgot how to breathe. My lungs protested so I gulped in some oxygen while I gawped at him in amazement. 'What do you mean you were there?' I squeaked.

All the conversation at the table had stopped.

'I'd just finished my first tour of duty in Afghanistan. Flew into Kuala Lumpur and met up with, Chappie.' He nodded to his step-brother and my cousin across the table. Chips eyes were as big as saucers as she stared at me in concern. I gave her a faltering smile to show I was okay and the tension in her shoulders relaxed a tad.

'We'd hired a couple of motorbikes so we could trek around Malaysia and had just pulled into Kuala Nerang to fuel up when there was a news flash on the radio in a local shop. As we were already on the border between Thailand and Malaysia, only two hours from Hat Yai, Chappie and I got straight back onto our bikes and headed there to help with the search and rescue efforts.'

'Wow, that's where my parents were,' I said, as I rubbed at the tension lines on my forehead with the heel of my hand. Ryan handed me my glass of beer. I shot him a smile of gratitude and took a large gulp of the cold amber liquid. The normality of the action helped to ease the raw emotions that clutched at the back of my throat.

'Thank you for going to help...'

'I'm just sorry there was nothing we could do for your folks, and I'm really sorry for raising such a painful subject for you both.' Ryan tilted his head to include Chips in his apology.

'How about you change the subject then,' snapped Chips, shifting into mother hen mode.

'Yeah, I think that's a good idea,' agreed Ryan. 'How about, Cutie, you give me the third degree about my life. Go on, ask away. Do you want to know what song I sing in the shower or how many wears I can get out of a pair of socks? No, I know, the most important question on everybody's lips. Pizza - with or without pineapple?'

I appreciated his efforts to change the subject to something lighter. I took another sip of my beer before replacing the glass on the table. As I watched the beads of moisture run down the outside of the middy glass, I took the time to compose myself and get my emotions back in check.

'By the way I hate pineapple on my pizza, so I hope that's not a deal breaker,' finished Ryan in a tone that brooked no argument.

That bought a grin to my lips. 'Not at all, as long as you're not grossed out by pepperoni with beetroot, pesto and goat's cheese.'

'You're pulling my leg, right?'

I chuckled. 'Nope. Not even a little bit. And I adore chocolate.'

'Who doesn't?' Ryan flashed me a beautiful smile and rubbed a hand over his flat belly.

Wanting to know everything about this man seated next to me but being careful not to dive in too deep or open a fresh wound with my questions I went for the mundane first. 'Can you talk about your job?'

He rocked his hand back and forth. 'A little...I can't always go into detail. What is it you want to know?'

'Well for starters, are you stationed locally or overseas?'

'Now, that is a question with no real answer. Tennille and I were based at Kapooka. We've been working there for the last twelve months.'

'Doing?'

'Drilling new recruits. My job was to toughen them up and prepare them for military life.'

'Kapooka, that's in New South Wales, right?' My hopes that Ryan lived somewhere nearby, fell with a clang along with my heart.

'Yeah, just outside Wagga Wagga.'

'You said there's no real answer to where you're based. Why's that, has something changed?'

'It has. I'm on bereavement leave at the moment. Once I've sorted out Dad's affairs, my commanding officer wants me to report in for a special assignment. I don't know what's on the cards for me or even where I'll be going.'

'Gosh, that must be hard?'

'Well, it hasn't been until now.'

I lifted an eyebrow in surprise. Was I misreading him? Being a coward, I didn't ask, instead I steered the conversation to something else I was very curious about. 'What happens to Tennille if you're sent to the Middle East or receive some other overseas posting?'

'Chappie takes her. He's based at Pearce Air Base and lives in Perth, most of the time. But I doubt I'll be going back to Afghanistan. Operation Highroad is being wound down. Most of our troops have already been redeployed to other trouble spots or returned home.'

'Oh good, I wouldn't like to think of you in any danger.'

Ryan smiled at my naivety, so I changed the subject. 'Do you have a wife or a girlfriend?'

'No, if I did, I wouldn't be here with you, like this. Loyalty, fidelity and honesty are the Holy Grail in my book. I learnt that lesson the hard way.'

His face turned stony, my eyes widened, full of unspoken questions. Ryan gave a wry chuckle.

'Fairs fair - I was engaged to be married once. My fiancée, Janine, found comfort in the arms of someone else during my second tour in Afghanistan. I caught them in my bed together when I came home early on leave.'

'Wow, that's rough.'

'It was. You're looking at a very jaded and distrustful man, Burger. What about you?'

'No, I'm not jaded or distrustful. I have no wife unless you put Chips in that class, though she acts more like a mother hen.' Ryan's throaty chuckle, at my description of my cousin and my relationship, sent a thrill down my spine. 'I lead a fairly dull and boring existence. Most of my time is spent studying, especially on the long, late nights at work.'

'What are you studying?'

'Criminology and Psychology, I hope to qualify as a forensic scientist.'

'Wow. Got your work cut out for you haven't you. You're both from Perth right?'

I nodded, not understanding where the question was going.

'So how come you're attending university in Albany and not a campus in the city?'

'Because,' I said with a sarcastic laden drawl, 'UWA overbooked this year's classes. Go figure. We had two choices. Attend campus here in Albany or defer for twelve months. You know what happens when you defer, other things in life get in the way and you never go back to what you were doing.'

Ryan nodded and took a small sip of his beer. 'And do you enjoy life in Albany?'

'Most of the time.' Ryan's eyebrows lifted in a question but not wanting to drag the conversation down again, I shrugged and avoided talking about the problems I was having with the sleazy campus security guard, Russ Johnson. To distract him, I said in a rush, 'Let's try twenty questions. I'll go first...why do you call, Adam, Chappie?'

'Because he calls everyone old chap.'

I chuckled. 'As simple as that?'

'Yep, sure is. But isn't that always the way with most nicknames? My turn - do you have a favourite movie or TV show?'

'There's a few. I enjoy those superhero adventures, especially *Thor*. Chris Hemsworth's chest is so drool worthy. The *Harry Potter* and *Star Wars* movies were awesome. *Bridget Jones's Diary* really tickled my funny bone, but I suppose as I love a good murder mystery, shows like *CSI* and *Vera* really play to my snoopy side.' I stopped to think, trying to pick a favourite. I gave up and shrugged my shoulders, 'Nah, can't pick a favourite. What about you?'

'I agree with you about *Star Wars*. I like anything that stays with you afterwards. *Shawshank Redemption* is probably a perfect example. Think about it - no matter how big a mess you face, if you work at it, you can make things a little better each day until you're back in the game. That's the message I took from that film. That and to take advantage of the opportunities you have and not dwell on the ones you wish you had.'

'Wow, that's deep. I hadn't thought about the meaning of the story...but yeah, you're not wrong.' I was amazed that I had missed the whole message behind the movie.

Ryan gave me a lopsided grin. 'Being bunkered down in the sand pit gives you a lot of time to think,' he said.

'Sand pit?'

'The desert. Afghanistan.'

'Oh, right.'

'I'm almost afraid to ask the next question,' said Ryan, rubbing his thumb in a gentle circle on the back of my hand. 'What type of music do you enjoy?'

I grinned, 'Anything easy listening or rock. I don't really have a preference. Why are you wiping your brow?'

'Whew.' He flashed me an endearing smile, 'I thought you were going to name some pretty boy band.'

I snorted, 'Music snob! Alright smarty pants tell me who you consider the best singer past or present?'

'That's easy, Freddie Mercury of course! He had an unbelievable four-octave vocal range that extended from bass low F to soprano high F and those notes came with pure emotion, passion and charisma. Of the numerous female singers I admire, I'd say the queen of soul herself, Aretha Franklin is my favourite. She has a dramatic falcon soprano voice and a no-nonsense attitude. It's impossible not to be moved by her vocals, though I do think Adele gives her a run for her money.'

'I don't know what half of that means but I can't argue with your choices. You seem to know a lot about music - do you sing or play an instrument yourself?'

'Some. I'm not that good. Not like Dad was. He spent his youth playing saxophone and singing Jazz. Made his fortune and retired.'

Chappie leant forward and with a wide smile said, 'Don't you believe him, Burger. Shanks has a fantastic voice. When he and Dad combined, they were awesome.'

I stared in fascination as a pink flush tinged Ryan's cheeks.

'I'd love to hear you sing sometime.' I said. Ryan was saved from further discussion on the subject by the arrival of our food.

* * *

The sun peeked out from behind a charcoal grey cloud. It enticed Ryan and me to stroll up the hill to his house, while Chips and Chappie went for a spin out on the highway in Kasam. I knew the pleasant weather wouldn't last so I made the most of the sunshine by holding my face up to the sky to absorb the warm rays deep into my bones.

'I love the sun,' I said, almost purring. 'If I had a choice I'd live where it was warm most of the year round.'

Ryan's soft chuckle sent a thrill up my spine. 'You remind me of a contented kitten.' He took hold of my elbow and guided me along the footpath so I didn't stray in front of any oncoming foot traffic.

As we strolled into Grey Street I studied the For Sale sign in front of his house and had to ask. 'I see you're selling. Was putting the house on the market a tough decision to make?'

'Dad was the one who is selling, not us. It was a strange thing for him to do.'

'Strange. Why?' I asked, as Ryan tugged a notebook and pen from his pocket and made a note.

I tried not to be too obvious about it as I craned my neck for a sticky beak over his shoulder. He noticed my glance anyway and held the pad towards me so I could easily read it. 'A list of things I need to sort out Monday.' In bold untidy print he'd written lawyer, funeral director and real estate agent. 'Dad selling the café I understood. The long hours behind the grill played havoc with his arthritis and the pain of it kept him up most nights. It was a relief for him to give up work. But the house, now that's a different matter. He loved this place with a passion and swore he'd never part with it. Plus, he knew both Adam and I were planning to come back and settle down here when our military careers were finished.'

'Do you think he was ill and needed the money for treatment?' I asked, wondering how exactly Ryan's dad had died.

'No, Fuzzy wasn't sick. Besides, he knew we would give him the shirts off our backs if he needed it. He only had to ask.'

'Yes, but would he? Ask that is. You know pride and all that.'

Ryan shrugged.

'So, how exactly did he die?' Blunt, I know, but my investigator nose had begun to twitch.

'He took a tumble down the stairs. His cleaner, Helen, found him when she arrived for work on Wednesday morning. He was ice cold and blue, but still breathing. He must have hit his head on a step or the railing when he fell because he had a nasty gash to the back of the head. The blood around the wound had congealed so he'd probably lain there all night.'

'Did he trip or was he pushed?'

'I asked the police that very question. Because there are no signs of a break in and as far as I can tell nothing is missing. The police say all the indications are that he tripped and fell.'

'And do you believe that? Is it likely that a man who lived in this house for years would have trouble negotiating his own stairs?'

Ryan nodded. 'It's possible. Fuzzy always slopped around the house in a pair of old tartan slippers that were two sizes too big for him. He wouldn't replace them because they were a gift from us as boys. You see, arthritis first came to visit Dad when Adam and I were about twelve years old. That time, his toes and ankles swelled so bad he could barely get his shoes on for work. To help him out, we whipped around the neighbourhood mowing lawns until we'd made enough money to buy him a pair of slippers he could wear to work. Fuzzy reckoned they were the best thing since sliced bread and wore them every day until the swelling in his feet went down. After that they were the first thing he put on when he stepped in the door and last thing he took off at night.'

A small pain of loss twisted like a sharp knife in my breast. I flicked a tear from my eyelash with my knuckle. 'What a sweet man. I'm so glad you got to say goodbye to him. That's something I missed out on.' I stared up at the beautiful home and added, 'I'm astonished the house hasn't sold yet considering how appealing it is.'

'Well, that's another weird thing. I found a box sitting on the dining room table. Inside was a folder that contained three different offers to buy. All for cash. All from the same bloke.'

'That is strange.'

'That's not the most bizarre part. Dad had knocked back the first two offers, even though they were way over the asking price and the third one was torn in half. There was a note from the real estate agent telling him he had to sign the paperwork this time. It's like he was being forced to sell to this Zelinski guy. Anyway, Adam and I have decided to take the house off the market. Chappie knows of some people who are willing to lease it fully furnished for a couple of years.'

I nearly choked when Ryan mentioned who the offer was from. He gave me a startled glance. 'What's wrong?'

'Did you say Zelenski? Not, Brian Zelenski?'

'Yeah, I think that was his name. Why?'

'Brian Zelenski is the manager of The Mariners café!'

Ryan halted in his tracks. He stared along the street. A chill ran up my spine and I wasn't sure if it was from the cold wind that chose that moment to whip up behind us or the stern expression on my companion's face. I began to shiver. Ryan must have noticed because he wrapped his arm around my shoulder and steered me towards the house. 'Come on, Cutie, let's get you inside where there's a fire blazing in the hearth and a mug of hot chocolate with your name on it.'

* * *

The inside of Lamb Lodge, as I had begun to think of it, was every bit as impressive as the outside. The entrance hall was carpeted with a fine Turkish rug upon which sat a beautiful walnut side table. Set upon this was a lead crystal vase full of sweetly perfumed garden flowers. It was warm and welcoming.

I followed Ryan along a short passageway of polished floorboards and dazzling aboriginal artwork into what he called the family room. A large double-glazed feature window took up the entire length of one wall and overlooked the magnificent garden growing in the rear of the property. The picturesque view added a sense of serenity to the room. It made sense to me that a music stand, saxophone and stool should be set in front of the plate glass, as it would be the perfect place to make music. Three dark brown leather couches had been positioned around a glass-fronted fireplace and offered a comfortable viewing platform for the wall-mounted, big screen television that was bolted to the wall above the hearth.

'Hey lazy bones, we're back,' said Ryan to the dog sprawled on her back, taking full advantage of the blazing fire to roast her belly. The tip of Tennille's tail wiggled a greeting but she didn't move from her coveted position. I made my way over and gave her a gentle rub on the chest. She gave me a happy pant, rolled to her side and began to snore.

I laughed in delight. 'Good watchdog you have here.'

He rolled his eyes. 'Yeah, give her a fire and she goes on strike. Make yourself comfortable, Cutie. We can check out the realtor's paperwork while we sip our drinks. Maybe you can give me some fresh insight.'

* * *

I nestled back into the buttery softness of the couch and sipped at my hot chocolate in quiet contentment. Holding up the taped pieces of paper that made up the real estate Offer and Acceptance form I gave it a thorough examination. There were two items in the O&A that really stood out. First the 2.5 million dollar offer, with a fourteen day settlement, was $500,000 over the asking price. Second the offer was for cash.

*Wow, who has that much money just lying around in ready notes?*

Curious as to how the sale of the business had been handled, I turned my attention to the Beach and Rock Café sale document.

'Is this your Dad's handwriting?' I asked, swiping my finger underneath the vendor's details and signature.

Ryan slid closer to my side and our arms brushed. 'Yep, that's Dad's hand alright. He didn't have much in the way of formal schooling when he was young, so was always careful to print in clear block lettering.'

The warmth of his nearness filled me. I gazed with longing at his close-shaven chin and delicious mouth as he studied the neat and laboured print over my shoulder. He caught me staring and flicked me an amused glance. Flustered I lowered my gaze and fumbled through the document to the purchaser's signature page.

In an attempt to cover my embarrassment I zeroed in on the first thing to catch my attention. 'Have you ever heard of Bearcub Enterprises?'

Ryan's attention returned to the document in my hand. 'No? Should I have?'

'Well, yeah. They're the ones who bought and paid for the café. Not Brian Zelenski. According to this he only acted as their agent.' I tapped my chin and mumbled my thoughts out loud. 'So Brian is managing the cafe for this Bearcub Enterprises. I wonder if it's the same for the house? Is Brian acting as an agent for the purchaser or does he want to buy the house for himself?'

I stared at Ryan. He stared intently back. I so wanted to lean forward and taste his lips. The pull was strong. Shyness overtook me. I dropped my gaze back to the O&A and studied the frugal information it contained.

'Ryan, the offer for the house is for cash. On Friday night, Brian was in the office at the café, counting big wads of the stuff. I'm curious as to where it all came from? Maybe I could have a poke around next time I'm at work and...'

'That's not such a good idea,' Ryan interjected before I could finish my musing. 'I don't want you to do anything that could put you in danger.'

I shot him a startled glance. 'Why would you think it dangerous? All I'd be doing is looking for paperwork. Besides Brian is hardly ever there. He spends most of his time at one of the pubs or nightclubs he has a hand in.'

Ryan opened his mouth, but whatever he was going to say remained unspoken because Chips and Chappie breezed in the door bringing with them the cold outside air and warm laughter.

# 6

## Chapter Six

Chips stuck her head around the door and barked, 'Have you still got your nose buried in that damn computer? What are you doing?'

Jolted from a long, deep delve into the internet, I took the opportunity to stretch my back. After reaching for the ceiling I let my hands fall into my lap and began to stroke the tortoiseshell cat curled up asleep there. Fleabag rumbled out a loud purr of approval. I flicked a glance at my cousin. She was dressed in black winter-weight running tights, a white, long sleeve top with an interesting fleck pattern all over it. She looked fabulous and I didn't understand how she did it. If I pulled on the same gear I'd look all misshapen and mismatched.

'Research. You should try it.'

I knew she didn't have to. My cousin had been blessed with an astute intelligence and the ability to speed read and memorize text, so she had no problem with course work or cranking out assignments that scored high marks. I, on the other hand, had to slog away, word by word, struggling to absorb the salient points from which to produce a coherent and readable assignment. My comment to her wasn't fair. Yes, I was doing research, but not for any university assignment. And, I was being snippy because I couldn't find the answers I wanted, getting more frustrated by the minute. For the entire morning I'd had my nose buried in the Australian Business Register seeking details about Bearcub Enterprises. Information was limited. All I'd managed to uncover so far was that the business was owned by an international group called Nimble Investments.

My bad mood didn't affect my cousin's happy one. She just gave a tinkle of amusement. 'You've got square eyes, Burger. Take a break. Let some of that information sink in before you add more guff to the pile you've already crammed into your brain. Here's an idea. I'm off to the beach, why don't you come along?'

Beach walking with Chips was like competing in a marathon. She wouldn't casually stroll along the water's edge for half an hour, occasionally dipping her toes in the cool surf. On the contrary, she'd set off at a brisk pace, that was impossible for me to keep up with, and cover at least ten kilometres without raising a sweat. The show off would then jog back and still look as immaculate as she did now.

I rotated my stiff neck in a half circle. She was right. A break would be good.

'I will, if, and only if,' I waved my forefinger at her, 'you let me do my own thing while you play at being wonder woman.'

Her face crinkled in a pleased smile. My mobile phone began to dance in a mad buzzing circle on the desk in front of me. I glanced at the caller ID. 'Hang on a sec. It's Ashley.' The happiness left her face. 'Hello, Ashley. How are you today?'

'Feeling lonely and neglected, I miss you.'

I giggled. 'Don't be silly. How can you miss me, we only met on Friday.'

'And what an introduction, you really rocked my world, Sunflower.'

'You're so sweet.' Chips shoved her finger down her throat and pretended to gag. I flipped her off. 'What are you up to?'

'Driving around, waiting for you to text me your address. It is Sunday, you know!'

'Sure it's Sunday,' I replied, wondering what the day of the week had to do with Ashley driving around the streets.

'Our date, remember. Don't tell me it's off because I'll be devastated. I was working on a very juicy scene in my manuscript. I put it aside, just for you!'

I was speechless. Had I missed something Friday? I didn't recall making a definite date with him but then my brain had been a mound of marshmallowy goo at the time. 'Oh no, I'm looking forward to it,' I managed to blurt out in a fairly convincing tone. 'I was just so caught up in some research I was doing that time got away from me. Where are you at the moment?'

'Little Grove. So, we're still good?'

I pictured the cute dimple that appeared at the corner of his mouth when he smiled and decided it wouldn't be a hardship to see it again. 'Sure. It'll be wonderful to get out of the townhouse and brush away a few of my study cobwebs.'

'Fantastic. Text me your address. I'll pick you up in ten minutes.'

I thought about the cat fur plastered all over my scruffy track pants and the rats nest state of my hair. 'Can you make it fifteen? I have a couple of things I need to finish here first.'

'Only if you promise you won't keep me waiting a minute longer. If you do, I'll have to punish you.' His low seductive growl drew a silly giggle from my lips.

'Idiot! Course I'll be ready and waiting for you out on the front kerb.' I crossed my fingers that I wasn't stretching the truth too far, 'Promise.'

'Awesome, see you in fifteen.'

After hanging up I shot him off a text with my address, dumped a protesting Fleabag onto my bed and made a beeline for the closet.

'So, no beach with me, huh?' said my cousin, her expression blank.

'Sorry, but it seems I promised Ashley I'd go out with him today. He's already on his way, so it wouldn't be right to fob him off.'

'No, I'm sure. Make sure you rug up. The breeze outside is icy.' I stared at her retreating back in bemusement as I bundled myself into a clean pair of jeans. What was her problem?

Neatly groomed and warmly dressed as instructed by my pseudo mother hen, I made it out to the front of our townhouse with a minute to spare. As usual, Chips, was right. The wind blasted like the ice-chiller's door had been left open. Big fat charcoal clouds scudding across a bleak sky held the promise of snow. I huddled deep into my sheepskin-lined, leather bomber jacket and flipped up the collar to keep my ears warm as I watched a black BMW glide along the street. To my surprise it halted in front of me. Ashley leapt from the driver's seat. He'd dressed for the climate in designer jeans, a thick, cream-coloured polo-necked sweater and Italian hiker boots that must have cost a fortune.

'Hello beautiful,' he said, hurrying around the front of the car to plant a soft kiss on my cheek. His warm lips scorched hot against my near frozen skin.

'Hi, yourself,' I said, with a hesitant smile. Bashfulness overwhelmed me because my memory of him hadn't been faulty. He was gorgeous and I had to lock my knees, so I didn't become a puddle at his feet. 'Did you have any problem finding me?'

'Well, I have been looking for a long time,' he joked with a pleasant laugh.

Heat invaded my cheeks. Being a down to earth girl, I was stumped for words because I wasn't any good at this flirting stuff.

Ashley studied my face, a small smile played on his lips. 'You look like a girl who could use an *affogato al caffe*.'

Along with hot chocolate, Ashley had just nailed another of my favourite hot beverages. I gave him an uncomplicated smile of appreciation, 'Sounds heavenly.'

He opened the car door and took a bow. 'Your carriage awaits, milady.'

Touched and amused by his chivalry I clambered in, grateful to get out of the breeze. Ashley slid into the driver's seat, captured my hands in his long, warm fingers and leant towards me. I thought for a moment he was going to kiss me. I wasn't ready for that level of intimacy. In the back of my mind an image of Ryan and the high moral standard of loyalty, honesty and fidelity he would bring to a loving relationship rose. I so wanted to share that with him. I sank back into the leather seat, away from Ashley's intensity. A shiver caught me by surprise.

'You're cold.' He reached across to redirect the air vents in my direction and flicked the car's heating up to full throttle. I tugged my fingers from his grip and held them up to the blast of hot air. From the corner of my eye I caught a small pout touch his lips before his face went blank.

'Thanks Ashley. The Antarctic is really sharing today.'

Ashley hooked a lazy wrist over the steering wheel and sedately manoeuvred the luxurious car down the street.

'So, how's your day been? Has your writing been going well?' I asked, in an attempt to kick start a conversation.

He flicked a quick glance my way. 'My plot is still in the early development stages, but has a lot of potential. Let's not talk about that or me, it's boring. Let's talk about a much more interesting subject - you.'

Heat rose in my cheeks, *again*. To hide my discomfort at being the centre of attention I began to waffle on a little with the standard information - where I went to school, why we moved to Albany and the type of study I was doing. I didn't feel the urge to share any in-depth details like I had with Ryan. When I mentioned that my parents were dead, Ashley didn't ask any questions and I didn't elaborate.

'How about you? Are you a local lad with a relative living on every street corner?' I asked, curious to get to know him a little better.

'Nope. Just like you, I'm from Perth,' he replied.

That was it. Short and sweet. Before I could ask him to give a touch more detail, he drew the car to a halt and leapt from the driver's seat. Racing around the bonnet of the car Ashley opened my door before I could get my hand on the handle. As I stepped onto the footpath, he took a firm grasp of my elbow and guided me into a pretty, cottage style café. There were lace cloths on the tables and a pot-belly stove blazed cheerfully in the far corner. The room was crowded but one table next to the fire had a reserved sign on it.

'Oh, how lovely,' I said, taking in the pretty garden prints on the walls, the display of fine china in a glass cabinet and the enticing scent of freshly brewed coffee 'I didn't know this café was here. How'd you find this place?'

'I have my spies,' smirked Ashley. He guided me over to the reserved table, pulled out a chair and made sure I was settled into the seat closest to the warm blaze. 'Do you want anything to eat with your coffee?'

My stomach growled, informing me I'd missed lunch. 'A slice of cake would be nice.'

'Sweets for the sweet. No problem. I won't be long.'

My gaze followed his tall, athletic figure as he stalked over to the serving counter. He walked with his shoulders back and elbows out like he owned the room. His manner was different from Ryan who glided like a silent, stalking cat. At that moment my phone buzzed in my pocket. When I pulled it out I had to laugh. One thought of the man and he'd sent a text.

*Are you okay, snoopy? (Sheep emoji.)*

My thumb danced across the screen and my lip lifted in a goofy grin as I shot off a reply.

*(Thumbs up emoji), Snoopy did find out some stuff – no danger involved! (Blood-stained dagger emoji). Bearcub Enterprises is a subsidiary of Nimble Investment. Mean anything to you?*

The reply came almost immediately.

*Nope. Hot chocolate? Icecream? Tennille misses you.*

*Sorry, Snoopy has her flak jacket on and is currently out for coffee with a friend. Raincheck? (Storm cloud emoji.)*

*It's supposed to be pouring tomorrow. Lunch together at Noon? Six Degree's Food Laneway?*

My heart began to glow.

*Lovely. See ya then. Tell Tennille, I miss her too. (Heart emoji). Gotta fly, I'm neglecting my friend. (Horror face emoji)*

I logged the date with Ryan into my calendar app and was slipping the phone back into my jacket pocket when Ashley returned to the table. He slid a dainty plate with a delicious looking wedge of malteser cheesecake in front of me.

'Wow, my favourite. Thank you.'

He gave an even-toothed smile and the dimple appeared in the corner of his mouth. My heart stuttered in delight.

'The coffee will be here in a minute.' He nodded to the pocket where I had shoved my phone. 'Problem?'

'Oh, no, just a friend wondering if I'd like to go out for a hot chocolate. I told them I was already taken.'

'Damn straight,' he said.

My eyebrows shot up at the possessive tone he used. Deciding it wasn't worth an argument, I changed the subject.

'Now, how about you tell me some stuff about yourself, like are you a full-time writer or do you have to juggle your writing around a career? Are you published? How long are you in Albany for? Where in Perth did you grow up?' I took a deep breath and continued, 'Do you have a brood of brothers and sisters?'

Ashley began to laugh and held out a hand to stop the flood of questions. 'Whoa up with the inquisition, Sunflower. Let me give you a quick synopsis and leave you to find the rest out over time. I'm twenty-four years old. Yes, I do have a family – a mum, a dad and no siblings. I work with my father in the family business and write in my spare time. And before you ask,' he said, flicking the tip of my nose with a gentle finger, 'we invest in failing businesses. Provide guidance and structure and turn them into profitable ventures.' He pointed around the room. 'This cafe is a classic example.'

'You own this place?'

'Not own, no. I just provide restructure and business guidelines. In return they pay me a gratuity.'

'Wow. Is that why you're here? To check up on the cafe?'

'Not really. This place is doing exactly as it should. I'm more fishing around for new opportunities and to work on my plot of course.'

'So how long is all that going to take?'

'What the plot or sourcing opportunities?' Ashley asked, with a hearty chuckle. 'How long's a piece of string? It all depends how everything goes, probably a few months. Now, enough about me, I have a question for you?'

'Fire away.'

'Why was that university security bloke giving you such a hard time on Friday?'

I rolled my eyes. 'Oh, that loser! Well, it all started at the beginning of the year when, unfortunately, RFW took a shine to me. I'm positive he took to hiding behind bushes and doors, watching and waiting for any opportunity to corner me. Whenever I was alone he would materialize at my side to whisper insubstantial endearments into my ear. It was revolting and creepy.'

'I bet. What does RFW mean?'

'Rat-faced weasel!'

Ashley roared with laughter. 'I love it. So, what did you do?'

'I threatened to report him to one of the councillors for harassment so he changed tact. Now he watches my every move and issues fines for any wrongdoing.'

'Can't you report him for that?'

'Not really, mainly because I've usually done the things I'm in trouble for - like running for class and crashing into you. And I must apologise once more. I hope I didn't hurt you.'

'No, it would take more than a beautiful girl throwing herself into my arms, to do that,' he said, with an amused grin on his face. 'And don't feel guilty, either. You, my beautiful sunflower, can crash into me anytime you like.' Ashley pulled his chair a tad closer, placed his hand on my forearm and gave it a soft squeeze. 'Do you want me to have a word with this RFW and point out to him the error of his ways?'

I leant back into my seat, away from the intimacy he was trying to create between us. 'That's really sweet of you, but...'

Ashley's smiled dimmed. He waggled a finger in front of my nose. 'No buts.'

'Thanks for the offer, but I think you better leave it. It might make matters worse.'

He grunted but at that moment the waitress arrived with our coffee and put a stop to the fruitless conversation. I took advantage of the moment to draw my arm away from his light grasp and placed my hands in my lap to clear a space for her to put my cup. Our waitress flashed her eyes and cleavage at Ashley as she placed a china teapot in front of him, but he didn't seem to notice. She dumped my coffee in the middle of the table, glared at me and stalked away. Amused by her antics, I asked Ashley an inane question and we began to chit chat about the things we liked doing. Me: reading, solving puzzles and spending time with friends. Ashley: writing, jogging, working out at the gym while watching sport and sorting out business challenges which he considered much like my puzzle solving. Suddenly a cold breeze hit us as the café door was flung open. Colin Faraday rushed in and came barrelling across the room. He was talking before he even reached our table.

'Hey Burger, so glad I spotted you as I was passing by. I want to let you know that I'll be late tomorrow. I've got a blasted dentist appointment that I forgot about when we made our plans Friday.'

'Hi to you too, Colin,' I said, pulling out my phone to check my calendar for the next day.

'Oh, yeah, sorry. Hi!' he replied, with a lopsided grin. Ashley didn't return the smile.

'You're always in a flap. If you slowed down a touch and wrote a few things down you mightn't get in these pickles,' I said. Considering how disorganised he was, I was amazed Colin actually managed to show up to any of his appointments.

With a first-class display of the braces on his teeth, Colin chortled. 'You sound like my mum.'

I nearly choked. Oh, god! I was also starting to sound like my cousin, the mother hen.

'How late do you reckon you'll be?' I asked, flicking open my phone calendar.

'An hour, at least. Say three-thirty to be on the safe side.'

'That's fine, suits me better anyway as I won't have to rush my previous appointment, but don't make it a habit, okay!' I waved a good-natured finger at him. I didn't let on that I was delighted with the time change. It would give me an extra hour for lunch with Ryan.

'Do you log everything into your phone calendar?' asked Ashley, leaning over my shoulder to watch me make the adjustments to my day.

'Sure do. It's something I'm pedantic about. I have a busy life, what with work, study and other stuff. I'd never be on time for anything if I didn't log it.' I flicked my glance up and took in his steely grey eyes as they studied my colour co-ordinated schedule for the next day. I turned the screen away and held it up for Colin to see. 'Three-thirty Colin, okay?

'Yes, Mum. Thanks, gotta dash. I'll see ya tomorrow after the chomper butcher.' With a wild flap of his hand and a rush of feet, Colin was gone.

I laughed. 'That was Colin.'

'So I gathered,' Ashley said, with raised eyebrows. 'He's quite a whirlwind. Are you going out on a date with him?'

'Not quite. We're conspiring together on a crime!' I had to giggle when his eyebrows shot high and his eyes widened. He looked shocked. 'Only on paper my friend. Colin and I have teamed up for this term's assignment. Every team must create some sort of crime scenario. The other students in our class have to try to solve the puzzle by deciphering the forensics clues we give them. Tomorrow is our first planning session.'

'Sounds like fun. What are you thinking of doing?'

'Not sure yet...' A thought suddenly struck me. 'You know the ins and outs of business, right?'

He nodded, and his eyes narrowed with a look of wariness. 'Sure, what do you want to know?'

'How would I make a load of ready cash?'

'I take it you mean nefariously obtained money?'

Not really sure if the money I was thinking about was the proceeds of crime or not, I decided to go with the flow. 'Yeah, something that produces a regular income.'

'There's the usual ways I suppose. Selling drugs, extortion, gambling, skimming profits, loan sharking, embezzlement or just plain old bank robbery.'

'Well not bank robbery. It's too public. Besides I don't have any knowledge of how to break into a vault.'

'Making the money wouldn't be your biggest problem.'

'It wouldn't?'

'No. Your problem would be to legitimise it.'

'As in launder, you mean?'

Ashley nodded. His eyes glazed over as if in deep thought. The corners of his eyelids crinkled up as if what was going on in his mind amused him. 'Hmm, here's a scenario for you. Say you're a profitable drug dealer. You have all this cash from your sales but no way to show where it came from. You could take out a small bank loan and buy a couple of cash type businesses.'

'I could? Why?'

'By falsifying the books, it would seem like the businesses are really profitable. That would account for some of the money, but you need to establish some sort of elaborate invoicing system to charge the business for goods not sold and services not rendered. And, you must pay tax, otherwise the ATO auditors will come down on you like a ton of bricks.'

'Why couldn't I just bank the cash?'

'You could. But you'd have to set up a raft of accounts and keep them all under ten grand. Your other problem is that all banks require more than one form of identity when you establish a new account. So, you'd need lots of fake ID's for it to work.'

'Why keep the accounts under $10,000?'

'There's a Government requirement that for any transaction or holding over ten grand the financial institution has to submit a Threshold Transaction report, commonly known as a TTR, to AUSTRAC.' Ashley took a sip of his green tea before continuing. 'I suppose you could use a shell company. Do you know about them?'

'I've heard the term, on the tellie I think, but I don't really know what a shell company is.'

Fascinated, I propped my elbow onto the table, cupped my chin in my palm and waited for him to go on.

'A shell company or corporation is a company without any active business operations or significant assets. They exist only on paper and are mostly used to make financial transactions.'

'Is that even legal?'

'Oh yeah, totally. Unless, of course, you're using the account for criminal purposes. One of the biggest challenges to a money launderer is how to get the funds out of the country, wash it clean and transfer it back, in such a way, so as not to raise suspicion.'

'Why send the money overseas?'

'So it can be smurfed.'

'Smurf did you say? What have little blue men got to do with it?'

Ashley cocked an eyebrow and gave me what I can only describe as a stinky eye. 'Smurfing, my dear sunflower, is the term used when cash is smuggled overseas and moved from country to country as its washed clean through various investments in things like property, art, jewellery or what would be my favourite choice - racehorses and luxury boats.'

'So, what happens then? I mean you're stuck with all this stuff...'

'Well, you off-load it. The money is considered clean because you have a tangible way of showing where it has come from.'

'Wow! How would I go about finding out about these shell companies? Like, for example, who the owner or the directors are?'

'You can't! Shell companies and the off-shore accounts they are associated with are usually set up in tax havens like British Columbia or Switzerland. The details are kept anonymous and very, very secret, otherwise those countries would lose what, for them, is a very lucrative industry.'

'Bugger.'

I sat back in my seat and blew out a gusty sigh. Maybe that's why I couldn't find anything on Nimble Investments, it was a shell company.

'Why bugger?'

I was tempted to tell Ashley about the cash I'd seen Brian counting on Friday night, but I really had no real proof that what he was doing wasn't legit. Besides the house he was trying to buy belonged to Ryan and Adam and it wouldn't be right to discuss their finances over coffee with a stranger without their permission.

'I had an idea, but it won't wash. Colin and Jess, that's the other member of our team, and I, are working to a tight schedule. It would take too much time and effort to design a scenario that involved a shell company. Besides I can't see what type of red herrings or clues I could create that would lead the class to solving the puzzle. Nah, my idea's for a project need a lot more thought. Thanks for the info though. It was interesting to learn about the internal workings of the rich and infamous. How come you know so much about money laundering?'

'I invest in businesses. It's important to know how the world works.'

'Yeah, of course,' I said, pushing my empty coffee cup away from me. 'It was a stupid question. Sorry.'

Ashley grinned at me. 'Did you think I was a big bad crook?'

I cocked my eyebrow at him. 'Oh, ho ho.'

He roared with laughter. When his amusement was under control, he asked, 'Where would you like to go now, my little criminal? How about we take in a movie and then I'll take you out for dinner?'

I glanced up at the clock above the counter. Five o'clock.

'Holy hell, look at the time! I'm so sorry. I'll have to take a rain check. I've got the evening shift at the café tonight. I need to hurry or I'll be late but I do want to thank you Ashley for a fascinating afternoon.'

I stumbled to my feet while yanking my wallet from my back pocket at the same time. My feet tangled. Ashley put a hand under my elbow to prop me up because I nearly fell flat on my face. My cheeks blazed with hot embarrassment.

'Thanks. I'm such a klutz. How much do I owe you for my coffee and cake?'

He looked thunderstruck. 'Put your wallet away, Sunflower. I take care of my girl.'

I was about to argue but the look on his face said it all. I lifted myself on tip toes and kissed his cheek. 'Thank you.'

Ashley smiled and slipped his arm around my waist. He pulled me close and squeezed me against his side as he guided me through the now almost empty café. Releasing me, he opened the door and waved me through. I looked up at his face and smiled as I stepped out onto the footpath and almost collided with a man who wore trendily slashed jeans and an unzipped black-leather biker jacket that revealed a faded ACDC tee shirt underneath. His long, untidy auburn hair hung across most of his face like a curtain but there was no disguising the drunken troublemaker from Friday night.

He leered at me. Alcohol fumes blasted my face as he shoved his ugly mug close to mine and breathed, 'Hello, sweet-cakes. How's about giving Slugger that kiss now?'

I jerked away from his grasping hand, stumbled and nearly fell. Suddenly I was in Ashley's arms. He swung me aside and took a stance between me and my aggressor.

'Leave my lady alone,' he said, in a voice so cold and hard it nearly froze the air around us. I leant around his broad back to stare at the man called Slugger. He stared up at Ashley with terror across his face.

'Sorry, mate. I didn't mean nothin'...'

'I'm not your mate,' interrupted Ashley, his voice now arctic. 'If you ever come near my lady again it will be the last thing you do. Understand?' The colour bleached from Slugger's face. He nodded. 'Now get lost.'

Slugger spun on his heel and bolted in an uncoordinated scramble down the street.

I was shaken. Ashley pulled me hard against his chest. I clung tight, and snuggled into the soft warmth of his jumper. Emotion swamped me and I began to cry.

'Are you okay,' he asked, handing me neatly folded white handkerchief.

I hiccupped, wiped away my tears and gave my nose a lusty blow before feeling in control enough to answer. 'Yes, thanks. He caught me off guard and not for the first time.'

Ashley's finger lifted my chin. His eyes bore down at me. 'Has this happened before?'

I gave a watery smile and nodded. Tears welled in my eyes as I remembered the fear the Friday night disturbance had caused in me. The bell on the door behind us tinkled and someone murmured, 'Excuse me, can I get past, please?'

The realisation we blocked the café doorway helped me tamp down my emotions. 'Oh sorry,' I hiccupped.

Ashley didn't say a word, instead he slipped an arm around my waist and led me to his car. He reefed open the door and fussed around ensuring I was settled comfortably into the passenger's seat before sliding in beside me and switching on the car's heater.

'Thanks,' I said, letting the warmth do its work. Slowly the shakes left my hands and I was finally able to breathe without sniffling.

'Tell me,' he ordered.

I recited the whole sorry tale leading up to Friday night's debacle but didn't give any personal details about Ryan or Adam as I was still concerned that their involvement might get back to the military and cause them problems. 'So lucky for us, no one was hurt and two of our customers managed to shove the troublemakers out the door.'

Ashley drummed his fingers on the steering wheel as he listened, his face a picture of anger. 'I'm sorry I let that little prick off so easily...Oh, sorry, Faith, excuse my language,' he said, taking my hand and pulling it to his lips. 'If he ever bothers you again, let me know, I'll...'

'It's over Ashley. I think you scared enough years from him to deter him for a lifetime.'

'Good,' he said with a smug grin. 'Now, we'd better get you home, milady, or you'll be angry with me for making you late.'

'Oh, I don't think I could get angry with you for looking after me,' I said, shooting him a grateful smile.

Ashley started the car and drove me home with a self-satisfied look on his face.

# 7

## Chapter Seven

The café was as quiet as a graveyard. I hadn't had a customer in over two hours. The clock had just ticked over into the early hours of Monday morning. It was now half-an-hour past my scheduled knock off time and Brad, who was supposed to man the grill from midnight to six a.m., still hadn't arrived for his shift. I bit the bullet and called Brian.

'Well, young lady it looks like you get a couple of extra hours tonight. You'll have to cover for Brad until...' he paused, I presumed, to consult his copy of the roster. 'I see Lucy and Jim start at 3 a.m., so stay until then.'

'But Brian, I'm all alone...' I was wasting my breath. He'd already hung up.

I took in the quiet state of the café, shook off the heebie-jeebies and focused on the naughty devil perched on my shoulder.

*'Now is the perfect time,'* she whispered in my ear.

Not really convinced, I took a shifty out the window to make sure I was alone before I dared step out into the car park to double check no one was heading my way. Soft misty rain, highlighted in yellow by the lone streetlight, fell on a silent street. The ocean, lapping at

Middleton beach five-hundred metres down the road, had quietened with the arrival of a dense, sea mist that muffled its calm rhythmic thrum. I checked beyond the dome cast by the streetlight. Houses were dark. Cars stood idle with their windows fogged from the cold. There was no movement in any direction. Reassured the town was asleep I hurried back inside and jerked open the storage cupboard. I dragged out a mop and bucket. With a cocky nonchalance I didn't feel, I whistled my way to the office door and glanced in. To the left, standing like a grey sentinel on the grubby black and white tiles, was a metal filing cabinet. Against the opposite wall a black-melamine desk had been shoved into the corner. The desk had seen better days. The top, chipped and scarred, had numerous sticky rings that had gathered dust bunnies along its battered surface. I glanced at the three lockable filing drawers on the left side of the desk leg well.

'Now what do you suppose Brian keeps in there?' I asked the oversized framed portrait of Fuzzy Lamb which hung in pride of place on the wall near the desk. Fuzzy continued to grin at me and I noticed Ryan's resemblance to his father in the shape of his jaw line and the flare of his nostrils. I gave the portrait a cheeky salute and backed out of the room.

As the entire back area of the cafe was in dire need of a good scrub, I hurried over to the large steel trough next to the back door and filled the bucket with bleach and hot water. Starting at the sink I slung the mop over the floor tiles until they shone, all the while trying to build up enough courage to tackle the task ahead. Every few swipes I paused to listen. It remained quiet. Even the fridges seemed to be asleep.

'Come on Burger. There's no one around...just do it already.'

I sucked in a lungful of air, retired my mop against the office door frame and slipped into the room. I don't know why, it wasn't like it was going to bite me, but I found myself tiptoeing to the desk.

'Idiot,' I snarled, and with a flick of my wrist, I yanked open the top drawer.

It was empty.

I slammed it shut. My heart stuttered in fright. I raced back out into the passageway to check if anyone was around to hear the sounds of my search.

I was met with silence.

'Get on with it, you ninny. The sooner you do this the sooner you'll be finished,' I muttered to myself.

The lecture seemed to give me courage. I strode back to the desk with more confidence and yanked open the next drawer. I found a bent paperclip in an otherwise empty drawer. Disheartened but now fully committed, I launched myself at the filing cabinet. It too, was unlocked and contained only two hanging files. Surprised the café business had only produced enough paperwork for two hangers I took a quick gander. The first folder was very thin and held a single sheet of A4 paper. I held it up and saw it was a copy of this week's work roster. To my disgust I noticed Chips and I had scored Friday night's grog sop shift again. I shoved the paper back into its folder and drew out the second hanger. It was fat and bulky.

'Now this looks more promising,' I said to Fuzzy. 'What do you reckon? Have I hit the jackpot?' I took his grin to mean go ahead and have a look.

I thought about Ashley and his comments about forged invoices and gave the mismatched pieces of papers a thorough examination. To my amateur eye everything seemed to gel with what we had stocked and sold. Disappointment kicked me in the guts.

'Bugger,' I snarled. Frustrated I slammed the drawer shut. It echoed throughout the building with a loud clang. Startled I sucked in a breath. 'That was plain stupid, Burger. What if someone hears you?'

I decided to double check that I was still alone before taking a further snoop around. I grabbed the mop, gave it a wiggle across the tiles just outside the office door while I craned my neck to check for gangsters sneaking up on me. The café was still empty. With a hefty sigh, I gave my heart a few moments to settle into a more reasonable rhythm. The silence of the café continued. With the return of my courage, I made my way over to the portrait of Ryan's dad. Fuzzy Lamb must have been in his fifties when the photo was taken. His kind face was wreathed in a huge grin, and I could see how he got the nickname. A cloud of wild, wiry-white curls surrounded his face like a halo. I slipped my phone from my pocket and took a photograph.

With an apology I lifted the frame from the wall to study the small wall safe behind. It was black, about a half meter square. It had a digital keypad and a chrome silver handle on an anodized white plate. I wondered about the combination. Unlike the movies, there weren't any numbers conveniently sticky taped inside or under the desk drawers. The only thing behind the picture was an out-of-date calendar with a few meaningless dates circled in red and black ink. Discarding the dates as insignificant, because there were too many circled, I gnawed at my thumbnail and stared at the nine-digit keypad. Taking a punt, I punched in the five numbers that corresponded with the spelling of the name BRIAN. My heart began gallop as each button I pushed stridently echoed around the quiet room. I sucked in my breath and gave the handle such a hard tug that I nearly dislocated my fingers. The lock held.

'Jeez, a little help would be nice.' I glanced down at the portrait at my feet. A loud hiss sounded. I almost leapt out of my socks. 'Shit, Burger,' I snarled. 'Get control of yourself. It's only the compressor on the drinks fridge kicking into action.'

The jitters returned. With shaky fingers I snapped a photograph of the safe and the calendar, muttered another apology to Fuzzy and rehung him back onto the wall where he belonged. Staring around the office I could see nothing else worthy of investigation.

With relief I slipped back into the corridor and picked up the bucket. I strolled out into the customer's dining area and began to mop in earnest while I thought about combination possibilities. My main problem was I was thinking like me, not Brian. I made a final pass of the mop under the fridge. As I stretched my back a thought rammed its way to the front of my brain. Was the five-digit safe combination FUZZY? I stuck the mop into the bucket, spun on my heel to shoot back into the office.

I screamed.

Brian stood right behind me.

'Bloody hell, Faith, is that how you greet all our customers?'

With my hands clasped over my pounding chest, I gasped, 'Jeez Brian, you nearly gave me a bloody heart attack. Where the friggin' hell did you come from anyway? Not in through the main doors that's for sure. I was standing right here mopping and would have seen you.'

Brian's belly wobbled as he chortled. 'I came in via the back door.' He rocked his portly frame back on his heels, pushed the laptop slung across his shoulder aside and strutted over to a table. He settled into a seat. 'I'm glad to see you weren't slacking off while it was quiet. Carry on with your cleaning. I'll watch the counter while I do my bookwork.'

I nodded and with trembling fingers reached down to grab the bucket.

'Oh and, Faith...' I waited, unsure of what was coming. 'For god's sake give the office a thorough clean will you. It's filthy!'

# 8

## Chapter Eight

The hair on the back of my neck rose. I had a sensation I was being watched. I scanned the car park, expecting to see the rat-face weasel or the creepy Slugger lurking about, but except for a row of parked cars the lot seemed quiet and deserted. Actually, when I came to think about it, I hadn't seen RFW at all today. I began to speculate about that. When the prickle of awareness stayed with me, I took another gander around and saw nothing untoward. I gave myself a mental shake and decided to ignore my over fertile imagination. Adjusting the load of textbooks in my arms I smiled. I had a date with Ryan. We were to meet at the pub across the road from the university. I decided to dump my gear into the boot of MC and leave her parked where she was. As I stepped past the first row of parked cars an arm fell around my waist. I was jerked backwards. I let out a loud squeal. Moments later, a dark four-wheel drive flashed past and roared away.

Heart pounding I spun around to stare at the owner of the arm. His eyes were as wide as saucers. He pulled me tight against his chest and wrapped his arms around me.

'That was close, Sunflower. You were nearly a splat on the bitumen.'

I gulped in a deep breath and snuggled against his broad chest for comfort.

With a mouthful of the soft wool jumper he wore I gasped, 'Thank you, Ashley. That bloody car came out of nowhere.'

He was silent. I looked up and our eyes met and held. His were an intense grey. Before I could analyse his intent, Ashley's lips covered mine in a searing, demanding kiss. My heart flipped. I slung an arm around his neck and parted my lips. The kiss was deep and wonderful but didn't feel right. I gently drew away.

Ashley hands came up to cup my cheeks. 'I thought I'd lost you.'

'I want to thank you from the bottom of my heart for the rescue. I must have crossed the wrong side of a black cat or something because that's the second time in two days you've had to save me. We can't go on like this. I don't think my heart will take it'

'You're my girl. I'm always going to watch out for you.'

I didn't want him to think of me that way. While it saddened me, I had to say something. 'As for the kiss, it was delightful...but, well you see...I've met someone and we are dating.'

Ashley's palms dropped away from my face and settled on my hips. He placed his forehead against mine and sighed. It was a forlorn sound.

'Does he make you happy?'

Warmth bloomed in my breast as I thought about Ryan. 'Yes, he does.'

'Good. A terrific girl like you should have someone nice.' His smile was melancholic as he cupped my cheeks with his warm palms. He leant forward, kissed the tip of my nose before stepping back and holding out a hand, 'Friends?'

I placed my hand in his, relieved he understood. 'Definitely, friends. Good one's I hope.' Hopefully he hadn't been hurt by our little interlude. As I gazed up, I decided to lighten the moment. 'Besides I need to keep you around so you can continue to save my sorry butt.'

He chuckled, 'Always a pleasure, milady. So where were you off to in such a hurry?'

'I've got a date at the pub with Ryan.' I pointed to the cream and brick arched windows of the busy and lively, Six Degrees across the street.

'Ryan, huh. What's he like? Oh, that's silly. He'd have to be nice if you're dating him,' said Ashley, with a crooked boyish grin.

My lips tilted up in a return smile but my heart hurt as I could see the flicker of pain in his eyes. 'Yeah, he's great. Look I'm sorry. I can't stop and chat right now. I'm running a bit late.' I spun on my heel to rush away but before I could take a step in the direction of my car Ashley reached around and removed the books from my grasp.

'I'll walk you. I want to make sure you get safely across Stirling Terrace.'

'That's sweet, but you needn't bother.'

'It's no bother.'

I tugged at the bundle of books in his arms. 'I'll be fine.' Ashley held tight, delaying my departure further. 'Ashley, please. I really must go.'

He let go.

'Sorry, Faith, I'm just trying to help.'

I reached up and patted his cheek in an affectionate gesture. He pulled me close. I thought he was going to kiss me again. Before he could take it any further, I put a hand on his chest, pushed back and stepped out of his arms. 'You're a sweetheart but I really need to go. I'll catch you later, okay.'

'How about coffee - tomorrow?' he yelled, as I jogged towards my car.

I gave a thumbs-up over my shoulder, opened MC's hatch and threw my books into the cargo space. I needed to let Ryan know I was running late so I reached into the back pocket of my jeans and fumbled for my mobile. It wasn't where I expected it to be. I patted all my pockets. Nothing. I started a frantic search through the car to see if I'd dropped it inside the vehicle by accident.

'Awe crap...' I growled, as I crawled around on my hands and knees hunting under the driver's seat.

'What's the matter,' Ashley asked, leaning over my upended butt and staring down at me.

'I can't find my phone.'

'You mean this one?' he said, holding out my glitzy pink phone case.

I leapt to my feet and threw my arms around his neck, squeezing tight. 'Oh, you really are a life saver, Ashley. Where would I be without you?' I squealed. 'Where'd you find it?'

'It was lying on the ground between those cars. You must have dropped it when you were almost mown down.'

'Thank you, thank you, thank you,' I breathed. My fingers swiped the screen to wake up the phone. No pesky screen lock for me, it was too much trouble. Ryan's contact page was already up. I must have forgotten to close it down when I was drooling over his photo that morning. 'I'm lost without my phone – most of my life is in it!' I said, as my thumb danced over the keys with a message.

*Sorry (frowny face, running feet emojis) Burger (heart emoji)*

In a whirl I pressed send, gave Ashley a quick peck on the cheek, locked MC and hastened up the pedestrian ramp. Three cars were slowly idling down Stirling Terrace making me wait. I tapped my foot, impatient to be off. Behind me I could hear Ashley nattering to someone on his phone.

'Did you get a good shot? Yeah, I got his phone number. It'll be interesting to see what happens when we send the photo.' A pause, then, 'No, don't you send it yet. I may want to do some photo shop magic on it. Just save it and I'll take a gander when I get home.'

I glanced around curious.

'Hang on a sec, mate.' He placed a hand over the phone's receiver, rolled his eyes and mouthed, 'New business.'

I grinned.

Ashley shook his head and blew me a kiss. He really was gorgeous and such a sweetheart but the moment he'd kissed me I knew what my heart really wanted, and it wasn't him. At that moment the traffic cleared, with a wave I sprinted across the road.

I found Ryan and Tennille settled under a red and white stripped umbrella in a sunny nook of the beer garden. A pot was keeping warm over a candle and two cups sat in front of the man and a bowl of water in front of the dog. Ryan glanced up from the pamphlet he was reading, spotted me wending my way towards them and smiled. He rose to his feet and drew a chair out for me. My heart leapt and warmth invaded my soul. Feeling bold I landed a soft kiss on his cheek before I flopped into the seat, probably a little more shaken by my close encounter with the speeding car than I cared to admit.

Tennille rose to her feet and settled her head in my lap. She stared at me with soulful eyes. I rubbed her ears and murmured a greeting, 'Hello, beautiful.' She gave her tail a lazy twirl, closed her eyes and sighed in delight at the petting. When I stopped stroking her silky coat she opened her eyes, gave me a disappointed look, turned three circles and settled onto my feet, as if claiming me. Almost immediately she began to snore.

I laughed and glanced up at Ryan who stood at my side with his hand on the back of my chair. He smiled as if I'd just handed him the moon and stars. My heart gave a flip.

'I'm so sorry I'm late.' I said, as he settled in the chair opposite me.

Ryan took my hand and stroked his thumb over the back of it. 'No worries, Cutie. You're here now. That's all that is important.'

I felt bereft when he let go of my hand to pour out a cup of hot chocolate from the pot. As he passed it to me he grinned, 'Thought you might be ready for this.'

I accepted it gratefully and took a great gulp. 'Ahh, yum. That really touches the spot. Thank you.' I nodded at the pile of papers on the table in front of him. 'Busy morning, huh?'

'Brain numbing. Forms, forms, forms. The Bank, social services, council, just to name a few. All of them ask the same questions. And, it doesn't end there either. Each institution has a register of other associated bodies I need to contact, and they have their own forms that must be completed before matters can be finalised. My list of jobs has gone from this,' He held up finger and thumb indicating a gap of about two centimetres, 'to this.' Ryan spread his arms wide and grimaced. 'This arvo's going to be worse. Adam and I have a meeting with the funeral director at three and then with a very un-happy realtor at six.'

I leant forward and clasped one of his hands. 'Is there anything I can do to help?'

Lifting my knuckles to his lips, Ryan kissed them. 'Thank you, Faith, but your company for lunch is enough for now.' I squeezed his fingers and with my other hand cupped his cheek. Ryan leant into my palm and closed his eyes. The world around me stopped and I bathed in the glory of the moment. He slowly opened his dreamy eyes, smiled and kissed my palm.

'So, tell me snoopy, did you take a look around the café's office last night?'

I sat back, nestled my hands in his and smirked. 'Of course, I did.'

His top lip twitched in amusement. 'I thought you might. And?'

'And – nothing. The desk drawers were empty except for a bent paperclip. There wasn't even an old pen rolling around. Who the hell runs a business with no stationery? The filing cabinet had one promising fat file, but it turned out to only contain this weekend's delivery dockets. But...I did get this for you.' I swiped my phone and held up the photograph I'd taken of the office wall. Ryan took my phone and studied the picture of his dad.

'Is it a painting or a photo?'

'A print...and here is the name of the local photographer who probably still has the negative.' I texted him the details I'd taken from a label on the back of the frame.

'I hate to ask where you got that - not safe cracking I hope?'

'Nope, my skills don't extend that far, though I did give it a whirl.'

'Of course, you did.' He rolled his eyes. 'Burger, you must be careful. This is not a game and opening that safe is not strictly legal.'

'I wouldn't have taken anything.' I sighed, but knew he was right. I'd nearly come a cropper last night. A minute later and I'd have been caught by Brian taking a second crack at the safe. 'There is something else I need to tell you.'

Ryan sat forward and locked his gaze to mine. 'Go on...'

I told him everything I'd learned about the art of smurfing and money laundering from Ashley. 'Do you think that's what's going on with the café and your house? Is Brian laundering money?'

'I bloody hope not, otherwise it means we're messing around with an organised crime mob and that is some serious shit. People involved in those types of enterprises kill to protect their turf.'

A lead weight settled deep in my belly.

'Please, Burger, no more snooping. I couldn't bear it if you were hurt.'

I squeezed his hand. 'Okay, I'll stop poking around at the cafe. I promise, but... I can still do some internet research into Bearcub Enterprises and Nimble Investments. That should be safe enough.'

Ryan sighed and shook his head. 'I've created a monster.'

I grinned, so pleased he didn't try to boss me around or order me to stop.

'What would you like for lunch, lasagne, chicken schnitzel or a beetroot, goat's cheese and pesto pizza?' His words showed me he had my priorities right.

* * *

Stuffed to the gills from the delicious pizza we'd shared for lunch, I went to collect a notebook from my car for the planning meeting with Colin and Jess. A piece of paper was wedged under MC's wiper blade.

'Oh, so RFW's still lurking around campus. I hope this is not another bloody fine because I've done nothing wrong.'

I snatched up the offending object ready to tear it to shreds. It wasn't a fine.

*Hope u like poisin - the hand of deaf.*

I read the line of neat, carefully formed print that had been crafted in black ink on a torn piece of legal pad and smudged with dirt. What the hell?

A gust of wind tried to snatch the scrap of yellow paper from my fingers. I tightened my grip. My guts twisted. I stared up at the university clock tower deep in thought and nearly leapt from my skin when a car zoomed into the parking space next to me. Colin rolled from the driver's seat with a cheeky grin and ambled to my side.

'Hi, not late am I?'

I stared at him with unfocussed eyes and slowly shook my head. He glanced over my shoulder to see what I was holding.

'Awe cool!' He rubbed his hands together in excitement. 'Our first anonymous letter. The games afoot, Sherlock. The next couple of weeks are gonna be such fun.'

A light flicked on in my mind – of course, the bloody assignment. No wonder the words didn't seem real. I took stock of the note. Neat handwriting. A tiny love heart above the letter I in the misspelled word poison. Poor spelling. Good punctuation.

'And easy – too easy, I think, Colin,' I said, as we wandered side by side towards the university's main entrance. 'This is a fair representation of Penny Jones's handwriting. See the love heart over the I. It's like her trademark. But we need to ask ourselves a question - is this a slip on her team's part or is it really a red herring? Could another team be trying to misdirect us down a false trail?'

Colin held open the front door and waved me through.

'I don't believe that Peter, Penny and Paula...' My tongue stumbled over the mouthful of P names.

'Let's call them the P Team,' said Colin. 'It's easier than having to stutter over Peter, Penny and Paula, all the time.'

I grinned, 'Good idea. Anyway, would the P team make such a fundamental mistake as that and just hand us the answer as to who wrote the note? I know sometimes people aren't necessarily the brightest crayons in the box, but this is a little obvious, don't you think?'

Colin sucked on his bottom lip before poking at it with a finger. He saw me staring. 'Does my lip look huge?' he asked. I shook my head. 'Well, it feels like it, and it's still numb from the needle the dentist shoved in. Hey, there's an idea, we could stage a murder in the dentist's surgery...' Colin prattled on as we made our way into the student's lounge where our other team member, Jess was waiting for us.

\* \* \*

'So, it's agreed. Tomorrow we'll do a forensic examination of everyone's notebooks, looking for the torn strip that matches our note. Can you create a search warrant for that, Jess?' Jess was the computer guru of our investigative team. She gave me a happy smile and nodded. 'Fantastic. It's a long shot, I know, but no stone unturned, remember. I'm told it's the little things that catch people out.'

I ran a finger down the list of tasks I'd made during our planning session. 'Colin, as you usually have lunch with the P team girls, can you craftily find out what Paula and Penny were doing between noon and three today? I can be specific with the time parameter because that slip of paper wasn't on MC when I put my books in her cargo hold at twelve and I was staring at the clock when Colin pulled up at three.'

'I'll take on Peter,' said Jess. 'He coaches my son's footy team. His boy and mine are great friends and we often meet for pizza and other adult stuff.'

Colin and I both stared at her in surprise.

'What? He's single, so am I. I'm entitled to a booty call now and then,' she grinned.

Jess was a dark horse. I patted her on the shoulder in approval. 'You sure are.'

I jotted my name next to a task on the to-do list. 'My boyfriend's just given me an awesome photo shop app,' I said. 'Tonight, I'll have a go at creating a picture of a dentist's office with an open safe and add those clues we discussed.'

Colin rubbed his hands together in delight. 'Awesome, let's see if anyone can work out how we got the safe open.'

I'd have to be very careful about where I hid the clue to the safe combination, because as a result of my planning session with Colin and Jess I now had a fair idea where to find the one that opened The Mariners Café safe. It wouldn't pay to advertise that little gem.

9

# Chapter Nine

After a short three-hour nap at home, I headed to work. When I breezed through the main doors of The Mariners, I was greeted by the sight of Jim wiping down an already clean table in an empty cafe.

'Hi, Jim, is Brad on strike or something?' I asked, because up till now the kitchen had been Jim's domain and he'd never crossed the line into Brad's work area. I glanced around for the elusive teen.

Jim's fist clenched around the cleaning cloth grasped in his long slender fingers and he hung his head. 'Guess you ain't heard.'

'Heard what?'

'Brads in the hospital – overdose.'

'Holy cow! That's terrible news. Is he going to be okay?'

'His mum reckons its touch and go.'

'Bloody hell. How did he get mixed up with the drug scene?'

'Brad never took no drugs before that fella' blew into town and introduced him and his school mates to all sorts.'

'What fella? Who exactly are you talking about?'

Jim, shy and usually economical with his words, gave me a mournful look. To my amazement he began to elaborate using more words than I'd heard him speak all year.

'That skinny dude, the one with the ferret face – don't know his real name. Young Brad always refers to him as Rattler. Idolises him, he does. It's always Rattler this, Rattler that, Rattler said. Raised the hackles on the back of my neck, I can tell you. Especially when this Rattler bloke introduced Brad to a couple of the Huntsmen gang members. They chummed up, next thing you know the young whipper-snapper went a little wild.' He stared at me, his brown eyes wide and his dusty eyebrows furrowed. 'The Huntsmen are not a group I like an impressionable lad like Brad to be hanging about with. I did try to give him a gentle warning, but who am I to give advice. I'm not his father. I'm just some old codger he works with. The lure of being considered a bad boy, biker friend, amongst the teens made Brad feel all grown up and significant.'

There was a hitch in the back of Jim's throat and his raspy voice shook as he enlightened me about the recent motivation behind all Brad's nocturnal goings-on. I reached over and lay a gentle hand on his shoulder. Jim patted it and coughed to clear his throat.

'Sorry,' he murmured.

'Don't be sorry. Brads a terrific kid, but even the best kids in the world can lose their way. We can only offer up advice. It's up to them whether they listen or not.' My heart bled for his family and the turmoil affecting them all. 'Are you going to the hospital to visit when you knock off today? If you do, give him my best and tell him I'll come in for a visit on my day off on Sunday.'

Jim shook his head. 'I can't go today. Brian's got me doing a double shift. After last Friday's fiasco, he doesn't want you girls to be alone in the café late at night anymore.'

'Well, that's a step in the right direction, I suppose. What about the early morning shift he has Chips on this week? You can't possibly be expected to cover that one as well.'

'Sam's coming in early to act as her offsider. And from next week we'll be overlapping the shifts to cover grog sop.'

I sighed in relief, grateful for the security his presence would offer but also disappointed I wouldn't have an opportunity to test my theory and have a go at cracking the safe combination. Probably just as well. I'd made a promise to Ryan.

The doors behind me swished open and a customer entered. I hurriedly pulled on my apron and got to work, all the while praying that Brad would get better and that I could get through the next twenty-four hours without having to add another funeral to my calendar.

\*\*\*

Built between 1841 and 1844 St John's Church is the oldest consecrated church in Western Australia. It is a beautiful stone building with a shingle covered, gabled roof and is surrounded by well-tended parklands and shady peppermint trees. It was a fitting place for Ryan and Adam to farewell another Albany institution, their father Arthur 'Fuzzy' Ryan Lamb.

Ryan and I had spent all our spare time together, roaming the district and the beaches, getting to know each other on a deeper level. I was happy to forgo a lot of sleep to cram in as much time with him as I could, because I knew it wouldn't be long before he would have to return to his soldiering work. I kept my fingers crossed, but deep down knew it would be unlikely his new posting would be somewhere nearby. But no matter where he was sent, I would wait for him, pray he would be kept safe and that one day he would return to me.

On the morning of the funeral the sun shone but the threat of a storm hovered on the horizon. When Chips and I arrived at St John's we were greeted by a long line of people snaking along the gravel apron leading up to the churches double-arched wooden doorway. The line put paid to my expectation that the funeral was going to be a quiet affair. We slipped past a chattering group who were enthusing over Fuzzy's musical prowess and signed the attendance register.

Feeling a bit overwhelmed by the mob already crowded inside I turned to my cousin and said, 'Do you mind if we hide in the back row, Chips?'

The female usher, whose job it was to escort everyone to their seats, looked at our names in the register and murmured, 'Excuse me ladies, but Captain Lamb and Flight Lieutenant Best-Lamb have requested for you be seated in the front row with the family.' I gulped. There goes that plan.

We followed the usher. My cheeks began to burn as people turned to stare at us as we were escorted along the stone aisle to the front pew. I twitched at my skirt. Chips reached over to grab my hand to stop me. She squeezed my fingers and whispered, 'Chin up, and stop fidgeting. Be the beautiful and mysterious goddess you are. It works for me.'

I glanced down at the grey, split print frock I wore and then over at her similarly styled, navy dress with a white flash. It's always good when Chips did the shopping for me because she has immaculate taste in clothes. Outfitted by her, I did feel lovely. She certainly looked it. The usher waved us to our seats. I halted and waited for Chips to slide decorously in beside Chappie. She cupped his hands and began to whisper in his ear. He seemed to gain support from her words because the glazed look left his eyes and his shoulders straightened. Being careful not to trip or do any of my usual clumsy stuff I managed to negotiate the floor space between myself and Ryan without causing a major incident. Relieved, I took my seat and gave him a compassionate smile. He held out a hand and I placed mine in his.

'Thank you for coming. We don't know half the people who have shown up today,' he whispered, flicking his index finger between himself and Adam. 'They must be from Dad's youth and music days, and there are so many. The Afghanistan sand pit was a cake walk in comparison to this.' I heard his breath hitch in the back of his throat as he confessed, 'I don't know if I can do this.'

His voice was even more gravelly than usual as he held a tight rein on his emotions. I cupped his blunt, work roughed hand with both mine and cradled it to my chest. 'Today will be hard, but you've got this. Remember your dad as the good man he was. A proud father, who loved his sons so much he wore a daggy pair of slippers long after their use by date because those sons loved and respected him so much that at a time when he needed a helping hand, they went out of their way to earn enough money to buy them for him.' I looked at the crowded pews and row upon row of people standing at the back of the church. They were young and old, some in military dress, others wearing flamboyant outfits or tactfully respectful in black, quite a mixed bunch in fact. 'And judging by the crowd that have shown up today, Fuzzy was a man who touched many lives, as have you and Chappie, hence the attendance of your colleagues. When you're standing up at the front of the church addressing everyone, just share what's in your heart. They'll understand.'

Ryan took a deep breath and squeezed my hand.

A solemn faced funeral director glided over. He was resplendent in a two-piece black suit, purple satin waistcoat with matching tie that covered a crisp, white, long-sleeved shirt. His cuffs were fastened at the wrist with company engraved, gold cuff links. I was dazzled by the shine he'd achieved on his black leather shoes as they competed with the brightness of the overhead lighting.

'It's time, Captain Lamb, Flight Lieutenant Best-Lamb,' he murmured in a discreet tone.

Ryan gave my hand a final squeeze and rose to his feet. With Adam flanking his left, Ryan strode with dignity to the lectern. My heart swelled. Both men looked magnificent and distinguished in their military dress uniforms, complete with the raft of campaign medals arranged in perfect alignment across their chests. Warm sunlight filtered through the stained-glass window from high above the altar, reflecting a golden glow over a spray of sweet-smelling, white carnations that lay atop the gleaming walnut coffin. I stared at the enlarged photo that had been propped on an easel next to the lectern. It was a picture of Fuzzy and he was grinning from ear to ear as he hugged his beloved saxophone. It struck me how strongly Ryan's eyes resembled that of his father and it really saddened me that I would never get to meet the man who had raised such decent and endearing sons.

A hush descended over the muted conversations being held around us when Ryan took the stand. He opened his mouth and in a steady, strong voice said, 'Thank you everyone for coming to say farewell...'

The eulogy the boys gave was tender and full of hilarious reminiscences of times past. The recap of Fuzzy's life was accompanied by a scrolling slideshow of photographs shown on the large TV screens mounted on stone pillars around the church. Tracks of music, mostly from Fuzzy's own albums were played. His friends joined in by singing and clapping along with the music. The service was a wonderfully bittersweet celebration of a sweet man's life. I found it heart-wrenching. Especially when Ryan, accompanied by Adam on the guitar, used his amazing baritone voice to sing, *Time to say goodbye,* as the coffin was borne away.

* * *

A magnificent sea eagle was perched on the branch of a leafless tree near where I stood with my shoes in one hand and Ryan's hand gripped in the other. We were both wrung out and exhausted after having successfully weathered the social chit-chat and heartfelt condolences handed out by everyone at the wake. It had seemed like an eternity before we'd been able to slip down to the beach for a breath of fresh air and some peace.

Waves pounded thunderously along the sand cove, churning the surf into an enormous froth of foam that extended the length of the shoreline. I stood blind to the threatening tempest out at sea while I listened with a heavy heart to the news I'd been dreading ever since Ryan and I had met.

'I'm sorry, Faith. I received my marching orders this morning. I can't tell you where I'm going, only that I may be gone for a very long time. Possibly twelve months or more.' He cupped my face gently with his hands. 'I want you to know that you are the best thing that has ever happened in my life.' I opened my mouth to speak but he placed a finger over my lips. 'No, I don't want you to say anything or make me any promises. All I ask is that you give me the next twelve hours so we can spend them together.'

A tear rolled down my cheek. 'Of course, I'll give you that, Ryan. I'll give you the rest of my life. You only have to ask.'

'That requires loyalty, honesty, fidelity and a lot of loneliness. I can't ask that of you.'

'Yes, you can, and I'll give it to you freely and unstintingly whether you ask or not. There is no one else for me, and never will be.'

'Are you sure?'

'Yes.'

'Then I'll take it because I love you.'

My reply was cut off by his hot, sweet lips. It felt like coming home.

\* \* \*

Ryan had asked me to meet him for dinner at Six Degrees, and after that he had a bunch of surprises planned to fill our time and make our last evening together memorable. I was not to ask any questions, just go with the flow. That suited me. As long as I was with him I didn't care what we did. In anticipation of being pre-pared for what I hoped would be a major part of the plan, I packed a thigh hugging, silk nightdress into an overnight bag, stowed it into MC's cargo hold and drove her at speed into a very busy city centre. I had to circle the streets numerous times before a vacant parking spot finally became available at the far end of Stirling Terrace. I swerved in and with excitement leapt from the driver's seat. I had to wait for half a dozen cars to pass before a gap emerged big enough for me to cross. I was about to scuttle across the street when I spotted my handsome soldier shoot out of the pub's main door. He stormed away in the opposite direction from where I was standing. The ramrod set of his back screamed of anger. I wondered what the hell was wrong. I shoved out a hand to stop the cars and tottered across the road in my troublesome heels to give chase as best I could. A group of people surfaced from a parked car and stood in a huddle on the sidewalk, blocking my path, while they discussed whether to go to the hotel or around the corner to the bar and grill. I shoved my way through the group, not bothering with apologies. Kicking off my shoes, I snatched them up and began to run barefoot along the cold cement pavement. When I reached the corner, Ryan was nowhere in sight.

I speed dialled his mobile. The call went straight to message bank.

'Ryan, its Faith. I just missed you at the pub. I'm worried? Call me back will you.'

I stood like an island in a sea of pedestrians wondering where he'd gone. Ryan and Adam had stored all their personal gear at a lockup facility and had closed-up Lamb Lodge. It now stood ready and waiting for its new tenants, so he wouldn't have gone there. Had he gone to The Mariners Cafe? I'd be surprised. There was nothing left of his father or their life in the place anymore. Maybe he'd gone to the motel where he'd stayed the previous night with Adam. As it wasn't far from where I stood, only half-a-block from the main street, I took a punt and jogged around the corner. Entering the grim, grey slate motel courtyard I glanced around. Remembering the pretty café where I'd had coffee with Ashley, I wondered if this was the type of business he was looking to invest in. It could certainly do with an injection of guidance on how to look attractive to guests. The quad area was overlooked by a bank of blank, non-descript charcoal-coloured doors that opened onto an uncovered outdoor balcony. The walkway was framed by an uninspiring paint-flaked, wrought-iron balustrade. The whole place was as ugly as sin and could have benefitted from a coat of bright paint and a spruce up. It wouldn't hurt to mention the place to Ashley next time I saw him.

Still clutching my shoes in my left hand and feet aching from the cold, I galloped up the bare concrete steps two at a time. I was wheezing and desperately trying to catch my breath as I emerged onto the second-floor landing.

'I really needed to get fit,' I grunted, as I hurried along to room 217.

With my toes tingling painfully, my neat hair awry and my chest heaving I pounded on the door and waited. There was no answer. I plastered my ear against the wood to listen. It was quiet inside. I thumped again but got no response. Snatching my mobile from the depths of my quilted clutch purse, I dialled Ryan's number. This time it rang, but no sound emerged from inside the room. Tears of frustration welled in my eyes before cascading down my cheeks. My chest stung as though shattered glass was doing its utmost to slice my heart apart. I could feel my composure slipping as a huge sob swelled in my gut and threatened to overwhelm me. I sucked in a deep shuddering breath to tamp it down. When I felt control coming back, I reached up to scrub the moisture from away from my eyes and cheeks with my knuckles, smearing my mascara in the process. Blindly I dug into my purse to reef out a fine lace hand-kerchief and ran it under my panda eyes in an attempt to blot up the mess, ruining the pretty cloth in the process. Sighing I returned the sodden mess to the depths of my purse and stared up at the grim sky while trying to decided what to do next. The ache of my cold feet finally penetrated my fogged brain. I slipped my shoes back onto my frozen feet and leant over the balustrade to study the courtyard. I spotted a sign for the motel's reception. Being careful in my heels I tottered back down the stairs to the office. The chime over the door chirped as I entered, adding more gloom to the cloud that hovered above my head. The seat behind the counter was empty. I could hear a console game blasting away somewhere in a back room. I struck the bell on the counter forcefully a couple of times trying to attract some attention.

'Yeah...yeah,' called a cracked and grumpy male voice. 'Be there in a sec.'

It was almost a full two minutes before an overweight, red-headed youth in desperate need of a tube of anti-acne cream sauntered in. He looked affronted at being disturbed.

'I'm looking for Ryan Lamb. Room 217,' I spat out before he could inquire as to what I wanted.

Acne boy fiddled with the computer keyboard for a moment.
'Checked out.'

'Checked out? What do you mean, checked out?'

'Checked out, as in gone...vamoosed.'

'But he wasn't due to leave until tomorrow. It doesn't make sense.'

Acne boy shrugged his chubby shoulders and looked bored with the conversation.

My mind buzzed. How the hell could Ryan have gotten his bags, checked out and left the complex in the short time it had taken me to lumber around the block?

'What time did he leave?' I asked.

'At about five p.m.' It was seven now. So he packed up after we'd been to the beach. The red head eyed me up and down and smirked. 'Done a runner on you has he? Well, if you're looking for a replacement fella, I'm available.'

I glared at him. 'You might be, but I'm not!'

His grin widened. 'No harm in trying,' he said, reaching down and adjusting the front of his trousers.

Disgusted I stormed outside before I vomited all over him.

Sucking in a lungful of night air, I leant against the building's brick wall and tried to make sense of everything. According to the pimple faced, wannabe gigolo inside, Ryan had packed up after we'd spoken at the beach. So, what was it he'd planned for us tonight? Had it really been Ryan I'd seen striding away earlier? Maybe he was still sitting in the pub with a whole special date planned and with all the noise in the busy pub he hadn't heard my phone calls. Delusional I know, the military uniform was hard to mistake, but I had to check.

Rain began to fall in a steady drizzle as I dogtrotted back along Spencer Street. I took a shortcut past the backpacker hostel and took advantage of the pedestrian cover on Stirling Terrace as I hurried towards the pub. Shoving my way into the crowded bar I wove around the cluttered tables and scattered chairs while examining every male face in a mad hunt for Ryan's familiar one. It was a pointless exercise. In my heart I knew he wasn't here. Even so I intended to be thorough. I even went to where the angels feared to tread - the men's room.

I took a quick peak around the door and surprised a bloke emerging from one of the stalls. I ignored him. 'Ryan,' I yelled. 'Are you in here?'

No reply.

Puzzled and hurt I left the deafening din of the barroom behind and raced back out into the street. Rain now hurled from the sky in great blobs. I huddled in the doorway of a closed shop and tried Ryan's mobile again. My call was immediately diverted to message bank. My usually docile temper exploded. I left an abrupt message.

'Ryan, its Faith. After everything you just said to me and the promises we made to each other at the beach, you've gone and left me high and dry, buddy,' which was ironic seeing as I was now soaked to the skin. 'What's going on? Call me when you can be bothered to explain.'

My anger gave me momentum. I stormed along the street, all the while scanning the passing faces for his familiar one. My phone dinged. I glanced down. Finally, I'd received a message from Ryan. With water dripping from the tip of my nose and the ends of my sodden hair, I halted in the deluge and fumbled with my phone to open the text.

*Loyalty, honesty and fidelity - my commitment to you. I have been sent proof that you don't hold those same values. It was the boots that gave you away. Have a nice life. Ryan.*

What the hell! Of course, I had the same values. Hadn't I just bared my soul to him? I texted a question mark and waited. Ten minutes later I was still waiting for a reply. The rain had eased but a cold breeze whipped up and swirled around my ankles. Soaked from head to toe and now chilled to the bone, I began to shiver. Whether from the cold or my inner turmoil it didn't matter, I couldn't stand here all night. Wrapping my arms around myself and my broken heart, I hurried to where I'd parked MC. I fumbled around in my clutch for my car keys. Had trouble locating them. In fury I gave a frustrated tug on the door handle as I screamed into the night. To my surprise my car door swung open. Surely I hadn't forgotten to lock it. Puzzled, I looked inside as if that would give me the answer and saw a piece of paper lying on the driver's seat.

'Oh, not another stupid, P team, letter,' I snarled. Staring around the car park I yelled into the night at anyone who might be listening. 'Now is not the time, people.'

Snatching up the offending missive, I was tempted to tear it up and leave it shredded on the street for the P team to clean up, but curiosity got the better of me. I tilted the page towards the faint dull glow coming from the streetlight. The muscles in my chest clenched so hard I almost couldn't drag any oxygen into my lungs. I was staring at a photograph. It was a very personal shot of Ryan and I. We were sitting very close together sharing a moment. We'd been having a picnic in the park. Over a wedge of apple pie, Ryan had been recounting a tale about some not very ingenious army recruits and the appalling manoeuvres they'd attempted in trying to sneak off-base for an evening out at a local pub. Our laughing images had been altered. Razor sharp canines had been added to my mouth and what looked to be blood droplets dripped from my teeth and ran down my chin. Ryan's face had been erased and replaced with a snake's face. Underneath, in bold print was written – **dedicated to my Faith.**

The longer I stared at the image the harder my heart thumped against my rib cage. Bile scorched the back of my throat. This wasn't a cosy mystery letter from the P team. This letter was meant to frighten.

Was it a new campaign by the rat-face weasel? Surely not!

How the hell did he, or anyone, find me tonight anyway? Was I being followed? And why was my car unlocked?

Suddenly the street noises snapped me from the shocked fog I was wallowing in. My fingers began to tremble and the photo clutched in my hand shook uncontrollably. I took stock of where I was and realized I was standing all alone in a dim, deserted car park. Terror suddenly overrode all other emotions. I dove into the relative safety of MC. My teeth clattered and echoed in the confines of the quiet car as I slammed all the locks into place and took a quick scan of the street. I spotted no sign of anybody nearby showing any interest in me or my car, but that meant nothing because, except for the occasional tingle on the back of my neck, I hadn't known I was being watched and followed at all. My heart squeezed. Despite sharp panicked breaths I valiantly fought to squash my terror and get my fumbling fingers to work properly. It took two aborted attempts before I succeeded in shoving the key into the ignition slot. MC purred to life. I didn't bother warming her up I just planted my foot on the accelerator, swerved around some parked cars and raced out onto the main road. I nearly ran up a gutter because my gaze was glued to the rear-vision mirror instead of where I was going. Sucking in a jagged breath, I forced myself to focus on the road. I didn't want to kill some poor innocent sod through inattention. With tears blurring my eyes I had difficulty seeing where I was going. I gave them a vicious swipe along with a series of rapid blinks to clear my sight as I randomly turned MC into one suburban street after another. A precautionary manoeuvre, in case I was being followed. We raced through mostly quiet empty suburbs for about half an hour before I felt it was safe enough to point the car towards home.

MC roared up the townhouse driveway. When her nose was nearly touching the garage door I slammed on the brakes and skidded to a halt. Double checking my surrounds, I bolted from the driver's seat to fling open the roller door. A sob of relief escaped my lips. Kasam was parked in her usual spot. Chips must be home! Or was she? Maybe Chappie had taken her out somewhere in his car. I prayed they were both here and Chappie could enlighten me as to what the hell was going on with Ryan. After all they were brothers. Surely they told each other everything. I know Chips and I did.

I nosed MC in beside Kasam. Abandoning my overnight bag, I flung myself from MC. After taking a precious moment to ensure car and garage were locked I tore down the footpath to the front door. I think if anyone had walked past or spoken to me in that moment, I would have died of a heart attack. I burst in the entrance and was confronted by normality. Chips was alone and curled up on the sofa painting her fingernails scarlet red. Startled by my unorthodox entry her reddened eyes widened. She had been crying. I don't know what my face showed but in silence she opened her arms. I tumbled into them bawling.

* * *

After days of silence from Ryan the pain in my heart hadn't eased and I was a wreck. To top it off I had developed a terrible head cold from the soaking I'd received. As a result I couldn't sleep and food tasted awful. My clothes, when I bothered to dress, hung limply on my frame.

But the silence from Ryan was worse.

Not knowing what I'd done to deserve such treatment, hurt.

Rejection of my love, hurt.

Resembling a discard from tramp school, I dragged myself into my cousin's room to curl up on the end of her bed and stared at her forlornly. Chips took one look at me and pulled out her phone.

'Come on flyboy... answer,' she snarled at the room in general. Her call went unanswered. Chappie had left town almost immediately after the wake. According to my cousin he'd been recalled to duty for an urgent mission. Chips had received only one message from him since his departure to let her know he'd received her text about Ryan but hadn't yet had a chance to speak with his brother. He'd tried but Ryan's phone was off, a strong indication he'd been deployed already. 'Adam's still not answering. Right...that's it! Enough is enough! I'm off to Perth. I'll storm Pearce Airbase if I have to, but it's time to track the guy down and get the real story. Ryan can't breeze into your life like this, play with your feelings and then breeze out again.'

Chips leapt to her feet and began to stuff clothes into an overnight bag.

'Don't do anything that will get you arrested, Chips.'

'Will torturing the truth out of the fly boy about his brother get me arrested do you think?'

I stared, not sure if she was joking or not, because when Chips is on a roll there's no telling what she will do.

'Maybe I should forego my up-coming presentation and come with you.'

Early in the second semester Professor Murray had assigned me the task of conducting a lecture in front of my peers about the value of forensic science in police work. The afore-mentioned presentation would earn me extra credits towards my Masters' degree. I hadn't planned on a taking a Masters degree, but Professor Murray insisted I should. He was a hard man to argue with and had stood over me to make sure I completed the application then and there.

'Don't you dare forego anything. I love you with all my heart, but sometimes you're an idiot. You mustn't destroy all your hard work, over Ryan...or any other man for that matter,' snarled Chips. She cupped my face with the palms of her hands. Her fingers were icy cold. She gave me the gentlest of smiles but her eyes were hard. 'I'm going to flay soldier boy alive when I get a hold of him...he had no right to walk out like that, without an explanation.'

'Chips...please...'

'It's all right, I'm only kidding. I promise I won't do anything too disastrous.'

I studied her beautiful face and noticed pain lines had taken up residence in the corners of her eyes. I mentally kicked myself. I'd been so wrapped up with my own misery and despair I'd forgotten how the situation with Adam and his continued silence affected her.

'You really love Chappie, don't you?'

She gave a short, sharp nod and abruptly turned away to delve in her underwear drawer. She wasn't quick enough. I caught a glimpse of the tears pooling in her eyes.

'I need to make sure he's not playing a game with me as well. I'll only be gone a couple of days. Can you cover my shifts at work?' she asked.

'Yes.'

'And promise me you'll look after yourself – eat properly and for God's sake take a shower.'

'Yes, Mum. I promise,' I said with a lopsided, half-hearted grin. 'Are you going to Tyrell Street or stay in the South Perth apartment with Unk?'

'I'll go stay with Popsicle. There's no point in opening up the Nedlands house just for a couple of nights. And yes, I promise I'll give Dad a big smooch from you...and tell him how much you miss him...and that you love him.'

My half-hearted grin warmed. Unk really was the love of my life. 'Thank you, Chips darling. Now promise me you'll drive carefully. I couldn't bear it if anything happened to you.'

# 10

## Chapter Ten

Ryan's phone vibrated in his pocket, bringing a smile to his face. He expected it was Burger, to let him know that she'd parked MC up a tree and was now on her way after hitching a ride on a camel or something equally bizarre. The girl certainly loved to send cryptic messages about her movements. Usually, he found the constant demands on his attention by the women he dated annoying – not so with this one. She was fun and made no demands. Her texts never required him to provide a constant reassurance that he cared for her or that he should switch his brain off and text soppy mush. Burger's messages usually consisted of an amusing emoji or two to describe her current situation, leaving him the luxury of interpreting their meaning. Like the one she'd sent the other day – a magnifying glass, a phone, a brain exploding and a girl on the run, all to tell him she would be late because she mislaid her phone. Ryan found this type of communication fun and thought provoking. To help craft his own replies to challenge her he'd gotten them both a photo shop app. He was eager to use it to create some fun messages that would stop her worrying about him while he was away on deployment.

His grin dimmed. He was going to find this latest assignment difficult. He'd miss his beautiful, fun-loving Faith. There was no doubt about it, he'd fallen for her, hard.

He eased the vibrating phone from his uniform trouser pocket expecting to see an emoji but the text wasn't from Burger. It was from his commanding officer.

*Mission time moved up to 0100hrs. Report for briefing 2330hrs.*

He flicked a glance at the time. Crap, time was tight, and he still had the long drive to Perth to contend with. He had to leave within the next half-hour to make the briefing in time. He cursed floridly under his breath. He'd planned such a beautiful evening, as it would be their last for a very long time. A quiet dinner followed by a glass of champagne on the balcony overlooking the ocean in the cosy apartment he'd booked into that afternoon. Ryan had changed his accommodation, not wanting to cheapen their first night together in the soulless, motel room he and Adam had been using since they'd shut up the house. None of that was going to happen now.

With a heavy heart, Ryan thumbed a text to his brother.

*Chappie, my mission's been moved up.*
*Those magnificent men in their flying machines*
*They can fly upside down with their feet in the air*
*They don't think of danger, they really don't care.*
*Please don't be like them and look after Faith for me.*

His brother would understand the song reference. And the veiled request that he not take any unwarranted risks with his life. Ryan was aware that Adam was about to embark on a potentially dangerous job in Afghanistan. As was he.

Damn the bloody terrorists.

Damn the reassignment overseas.

Damn having to leave Faith.

He gathered his things together and decided it would be best to wait for Burger outside. A noisy pub was not the place to share his bad news. As he headed for the door Ryan's phone buzzed again. He didn't recognise the number, and opened the message expecting more instructions about the mission.

Instead, his screen was filled with a photograph.

Faith stood with her arms flung around the neck of a tall, dark-haired man. His hand was in the back pocket of her jeans. She wore the fancy boots her cousin had given her and the pair had locked lips in an intense and passionate kiss.

Underneath the photo was a message.

*I miss you lover. Here's a goodnight kiss. Faith*

Ryan's heart shattered.

In fury he shoved away from the door and stormed down the street to his car.

* * *

His phone buzzed. Ryan ignored it. It went off again. He pulled the car over to listen to the message. Faith's sweet tone sounded worried.

*'Ryan its Faith. I just missed you at the pub. What's going on? Call me back will ya.'*

He switched his phone off, threw it to the floor of the car and planted his foot hard on the accelerator. Anger and betrayal waged a fierce battle in his chest. The girl, with her gorgeous, unruly hair and cheeky grin, had played him for a fool. The photo was evidence of that. While promising herself to him, saying there was no one else, on the side she had been playing the field. It was his ex-fiancé, Janine, all over again. Well never again.

After stewing for a few kilometres, he had to let the emotion out. He would do it in a text. He knew exactly what he wanted to say to her. Slamming his foot on the brakes he jerked the car over to the verge and came to a skidding halt. He grappled around on the floor to locate his phone. The raft of missed calls and message notifications that flooded in when he switched it on surprised him. He took a closer look. None of them were to do with his mission; they were all from Faith. Ignoring them he thumbed out an angry text.

*Love, loyalty, honesty and fidelity - my commitments to you. I have proof that you don't hold those same values. It was the boots that gave you away. Have a nice life without me. Ryan.*

Almost immediately she replied.

*?*

A cold hand squeezed his heart. Ryan had thought that sending the message would have been a cathartic act, but all it did was make him feel like a bastard. A real man would have waited, had it out with her, face-to-face. He should go back, and do just that. Ryan glanced at his watch and realised he didn't have time. He was already running late. Besides what did she mean by sending a question mark anyway? What sort of an answer was that he growled to himself as he planted his foot on the accelerator? The car tore down the highway and away from the source of his fury, but it didn't ease the pain.

\* \* \*

Mid-flight, Ryan's team mates, Sergeant Luke 'Seadog' Baxter and Sergeant Marcus 'Rowdy' Stone had spread out and were asleep. Ryan unhooked his seatbelt and made his way to the cockpit. From the pilot's seat of the RAAF C-130 Hercules, his brother, Adam, grinned up at him.

'We've just gone dark on the radar. Six hours and we'll be at Harmid Karzai airport.'

Ryan grunted. Six hours, six days, it made no difference. The shit storm that was Afghanistan would still be waiting for them. Seeking a distraction, Ryan said, 'Tell me about your mission, Chappie.'

'Evacuation detail. The Kabul ground team have got twenty-six personnel ready for me to transport to the Arab Emirates. Then, as soon as the yanks get their shit together and give us a regular landing timeslot, we'll start pulling out our troops.' Chappie reached up and squeezed Ryan's forearm. 'Don't worry about me, Shanks. I got your message. I'm not about to take any unnecessary risks. Not with a beautiful woman waiting for me back at home. I'm the one who should be fretting...because man, you're going deep into the belly of the beast and it won't be pleasant. What's the brass thinking?'

'Well, someone's got find out what the bloody Taliban are up to.'

Chappie grunted. 'I hope you've got your head in the game, Shanks?'

Ryan nodded. 'Yeah, mate, it's in. Losing Fuzzy was rough, on both of us...then this thing with Burger, even rougher. But I've compartmentalised, bro.'

Chappie's eyebrows rose. 'You sound like one of those fucking motivational gurus the brass push at us whenever there's dirty work to be done. Compartmentalise those feelings people – emotion will only distract you from your goal.'

Ryan snorted.

'Do you want me to tell her where you are?'

'No, bro. I have my orders. It's a clandestine op. The team must stay dark. No one is supposed to know we're staying behind. Bloody fortunate for me you're the one flying us in though. It didn't seem right not being permitted to tell you where I was heading. Listen, Chappie, if I don't make it back...'

'Fuck, Shanks. Don't go there, bro...It don't bear thinking about.' Ryan lifted an eyebrow and eyed his brother off. Chappie sighed. 'You know I'll take care of her, even though she's done the dirty on you. You are sure, aren't you...that she did do the dirty?'

'Yes...no...oh, I don't fucking know. My knee jerk was to think it was Janine all over again but now I've had time to think about it...it just doesn't seem to sit right. Burger doesn't seem the type. I'm so bloody confused and it's not something I can afford to dwell on right now.'

'What do you want me to tell her?'

'Nothing, mate. You haven't heard from me and you don't know where I am. Leave the whole sorry mess alone – I can't go through another Janine fiasco. And I mean it – don't even discuss it with Chips.'

Adam cocked an eyebrow. 'That's a tough ask, Shanks, I can't help myself. She crooks an eyebrow and I tell her everything.'

'You're well and truly sunk, Chappie...it'll be wedlock next.'

Adam gave a happy sigh. It brought a sad grin to Ryan's face.

'Lucky bastard.'

# Chapter Eleven

Chips left and the house was silent. I was lonely. Even the bane of my existence, the neighbours' cat, Fleabag, had deserted me. I rattled around the townhouse all morning, restless and unable to concentrate on anything. In the end I curled up on my bed in a funk. Sunshine streamed in through the window sending dust mites dancing for joy in its golden beams. Disgusted by the happy sight I pulled the duvet over my head and nursed my pain. I took out my phone and with tear filled eyes stared at the laughing faces of Ryan and myself. We'd taken the photo at the beach after that phenomenal kiss. A sad smile touched my lips as I fell into the memory. The buzz of my phone still clutched in my hand startled me back into the moment. I tried to focus my blurred eyes on the caller ID, gave up and answered instead.

'Lo.' There was silence at the other end of the line. I was just about to hang up when Ashley spoke. 'Sunflower is that you?'

'Oh, hi, Ashley,' I croaked, in a slightly stronger tone.

'Is something wrong?'

'Chips had to go away for a couple of days and I'm all alone.'

'I'll be right over.' Ashley hung up before I could tell him I had a cold and would be lousy company.

I rose from the confines of my rumpled covers and slopped my way to the bathroom to splash some water over my face. I stared in the mirror and was shocked by the image that greeted me. My hair resembled an unkempt rat's nest, my eyes and nose red from crying and I looked drawn and haggard.

'You're a dumbass. Chips is right. You can't give up on life because the person you love doesn't return your feelings,' I chided at the reflection in the mirror. 'Now remember the promise you made to her, as half-hearted as it was. Enough is enough - pull yourself together.'

To reinforce the first positive thought I'd had in days, I threw some paracetamol down my throat for the crying headache behind my eyes, stripped off the clothes I'd been slumming in for days and dove into the shower. Using a generous portion of soap and shampoo I scrubbed myself from head to toe. The girl who emerged from under the hot spray felt slightly better.

With my body wrapped in my fluffy gown I hurried to my room, flung open the wardrobe and tried to think like fashionista Chips, but it was hard. The sound of a car roaring into the street startled me from my musings so I grabbed an emerald and rust patchwork peasant blouse and white jeans from the shelf and pulled them on. I scooped my wet hair into a coil on the back of my head and stabbed it into place with a pewter chopstick hairpin before giving myself a quick spritz of perfume. The alluring scent of gardenias filled the room, replacing the musty sour smell it had acquired over the last couple of days. I wrinkled my nose at the underlying fug and flung open the bedroom window to let in some fresh air.

The doorbell began to peel persistently as if someone was leaning on the button. As my bedroom window faced the front of the house, I leant out and yelled down at the person hanging off the doorbell. 'Hold your horses, will ya. I'll be down in a minute.'

As I made my way barefooted to the front door, Ryan's voice sounded a warning in the back of my mind. *Always check the peephole before you open the door.* Without hesitation I obeyed his command and saw Ashley standing on the front porch with his hands shoved deep into the pockets of dark blue designer jeans. He was staring down at his shoes. Today he'd dressed in a red and white stripe Red Sox baseball shirt and cap. It made him look cute, bashful and boyish. Determined to be the new me I flung open the door and gave him a dazzling smile.

'Hi.'

He seemed stunned by my greeting.

'Wow you look fab,' he said. Before I could stop him, he stepped forward, pulled me into his arms and placed his lips gently over mine.

*Well, why not.*

I slung my arms around his neck. His grip tightened, my back hit the wall and he leaned into me as his tongue delved and danced inside my mouth. A flutter of something rose as he pressed himself even closer. Slowly he ended the kiss. 'Now that's a greeting,' he murmured, nuzzling at my neck.

'Sorry...' I placed my hands on his chest to push him back a step. This wasn't what I wanted. It was too much, too soon.

'Tut, tut,' he said, wagging a finger in my face. 'Never be sorry.' His gaze, full of desire, raked me from head to toe. 'Beach, I think!' he said, and surprised the hell out of me by picking me up and throwing me over his shoulder.

I squealed in protest as he strode down the path towards his car with me hanging like a limpet. 'But Ashley I don't have any shoes on.'

'That's ok, it's just how I like you – barefoot and...'

'And, what?' I asked, curious as to his thoughts. He set me gently on my bare feet at the door of his immaculate BMW. 'Mine!'

Oh crap! One impulsive action on my part had given him the wrong impression.

'We're just friends- remember.'

'Of course, Sunflower,' he replied, and dropped a peck on the tip of my nose. He opened the car door for me. 'Now hop in, the day's a wasting.'

He drove with care and precision to the beach at Two Peoples Bay Nature Reserve. Except for a dozen pink-billed pelicans that floated along the water's edge enjoying the warmth of the day we had the shore to ourselves. Ashley took my hand as we strolled along the wooden boardwalk that led out to the two large granite boulders. They looked as if they'd been left behind by some giant playing a game of marbles. I think I must have overdosed on the headache tablets because when we reached the damp sand, I broke away from him and raced into the surf, not caring that my jeans got soaked in the process. Crisp fresh air brushed my face. Even though the sunshine was glorious after my self-imposed hibernation it didn't do much to burn away my grey, brooding thoughts. A wave splashed my chin and wet my face. I glanced down in surprise. I was chest deep in icy seawater. The temptation to keep going until it covered my head gave me a fierce nudge. A sea eagle swerving on its wingtip right in front of me snapped me away from those dark thoughts. I watched in awe as the raptor rose, high into the cloudless blue sky, folded its wings and dove into the pistachio coloured ocean. A moment later it surfaced with a fish clutched in its talons. The beauty and awesomeness of nature filled me and eased a little of the pain that had settled around my heart.

Ashley called out, 'Come back onto dry land you crazy woman. That cold water can't be good for you.'

Realizing he was right and what I was doing probably wasn't the best remedy for my mental state, I waded away from temptation and back onto the beach. When I reached his side, Ashley slipped an arm around my waist.

'Bloody hell, you're soaked to the skin and frozen.' He tugged me close and quickly walked me to a sheltered nook out of the ocean breeze. 'Strip off your jeans and your top. I'll spread them out on this rock so they can dry in the sun. In the meantime you can have my shirt. Put it on, it'll keep you warm. We can't have you getting ill.'

Ashley ignored my murmur of protest. He shoved his shirt into my reluctant fingers, turned his back to give me a modicum of privacy and stood with arms folded across his chest, patiently waiting. Defeated, I stripped off my wet gear.

'Okay you can turn around now,' I said, once I was decently covered.

Ashley settled into the sand and patted a spot at his side. 'Come sit, its lovely and warm here. Then you can tell me why you've been crying?'

I tore my gaze away from the toned muscles of his chest, drew his shirt tighter around my body and slumped into the sand. 'Ryan dumped me.'

'The man's a fool,' he said, taking my hand and giving it a gentle squeeze. 'Tell me what happened.'

I took a shuddering breath and related to him the whole sorry event. 'It's over now, and no good will come by dwelling on it,' I said. Determined not to discuss my recent turmoil any further, I steered the conversation away from my personal life by asking, 'How's your book coming along?'

Ashley smiled. He plucked a tuft of dry grass from under a wavy leaf saltbush and ran the tendril of grass along my forearm. 'Slowly,' he said.

'What's it about?'

He flicked the grass tip at my nose. I swatted it away and he grinned. 'I'm not telling. You can read it when I'm finished.'

'Is it hard to write a novel?'

'Yes, especially when your characters don't fall into line with the plot.'

'Does that happen a lot?' I asked, intrigued by the thought that a writers characters could hijack the story line.

'It has in recent times, but I sorted out the problem and now everything is back on track,' he murmured with a far-away look in his eyes. 'Anyway, let's not talk about that right now.' The far-off look remained in his eyes. I studied his face and noticed a furrow developing in his brow.

'Is something wrong, my friend?'

He refocused his gaze on me. 'Wrong, what could possibly be wrong? The spring sun is showing her face and it's a glorious day. You're here and we have the whole afternoon in front of us.' His words didn't quite ring true, but I decided to wait him out. When he was ready Ashley would tell me what was on his mind. 'But there is something I want to discuss with you.'

Ah ha, I knew it. I leant back on my elbows, closed my eyes and held my face up to the sun so he wouldn't notice how curious I was. 'Hmmm...sure. What's up?'

'It's about your Christmas break?'

Startled, my eyes shot open. I stared at him in surprise. Not what I was expecting at all. 'What about it?

'Once you've finished your exams and that damn presentation the Professors got you slaving over - how much time will you have before next year's semester starts?'

'Around three months. Why?' I asked, rolling to my side and crooking my elbow so I could prop my cheek in my hand and study his face.

'I have business in the north of the state that needs my attention. I want you to come with me?'

'Ashley...'

'No strings,' he said with his hands held out as if in surrender. 'Just a nice holiday break for us both. We could spend Christmas day with the dolphins at Monkey Mia, or go for a sunset camel ride in Broome, or sightsee some country towns and seep ourselves in the local culture they have on offer. Race meetings, local fairs, bird watching - anything you want. My time is flexible in that regard.'

'Well, I don't gamble, and know next to nothing about horse racing, but the rest sound delightful.' I heaved a loud sigh. 'Can I take a rain check, my friend? I don't know what Christmas plans Chips and Unk have made for us. Plus I still have to work. At the moment I'm covering for Chips at the cafe as well. I don't know how long she plans to be away. Besides I'm gun-shy because of Ryan and I'm waiting...' Damn it! I hadn't meant to bring Ryan into the conversation. I cut off what I was going to say. There was no need to tell Ashley that Chips was trying to get some answers for me.

'Well, when your cousin gets back, she could cover a couple of your shifts, couldn't she? I mean, look at all you're doing for her! You give so much of yourself to others, Faith. It's high time you did something for yourself.' Ashley glowered at me.

I opened my mouth to protest. 'Christmas without my family is a big ask, Ashley. It would be the first time ever. And what about your family, surely you want to spend time with them?'

'I promise I'll work around what suits you but I really need to spend the next few months with just you. So would you mind very much, giving up Christmas with your family, just for this year? Please...' there was a catch in his voice. I studied his face as he stared off at the horizon with cold eyes and a blank face. It hurt me. I could see something was causing him pain. I reached over and touched his hand.

I stared in shock as tears pooled in his eyes. 'Tell me, my friend, what's really going on.'

He rolled to his side and faced me. 'I...I...all this year I've suffered from extremely bad headaches. I saw a specialist about them last month and he said they were just migraines but sent me for a couple of precautionary tests to rule out anything else. That's really why I came to Albany, to take a break from things, like he recommended. The neurologist called me yesterday with those test results. Faith, darling...I...I...I don't know how to say this.'

'Just spit it out. We'll deal.'

'Okay - I have a brain tumour.'

'Ashley, NO!' My heart clenched and almost broke. Could things get any worse? First, I'm rejected by the man I love and now another friend who also holds a special place in my heart was in crisis.

'Faith, my beautiful sunflower, he only gave me twelve months to live.'

His answer to my unasked question came like a smack in the face. I flung my arms around him and squeezed tight. 'Ashley, I can't lose you, too.'

In response his arms clenched firmly around my waist and gathered me close. I began to sob against his bare chest.

'Please tell me there is something they can do for you,' I managed to choke out through my anguished tears.

He shook his head. 'No, there's not. Evidently the growth is inoperable,' he muttered. 'Please, don't cry. I didn't tell you to cause you pain. It's just that you're very special to me and now that you're free, I thought we could spend the little time I have left, together.'

I hesitated for a moment. 'You're special to me as well.' In that instant I made a life altering decision. 'I'll share what time I can with you.'

'Thank you, my sweet, beautiful flower.' He tugged me even closer and kissed the sweet spot behind my ear. I responded with a watery smile.

We lay in each other's arms in the sunshine for hours, and in an unspoken agreement talked about anything and everything except his pending demise. Time passed and the sun began to set. It bathed the ocean and blue sky with whispers of purple and orange. Overhead seabirds flocked together in a noisy group and charged out to sea. A dolphin crested a wave and leapt high into the air before disappearing below the surface. All the glorious sights were tainted by the sadness lodged in my chest.

The sun sank and, with the emergence of sparkling stars in an inky black sky, came an evening chill. I began to shiver from the cold. Ashley noticed.

'It's time to go,' he said.

Through chattering teeth I managed to push out an almost decipherable response. 'Yes please. I'm feeling the bite of the Antarctic.'

He wrapped his arms around me to warm me. 'How about we go to your place for dinner,' he whispered close to my ear. It was too seductive and raised a few goose bumps on my skin even as the request caught me by surprise. Ashley had never invited himself into my home before. In fact, he'd never even crossed the threshold of our jolly little townhouse the few times he'd been around. And maybe that was because he clashed with Chips, and it made their encounters uncomfortable for us all. I glanced up at him with a raised eyebrow.

'I'm starving, Sunflower,' he explained. 'I missed my breakfast and lunch to be with you.'

Guilt washed through me. He really needed to take better care of his health.

'I might be able to dig out a ready-made lasagne from the freezer,' I said, embarrassed by the shortage of healthy food options my usual diet offered. There was also my dearth of skill in the cooking department. 'If you're asking me to cook a wholesome meal, you're flirting with death. I'm only capable of microwave meals and the stuff we sell at the café!'

'I don't do carbs, babe. Do you have any salad or vegetables?'

Taking a punt, as my cousin lived off green stuff and usually had a ready supply in the fridge, I nodded.

'What about a couple of juicy steaks?'

I shook my head.

'Okay, we'll stop at the supermarket on the way home and buy some. Can you pull together a tossed salad without killing us?'

'Maybe...' I gave him a lop-sided grin, not willing to tempt the mischievous gods.

Ashley smirked. 'Fantastic. I'll grill us a steak each. I know exactly how I like it.'

* * *

Ashley nosed the BMW into a parking bay right outside the supermarket entrance. He leant across in front of me and popped opened the glove box. Inside sat a bulging black leather wallet. Ashley extracted two $100 notes from a wad of cash and handed one to me. I tried not to stare as he tossed the wallet back into the compartment and slammed it shut. Wow, so casual with so much money. I kept my lips zipped. His money wasn't really something I felt comfortable discussing.

'While you duck inside and grab us a couple of T-bones, I'll nip across to the Bottle-O. What type of red wine do you like?' he asked.

'I don't. Wine and I don't play well together. I'm more a beer girl.'

He crinkled his noise as if he'd smelt something disgusting. 'More carbs! Well my dear sweet girl, you cannot have steak without a glass or two of red wine. I have a special one in mind that you will enjoy. It releases a wonderful aroma of berries when you decant it and will leave a subtle tang of liquorice on your tongue.'

'That sounds nice, I suppose.' My unenthusiastic remark was greeted by raised eyebrows and pursed lips. The thought of Ashley drinking alcohol worried me. I broke our unspoken rule, 'Should you be drinking?'

Ashley ignored the poignant question. Instead, he pulled me close and began to poke me gently in the ribs. 'Nice! My darling girl, you should breathe in awe and say something like, "That sounds divine, Ashley" or you could expound in a haughty tone, "Darling, my taste buds are twirling in a delightful dervish of anticipation."'

The ridiculous comment along with his finger against my ribs caused a bout of giggles to escape my lips. 'Stop, please stop.' I pleaded.

His finger ceased its torment. I took a deep breath. 'I'm excited at the prospect, okay?' I gasped. 'How's that sound?'

Ashley rocked his hand back and forth. 'It's a start. But tonight I will give you a course on wine appreciation and descriptive language. I intend to re-educate you, young lady.'

* * *

When I emerged from the grocery store I spotted Ashley across the street exchanging chit-chat with a heavily tattooed, leather clad man who was mounted on a Harley Davidson motorbike. Ashley spoke to him for a long time. The biker held his head cocked to the left and seemed to be listening intently. Occasionally he'd nod but, on the whole, barely spoke a word. At the end of the one-sided conversation Ashley offered him a thick envelope. In return he was given what looked to be a roll of banknotes which Ashley quickly slipped into the front pocket of his jeans. The two men touched fists. Ashley tucked a wine bottle more firmly under his arm and without a backward glance strode over towards where I waited.

I studied the man on the Harley as he rode away. Across the back of his sleeveless leather jacket was an embroidered emblem of two crossed axes. The words *Huntsman* was arched over the top of the axes.

Curious I nodded after the motor bike. 'A friend of yours?'

Ashley glanced over his shoulder and turned to give me a blank look. 'What?'

'The guy on the Harley. Is he a friend of yours?'

Ashley studied my face with a cold stare. I began to feel uncomfortable and jigged from foot to foot. He blinked and the animation returned to his face. 'Oh, Craig,' he said. 'No, I was just asking some questions about his bike. Good fodder for my novel.'

His reply seemed a little glib. The exchange had looked more than that to me. I opened my mouth but immediately closed it again.

Really it was none of my business.

\* \* \*

Ashley served our steaks rare. Too undercooked for my taste but he seemed to relish each bite and had soon devoured his meal. It peeved me that when it came time to clear the dirty plates, there was no offer of help from him. Instead he lolled back in his seat and watched me clean up the kitchen. Done, I resettled onto my chair to chat with him.

I took a tentative sip from the full glass in front of me, but didn't enjoy the taste. The flavour seemed different, more metallic.

'Tell me a little about your family, Ashley.'

'What do you want to know?'

'Well, what are your parent's names for starters. And what are they like?'

'Dad's name is Robert. He was raised by his widowed mum but doesn't talk about his childhood much. Only that he left school at a young age and did what he could to help Gran put food on the table. He once told me that growing up poor can drain you of motivation and self-respect if you let it. He didn't. He's now a self-made entrepreneur.' The admiration in Ashley's voice as he spoke about his father was hard to miss.

'You have a good relationship with your father then?'

'The best.'

I picked up my drink to take a sip. Ashley nudged the stem of the glass, so I ended up with a mouthful.

'Nice drop...' he said, topping up my glass.

'And what about your mum?'

'Sasha's very frail and is in and out of hospital a lot. She's a very quiet and sweet-natured woman. You'll like her.'

I opened my mouth to ask another question but Ashley held up his hand.

'What's your uncle like?' he interrupted.

Ashley showed intense interest as I began to waffle on about one of my most favourite people in the world. He asked at lot of questions about Unk's work and pastimes. I must have drunk a lot, despite the care I took to only sip from my glass, because suddenly the bottle was empty, my brain real fuzzy and my words didn't come out properly. I couldn't figure out what was wrong for I could have sworn I'd only managed a few mouthfuls.

In the end I had to confess, 'I think I'm tipsy,' I slurred with an inane giggle. Ashley gave me an indulgent smile, rose from his seat, came around from his side of the table and lifted me into his arms. I slung my arms around his neck to keep my balance and tried to focus on his face, but it was blurry. 'Why won't you come into focus?' I asked.

'Too much wine, I guess,' he grinned.

'Tut, tut, naughty boy.'

'I'd like to be a lot naughtier,' he murmured, against my lips. His mouth was warm and inviting and I sank into the kiss. Our tongues danced. Heated desire sizzled in me, and I could hear a moan growling deep in my throat. Ashley broke off the kiss. 'I'm sorry beautiful. I can't...'

'Bugger,' I slurred, staring at him in disbelief. 'Not even a little bit?' I asked.

He gave me a crooked grin, 'No, not even a little bit.'

I laid my mouth on his and began to lick his lips. 'Are you sure?'

He groaned, pulled me hard against his chest and walked towards the stairs. 'God Faith, I want you so badly I can't see straight, but you see it would ruin the plot.'

What an odd turn of phrase. I lost the thread of my thoughts when Ashley began to ascend the stairs. 'Where are you taking me?'

'To bed.'

'Oh goody...' I murmured and tried to concentrate on nibbling his jaw line.

'Which room?'

Ashley strode in the direction I indicated and deposited me on my mattress. I reached up to draw him down next to me, but he gently removed my arms. With heavy eyelids I gazed up at his handsome face and watched as he shoved Fleabag aside. The cat hissed at him and took a swipe.

'Go on scat,' he growled. Fleabag stalked away, back arched in disgust.

I tried to focus on Ashley as he picked up my phone, but it was really hard as my brain didn't feel like mine. 'What are you doing?'

'Setting your alarm – you've got work remember.'

'Thank you, you're so sweet, but I think it's already set.'

'I'll just double check.' It seemed to take him ages to set my alarm. My eyelids kept closing. I found it almost impossible to drag them apart. I drifted. Ashley's warm body settled next to me, and his lips brushed mine, gently at first and then with more demand. I locked my arms around his neck and his hand slid inside my shirt.

His pocket began to vibrate against my leg. 'Oh, that's new,' I slurred against his lips. 'Never had one that vibrated before.'

Ashley cursed and rolled away, pulling his phone from his pocket in the process. 'What?' he growled. I leant over and fumbled with his top shirt button. 'I'm busy. Why can't you take care of it?' He listened for a moment, and I finally succeeded in getting the damn button through the button hole. Just as I started on the second one, Ashley's hand halted me. 'I have to go.'

'Something wrong, Ryan?' It was hard to get the words out. My tongue felt weird.

'Ashley...I'm Ashley, remember.' His voice was laced with anger.

'Of course, you are. You must have had too much wine if you can't remember who you are.' I rolled to my side and began to trail soft kisses along the frown line that extended from his lips to his jaw.

'I really need to leave,' he sighed, climbing out of bed. 'My cousin's gotten himself into a troublesome situation. Go to sleep, Faith. I'll see myself out.'

I vaguely heard the front door slam. Fleabag settled at my feet. 'Night', Ryan. I love you,' I slurred.

* * *

I awoke to an incessant clamour. My alarm voiced its presence on the pillow beside me. I wanted to throw it across the room. It was three in the morning, an ungodly hour for anyone to get up. I lifted my head and groaned. My brain ached. I had a sour mouth and churning stomach. I cursed the inventor of wine and stumbled out of bed. A hot shower and a liberal application of toothpaste didn't help the bitter turmoil in my stomach or the thump in my head. With squinted eyes and tentative movements, I fell into my white skivvy and black pants, and headed to the cafe. As I drove, I tried to recall the events of the previous evening but my memory was beyond hazy. Had I really invited Ashley to my bed and called him Ryan, or had that just been a dream?

With careful footsteps I entered the café. My head hurt and stomach roiled with each step. I pulled up short when I spotted who was seated at table one. Dressed in running shorts and tee shirt, with a pot of tea and the newspaper spread out in front of him was Ashley. He grinned, rose and strode towards me. He scooped me into his arms and planted demanding kiss on my lips.

'Morning, Sunflower. How are you feeling?'

I stared up at him, wondering what the hell was going on. How had our relationship developed to this so quickly? I wasn't ready for it.

'Fragile,' I said, taking a step back.

Ashley's brows beetled together in a small frown at my action. Not wanting to get into an argument right at that moment, I backed away further. 'Don't you ever sleep or suffer a hangover?'

He grinned. 'Sore head, huh? Come and have a cup of tea.'

'I can't. I have to start work.'

'Not for ten more minutes. I checked. You've just enough time to have a restorative hot drink.'

Before I could protest, he took my hand and guided me to the table. I glanced down at the newspaper laying open at the racing section as he poured out the hot brew.

'I see you like a flutter.' I pointed at the circled races and horses on the page.

'Not me. I borrowed this from your cook, Jim,' he said, handing me a warm cup of tea and two white pills.

I raised my eyebrows in query.

'Paracetamol,' he said.

I grinned sheepishly. 'How'd you know?'

'My body is tuned to you.' He lifted my fingertips to his lips, gave them a soft kiss. 'Drink your tea, Faith. It'll help.'

'I need milk and lots of sugar.' I said, casting a glance over the table searching for a milk jug.

'No, you don't,' he said, as he nudged the cup towards my lips. 'It's green tea. You drink it just as it is. It's much better for you than that swill you usually pour down your throat.'

'There's nothing wrong with a good cup of coffee with lots of sugar. It can be very restorative,' I muttered, not believing him. I took a large mouthful, along with the pills and discovered he was right; the tea did seem to settle my stomach. I sighed. 'Why aren't you at home in bed?' I asked, curious as to why he was at my workplace at almost four in the morning.

'I'm going for a jog on Middleton beach. You can join me in future.' He ignored my shaking head. 'We'll start tonight. I'll pick you up at five.'

'Ashley...'

'Hush,' he interrupted. 'It's important for us to keep fit. I'm heading off now because I won't be able to keep my hands off you otherwise and you need to start work.'

I gave a start and cast a quick glance at the clock above the counter – it was one minute to four. I leapt to my feet but before I could go Ashley pulled me close.

He stroked his forefinger along my cheek. 'Will you change a couple of $100 notes into fifties and twenties for me? I'd do it at the bank later today, but I really need to buckle down to my writing.' He seemed hesitant to ask the favour because he suddenly changed his mind. 'No, don't worry about it. I'll make up the time later somehow.'

I knew Ashley's accommodation was a good twenty-minute drive from the CBD and driving into town would take a big chunk out of his work day. 'Don't be silly, Ashley,' I said holding out my hand. 'I'm sure there's enough cash in till. Give me your money and I'll change it.'

Ashley dropped a light kiss on my brow before I hurried away with his cash clutched in my fist.

# Chapter Twelve

Exhausted from my hangover and the double shift I'd just completed, I dragged myself to the university to attend a full afternoon of lectures. As I pulled MC into a parking bay my phone buzzed. It was a text message from Chips.

*Just got a coded text from the Flyboy. He's away on a hush hush...that's why the silence. Oh goody, just got a second one – not coded this time. Oh boy, he loves me!!!!! C XXX*

My eyes filled with tears. I swiped them away with the back of my hand and texted back.

*(Happy face emoji and a row of hearts) Awesome. When are you coming back? Or should I come home to Perth.*

Her reply was prompt.

*Stay. I'll only be a couple more days. I want to get you some answers. I'm hunting mutton atm.*

A sad smile touched my lips and my heart ached – Ryan was in so much trouble. Before I had time to answer the first text, a second came through.

*Are you looking after yourself? Growly face C.*

I replied with a thumb up and a throbbing heart. Not up to playing my usual texting game I added a short message that I knew would amaze her. *Going jogging tonight!*

Chips responded with a string of amazed emoji faces.

I sent her a pile of poo.

\* \* \*

I struggled to jog the one hundred metre warm up without throwing up. Ashley frowned at my pathetic attempt and pointed at a circle that encompassed the entire oval. 'We are not leaving until you make one full lap. Off you go.'

I glared at him. He reached forward and gave me a determined shove. I jogged a few steps then walked a few. As I rounded the back straight, I spotted him leaning on his elbows on the window frame of a red, souped-up, muscle car. The driver handed Ashley a zip up wallet that resembled the ones the courier driver had delivered to Brian a few months back. The car drove away. Ashley strolled to his gym bag, secreted the wallet away, and pulled out his phone. He picked up a drink bottle as he chatted. When he'd finished the call he sprinted around the track, covering the ground I'd just staggered along, at a fast clip. I continued my slow totter and scowled as he rapidly caught up with me.

Jogging in place at my side, Ashley handed me the water bottle. He hadn't even broken out in a sweat and I hated him for it.

'Show off.'

'Have a mouthful of water,' he grinned.

I glared in disgust and took a gulp from the bottle. I winced at the metallic taste. When I'd caught my breath I nodded towards the road. 'Who was in the ute?'

Ashley ignored my question and tapped my shoulder. 'Come on, I'll pace you.'

Every time I slowed to a walk, he slapped my butt. 'Keep going, you're nearly there.'

By the time we arrived back to where he'd left his bag, I hated him even more. My clothes were soaked in sweat and my leg muscles burned with pain. I collapsed onto the grass, prepared to never move again.

'Good work,' said Ashley. He reached down, grabbed my wrist and hauled me back to my feet. 'Now, home with you. Time for a hot shower. We'll do this again tomorrow and you'll run the entire lap.'

'God no, I can't do this again,' I gasped.

'Yes, you can. By the end of the week, you'll be running two laps without a single stop.'

I glared at his back as he strode nonchalantly towards the car. I staggered after him and fell in the door he held open for me. I sank into the BMW's soft leather and closed my heavy eyes, desperate for sleep.

* * *

I awoke on my couch. Confused, I tried to sit up, but every tormented muscle in my body screamed out an agonised protest. Across the room my blurred vision spotted Ashley. He was settled in a chair sipping hot liquid from a mug and watching television. I groaned as I struggled to throw away the blanket I was tangled up in. My head thumped as I tried to rise. It was weird how tired I was all the time. Ashley put down his mug and made his way over to my side. He reached down and helped me negotiate my way out from under the blanket and up into a sitting position.

'Welcome back, sleepy head.'

I brushed my crazy mop of hair away from my face and rubbed at my crusty eyes with the heel of my hands. 'I feel like crap,' I moaned. 'How long was I out for?'

'Fourteen hours. I was beginning to think you were never going to surface. I hope you don't mind, I used the shower,' he said, handing me the mug he'd been sipping from. 'Green tea,' he said, when I sniffed at it suspiciously. 'Go on, it will do you good.'

I took a large gulp to clear the fuzz from my teeth and the dry scum in my throat. My eyes focused. I noticed Ashley was dressed in a beautifully cut black suit, white silk shirt and silver tie. I, on the other hand, still wore the clothes I'd been jogging in. I lifted an arm and sniffed my armpit. I stank of stale sweat.

'Eww.'

Ashley laughed and cupped my face with his hands. 'You smell divine.'

I snorted. 'Yeah, right. What time is it?'

'Almost eight-thirty.'

'Aw...crap. I've got a class in an hour.' I struggled to my feet. 'What about you, Ashley. What's on your dance card today?'

'I've got a day of meetings.'

'Hence the knock-em' dead outfit,' I said, eyeing him up and down in approval. 'You look classy. Do you want something to eat before you go? I think there's some muesli left. I really must find the time to shop.'

'Don't worry about it, Faith. I've already eaten. And I've taken care of the shopping. Now I must leave,' he said, pulling me close, 'but I'll see you at the oval at four this afternoon. Don't be late.'

Ashley kissed me thoroughly and was off out the door before I had a chance to ask what he meant by he'd taken care of the shopping, or even lodge a protest about ever jogging again. I was ready to die. Since I was already on my feet, I stumbled into the kitchen and opened the fridge seeking a plate of lasagne to help fortify me for the day ahead. I pulled up short.

*What the hell!*

The shelves were loaded with fresh fruits and salad, tubs of yoghurt, bottles of juice and a package of butcher's meat. I flipped open the freezer – all my microwave meals were gone.

* * *

I let rip with every swear word I could think of as I strode to my car after a round of lectures. I cursed some more when I noticed the back tyre was flat. Convinced RFW had something to do with it I stared intently around the car park ready to give him a piece of my mind. I saw no sign of my nemesis. In disgust I yanked open MC's hatch and pulled out the jack. A car drove into the bay on my left and the driver's window buzzed down.

Professor Murray stared at me over the top of his glasses. 'Is everything all right, Miss Bergman?'

'Yes thanks, Prof. I'm just changing a flat.'

'Do you want me to call the campus security guard? I'm sure he'll be happy to change the wheel for you. I'd do it myself, but I have a bad back.'

'Thanks, but no thanks. Russ Johnson and I don't really see eye to eye,' I said, not wanting to have an encounter or even be beholden to old rat-face.

'Russ Johnson? Oh, you mean the janitor,' said Professor Murray. 'Easy mistake to make, the uniforms are very similar. No, our campus security guard is Steven Thatcher, and I can't imagine him not getting on with anyone.'

I stared at him, surprise and something I identified as anger, fizzed to life in my veins. So, Russ wasn't campus security. And all those stupid on the spot fines he'd plagued me with were bogus. I bet he'd pocketed all that money feeling very smug. Bastard!

I dragged myself back into the moment because the professor was giving me a puzzled stare. I smiled at him to ease his concern. 'I'm fine thanks Prof. I can do this,' I said, as I hauled the spare tyre from the wheel well.

By the time the wheel was changed I was late for the run with Ashley. *This is your love – answer the phone* blared from my mobile as I raced MC towards the jogging track. I glanced down in surprise. Ashley's photo was on the screen. I didn't even know that ringtone had been assigned to his profile. He must have added it when he set my alarm the previous week. It made me cross that he'd fiddled around with my phone settings, so I chose not to answer the call.

In a flurry of gravel, MC skidded to a halt beside Ashley's BMW. He was pacing up and down, wearing a new track in the grass with his phone jammed against his ear. He looked angry.

Not one for scenes, I decided to defuse the situation as I leapt from the driver's seat. 'Sorry, sorry, sorry. I had a flat tyre.'

The tension left his face, and he covered the gap between us in a rush. He scooped me into his arms and growled, 'You should have called.'

I tried to step away from his firm grasp, but he held my upper arms in a tight grip. I wriggled in an attempt to break his hold. His response was to slam his mouth hard against mine in a bruising kiss.

When he broke contact, intensity oozed from him in waves. 'I was worried,' he growled.

'Calm down. I'm sorry, alright. I came as soon as I'd changed the wheel.' I glanced down at the time on my phone. 'Why all the drama anyway, I'm only five minutes late.'

He pulled me hard against his chest, 'Sorry, Sunflower, I was worried something had happened to you.'

With a mouthful of shirt I mumbled, 'Why should anything happen to me. Come on, ease up will you.' I shoved hard against his chest with the palms of my hands, attempting to put some breathing space between us. It was like trying to move a solid brick wall. 'Look, do you mind if we give this running lark a miss for today.'

'No! You'll set your program back if you miss a day.'

'But I need to take my tyre in for repair.

'Here, let me check it out for you,' he said, finally releasing his tight hold. I rubbed my upper arms where I'd been grabbed. I was going to be covered in blue-black marks.

Ashley strode around to the back of MC and opened the hatch. He stared at my wheel and fiddled around. 'There's a bloody match stuck in the valve, probably just some kid's idea of a joke.'

Words exploded from my mouth before I could stop them. 'That bloody RFW!' Ashley spun around and stared at me.

'RFW?'

'The rat-faced weasel - Russ Johnson. Don't you remember? You spoke to him the day we met. I just found out he's a fake.'

Ashley rubbed the heel of his hand over his forehead as if it pained him. His gaze was sharp but the rest of his facial features blank. 'What do you mean fake?'

I meant to ask him if he was okay or if his head hurt, but my anger had me blurt out details of my recent discovery instead. 'Fake as in not real. It seems RFW is the janitor not the security guard he's been portraying himself to be.'

'Are you sure?' Ashley barked.

'Yep, I just met the real campus security guard. Professor Murray must have called him when he saw me struggling with my flat, because he came by to check on me as I was reloading my tools back into the car. We had a lovely chat. Steven Thatcher is a 50-year-old sweetie, with a jolly laugh who has worked at the university for ten years.'

'So, who do you think this Russ Johnson is?' Ashley asked, spacing the words in a cool level tone.

'A creep! I don't know...but I'll tell you something, he's made a shit load of money out of me. Do you know when we first met he tried to get me to date him.' I gave a revolted shudder. 'Then he kept calling me. I told him to stop, or I'd report him to the student welfare councillor for harassment. In retaliation he began to issue on-the-spot fines. They cost me a bloody fortune.' I looked at Ashley, concerned. 'I already told you all that. Don't you remember?'

'No, you didn't,' he said, dismissing my statement as if I was the one with the memory problem. 'How can I possibly protect you if you don't tell me everything that is going on in your life?'

'But I did, Ashley. Maybe you just forgot.' I didn't like the way this conversation was going. 'Are you feeling, okay?'

'What I don't understand is why you think this RFW would let your tyre down,' said Ashley, ignoring my question.

'Well, recently anonymous notes have been placed on my car windscreen, now this. It must be him. Who else could it be? I think I'll go to the police and have him charged.'

'You can't. You don't have any evidence.' Those five words took the wind right out of my sails. Deflated and defeated, my shoulders sagged. Ashley was right. Unless I could catch Russ Johnson in action, I had nothing to go to the police with.

'And I knew you weren't telling me everything. What you need is my full-time protection. From now on I'm going to drive you anywhere you need to go and walk you to all your classes. This guy is not going to get anywhere near you ever again.'

I stepped back, pulling away from the smothering force of his over-protectiveness. I held up my palm. 'Whoa there, buddy, back the truck up. There's no need to go overboard. One flat tyre and a couple bits of paper don't constitute full time security. I'm perfectly safe. Chips will be home in a couple of days, and I'll stick close to her. Besides he has no idea where I live or work.'

'Faith...'

'No Ashley, you're going overboard.' I turned and stomped away.

* * *

That night I sat down and held a serious internal debate with myself. Do I throw in the rest of the semester at uni, pack my bag and go join Chips and Unk in Perth or should I stay to brazen out the whole anonymous letter thing. Ashley's intense possessiveness was another issue I needed to address. I could take the easy route and just walk away from him and our friendship. I was more than tempted, but if I did I wasn't being a good friend to someone with a terminal illness. When things get tough a good friend doesn't desert the relationship, she works on it, to rectify the problem. Plus, I'd given him my word that I would spend what days he had left with him and I'm a girl who always keeps her promises. Maybe I could drag Ashley back to Perth by suggesting he visit his family and meet my uncle Alex. The change of scenery might even be good for him. With family around it might help defuse his over-protective instincts. At the same time, I could convince him to pay a visit to his doctor because his recent memory lapses had me concerned. My biggest hurdle there was that I didn't know how to approach him on the subject. His brain tumour was still a taboo subject.

I decided to call Chips. The sensible girl she was, she always gave good advice. I picked up my phone. It rang in my hand. I laughed when I saw the caller ID.

'Well, speak of the devil,' I said. 'I was just about to call you. I was thinking of coming home for a few days.'

'Don't,' croaked my cousin.

'God, you sound awful. What's wrong?'

'Both Popsicle and I have come down with the dreaded COVID.'

'Oh God, no. Poor you. How sick are you both?'

'Me not to bad, feels like a crappy case of flu, but Popsicle is very sick. He spent all night coughing and hacking up the lining of his lungs. He says his body aches like he's being pummelled by a boxer intent on recouping a world championship. I had the doctor call around this morning. He told Dad it's going to get a lot worse before it gets better, and it could be weeks before he's well enough to go back to work.' Chips began coughing and it was ages before she could catch her breath and continue. 'We're in isolation at the moment. Have to stay that way for a couple of weeks. When that's over, I'm still going to stay on here until Popsicle is fully recovered. I've spoken to my study co-ordinator and mentor. She's organised for me to take all my classes online for the rest of the semester. As for my exams, I can do those at the Curtin campus.'

'What do you want me to do about your job?'

Another prolonged bout of coughing ensued. 'Throw it in if it's too much for you. I'll be moving back to Perth next year anyway. I'll borrow some money from Popsicle and pay you for my share of the utilities.'

'I think I'll keep covering your shifts as long as I can. The extra cash will be handy for me for Christmas,' I said, thinking about Ashley's travel plans.

'You don't need to run yourself into the ground, Burger. You know you can draw from your trust fund, right?' said Chip, alluding to the large inheritance my parents had left me.

'Yeah, I know but that won't teach me self-reliance will it.' I didn't want to discuss my finances so changed the subject. 'Do you hear from Adam much?'

'He's sporadic. Just quick short missives to let me know he's fine. There's no substance in his messages as the Air Force is keeping a tight lid on all communications so as not to compromise their mission. I've also had no luck getting any info about Ryan.'

I thought long and deep for a moment and finally came to a decision. 'As much as I love him, I don't want you to bother about him anymore. I need that wound to heal. I've decided to move on with a life that doesn't include him.'

Chips was silent for a long, long moment before she asked, 'Are you're sure?'

'Yes, no…oh, I don't know. Just let it go, Chips. And keep me posted how you and Unk are faring. If you need me, I'll pack up and come home, okay?

'Love you, darling,' croaked Chips.

'I love you too. Give Unk a big smooch from me. Now, go, have a hot lemon drink, some flu tablets and go to bed. You sound bloody awful.'

# 13

## Chapter Thirteen

My dogs were biting and ached like a bitch. I'd just completed another double shift in a long line of double shifts. To top it off the day had been a scorcher and the café hot and stuffy. I would have preferred to have been out with the masses who'd seeped from the woodwork to swamp the beach to enjoy a frolic in the sun, rather than to be kept on my toes in the airless café attending to the constant demands for food and drink. I let out a huge sigh of relief when I handed over the reins to the oncoming shift and hung my apron up in my locker.

I turned to Jim, my work partner of the day. He stood with a bamboozled look on his face as he stared at the timesheet clipboard in his hands. Concerned his dilemma might be associated with Brad, who was still in hospital. I sat, hooked my right foot onto my left knee so I could rub at my tender ankle, and eased into the subject.

'Are you going to the hospital to visit Brad? I can give you a lift if you like, I'm planning to pop in myself.'

'Brad's not in the hospital anymore. His mum, Paula, discharged him this morning and has taken him to a rehab clinic in Perth.'

'Oh, that's good, isn't it? It must mean he's on the road to recovery.' Jim nodded. 'So, is it going to be a quiet night for you or have you got something interesting planned?'

Jim's face turned beetroot red, and he began to stutter. 'I've...um...got...got a tutor coming over.'

'Oh wow. What are you studying?'

'I'm, ahh, learning to...to read,' He blurted out in a rush.

Well, that explained the bewildered look on his face as he stared at the timesheet. 'That's awesome, my friend.' I cocked a bright smile in his direction as I swapped ankles and applied another soothing massage.

He looked surprised. 'You don't think I'm missing a few buttons on my remote control, because I'm not smart enough to read?'

I stared at him dumbfounded. 'What the hell has not being able to read got to do with being smart?' I leapt to my feet and laid a gentle hand on his shoulder upset he could think so little of me. 'I don't think that at all! You're a great bloke with a kind heart. To top it off, you cook some of the best food I've ever eaten – something, even with all my so-called education, I can't seem to manage. As for the reading, it's not hard and you'll soon learn.'

A happy, gap-toothed grin appeared on his tanned leathery face. 'I'd be glad to give you some cooking pointers anytime you like.'

'And I'd be glad to have them. Maybe we can practice a recipe or two together on some of those long boring nights when no one comes into the café. What do you reckon?'

Jim's face glowed in pleasure.

I glanced over his shoulder at the clipboard. 'Do you need a hand with that?' I asked, with a flick of my finger at the clipboard.

'No, I can do numbers, but...' He held up a plain white envelope that had been clipped to his timesheet. 'I got this letter. Don't know who it's from. Would you...?' he stumbled over the request.

'Would you like me to give you a hand with a few of the words?' Jim's head bobbed up and down. 'If you wouldn't mind.'

'Of course I don't mind. We might as well do this in comfort, so let's go take a pew at one of the tables in the café while we have a gander.' Jim's top lip tilted sideways with a grateful grin.

As we wandered out to take a seat, he handed me the single sheet of paper he'd extracted from the plain white envelope. I gave the message a quick scan and rolled my eyes.

'It's a memo from our glorious leader, Brian.' My nose wrinkled in disgust at the affected language he'd used to convey a simple message. I pointed to one of the customer's chairs. 'Take a load off, Jim. This has been written in Brian's usual pompous and authoritarian style so it might take a while to decipher its actual meaning.'

Jim chortled, amused by my facetious lack of respect. We settled side-by-side at one of the booths and I spread the page out on the table between us. Running a finger under each word I let Jim read at his own pace. I only had to help him decipher some of the more grandiose words.

> All employees are to be on vigilant guard against the passing of fraudulent bank notes used in payment for the purchase of goods and consumables. If a team member detects the presence of a suspicious note in any transaction, they are to refuse to take cash payment and request that the customer either use a debit or credit card to settle their account and immediately report the incident to the Manager.
>
> Neither the bank nor the Australian Treasury will honour the value of any transaction made with counterfeit currency. Therefore, as management cannot recover the value of any

purchase made using fraudulent means and refuse to carry the loss, any employee who accepts such a payment will have the value of the transaction docked from their wages and their employment terminated.

Brian Zelinski,

Manager

The Mariner Café

Dumfounded I raised my head and stared at Jim. 'And here I thought that with the introduction of plastic money, counterfeiting had been eradicated in Australia. How is it possible to make dodgy notes?'

Jim gave me a knowledgeable look. 'Someone will always find a way to buck the system. Just ask that young man of yours.'

'What young man?'

'That Ashley bloke you've been hanging around with.'

I stared at him in amazement. 'Ashley's not my young man. He's just a friend. What the hell's he got to do with fake bank notes, anyway?'

Jim opened his mouth. The cafe door slid open, and the subject of our conversation strolled in. His gaze narrowed to hard lines when he spotted Jim and I seated together. The boyish grin left his handsome face.

My companion clamped his lips closed and leapt to his feet. 'Nothing at all. Thanks for your help. I'll get out of your hair now,' Jim rushed towards the employee locker room before I could ask him to explain his bizarre comment.

Ashley slid into the freshly vacated seat with a stormy look on his face.

'Oh, hello,' I said. 'This is a surprise. I wasn't expecting you.'

'Obviously.'

I didn't like the glower fixed on Ashley's face as he watched Jim hurry through the dining room with a backpack slung over his shoulder. 'Thanks for your help, Burger. I'll see ya' next shift,' he said, with a half-hearted wave.

'Bye, Jim,' I called out in a chirpy voice as he raced for the door.

Ashley focused his steely grey eyes on me in a fierce glare. 'What's going on, Sunflower? Why are hanging out with that loser?'

Anger fizzed low in my gut. How could he talk about such a nice guy in such a derogatory way?

'Jim is not a loser. And, I don't appreciate you referring to him as one.' I struggled to my aching feet, deciding that rather than get into an argument I'd walk away. Ashley had other ideas. His hand shot out. He grabbed tight hold of my wrist and gave it a yank. I landed with a thud back into my seat.

'Hey,' I snarled, snatching my wrist from his grasp to rub at the deep red mark his grip left. I shot him a filthy look.

'Did I hurt you, Sunshine? I'm so sorry, my darling. I didn't mean to. Please don't be mad at me. I don't know what's wrong with me. Yes, I do. I'm not feeling right and to top it off I'm worried about you. Please forgive me.'

Ashley took a gentle hold of my wrist and showered it in soft kisses, all the while batting his long dark eyelashes at me. He looked so contrite and cute I couldn't stop my amusement showing. When my lip lifted in the tiniest smile he leapt to his feet and gently encouraged me to mine. With loving arms, he cradled me against his chest.

'That's better, a smile. I love it when you smile,' he said, nestling his cheek on the top of my head and stroking a gentle finger up and down my arm.

I sighed. 'You were bullying me, Ashley. I don't like it when you do that.'

'I'm truly sorry. It won't happen again. I promise.' He reached down to take my hand but was hampered by the envelope clutched there. 'What's this?' he asked.

'It's a memo from our intrepid leader. It was the subject of Jim and my discussion.'

'Oh, I see. And does your boss have anything interesting to say?'

'Not really, he's just being a pompous ass as usual. This time he's carrying on about how it is the employee's responsibility not to accept any counterfeit notes, or some such nonsense. Brian claims he'll dock our wages and give us the boot if we do!' I opened the envelope and held out the page for him to read. 'Is that legal? Can he even do that?'

Ashley scanned the memo and snorted.

'What a twat.'

'You're not wrong!' Jim's comment about Ashley having knowledge about counterfeiting gave me a nudge. I decided to test the water. 'I wouldn't know how to identify funny money if I fell over it. Would you?'

Ashley sent me a slightly superior smile. He took me by the elbow and guided me out the door into the parking lot. 'Sure. It's easy if you know what you are looking for. A genuine note is made of plastic and it will bounce back into shape when you scrunch it up in your hand. That can't be faked.'

I stopped walking and stared up at him in amazement. 'Of course. Now why didn't I think of that? I really should pay more attention. How do you know all this stuff?'

'Research for my book.' He laughed, flung his arm over my shoulder and escorted me over to MC. 'But not all of us can be a font of useless information so, I don't want you to worry your pretty little head over the unimportant stuff, leave all that to me.' I lifted a quizzical eyebrow at him. 'Okay?' he prompted.

'Okay...I suppose...'

'Excellent. Now let's get you home and changed out of that ugly work clobber you insist on wearing and into a pretty dress. I've got a picnic basket full of delicious treats all packed up for us and a reservation on a quiet strip of beach.'

'Oh Ashley, that's so sweet, but...'

He sealed the rest of my objection behind a deep and serious kiss. 'Sunflower, you need this. You work too hard for an unappreciative boss...and a demanding professor. We don't get to spend nearly enough leisure time together. You're tired and need to relax.'

He was right about that. I'd been working and studying very hard lately and along with the harsh jogging routine and diet he had me on, I was exhausted.

'A picnic dinner sounds lovely. But I do need to be home by eight o'clock. I have another shift starting at nine.'

The smile left Ashley's face. 'And how long is this shift? Not another late one I hope.'

'No, only three hours, thank God. I'm due to finish work at midnight. Why?'

'That gives us hardly any time together.'

'Yeah, I know, but after tonight I've got a couple of days off. Maybe we could do something special together tomorrow night.'

His face broke out in a cheeky grin complete with wiggling eyebrows.

'Stop it, sir. Behave yourself. Putting aside the fact that red wine and I do not play well together, you know I'm not ready to take our friendship to that level...yet.'

A shaft of disappointment crossed his face. He reached over, tugged me close and kissed the tip of the nose. 'Please don't make me wait too long,' he whispered.

Guilt and concern stabbed me in the chest. I stroked soft fingers over his cheek. 'Ashley is everything...'

He cut me off by giving me a small gentle shove away. 'Off you go, Sunflower. Time to go get changed.' The phone in his pocket gave an insistent chirp. 'Sorry, I need to take this call. You go on ahead. I'll only be five minutes behind.'

I caught a snatch of his conversation as I idled past with my window down.

'No,' he said. 'I told you yesterday that cover is totally blown, buddy. I'll get the Scotsman to find a replacement for you. For now, I want you to stay where you are and finish the current batch we're working on. Then get the press ready for shipment. And lay off the fucking booze, will you, Cuz. I can't keep cleaning up your messes.'

Ashley dazzled me with his glorious smile as I glided past. My heart began to ache, knowing that I might not get to appreciate those gorgeous dimples for much longer. If today was anything to go by, his tumour was starting to affect him. Who knows how much time together we had left? With that sad thought in the forefront of my mind, I hung my hand out of the window and gave him a small wave that was tinged with sadness.

* * *

Ashley's much-anticipated quiet patch of beach wasn't. The whole shoreline was packed with barbequing and picnicking families. A large contingent of teenagers spent their time racing along the sand performing a courting ritual of kiss chase. I enjoyed watching the spectacle but could see my friend was disappointed our time together was being intruded upon by others. He scowled at the teenagers and snapped at me. No matter how hard I tried to make him laugh he wouldn't. A small sliver of ice settled around my heart as I realized that nothing seemed to please him today.

Breaking my vow of silence on a certain subject I asked, 'Ashley, do you feel okay?'

'Yes, why?' he barked. His bad mood hurt me. Tears welled in my eyes.

'No reason, you just don't seem to be enjoying yourself.' I held back on the tears that threatened to spill down my cheeks. To hide my unhappiness and to distract myself I collected together our used salad bowls and cutlery, and packed them in the picnic basket. When I was sure my emotions were under control, I turned to Ashley. 'Will you take me home, please? I need to get ready for work.'

'We still have another half an hour yet,' he said, as he crawled behind me and wrapped his arms and legs around me in a tight hug. He nuzzled the back of neck, igniting flickers of desire low in my gut as his fingers slid to just below my breast, causing my temperature to rise even further. I could feel his desire pressed hard against the small of my back. A loud squeal intruded on our rising passion as two young kids kicked up the sand as they raced past.

Ashley pulled away and rose to his feet. 'This is hopeless. Come on, Faith, let's go somewhere quiet.'

'I'm sorry but I don't have time...'

'Time...you promised me time but insist on giving it to others,' he snapped. 'Get in the car. I'll take you home.'

Ashley grabbed the picnic basket and stormed away. I followed in his wake, miserable and confused. I didn't know how to handle his mood swings.

* * *

Brian waddled into the café, an hour and a half into my shift, loaded down with a pile of green leather account books, a laptop computer and a sports bag. As he passed me on his way to the office he announced, 'You'll have to stay late tonight, Faith. Sam's come down with COVID and won't be in.'

'Can't you find someone else to cover for Sam? I worked all day. I've only had a three-hour break. If you're going to be here anyway maybe you could...'

'I've got other fish to fry. Just suck it up girlie and do as I say.'

My tired brain screamed, *NO, you ignorant moron and don't call me girlie*! I opened my mouth to tell him to shove his shift, but what actually came out was, 'Okay, but you can pay me triple time...'

'That's friggin' highway robbery.'

'Don't care,' I grouched, too tired to worry about being nice and retaining my current employment status.

'Fine!' Brian stalked off muttering under his breath. 'Bloody, pig-headed employees...'

I rolled my eyes and thought bad thoughts about pompous employers.

As was usual by midnight, custom had died down to zilch. The streets outside were deserted as everyone except me got to snuggle under their warm cosy covers for the night. Grumpy as all hell, I waved farewell to Jim, jealous that he at least would soon join that elite group of bed-dwellers. I trudged out into the back room and snatched up the mop and bucket. The office door stood ajar. Brian was shoving bundles of cash into the sports bag he'd toted in earlier. I didn't stop and stare. I knew the money wasn't from The Mariners Café takings as we didn't do enough business to generate that much cash. Maybe he was skimming from the other business's he was involved in, but I didn't care anymore. I was so fed up with everyone and everything. And, I was so God-damned tired. Ashley's moodiness tonight hadn't helped either. I was so ready to chuck it all in - even him - and go home to Chips and Unk. COVID 19 be damned.

The bell above the café entry chimed. I turned off the tap I was using to fill the bucket and wiped my hands on my apron. The chime played for a second time. Wow, busy night. I headed towards the noise but Brian, sports bag in hand, strutted out of the office and put up a hand.

'I've got this. You stay out back and mop the floors until I call you.'

Confused, I stared at his retreating back. That was weird, but as my care factor was at zero, I just shrugged and trundled into the office to take a look around. The safe door stood wide open. It was empty. The surface of the desk was clear and clean, not even a dust bunny marred its pristine surface. All of Brian's journals plus his computer gear were gone. He'd lugged them out into the café with him when he went to answer the doorbell. I gave the floor a cursory swipe with the mop as it was clean anyway, then returned to the corridor to lean against the wall with my eyes closed wishing I was at home in bed. My zoning out was disturbed by the sound of a raised voice that echoed down the short hallway.

'Don't make excuses, Brian. Revenue is down. Everyone seems to be behind on their payments.'

On tiptoes I ventured a little closer to listen.

'Tomorrow you will visit all our customers and remind them we are not a charitable institution. I want these deficits rectified by Friday or we will have more than words, you and I.'

Brian's voice quivered when he responded to the instruction, 'Yes, Cub.'

'Now what's the status on the real estate I wanted?'

'The owners took it off the market.'

'Well persuade them.'

'I can't, Cub. They've left town.'

I took another step forward and peaked into the dining room.

At a corner table, facing me, Brian sat across from two men. He was blotting sweat from his brow with a handful of serviettes. My movement must have caught his eye because he glanced my way, lifted his chin in a jerk to indicate I should go away. The man nearest me turned to stare.

It was Scotty, the Dash Deliveries guy.

He must have moved up in the world because he no longer wore khaki work clothes. Instead, he was dressed in a good quality black suit and dress shoes. His bulky, broad shoulders blocked my view of his companion who seemed to be studying the set of books Brian had been carrying earlier.

Scotty leant left, murmured to the man beside him, before rising to his feet to amble over.

'How about some hot drinks, lassie.'

'Sure...Scotty isn't it?' He nodded. 'What can I get you?'

'Tea for Cub, I'll have a large cappuccino.'

I tried to lean around his bulk to get a clear view of the boss, but Scotty hooked his elbow onto the cappuccino machine to block my view. He handed me a small pouch.

'Make the tea from this. It's Cub's special brew.'

While I sorted out a teapot and cups Scotty ran an appreciative glance up and down my body. He made me uncomfortable with his close scrutiny. My cheeks began to burn.

Scotty raised his voice so he could be heard over the hiss of the cappuccino machine. 'You're a *bonnie lass*, what time do you get off work? We could go for a *wee dram* and a *coorie* at my *aite*.'

The broad Scottish brogue rolled smoothly from his tongue and I had to pause to decipher the meaning of his words. I stared at the smirk on his lips and gathered he wanted to take me back to his place for what I bet was much more than a drink and a cuddle.

Surprised by his straight-forward attempt to bed me and not being at all interested, I said, 'I won't be getting off anytime soon.'

'Pity. I can put the hard word on Brian if you like,' he said, reaching over to run a gentle finger slowly down my throat toward my cleavage.

'No thanks.' I squeaked, taking a hurried step away from his inquisitive finger.

'You're sure, lassie? We could have some real fun together.'

I picked up his coffee and shoved the hot mug into his chest. 'I'm sure. Here take this. I'll bring over the tea.'

Scotty hooted in amusement at my manoeuvre, wrapped his left fist around the mug handle and smacked my butt with his right palm before strolling casually back to his seat. I followed behind at a wary distance and caught my first glimpse of the boss, Cub. He was dressed in a black Armani suit and a white silk button down shirt. He looked suave, sophisticated and classy. His handsome face was expressionless but the arms folded across his chest expressed displeasure. I glanced at Brian. He was giving a great impression of a wilted lettuce.

Cub spoke and his voice was as hard as tempered steel. 'Issuing a memo to be on the lookout for counterfeit bank notes was stupid, Brian. Do you want a visit from the federal police?'

Brian rapidly shook his head.

I gently placed the tea pot onto the table in front of Cub and said, 'Your green tea.'

# 14

## Chapter Fourteen

Cub glanced up at me and smiled. He rose to his feet, gathered me into his arms and settled his mouth over mine in a long kiss. I probably didn't respond with the ardour he expected because when he broke away his smile seemed forced. 'This is a lovely surprise. I thought you finished at midnight, my love,' said Ashley.

'Sam's sick – COVID. I have to cover for him.'

He tucked a wisp of air behind my ear and studied my face. 'You look exhausted.'

'I am.'

Ashley turned his head and glared at my boss. Brian's mouth flapped like a fish out of water at the sight of the man he called Cub cradling me in his arms.

'Brian, you will cover the rest of Faith's shift. I'm taking my lady home. And she is to have at least a week off so she can rest and prepare for her exams.'

I glanced at Scotty and found his reaction very interesting. His already white skin had paled significantly, but it was the terror in his eyes that had me baffled.

'Go get your things.' Ashley turned me around and gave me a gentle push. 'I'll drive you home.'

'Don't you have work to do?' I asked, pointing to the open, blue account book and printouts spread across the table.

'It'll wait. Nothing is more important than you.' Ashley glanced at his companion. 'Scotty, escort Faith out to her car. I want a final word with Brian.'

'Aye, boss,' Scotty said. He leapt to his feet and shoved some chairs aside to give me clear access to the door.

I stared down at Brian, uncertain if Ashley had the authority to order him around.

'Off you go Faith,' he stuttered. 'I'll call the next shift in early. And take some days off. Make sure you rest up.'

'Are you sure you can get someone to cover?'

'Yes, yes, of course. I'm a well-organised businessman, you know. There are plenty of people on my books I can call.'

So why didn't you call them sooner instead of working me to the bone I wondered as I rose onto tiptoes and kissed Ashley's cheek.

'Thank you,' I whispered and dashed to my locker to grab my stuff.

Scotty walked with a respectful distance between us and kept his hands to himself. He didn't speak until the main doors swished closed behind us. 'I'd like to apologise to you, lass. I didn't mean any disrespect earlier.'

'Just don't do it again, Scotty and we'll be fine.'

'Aye, I promise. Could I ask a wee favour of you though? Please don't mention my boorish behaviour to Cub?'

Remembering Ashley's reaction when I'd been confronted by the tattooed redhead, I murmured, 'No, I won't.'

A piece of paper flapped under MC's wiper blade. Scotty grabbed it before I could stop him. I gently removed the sheet from his tight grip and glanced at it. Not a neat printer job with a photo this time. This note had been hand scrawled in fury judging by the holes punched through the paper at each full stop.

*I'm angry with you, Faith. Why a cub when you can have me. Be ready, I'm coming for you, your devoted and FAITHFUL HUNTS-MAN.*

The word faithful was underlined three times. A shiver ran down my spine.

'What the fuck?' said Scotty, perusing the letter's contents from over my shoulder.

Behind us the café doors swished open. We both jumped at the noise. Ashley strolled out with the sports bag slung over his shoulder and a satisfied grin on his face. He spotted us huddled over the threatening note and the smile left his lips. 'What's going on?'

Scotty spoke up before I could fob him off. 'Someone's threatening your wee lass, Cub.'

Ashley plucked the paper from my fingers and glared at it.

'Get in the car, Faith. I'll take care of this.' He opened MC's passenger's door for me. As I clambered in, he growled to Scotty. 'This has gone far enough. I want you to take the BMW. Go find that little prick, Slugger. Obviously, he didn't listen the first time I told him to back off. Come get me when you have him.'

'Aye, Cub. Where can I find you?'

'I'll be at Faith's townhouse. You know where that is.'

'Aye, where I dropped the groceries off the other day. You sure this is the work of the red-headed git?'

'The letter is signed, faithful huntsman. Just find him and I'll ask.'

A shiver ran up my spine at Ashley's cold anger. He threw the sports bag onto the back seat of MC and folded himself behind the wheel. He held his hand out for my car keys. I placed them gently in his palm, disappointed to see his happy mood had evaporated with the arrival of the anonymous letter. I'd been receiving them for so long now they didn't upset me anymore, besides nothing ever came of the threats. I decided to distract Ashley and get him into a better mood.

'Can I ask you a question?'

'Sure, Sunflower. What do you want to know?'

'Is the cafe in financial trouble? Should I be looking for another job?'

'No. What makes you think that?'

'Well, I do remember you once told me that you and your father bailed out businesses in trouble, reshaped them into profitable ventures and I couldn't help but notice that Brian was showing you one of the sets of books he keeps. I thought he might be asking for help.'

Ashley took his eyes off the road and stared at me. 'One of the sets, does he have more than one set?'

'I think he must have, because he usually writes the cash he counts up in a green journal, but I noticed tonight he was showing you a blue one.'

'Ahhh, that might explain a thing or two,' he mumbled under his breath. 'Faith, I don't suppose you know where he keeps those other books?'

I was tired and lost interest in the conversation. An eye watering yawn escaped. My jaw almost dislocated. I snuggled down in my seat.

'Faith?'

'Probably in the safe, though I wouldn't have thought that was very secure. The combination to it is circled in red on the calendar he keeps on the back of the portrait on the wall.'

Ashley's gaze returned to the road and a cold smile touched his lips. 'Thank you,' he said, but didn't explain what he was thanking me for.

# Chapter Fifteen

Logging off from the university computer I stretched my back and let out a soft sigh of relief. I'd just completed my final exam of the year. I felt I'd done alright, considering my mind wasn't quite on the job. It had been more than a week since I'd received any form of contact from my stalker. I was on tenterhooks, curious as to whether Scotty had found Slugger or not. If he had, what had Ashley done to warn him off?

So as not to disturb the other students who still slogged away at their exams, I silently gathered together my things and tip-toed out of the room. With a spring in my step, I made my way across the street to the coffee house and took a seat amongst the anonymous crowd of outdoor diners as I revelled in the freedom of not being smothered by Ashley's intense over-protectiveness. I ordered a cappuccino. As much as I wanted a piece of cheesecake, I decided against it. Ashley wouldn't approve and would make me jog extra laps to atone for my transgression from the diet and fitness plan he had me on.

While I waited to be served, I pulled out my phone to check my messages. There was one from Chips.

*Exams finished. No probs sitting them at Curtin. Feel like I did well. You?*

I hadn't told her about my stalker, or Ashley's brain tumour, or even that he now slept on the couch at our townhouse. In fact, I'd kept stum about a lot of things going on in my life as she had enough on her plate looking after Uncle Alex and worrying about Adam.

I thought carefully about my reply before thumbing a broom and dustpan, two googly eyes and the letter U. Chips would easily decipher that I was all done and dusted and asking when I going to see her?

A shadow fell across the screen as I pressed send. It was the waitress. She placed my coffee at my elbow. I smiled a thank you just as my phone buzzed.

*Sorry, you'll have to celebrate surviving exams alone. (sad face emoji) Disappointed I can't be there for the big PRESENTATION. Popsicle is on the mend but his recovery is slow. He's planning to make an appearance at work on Monday but we'll see. Flyboy's mission is finally over and he's on his way home. So excited, I have pains in my stomach!!! He's coming for dinner, Sunday. Popsicle promises no interrogation...don't believe him. The mutton is still being elusive. Love you C.XXX*

I stared at the message and my heart ached. I missed her and her good advice, terribly. I was mulling over what to reply when the chair next to me was jerked away from the table. My head shot up in fright.

Ashley, his lips drawn in a tight angry slash, sat down and snapped, 'You didn't call me when you finished your exam.'

'I was just about to. I wanted a celebratory coffee first to clear my head,' I stuttered, wary of his tone. Were we about to have another day of anger from him because I didn't do everything his way?

'And didn't you think I might like to celebrate with you?' He leant forward and pushed my cappuccino aside. 'That stuff will rot your guts.'

'Why are you so cross, Ashley?'

He raised his hand to the waitress. 'Two green teas,' he demanded, before turning to me. 'In case you haven't noticed, a lot of weird stuff has been happening around you lately. I'm upset you didn't call. I had to ask your bodyguard where you were.'

'Bodyguard? What bodyguard?'

He pointed to a lightly built Asian lad who leant nonchalantly against a light pole further down the street. 'Sammy Chow. I hired him to watch out for you.

I indicated around at the crowd that surrounded me. 'I don't need mollycoddling, Ashley. I'm perfectly safe.'

'This time maybe, but that little prick Slugger is still out there. I don't want you going anywhere unprotected or without me at your side.' He picked up my phone and read the latest string of texts between Chips and me. 'You've had time to text her but not call me! What the hell does she mean by mutton is being elusive.'

My heart slammed hard against my ribs. I didn't like his over-the-top, bossy tone and I certainly didn't like him thinking he had the right to read my personal text messages. I trotted out the first lie that came to mind.

'If you must know she's planning a special meal for Uncle Alex and needs pumped mutton,' I snapped, snatching the phone from his hand. In fury I rose to my feet. 'You're being horrible and you're smothering me. I'm leaving. Going home...by-my-self.' I spaced out the words to give emphasis to my statement.

Eye's wide, the waitress, setting a stainless-steel teapot along with two tiny white cups and saucers on our table, drank in the drama.

Ashley noticed her intent stare and took my hand in both of his and fell to one knee.

'I'm sorry, darling. I've been going about this all wrong. It's because the joy you've bought into my life is more amazing than anything I have ever felt before. I want you beside me for the little time I have left.'

My cheeks burned in embarrassment. 'Get up, Ashley. You're making a scene,' I whispered.

He ignored my plea.

'I love you with a passion, Faith,' he said, flashing his dimples before opening his eyes wide and giving me a knee buckling soulful look. 'Will you please do me the honour of becoming my wife?'

I heard the waitress suck in an excited breath. I flicked a glance at her. She stared at me with hope aglow in her eyes. I cast a peek around at the people seated at the surrounding tables. They had all stopped their nattering and were busy ogling in our direction. The heat of their expectant gazes as they watched Ashley's very public marriage proposal made my cheeks burn even more fiercely. I gawped down at him. Fury raged inside me. I didn't love him like I did Ryan. Proposing like this in public had me trapped. I couldn't hurt or humiliate him by saying no. Nor could I discuss with him the challenge of our future as we dealt with his tumour. While I floundered for the right words, he slipped a ring on my finger. My eyes widened in astonishment at the huge diamond he'd placed there.

'Ashley, it's beautiful but it's too much...'

It was enough for Ashley, he leapt to his feet and shouted, 'Yes, she said YES.'

Chaos erupted around us as the crowd gave a loud cheer and began to applaud. To their delight Ashley swept me up into his arms, swung me in a full circle half a dozen times before taking possession of my mouth in a possessive public kiss.

Excited babble and calls of, 'You rock, man' and 'That's so sweet!' filled the air around us. I tried to break away, embarrassed and angered by the spectacle Ashley was creating, but he held me tight.

'Faith Bergman, you've just made me the happiest man on the face of the earth,' he announced in a voice loud enough to ensure everyone in the vicinity heard.

'Ashley, please...' I croaked. My insides churned in turmoil.

He stroked a finger along my jaw line, lifted my chin to lay his lips over mine and took ownership of my mouth. A mixture of confusion, anger and bemusement swirled like a category five cyclone in my gut. I had to fight the urge to push him away.

Ashley ended the kiss. 'Let's get out of here, there's something special I want to do with you,' He whispered against my lips.

Bemused by the speed of events I nodded. I would have agreed to anything in that moment, just to get away from the spectacle he had created. With a grin, Ashley reached into his pocket, extracted a fifty dollar note and threw it on the table. He grabbed my hand and tugged me along in his wake while responding to the smiling people around with a crow of, 'She said yes!'

My face began to ache from the smile I had plastered there. Ashley slung his arm around my waist, gripped hard and pulled me close in to his side as he guided me across the road to where he'd parked his BMW. I stumbled along in a befuddled cloud. He took MC's keys from my lax fingers and threw them to Sammy Chow.

'Take the lady's car home,' he commanded, while opening the passenger door of the BMW for me.

I was stunned. Everything was moving too fast. I tried to clear the fog that had accumulated in my brain and focus on what I really wanted for my life, because deep down I knew I wasn't ready for a controlled life of marriage with Ashley. While I cared for him as a friend, I didn't love him, and in the end, I had to be true to myself.

I needed to clear the air with him before things got even further out of hand. With effort I managed to unlock my tongue. 'Ashley, we need to talk to about this marriage thing...it's a big step, I don't...'

He cut me off by sealing my lips with a kiss followed by a trail of butterfly kisses along my neck. I pushed him away. 'Ashley, stop it will you. This is not what I want.'

'Sunflower you're just nervous. I understand. But as we love each other there is no reason why we can't move forward together.'

Dimples appeared around his uplifted lips. I scrambled through confused brain cells in an attempt to find the right words to put a stop to things.

'Let's go,' he said. 'The celebrant is waiting.'

'Ashley, I...what do you mean the celebrant's waiting?' I gasped.

He grinned, started the car and drove with speed down the street. 'Surprise!'

'No! Not a good surprise, this is not how I want to get married!' My voice rose to a squeaky pitch as pent-up words began to pour from my mouth. 'I have a family I want to include. I want a special dress. You've no right... I'm not even sure about this...'

'Calm down, Faith,' he growled, 'there's no need to yell. I have family too, you know. One that expects a great deal from me. And the dress is not important. I just want this special moment to be about you and me. We can do the big wedding and family rigma-role later.'

Furious and gobsmacked by his arrogance, I glared out of the car window, stumped as to how the hell I could get through to him that I didn't want this. Ashley turned the car into the beach parking lot where I saw Scotty holding a conversation with an elegantly dressed middle-aged woman. They both turned our way and smiled when Ashley guided the car to a halt.

'But I don't want to get married...' I cried out in a last-ditch effort to make him understand.

'Please, Faith,' he begged. 'The doctor says I don't have much longer...'

My heart broke. I took a sobbing breath and wondered how I could say no?

I couldn't.

\* \* \*

The ceremony was short. With a quick exchange of vows as an orange sun set over a turquoise ocean, I was suddenly wearing a gold band next to the diamond ring on my wedding finger. It was like I was in a sea of treacle. There was no escape now. My life had irrevocably changed.

With a smug look of ownership, Ashley tugged me across the sand towards his car. As I stumbled along in his wake my phone began to vibrate madly in the back pocket of my jeans. Startled, I yanked the offending object out and stared at the screen. It was my Uncle Alex. This was an unusual turn of events as he always rang me in the evenings. He'd only call during the day if it was important. I halted in my tracks and reefed my hand away from Ashley's tight grasp.

'It's my uncle calling. I have to take this.'

A frown beetled Ashley's brow and a pout formed on his lips. He stomped the final three steps to the car, leant on the bonnet and folded his arms across his chest. He glared at the phone in my hand. Stress began to claw at my gut. I was stuck between a rock and a hard place. I'd just upset my new husband...and then there was my uncle. What the hell was I going to say to him? How was I going to explain what had just happened. I couldn't just blurt out that I'd just gotten married. I needed time...time to pave the way, and time to plan the conversation. I decided to play it cool for now.

'Hello, Unk. Are you checking up on me to see if I've survived my exams? Well, I have...'

'Faith, my sweet girl, its Lucy,' he gasped, interrupting my inane prattle.

I took a startled breath. My heart squeezed painfully in my chest as I spat out, 'What's wrong with, Chips?'

'She's been rushed to hospital!'

'But we were texting only a short while ago. She was fine then. What's happened?'

'As she was leaving the university...she collapsed.' There was a catch of pain in his voice.

Tears began streaming down my cheeks. 'Oh my God, what's wrong with her?'

'I don't know, but this morning she grouched her stomach hurt. We put it down to nerves. I'm in the car, on my way to Royal Perth Hospital. As soon as I know something I'll call you.'

'Do that!' I grabbed Ashley's wrist and turned it so I could read the time on his fitness tracker. It was five in the afternoon. 'If I hit the road straight away, I should be able to make RPH by ten, depending on traffic of course.'

'You don't need to come, not until I know something...'

'Yes, I do!' I cut in. There was no way I wasn't going to be there to support him through this crisis. 'I wasn't able to be there when you had that horrible COVID, so don't deny me this. You're my family and I love you.'

'And we love you. Alright, but please drive carefully, my precious girl, I couldn't bear it if something happened to you as well.'

'I will. I promise. Text me the moment you get an update. See you soon.' I disconnected and with wet cheeks and moisture filled eyes I stared up at my new husband. He wasn't going to like this, being our wedding night and all, but life is like that. Not everything goes our way.

'I have to leave. Go to Perth,' I blurted out. 'Right now.'

His grey eyes turned dark, and his lips stretched into a long, thin scowl. The stress of it all got too much for me and I began to sob. I couldn't cope with his bad mood on top of everything else.

Ashley's face cleared of all expression, and he cupped my cheeks with his palms. 'What's wrong?'

'It's Chips. She's collapsed and has been rushed to hospital.' Ashley pulled me tight against his chest, close to his heart. I sobbed even harder when he handed me a handkerchief to sop up the mess. The gentle stroke of his hand on my hair was soothing and my crying jag eased. I gave my nose a lusty blow and murmured against his now wet jacket, 'I need to leave, right now!'

'Why don't you wait until morning?'

I pulled back and stared at him. His eyes looked cold and distant. Surely, he wasn't so intent on his own expectations that mine and those of my family didn't matter? An angry spark fizzed to life in my breast. 'Are you for real?'

The faraway look in his eyes disappeared and his gaze refocused. Ashley reached down and with his thumbs stroked the remaining tears from my cheeks.

'Take a breath,' he ordered.

I did as he asked.

'And now another.' I sucked in a deep lungful and slowly let it out. 'There you go – feel better?' I nodded. 'Good. I just meant that you're in no fit state to drive at the moment. Tomorrow would be better.'

The anger in my breast died as suddenly as it had surged. There was nothing but concern on his face.

'Sorry...' I said, contrite I'd snapped at him.

'It's okay...this time, but only because I understand how worried you are,' he said. 'I'll drive you to Perth. Do you need to call anyone or collect anything from the house before we go?'

'You don't need to...'

'Yes, I do! You're my wife. I meant every word when I said I always want you at my side,' he snapped. 'Sorry.' He gentled his tone. 'Now answer my question. Is there anyone you need to call?'

'I should speak to Professor Murray. Let him know I can't make the presentation, Monday. There's also my job.'

'Well, that's not important. As my wife you don't need to work anymore.'

I opened my mouth to argue, but now was not the time. 'No, but it's polite to let Brian know I won't be at work tomorrow and maybe for the foreseeable future. That way he can organize somebody to cover my shifts. And we'll have to swing by home as I need to collect, Fleabag.'

'Why the cat? That hissing ball of fuzz belongs to your neighbour, doesn't it?'

'They moved out last week. She stayed.'

Grouching inanities about bothersome pets and stupid pet owners, Ashley drove us to the townhouse.

* * *

'I'll just make a few phone calls while you pack,' said Ashley. He settled into a chair at the kitchen table and fished his mobile from the breast pocket of his suit jacket.

I caught a snatch of his conversation as I mounted the stairs.

'Hey cuz, where are you?' There was a long pause then his voice rose, 'What do you mean you've taken care of him?'

My heart leapt in fear at the anger in his voice. I stopped on the top step to listen.

'You stupid, bloody fuck-wit! I thought I told you to stay out of my business. You had one job to do after that kid overdosed. That was to keep your head down. No, I don't care whose fault you think it was, dipping into the product and selling it to line your own pockets is bad for business. Now, this! Pack your gear. Get yourself out of town.'

It went silent. I thought Ashley must have finished the conversation and hung up. I took a soft step towards my room but halted when he began to speak again. This time there was less anger, but his tone was sharp. 'No, I can't come and help you. I'm at Faith's. Yeah, we just got married. We're leaving for Perth within the hour. The cousin's been rushed to hospital. Look, don't you worry about my business, I know exactly what I'm doing... just make sure the Huntsmen get their shipment before you go.' There was a pause before Ashley growled. 'Fuck... take him with you and stash him with the others at the shack. I'll meet you there in a couple of days.'

I heard Ashley's chair scrape along the kitchen floor, and he let out a loud curse. Startled, I released the breath I was holding and tiptoed into my bedroom. What the hell were Ashley and his cousin into?

I let my gaze sweep around my room. Another layer of ice settled around my heart. As a result of Ashley's constant nagging this week, my personal space, along with the rest of the townhouse, had no personality left. Every item had been stowed away into cupboards and drawers, even the family photos that had once graced the wall unit along with my favourite books and knickknacks were gone. The shelves were bare and glowed from the daily application of polish I was expected to apply. The bed was so stiff and meticulously made that even Fleabag must have found it uninviting because she was nowhere to be seen.

I packed a few essentials and lugged my backpack to the top of the stairs. On the way past I flicked a quick glance into my cousin's bedroom, the only place left untouched by Ashley's strict house-keeping demands, in the hope of finding the recalcitrant cat but she wasn't anywhere upstairs. Ashley's voice carried up the stairs. He was still talking on the phone. I made my way to the top step and paused to blatantly listen.

'I scrutinized the real account book last night and have had a severe word with Zelinski. Yeah, he's certainly made a career-limiting move. Once the purloined money is returned, his days as manager are over. Keep me updated.'

I sucked in a large, quiet breath and let it out slowly. Things didn't sound too promising for Brian. I took what I intended to be a silent step forward and my toe caught on the stair tread. I stumbled, let go of the bag I carried to grab the handrail to stop my forward momentum. Freed, my pack tumbled noisily end over end down the steps. The loud thump drew Ashley from the kitchen with the phone still glued to his ear. 'Yeah, I'm heading to Perth. Come over and collect the BMW, I won't need it again.' He hung up and raised his eyebrows at me.

I gave a sheepish grin. 'Well, that's one way to get the luggage down.'

Ashley rolled his eyes, 'You're such a klutz, Faith.' He picked up my pack as if it weighed nothing and headed out the front door.

'Have you seen Fleabag?' I asked, following him out.

'No. Is this all you're taking?'

'If I need anything else, I'll raid my wardrobe at home.'

I looked down at my thin waist, or maybe not! My clothes swam on me these days. I made a snap decision that once my cousin was out of hospital and well enough, I would let her take me on a shop-ping spree.

The phone in my hand buzzed. I glanced anxiously at the screen hoping it was Uncle Alex with good news, but it was Professor Murray returning my earlier call. I sat on the front door step and chose my words with care. I avoided filling the conversation with the emotion that churned around in my gut because I knew the professor liked his facts clear and concise. I succeeded first time. He totally understood my dilemma without me having to clarify anything.

'Don't worry, Miss Bergman. Email me your presentation for grading. I'll get Colin Trasker to present his paper instead. Please pass on my regards to Miss Chippens.'

I sighed in relief and hung up. Really, under his gruff exterior the professor was a very nice man.

I dialed Brian's number. Our conversation didn't go so well.

'I can't have employees disrupting my schedule whenever they feel like taking time off, no matter who they are dating...'

I doubted he would act so pompously if he knew Ashley was nearby. I couldn't be bothered with his ego at that moment, so I cut him off mid rant. 'Brian this is an emergency. Lucy has been rushed to RPH. I need to be there for her.'

'Be that as it may, I still have a business to run. Replacement staff are a dime a dozen. I've had numerous enquiries from people looking for work.'

'Well use one of them to cover until I get back.'

'Not an option. There's so much paperwork involved in taking on temporary staff and I'd have to change the schedule, spend an hour training them,' proclaimed Brian becoming more bombastic by the moment. 'No, if I have to go to all that effort then I can't guarantee you'll have a job to come back to. Choice is yours.'

'There is no choice, Brian. You can stick your job – Chips is more important to me than you are,' I snarled and hung up.

Ashley wandered back around from stowing my luggage in the rear of MC and reached down to brush a stray wisp of my hair behind my ear. 'Is everything okay, darling wife?'

My cheeks burned with suppressed anger at Brian's callous and bullish behaviour. 'I just got fired... no, I'll rephrase that! Chips and I are no longer employed because Brian didn't want to do some paperwork.'

Ashley pulled me to my feet and gathered me close. 'Don't worry about it. I hate you working those long, late hours. They eat into our time together and wear you out.' I opened my mouth, but Ashley forestalled any further discussion with a long, sweet kiss. 'As my wife you no longer need to work.'

'That's kind, Ashley, but I like to work. It gives me a sense of self-reliance and independence.'

'Let me reword it then. You're mine, Faith, and I take care of what's mine – so no more working. No don't argue,' he said holding up a forefinger to forestall me. 'Now, it's time for you to get in the car, so I can safely get you somewhere more important'

I cupped his cheek with the palm of my hand and gave him a grateful smile. He really was working hard on being a rock. As for the dictatorial attitude – I would slug it out with him once I knew my cousin was okay.

* * *

MC's tyres hummed monotonously on the bitumen highway as Ashley kept the car's speed five kilometres below the speed limit. In response to my plea for him to drive faster he reached across and gently squeezed my fingers.

'Relax, Sunflower. I'll get us there safely. Now stop stressing, you'll make yourself ill. Your uncle promised to ring if anything happened didn't, he?'

I glared at him and gave a quick nod. I knew I was being unfair by taking my worry out on him. Just because he was right didn't help soothe my mood or quell my fears. To add to my concerns there was the absent Fleabag. I'd had another scout around before we left and hadn't located her.

'It was kind of Scotty to offer to find and feed the cat for us. I wonder where she's got to?'

'Probably getting comfy on some other gullible student's bed.'

'You two don't like each other do you.'

I couldn't keep a slight smirk off my face. Ashley and the cat had a hate/hate relationship. A bit like him and Chips, really. My amusement fell away, and I began to gnaw at my thumbnail. Ashley reached over and pulled my hand away from my mouth.

In an attempt to distract my thoughts about my concerns over my cousin I began to babble. 'Have I been interfering with your writing, Ashley?'

He cocked an eyebrow. 'What makes you ask that?'

'Well, you've been at the townhouse for over a week, watching over me while I study. In all that time you've not done anything on your manuscript. And now with the wedding and this disaster it must be playing havoc with your creative thoughts.'

'Oh, yeah, my manuscript. No everything is going to plan. Phase one is complete.'

'What does that mean?'

'It means I'm now moving into phase two,' he said, with a raucous belly laugh. I stared at him, puzzled he wasn't worried that he might be running out of time. 'Look Faith, don't concern yourself. Everything is fine.'

I could see he wasn't going to discuss his writing with me, so I changed the subject. 'Can I ask about the business you're doing with Brian?'

'Now is not the time, Faith. Here have a drink of water,' he said, handing me an insulated water bottle.

I took a large gulp. It tasted metallic and stale. I dropped the bottle into the centre console cup holder in disgust. Warm rays of sunshine streamed in through the side window and fell on my hands clasped tightly together in my lap. I splayed the fingers on my left hand to study the rings adorning the third finger. This was the first time I'd actually taken a good look. The engagement ring, a rose-gold flower petal clasped around a glowing diamond, nestled next to a matching gold wedding band and flickered with a prism of glorious colour in the sun's bright beam. The diamond was quite large and not what I would have chosen for myself, but there was no denying the ring was beautiful.

'I hope the rings please you, Faith, because they so remind me of you - unique and exquisite.'

His tender words made my heart swell. I got all emotional and my eyes began to fill with tears. 'Oh, Ashley,' I sniffled.

'Now don't start to cry. I hate that. Here have another drink, it'll calm you.' I took another gulp of the water and wrinkled my nose.

'Eww! Why does your water always taste weird,' I asked, with a small shudder. Disgusted, I put the bottle back into the cup holder.

Ashley gave a small chuckle. I turned my head and gazed out of the window. After a while the mesmerising scenery seemed to lull the impatience and worry away. My head began to nod. I jerked awake and gave a loud yawn. Ashley patted his left shoulder.

'Lean your head here and close your eyes.'

As my heavy eyelids kept slamming shut, I didn't bother to argue, I just settled against his arm. Within moments I drifted off into a deep sleep.

\* \* \*

'We've arrived.'

I awoke with a start. My head felt like it was stuffed full of cotton wool and my mouth tasted like the cat had slept in it. I groaned as I jiggled my neck to alleviate the painful crick that had formed there.

'God, I must have bombed out.' I ran a raspy tongue over my dry scummy teeth. I glanced out the window, looking for a street sign in an attempt to get my bearings. 'Where are we?'

'We're about to turn onto Wellington Street. Where's the nearest all night car park?'

I did a search on Google maps. 'Moore Street. Access it off Lord Street.'

Ashley nodded, flicked a quick glance my way and said, 'Tidy yourself up, will you and slap on some lip gloss.' I stared at him. 'You look a mess. Your hair is all over the place and your face is rumpled. You don't want you to give your uncle a fright when he sees you. I think he has enough on his plate right now.'

I checked my visor mirror. Ashley was right. My hair was all lopsided and I looked haggard. I dug out a hairbrush and some cosmetics from my handbag and did the necessary repairs.

'Better?' I asked, turning so he could inspect my face.

He pulled the car to a halt at the car park boom gate, leant over and chucked me under the chin. 'You look almost ravishing, but at the next opportunity I'm going to take you shopping and buy you some decent outfits.'

I looked down and wondered what was wrong with what I had on, but kept my own council because Ashley's good mood seemed to be holding. 'You're so good to me, Ashley.'

A heart flipping dimple appeared in the corner of his mouth, and he gave my fingers a squeeze. 'Lucky you married me then.'

'About that.' Stress began to dance a jig in my breast. There was a slight catch in my throat as I dared to touch on a subject that was really worrying me. 'It's probably best we keep the fact that we've gotten married to ourselves for now. You know, until we know what's happening with Chips. It wouldn't really be right to show up in the middle of a crisis and nonchalantly announce we've just gotten hitched.' Ashley didn't say a word. I sighed in relief that he saw things my way.

I grabbed my mobile and hit speed dial to call my uncle. He answered almost immediately. 'Unk darling, how's Chips doing?'

'She's in surgery. And it may be hours before we hear anything. You're not phoning while you're driving, are you, Faith?'

'No. I'm in the multi-story car park near the McIver Train Station. Where can I find you?'

'This damn hospital is a rabbit warren. I'm not sure which ward Lucy will be on when she comes out of surgery so I'll meet you at the café on the Wellington Street overpass.'

'Okay...I'll be there in five minutes.' I disconnected and leapt from my seat ready to dash into the building.

Ashley took a firm grip of my hand. 'Slow down,' he said. 'Sprinting through the hospital won't help. All that will happen is you'll knock someone over or hurt yourself. A steady pace will get us there just a fast.'

Again, he was right, but it didn't stop me tugging on his hand to get him to increase our pace to a power walk. We ducked and wove around the slower pedestrians until I spied Uncle Alex standing by a tall potted palm. He looked grey and forlorn. He'd lost weight and had aged since I'd last seen him three months ago. His immaculately trimmed hair was now totally white and there were deep furrows on his brow that spoke of permanency. I unhooked my hand from Ashley's tight grip so I could race towards the man who meant so much to me. Uncle Alex spotted me and opened his arms. With a loud sob I flew into them.

'My darling girl, I've missed you so much,' he murmured into my hair, a hint of tears in the back of his voice.

I breathed in his wonderful spicy scent and buried my face into his strong, dependable shoulder. I was home. I clung tight. Tears welled in my eyes.

'I've missed you so much, Unk,' I managed to choke out. Uncle Alex gave me a tight squeeze before gently moving me to stand in front of him. He gave me a close inspection. 'What have you been doing to yourself, my darling girl? You're all skin and bones?'

Pleased he'd noticed the changes in me, I couldn't keep the pride out of my voice when I announced. 'I've taken up jogging. What's your excuse?

'Oh, nothing so drastic. Just a slight case of the flu.'

I stroked his cheek in concern. 'But you're better now, aren't you?'

He cupped my face with the palms of his strong, dependable hands and nodded. I gave him a blast of the special smile that I always reserved just for him. 'Good because I've been worried about you.'

At that moment Ashley's left hand slid around my waist and he gently drew me away from my uncle and close to his side. 'Aren't you going to introduce me, Sunflower?' he breathed in my ear, loud enough for my uncle to hear.

'Oh, I'm sorry. Uncle Alex this is Ashley...'

'Faith's husband,' he said, with a proprietary grin as he held out his hand to shake Uncle Alex's.

I saw a flash of shock flick across my uncle's face before the shutters came down over his eyes and his polite, business demeanour kicked in. Uncle Alex clasped Ashley's hand in a quick handshake.

'Hello young man. Faith, why you didn't say?' His eyes berated me for catching him unawares.

Angry heat flooded my face. I was gob-smacked that Ashley had broken my trust like that and not allowed me the privilege of telling my uncle about our marriage. I shot him a fierce glare that didn't quite show how much I really detested him at that moment.

'I'm sorry, Unk. It only just happened. Right before your phone call this afternoon, in fact. With Chips so ill, I didn't think it was quite the right moment to make the announcement.' Considering my cousin more important, and because I'm a coward and didn't want to discuss with him how I'd been railroaded, I began to pepper him with questions about Chip's health. 'So what is going on with her anyway? Why on earth is she in surgery?'

'Acute appendicitis. It must be removed before it ruptures. Routine surgery, the doctors reckon, but the op seems to be taking forever.'

Still angry with my newly acquired husband, I shook off his smothering embrace, took Uncle Alex by the hand and guided him to a seat at a vacant table.

'What do you mean, taking forever?' I asked, as Uncle Alex settled into a chair. 'How long has she been in surgery?'

Uncle Alex's eyes glazed over. He covered his face with his hands and took some shuddering breaths.

'Unk...darling. Are you okay?'

He nodded. 'Just give me a moment.'

I stroked the back of his head and flicked a glance at Ashley. 'Why don't you go do something useful, like get us all a hot drink while I find out what's going on with Chips.'

Ashley's eyes went a cold, dark grey. He didn't say anything, just stalked over to the counter. I didn't give him a second glance, didn't care if I'd upset him with my harsh tone – I was more than a little angry with him.

Uncle Alex cleared his throat and began to talk as if the interruption to our conversation hadn't occurred. I guess he was in shock.

'Lucy collapsed at the university not long after finishing her last exam. An ambulance was called and she was rushed to ER. I only got to see her briefly before they raced her to theatre. She looked terrible, and the pain...' He stared down at his watch with glazed eyes. 'That was three hours ago. It shouldn't be taking this long, should it?'

'It takes ages because she had to be prepped for surgery. The hospital also had to find a surgical team who were available to operate and an empty operating theatre. She's young, fit and healthy - everything will be fine.' I spouted the words of comfort as if I knew what I was talking about, when in reality I just wanted to fall into a sobbing heap and be told it was all over and Chips was fine.

Uncle Alex reached across the space between us and laced his fingers with mine. Unshed tears shone like bright stars in his eyes. 'Thank you. You are such a comfort and I'm so grateful you're here with me.' I leant forward and kissed his cheek. He cleared his throat and made a valiant attempt at normality. 'So, you've gotten married, huh. That's come as a bit of a surprise. Are you happy?' he asked.

'I haven't had time...'

Ashley dumped a loaded tray between us, interrupting what I'd been about to say. I flicked a glance at his purchases and was surprised to see two mugs of foamy, hot coffee and two plates containing fat slices of frosted carrot cake on the tray next to his obligatory cup of green tea. I peered up at him astounded. He crooked me a dazzling, boyish grin as he answered my unasked question.

'It's been kind of a stressful afternoon for you both. A few carbs and some caffeine to bolster your system will help you through the rough hours ahead.'

I reached out and grasped his strong fingers. I gave them a squeeze. 'Thank you, Ashley. I'm sorry I snapped at you. It's just the worry,' I said, my anger easing a tad to a wave of gratitude.

'I know.' He returned my grip with a gentle one of his own before drawing his chair close enough to sit with his arm around my shoulders. I settled back in my chair to take a small sip of my brew and wished he would remove it.

Uncle Alex's mobile buzzed. I gave him an expectant look. He shook his head. 'It's Rosie,' he murmured, as he answered the call.

'Who is Rosie?' asked Ashley, softly in my ear.

'My aunt.'

'I didn't know you had an aunt. I thought your Uncle Alex and your cousin Lucy were your only living relatives.'

'Oh, she's not a blood relation.'

Ashley gave me a puzzled frown. 'Neither is your uncle.' He rolled his fingers in a tumbling circle encouraging me to go on and explain what I meant.

'Well, it's complicated, but what it all boils down to is that Uncle Alex was married to my Aunt Lucille. Aunt Lucille and my mum were sisters.'

Ashley nodded. 'And?'

'After their dad, my Grandfather Sullivan died, my grandmother got remarried to Grandpa Bloom.'

'Nothing complicated about that.'

'But wait, there's more. Three years after they married, Grandpa's best friend and his wife died in a car accident, leaving their twelve-year-old son, Ian, alone in the world. Grandpa and Gran were kind and generous people. They opened their home and family to Ian and adopted him. Ian fitted well into the family. I know my mum adored him. Anyway, at the age of 21, Ian married Rosie Kettle.'

'So, Rosie and Ian are your step-step-aunt and uncle. Gotcha.' Ashley took a tentative sip of his hot tea. 'Go on, do tell, what are they like?'

'I never actually met Ian. He was only twenty-three, when he died.'

'When was that?'

I did a quick calculation. 'I'm almost 22 now. It happened three years before I was born. So, around 1998 or 1999. As for my aunt's personality, well...'

Ashley's eyebrows rose at my long pause as I sought the right words to describe her. He gave me a chin lift in encouragement. 'Go on.'

'How do I describe Aunt Rosie? She's very, very smart. I don't think anyone could ever pull the wool over her eyes. Her personality has been described as challenging and acerbic, but not in a bitter or sour sort of way, more, sharp and to the point. She never concerns herself about what others think or whose toes she treads on. She is most definitely not someone you want to get on the wrong side of, that's for sure.' By this time Ashley's eyebrows had nearly disappeared under his hairline. I snorted, amused by his startled expression.

'She sounds like hard work.'

I didn't agree with his summary. 'No, once you accept her for what she is, her company is stimulating and rewarding.'

'Did she have a lot to do with your upbringing?'

'Not really. Her work kept her away a lot but the few times I got to spend any length of time with her were inspirational and worthwhile. Aunt Rosie may not be a close blood relative but even after twenty odd years of being Ian's widow she's still considered part of our family. And if I ever need a strong advocate in my corner, she's who I'd choose.'

'How'd your uncle die?'

'He was murdered.'

Ashley's lips formed a circle. 'Oh, wow. What happened?'

'I don't know for sure and it's not something we've ever discussed in detail. All I know is that Ian's death is still a police cold case.'

'So, the cops never caught up with your uncle's killer?'

'No, not yet. It burns Aunt Rosie up. But she's in the right job to catch the murderer and one day she will. I'd happily bet my last dollar on it.'

'What do you mean? What job?'

Before I could answer, a movement over my shoulder diverted his attention. Ashley stiffened in his seat. His face went blank and his body froze.

'What's wrong?' I asked, following his gaze. I caught sight of a middle-aged woman with a sharp angular face. She was dressed in black cargo pants and a black, long-sleeved tee-shirt partially covered by a vest with the words police emblazoned across the chest. Her short, silver hair had been cut into a bob to frame her sharp vixen features. I leapt to my feet as she swept in on Uncle Alex and gave him a rib cracking embrace before swinging her attention to me.

'Aunt Rosie,' I cried, clinging tight to the woman who had once captured the media's poetic side and been nicknamed the Silver Dingo. 'I thought you were working up north somewhere.'

'I am. Only in Perth for the day, to give evidence at a murder trial. I fly out again on the midnight horror.'

'Not the *Well of Bones* case?' I gasped. Aunt Rosie nodded; a gleam of satisfaction shone bright in her piercing blue eyes. 'I read about that in the *West Australian*. Good job, you! Is the court case going well?'

'My lackey and off-sider, Constable Bayden did a bang-up job with all the evidence we collected. As did the forensic team. It's looking good. It's now up to the legal eagles to get a conviction. But enough of that, tell me what's going on with you?' said Rosie, casting an assessing eye towards Ashley.

'Ashley, I'd like you to meet my aunt, Detective Rosie Bloom.'

Under her intense blue-eyed stare my husband rose to his full height and swelled to tower over us. He spread his shoulders in that intimidating way he had as he shoved out a hand of greeting. 'Nice to meet you, detective'

They gave each other the briefest of handshakes.

'You look familiar, have we met before?' asked Aunt Rosie, not showing any sign of wilting under his domineering stance.

'No, I would have remembered meeting the Silver Dingo.' He abruptly turned to me and said, 'I'll leave you to catch up with your family, Faith. I must go and call my parents. My waste of space of a cousin has texted them to say we were on our way to RPH but didn't explain why. I need to ease their minds before they come rushing in expecting the worst.' He kissed me on the cheek and strode away before I could make any comment. My aunt stared at his retreating back with a puzzled frown on her face.

I took her hand to catch her attention and pointed to a chair. She blinked, gave me a small smile and settled at the table. I listened as Uncle Alex updated her on Chips and her condition. Just as he finished his phoned buzzed.

'ICU... peritonitis...I see, yes I'm on my way.' He hung up. 'Lucy's just come out of surgery. They're moving her to the Intensive Care Unit.'

'ICU!' I clutched a fist to my heart. 'Why? What's wrong with her?'

'Her appendix ruptured as it was being removed. She needs to be closely monitored for the next twenty-four hours while they pump her full of antibiotics as a precaution against sepsis. At this stage I'm the only one allowed at her bedside. I'm sorry Rosie, I have to go.'

She reached over and gripped his shoulder. 'I understand Alex...go, be with your daughter. I have a plane to catch anyway.'

'Faith darling, if Lucy has a good night and responds well to treatment, you'll be allowed in to visit tomorrow. But only you. The hospital has strict COVID restrictions in place and is only allowing two visitors a day.'

'I understand.' I flung my arms around his neck. 'Please tell her I love her.'

He clutched me tight. 'I will,' he murmured against my hair. 'Rosie, walk me to the elevator. I want a word before you leave.'

Rosie nodded.

My glance zipped between their expressionless faces. Something was going on. Was it something to do with Chips?

'Oh, and Faith,' said Uncle Alex, turning and holding out a key. 'Take the key to my apartment. Unfortunately, the painters are in at Tyrell Street at the moment, giving the house a spruce up, so it's not fit for occupancy. I'm sorry but my apartment has only got enough room for one...'

Ashley materialized at my shoulder and cut him off. 'Its fine sir, we're going to stay at my parent's house.'

Startled, I swung around. 'Oh, Ashley, I can't just lob in on your parents in the middle of the night, unannounced. I couldn't put them out like that...but you should go. I'll stay here at the hospital in case Uncle Alex needs me. If I get tired, I'll take a taxi to the South Perth apartment.'

Ashley hand tightened on my upper arm. I tried not to flinch at its firmness. 'My folks are expecting us, Faith. They are really excited about meeting my wife.'

Aunt Rosie's eyebrows rose. She mouthed the words wife to Uncle Alex. He gave a short sharp nod. Me, I was stuck between a rock and a hard place. I desperately wanted to stay but I couldn't fob off my husband and the new family responsibilities I'd acquired.

'Go, Faith,' said Uncle Alex 'There's no point in you sitting around on a hard plastic chair in a cold corridor all night. The doctor is happy with Lucy's condition. She said that ICU is just a precautionary measure. I promise to call you if her condition deteriorates.'

I unhooked myself from my husband's tight grip and put my arms around my uncle's waist. Placing my warm lips on his cold, pale cheek, I whispered, 'Are you sure? Can't I at least walk with you to ICU?'

He cupped my face and stroked my cheeks with his thumbs in a loving gesture. 'No, I'll be fine. You go and get some rest. You've had a busy, event filled day and a long drive. Come to the hospital at ten tomorrow morning.' He placed his cheek against mine and whispered in my ear, 'And when everything has calmed down, we'll have a good long talk so you can tell me what is wrong, so I can fix it.'

I buried my face into his shoulder and clung tight. 'Promise?'

'I do,' he murmured. Releasing me from his embrace, Uncle Alex turned towards a bank of elevators and strode away with Rosie at his side.

Ashley took a firm grip on my wrist and pulled me in the opposite direction. 'Come on, Faith. Let's go home.'

I fell into step beside him. Inside of me a raft of emotions tumbled over each other in such a churning swirl they made my head spin. The deep concern I held for my cousin melded with the unhappy anger I harboured because I hadn't been strong enough to resist Ashley's insistence we get married. I was also terrified at the prospect of meeting his parents and what they would make of our sudden marriage. My head dropped. Tears welled in my eyes as we strode towards the car. I knew that marrying Ashley today had been a huge mistake, but one I was going to have to live with, because I never broke a promise.

* * *

Ashley pulled up in front of a set of wrought iron security gates that protected the driveway of what I could only describe as a palatial mansion. He tooted the car's horn once and the gates slid open. MC rolled up a paved brick driveway and glided to a halt in front of one of three, closed, garage roller doors. Slowly I dragged myself from my seat, unenthusiastic and very nervous about meeting Ashley's parents. My new husband came around from the back of the car, lugging our overnight bags in one hand, the keys to MC dangled from the fingers of his other. I held out my hand to take the keys. He must have misinterpreted my gesture because he slid them into his trouser pocket and took my cold hand with a warm grip.

Eyeing me up and down Ashley said, 'Let's get you inside and in front of a mirror. You need to tidy yourself up.'

'What's wrong with me?' I asked, staring down at my rumpled A-line green floral cotton shirt and jeans. Depressed at the sight I brushed uselessly at the creases caused by the long hours of travel and sitting around the hospital.

Ashley dropped the bags at his feet and drew me into his arms. Removing the clip holding up my hair up he ran his fingers sensuously through the long strands to comb it out. A shiver ran the length of my spine. He fastened his lips possessively over mine and began to explore my mouth. When he finally broke free he looked down at me with a smile in his eyes.

'Absolutely nothing that a steaming hot shower and a fresh dress won't fix. We can't have you meeting my folks looking like a ragamuffin.'

I had to agree with him on that score. Not the best way to start the in-law relationship. Ashley took a firm grip on my elbow and steered me to a set of intricately engraved jarrah doors. Instead of a lock and a twisty door knob there was a latch with a fingerprint scanner on the button. Ashley applied his thumb. There was a beep. The door popped open. I stepped inside and my shoes sank into the deep pile of a luxurious white carpet. It covered an amazing open void, circled a sweeping staircase and ran up the treads to the rooms above. I craned my neck to stare in amazement at an ornate domed ceiling. It was grand, majestic and only the entry to the house. Overwhelmed I wanted to run.

The air around me was still, the entry lights on low and the house quiet.

'It's later than I expected,' said Ashley. 'It looks like my folks might have gone to bed. You can meet them in the morning.'

Giving me a nudge away from the staircase, he guided me past a variety of living spaces that opened into the foyer toward the back of the house.

At the end of a short corridor he announced, 'This is our room.'

I opened the door and nearly put a crick in my neck taking in all the features. A double mirrored walk-in-robe ran the entire length of one wall increasing the perception of a large room into a massive space. No expense had been spared on the furnishings or décor. Opposite the king sized wooden-framed bed, dressed in a nautical blue and grey striped quilt with dozens of matching pillows, a glass sliding door opened onto a stunning private courtyard. I flung open the door and stepped out into a sultry environment of an enclosed tropical flower garden, soft mood lighting and a very inviting hot-tub that was busily adding its steam to the atmosphere.

'Oh wow. A person could live out here.'

Ashley smiled, slid in behind me and slipped his arms around my waist. My hair was moved aside and soft lips were laid on the sweet spot just below my ear.

'It's the perfect place for us to wallow with a glass of merlot,' murmured Ashley, as he gave my neck his full attention. My heart flipped with anxiety at the hint of what was to come. I snagged my bottom lip between my teeth and began to chew. Unsure of myself I eased away from him and stepped back into the bedroom. There was an opening to the left of the bed head. I leant in the doorway to take a peek. The sight of a large, black and white marble ensuite drew me fully into the room. My eyes widened as I took in the enormous shower cubicle with a crazy amount of spray nozzles, the gleam of a white porcelain spa bath and the giant fluffy towels hanging beside twin sinks.

'It's all so beautiful,' I gasped.

With a seductive smile Ashley backed me hard against the wall and whispered softly in my ear. 'It's nothing compared to you, my darling.'

Suddenly my clothes began pooling at my feet as his warm hands began to explore my body.

* * *

The snick of the bedroom door woke me. I was alone in the massive bed. I blinked into the gloom, lit only by a soft light filtering in from the ensuite, and noted it was still dark outside. Confused as to where Ashley would be going in the middle of the night I rolled from under the covers and pulled on the first item that came to hand, my fluffy robe. Brushing my mop away from my face I gave it a quick twist and knotted it into an untidy bun at the nape of my neck. Gently easing the door open I took a quick peek into the corridor. The light was out but a bright beam shone from one of the rooms we had passed earlier in the evening. I cocked an ear and heard the murmur of male voices. Concerned there was something wrong, my bare feet melted into the thick carpet as I tiptoed to stand just short of the doorway. I didn't want to interrupt whatever was going on. I took up position opposite an ornate wall mirror that gave me a perfect view into the lounge room. Standing in front of a plush leather couch was a dark-haired, stocky man, whose facial features bore a remarkable resemblance to my husband. He handed Ashley a glass of red wine. A deep woody smell wafted from the room. Both men had big fat cigars clamped between their teeth and self-satisfied grins on their faces.

'It's good to have you home, Son.' His father clicked his brandy snifter against Ashley's wine glass before moving over to one of the wing-backed chairs grouped opposite the couch. He tossed the cushions arranged there onto the floor before taking a seat. 'Everything go alright in Albany?'

Ashley propped his socked feet up onto the coffee table and removed the cigar from his mouth.

'Mostly, Dad. I did manage to straighten out that business problem we had. And I was correct. Zelinski was systematically diddling the books. He will have to be replaced once he's repaid all the funds he purloined. As to the other stuff. A new distribution chain is now in place and seems to be running well. I picked up a few new businesses for our portfolio. I'll give you the details in the morning. As for personnel - the Scotsman has proven to be quite an asset, as do the Huntsmen.'

'And your cousin?'

'Still a problem, I'm afraid. He draws too much attention to himself and has a bad habit of helping himself to the merchandise. I missed out on the real estate deal I was after because he was too fervent in encouraging the owner to sell. I've sent him to the shack for now.'

'Good. His over-enthusiastic persuasion tactics have their uses but only as a last resort. Any more stuff ups from him and I'm going to have to step in.' Suddenly Ashley's father's face was wreathed in a large grin. 'So, you married her then?'

Ashley chuckled, 'Yep, today.'

'Good lad, I know she was being resistant. How'd you finally convince her?'

'Well, you see, Dad, I've got this brain tumour and only have twelve months to live.'

Ashley's father's body began to shake as he let rip a mighty roar of laughter. 'That's my boy. Is the uncle going to fall into line or will he be a problem do you think?'

I stopped breathing. My lungs began to burn and I had to force myself to suck in some air before I passed out. Tears welled in my eyes as I came to the realisation that Ashley had lied to me.

'I don't know yet. The cousin getting ill has changed the dynamic of what I'd planned. I'll give it a week before I try to draw him in. But the lease won't be a problem now. We do have another slight concern though.'

Ashley's father, taking a sip of his brandy, cocked his eyebrow over the top of the glass in a wordless question.

'Did you know about the aunt?'

'What aunt?'

'Exactly. Someone slipped up when they did the research for us. You're gonna love this, Bear. Turns out Faith has an aunt. It's none other than that copper known as the Silver Dingo.'

Ashley's father almost choked on his drink. He managed to swallow. His voice was raspy as he gasped, 'You're fucking with me, right?'

'Nope. I met her tonight at the hospital. She wanted to know why I looked familiar to her. What would that be about, do you know?'

Bear gave a small cough. 'Uhhum...yeah, well, it's been a few years, but we have crossed paths. She's smart and tenacious, so be careful, Cub. I don't want you doing anything to engage her interest.'

My heart clenched fiercely in my chest as I caught Ashley's blank gaze staring directly at the mirror. I froze, not daring to move a muscle. In silence I prayed he couldn't see my reflection in the glass. Bear Watson reached across and buffed his son's arm with a closed fist. Ashley's gaze moved to his father's face.

'What do you plan to do if the girl becomes a problem?'

'Mental health is a big issue these days isn't it, Dad. I wouldn't be at all surprised if I told Doc Myers she'd taken an overdose of tranquillizers, he would be happy to give her a long stint in one of the secure wards at Abbotsford Private Hospital. She'd be good company for Mum.' My husband's gaze returned to the mirror, a self-satisfied smirk on his lips. He winked. 'But it won't come to that will it, Faith, because if anyone tries to interfere in our marriage, I'll hurt everyone you love.'

Fear sizzled through my body. He'd known all along I was there. In terror I bolted back to our room.

# Chapter Sixteen

TWELVE MONTHS LATER.

Three men dressed like native Pashtun, in *Partug-Kamees,* woven from linen and traditional soft wool *pakol* berets, merged with the contours of the landscape as they crawled over sharp, grey shale and chai tea coloured sand, heading towards the peak of a high slope. The surrounding Afghanistan countryside, an arid sandy wasteland, was devoid of any greenery or human settlement. It was a hot, harsh environment in which to travel on foot, but needs must.

For over twelve months Captain Ryan Lamb along with his fellow soldiers, Sergeant Marcus 'Rowdy' Stone and Sergeant Luke 'Seadog' Baxter, had inserted themselves into the general population of Afghani life. Posing as local villagers they'd frequented the markets and popular gathering spots to listen to the unfolding gossip while they monitored the changes taking place in a community that was being forced to exist under the strict Sharia law that was being imposed by the new Taliban rulers. Ryan had watched in disgust as families who didn't want to live under the decree of the regime had their life choices and freedoms eroded by the extremist leaders and their gangs of brutal enforcers. He and his team were forbidden to intervene in any unfolding events, even when they witnessed an atrocity or injustice being carried out. Their brief had been to watch and report. Doing otherwise would put their lives, and the lives of others tasked with a similar mission, at risk. Ryan's team had done their job well, but now their part in Operation Meddlesome was drawing to a close. Seadog, Rowdy and Ryan had been ordered to rendezvous with a new infiltration team at the Iranian border. After bringing the new team leader up to speed they would receive the exact co-ordinates for their own extraction.

Ryan's gut churned in excitement - they were finally going home. He quickly tamped the sensation down. Now was not the time to allow eagerness in. It might distract him from the task at hand and put the lives of his team mates at risk.

As the sun settled low on the horizon, the group crested the peak of the hillock on their bellies. Ryan made his way over to a large, odd-shaped boulder and slithered to his feet. In the twilight he blended against the rock like a shadow. He studied the terrain with care. To his left was the Hindu Kush Mountain range - the border between Pakistan and Afghanistan. Pakistan had been their original objective but a mass gathering of Taliban soldiers in the mountains, to prevent citizens escaping to the safety of the neigh-bouring country, made that way impossible for them. His team had been rerouted by command to an alternative meeting point. He stared into the shaded valley below that marked an invisible line between the volatile Afghanistan and relatively calm but unfriendly Iran. Seeing nothing untoward Ryan checked his watch. They were early for their rendezvous. He was pleased. It would give them time to ensure the area was secure.

'We're here,' he announced. Not letting his guard down, he spoke to the team using the *Pashto* dialect. Seadog and Rowdy nodded. 'Check for curious eyes. I want this meet to go ahead without incident.'

His companions settled into vantage points along the crest and began to check their perimeter.

An excited thought filtered into Ryan's mind. In four hours, he hoped to have completed the handover. He was looking forward to snaffling some motorised transport from the incoming group and getting the hell out this sand ridden, waterless country.

'Where's our new extraction point, Shanks?' asked Seadog, dropping his elbows and looking at him over the top of his binoculars.

'Ten clicks south of Bandar Abbas. The yanks are going to send in a chopper to give us a lift across the Persian Gulf to Abu Dhabi.'

Seadog gave a soft sigh. 'Can't wait. I suppose we'll have hours and hours of debriefing with command to contend with before we get a decent feed or shower. What do you miss most, Rowdy?'

'Peace and quiet,' grunted Rowdy, who was always economical with his words. 'And time on my motorbike.'

'I don't suppose there are going to be any decent waves in Abu Dhabi?'

That statement summed up Luke in a nutshell. He loved to surf and would live in the ocean if he could. Ryan understood how hard the last year had been for everyone and what they had all sacrificed for their mission, but he had no intention of hanging around doing R&R in the United Arab Emirates before going home. No, as soon as humanly possible Ryan was going to be on the very next transport out of the Middle East. He was never coming back. The thought made him restless.

Ryan flicked a glance at Seadog. 'Cut the chatter. Now's not the time,' he growled.

Seadog nodded. Silence returned.

An hour slid by before the com clicked once in his ear.

Ryan shot a glance toward Seadog. He had a pair of field glasses trained in the direction they were expecting the incoming team to arrive from. Seadog flicked his fingers to indicate there was no sign of movement. He let his gaze drift over to Rowdy and was met with a thumbs up, meaning all was good on their tail.

'Stand down for an hour, Rowdy. Rest.' Ryan whispered. 'Seadog you've got first watch.'

'Roger that, Shanks,' said Seadog.

Never one to miss an opportunity, Rowdy sank to his haunches with his back against a rock. After tucking his long black beard into his shirt, he clutched a pistol to his chest and closed his eyes. Ryan grinned. Good man. Good soldier. Always at the ready.

As Seadog could be relied on to diligently watch over them, Ryan decided to take a break himself. He settled his gaze on the sun as it sank in a blaze of burnt orange. Darkness rapidly crashed in allowing luminescent stars to sparkle like diamonds in a clear night sky. A crisp cool breeze sprang up from the desert. It ruffled the long, thick growth that covered most of his lower face. Ryan copied Rowdy and tucked his beard into his shirt as he stared up at the magnificent heavens. He sighed as his mind filled with the image that was always there. A glorious mane of unruly caramel hair running riot around a gorgeous, happy face with a smile he desperately wanted to go home to.

His home.

His heart.

His Faith.

Ryan had his next mission lined up. As soon as his feet hit the deck in Australia, he intended to go find Faith and ask her for forgiveness. And if she'd have him, he'd never leave her again.

The com double clicked in his ear. Ryan shot to his feet. It was time to move.

# 17

## Chapter Seventeen

Detective Rosie Bloom's boots echoed on the polished concrete floor as she strode along the corridor of the Mount Ibour police station. Her silver hair, cut at chin level, remained perfectly in place even though the rest of her short, fit frame moved at a rapid pace. Constable Mark Bayden wrestled with an armful of boxes as he struggled to keep pace with her fast stride.

'Come on Bayden, shake a leg. We've still got the paperwork to finalise before we can close this case,' said Rosie, increasing her pace.

Mark, envious of his super ninja boss's superb fitness, decided that it was time to cut back on indulging in his wife's delicious cooking and go back to jogging in the evenings. While his tall, slim frame had no fat on it, the normal pace his superior moved at was a challenge to his current fitness level.

'Righto, boss,' he managed to puff out as he trailed along behind her.

'When's the prisoner transport due?'

'Seven, Monday morning.'

'Excellent. I'll be happier when that one is not only out of our cells but also out town.'

Mark gave her a grim look. 'You're not wrong. Once word gets out that our church warden and Sunday school teacher, Morton Patterson, has been arrested for paedophilia, the locals are going to go ballistic.'

Senior Sergeant Noel George stepped into the corridor. It was unusual for him to be here this late on a Saturday. He fluttered an urgent hand at Detective Bloom, indicating he wanted to see her in his office.

'You get on with sorting the transfer papers, Bayden,' she said, dumping the file that was in her hand on top of the load in his arms, 'while I go check what's got the Senior in such a flap.'

Mark, the font of all local knowledge and gossip, gave Rosie a cheeky smirk. 'Today was the REA cricket challenge.'

'REA?'

'Red Earth Ashes. It's held every year between Kelly Creek and Mount Ibour. Maybe Kelly Creek finally won. Senior wouldn't like that!'

'Why? What's the big deal?'

Mark's eyes almost bulged from their sockets in astonishment. 'You're joking right, Boss? Don't you know that Senior is a founding member of Mount Ibour Cricket Club?' Rosie folded her arms across her chest and began to tap her foot. Mark avoided sinking into his usual waffle and got straight to the point. 'He has a legendary determination to protect MICC's record.'

'What record?'

'Our unblemished one of course! Surely, you've heard of that?'

Rosie shook her head.

Mark expounded. 'Mount Ibour has won the ashes every year since the challenge's inception in 1980. And it really pisses off the Kelly Creek mob that they can't wrestle the urn from our grasp. Senior Sergeant George loves it, so of course he rubs it in. No player from Kelly Creek dares to set a foot out of line during the cricket season just in case the Seniors lurking behind some bush waiting to bring the might of the law crashing down on them. Many a players missed a game because they were wallowing in the cells waiting to front the magistrate as a result of his diligence.'

The corner of Detective Bloom's mouth tilted in amusement. Mark shuffled the load in his arms into a more comfortable position. 'Maybe we've lost the Ashes and the Senior wants to carry out a fully armed raid of every building in Kelly Creek in retaliation.'

'I wouldn't mind,' she chortled.

Mark juggled the boxes of evidence. A sense of satisfaction nestled into Rosie Bloom's chest. She was gratified at the fine police officer he'd developed into since they'd joined forces to solve her first mystery in Mount Ibour. It had been an investigation that had morphed from a cold case missing person inquiry, into one of abduction and murder, and had cemented a good working relationship between them. Not that Rosie would admit it to anyone but she had come to rely on Mark.

This past week he had done some stellar work on the Patterson case which had resulted in last night's raid and arrest of a despicable creature masquerading as everybody's friend. All that was left to do was dot their i's and cross their t's and hand the case over to prosecutions. Shouldn't be a problem, not with the raft of evidence they'd found at Mort Patterson's house and on his personal computer. The grin left her face as the thought struck her that something might be amiss with the arrest and that's why Senior Sergeant George wanted to see her.

'Alright, Bayden, you go and sort this lot out,' she said.

She strode into the Senior's office. Not averse to kicking a hornet's nest just to see what would happen, Rosie, didn't bother with a greeting. 'What's up Noel, did MICC lose the cricket today or something?'

A grin that could have lit the night sky bloomed to life on Noel George's face. 'Nah, Rosie. The lads did us credit once again. The ashes are exactly where they belong, locked up in the cricket club's trophy cabinet for another year.' His face glowed with happiness as he leant back into his leather chair and rubbed his hands together in delight. 'It's going to be a wild old night in Mount Ibour to-night. I've got every available officer out patrolling the streets and a booze bus set up on the main road between here and Kelly Creek. Happy days.'

'Is that what you want to talk to me about? Or is there a problem with the Patterson arrest?'

Noel shook his head. He reached across the desk and spun a newspaper around so the headline was readable to her. 'No problem with the arrest. Sterling work, Detective. You even made the front page of the national news.'

Rosie scanned the block lettering and felt her temper rise.

*SILVER DINGO SNIFFS OUT SCUM.*

'Why do the bloody press insist on using that stupid moniker all the time?' she snarled.

Noel let out a snort of amusement. 'You may not like it, Rosie, but it makes excellent press. It doesn't hurt our station's reputation, either. Which is a good thing, because it makes the Commissioner and Deputy Commissioner happy.' He held up his forefinger and went on. 'And if they're happy then our Commander is happy, which makes me happy. In fact, our boss is so happy he's just spent the last half an hour chewing on my ear in a long-winded prattle telling me how delighted he really is.'

'That's a lot of happy, Noel.'

Noel rolled his eyes, but his pleased grin didn't waiver. 'Oh, by the way, the Regional Commander asked me to pass on his congratulations to you and Bayden, so, well done you two.'

Rosie shrugged off the compliment and forged ahead with her own line of questioning. 'How did the press get hold of the Patterson story so fast?'

'The price of fame I suppose. It seems our local reporter, Piper Edwards, was following you around and witnessed the arrest of Patterson. She filed the story with the metropolitan city office immediately and it's been the lead story on the radio and television news all day.'

Rosie grunted. 'Nosey bloody snoop,' she muttered. 'Is that it, can I go now? I've got the paperwork to take care of still.'

Noel shook his head. 'The commanders approved a new job for you.'

The shaft of disappointment that speared Rosie in the gut surprised her. It made her realise how much she was enjoying her life in Mount Ibour. She'd even made some special friends in the district. Now she was about to be transferred.

'Where am I going?' she growled. 'How long do I have to pack?'

Noel's eyes widened in surprise, 'You're not leaving us, detective. In fact, the Assistant Commissioner and the Regional Commander and I have all come to an agreement. You're to remain stationed here as the Kimberley region's Senior Detective full-time. We can only benefit from having an investigator of your calibre on tap.'

Rosie furrowed her eyebrows and snarled, 'Do I get a say in these arrangements your all making on my behalf? Did you consider I mightn't want to stay in Mount Ibour.'

Noel looked flummoxed. 'I thought you'd settled in well here...'

Rosie couldn't hold back her grin. 'Just yanking your chain, Senior.'

Noel swore softly under his breath. 'God save me from fractious women,' he snarled as he snatched a blue folder from the tray on his neat desk and shoved it towards her. 'Here's something new for you to get your teeth into. In the last couple of days some dodgy bank notes have been found floating around the state. Yesterday a couple of them were handed over at the Bottomless Keg. It seems we have a counterfeiting ring operating in W.A.'

Rosie's eyebrows rose.

'I want you and Bayden to nip down to the pub and have a chat with the publican, Frothy Sinclair. I'm not holding out much hope that he noticed anything, like who actually passed the notes, because he's not the most observant or sober sod, but there may be some CCTV footage or one of the staff may remember something.'

Noel checked the time on his watch.

'Hmm...perhaps you better leave Frothy till morning because I'd say he'll be well and truly tanked by now.'

Rosie shook her head, 'How does he expect to run a business like that?'

'He doesn't. No-one can deflect Frothy from a beer or socialising with his clientele. His wife, Fizz, gave up trying to dry him out a long time ago. Unfortunately, twelve months ago she got quite ill and couldn't work anymore. After Frothy made a real mess of things he hired a bar manager to take over the reins.' Noel paused. 'On second thoughts, he's the one you should speak with. J-five, is his moniker. He's one smart cookie. From what I hear, he takes excellent care of the business. He'll have a handle on what's going on. According to Fizz, she doesn't worry too much about the pub while Frothy is busy bending an elbow with his mates when J-five's around.'

Rosie lifted her eyebrows, 'Frothy and Fizz makes sense, but J-five?'

'His real name's Jackson Michaels. Not hard to recognise, he's only got five fingers. A birth defect or something,' Noel shrugged. 'Anyway, you know what this place is like. Some funny bugger heard Jackson's name, saw his hands and thinks Jackson Five. It's easier to slur J-five after a couple of rounds so the name got shortened and stuck.' Rosie rolled her eyes. Noel grinned. 'I expect whoever passed the dodgy notes over the bar won't have hung around town for too long. But you need to check it out anyway.'

Opening the folder, Rosie balanced a pair of half-moon reading glasses onto the tip of her nose. She studied the faxed copy of two one-hundred-dollar notes. The details on the money were unclear. She flicked through the phone log record of the call, made by the Bottomless Keg's manager, Jackson Michael, requesting the police come take a look at some suspect notes when they had time. 'Is this all the information we have?'

'Yeah. With one thing and another, it's been a busy day. I haven't had anyone available to go take a statement. You and Bayden can do that tonight, before you knock off.'

Rosie sighed and clambered to her feet.

'What, no argument about not needing a partner?'

Rosie turned and glared at Noel. 'Would it do any good?'

Noel grinned and shook his head.

'Thought not...besides, Bayden has his uses.'

A contented look flitted across Senior Sergeant Noel George's face.

'Oh, one other thing, detective. Do you know some pushy girl named...um...er...' He hesitated over the name as he ran his finger under some untidy scrawl on the notepad in front of him. 'Chips, is it?'

'Chips? Yeah, I know a Chips. She's my husband's niece. Why?'

Noel's auburn eyebrows lifted so high in surprise that they would have melded with his hairline if he had one. 'I didn't know you were a married woman, detective.'

'Widow,' Rosie corrected, not offering any further information. 'Why do you want to know about, Chips?'

'Chips, hmmm... unusual name. Anyway, she rang me, demanding to speak with you.'

Rosie stared at him in surprise. 'She rang you?'

'Yeah, while you were in the interview room bringing Morton Patterson to heel.'

'What did she want?'

'Didn't say, just that it was important. I tell you that girl has more front than a large bloody city department store,' he grouched. 'Ringing and expecting me to take messages. Go call her and tell her I'm not your bloody answering service.'

Rosie smirked at Noel's pretence at gruffness as she strode from his office.

* * *

'Hello, Chips. It's Rosie.'

'OMG, Aunt Rosie, it's about bloody time. I was beginning to think you hadn't got my message.'

'I've been tied up on a case all day.'

'So I saw on the news tonight.'

Rosie grunted, recalling the lurid, but mostly accurate speculation printed in the evening edition of the newspaper. 'Tell me what's wrong?'

'Someone attacked Popsicle...'

'Shit...is Alex all right?'

'He's in ICU. The doctors have put him into an induced coma.'

Rosie's heart clenched as she paced back and forth across the meeting room she used as the department's investigation office.

'Talk to me,' she demanded. 'How badly hurt is he?'

Mark stopped sorting through the evidence boxes and looked up in concern.

In a voice choked with emotion, Lucy managed to strangle out, 'I'm so frightened he's going to die. He...he...did regain consciousness for a short while...managed a few coherent words, but wasn't making any sense. According to the nurse, the doctor is going to keep him under sedation for a couple of days in the hope that the swelling in his brain will subside. If all that goes well, they'll take him off the critical list and move him to a ward.'

'Any other injuries?'

'Along with the large gooseberry on the side of his head that's caused the swelling of his brain, Popsicle has got two busted ribs and a broken nose. The cops and doctors all agree he was probably kicked by someone wearing steel-cap boots. His stomach and kidney areas a kaleidoscope of black and blue bruises, and to top it off - his heart is beating weirdly. They're talking about inserting a pacemaker if it doesn't settle down.'

Rosie's gut clenched. Alex was a good man who held a special place in her heart. She chaffed at being so far from his side when he needed her help.

'Tell me what happened?' she growled.

'Not sure, only that he was taking a shortcut through Elizabeth Quay Park on his way to catch the 11 p.m. ferry last night. Someone must have jumped him.'

'What was Alex doing in the city at that time of night?'

'Working. That's where his office is located, at the Central Park Tower. He's been doing that a lot in recent times, working late that is,' said Chips. 'He's also taken to living full-time in the South

Perth apartment. Even before this attack I was worried about him, because he's aged so much in the last few months. He looks tired and cheerless.'

'Do you know why he's taken to working such long hours?'

'Nope, only that he's determined to destroy some criminal enterprise.'

'What criminal enterprise?'

'No idea. He won't discuss it.'

'Did the police find anything on the city scan CCTV footage?'

'There was none near the quay. A maintenance request was raised at noon because someone blinded the camera with paint and smashed the streetlight.'

'Hmmm...that sounds convenient,' mumbled Rosie, folding her lips together.

'That's what I said, but the police constable, who I spoke with, he just fobbed me off. Because Popsicle had $200 in his wallet and that was stolen the constable put it down as a random mugging.' A loud sob echoed down the phone. 'Oh, Aunt Rosie, he was laying there, on the cold ground, injured and alone, for hours.'

'Who'd you speak to in the police force?'

'The two constables who attended the scene...but a Detective, oh what was her name... hang on a sec, she gave me a card.' Rosie heard Lucy fumble around for something before coming back on the line. 'Here it is. Detective Anne Graves. Anyway, this detective came by the hospital a little while ago asking to take a statement from Dad. The attending physician told her, Dad's, not ready for that. When he is she's not to expect too much from him, because before they put him into the coma, he barely remembered his own name or details of his life. The doctor reckons it's likely that the events of last night will remain a blank.'

'For how long?'

'Could be for days or months or even forever.'

Tucking the mobile under her chin, Rosie leant over a computer keyboard and began checking the police profile of Detective Ann Graves. What she read made her raise her eyebrows. 'Hmm, I see that Detective Graves is a member of the Serious Crime Squad. Now I'm really curious as to what Alex has been poking around in,' she muttered to herself.

Straightening her back Rosie resumed her conversation with Chips. 'Is Faith with you? Are you both okay?'

The question was met with silence.

'Chips, you still there?'

'Yeah, I'm still here,' came a soft, sad reply. 'Aunt Rosie, we haven't seen or heard from Burger since I was in hospital with appendicitis last year.'

Lucy began to cry in earnest. Rosie moved the phone slightly away from her ear.

'Calm down, Chips. I want you to take a deep breath.'

'Sorry...*hic*...just give me a moment.' Rosie waited impatiently while her niece took some long shuddering breaths and blew her nose. Finally in a choked voice she continued, 'Here's what happened. Burger came to visit me at the hospital two days after my operation. Only she didn't look or act like our Burger anymore. She was thin and pale, had big black bags under her eyes that she'd tried to hide under a thick layer of makeup. There was a wild frightened look deep in her eyes. She was dressed like a Barbie doll, in a designer frock and very high heels, which surprised me because Burger always swore, she'd never wear shoes like that because she was clumsy, and it wouldn't end well. That git, Ashley...you know who I mean, I believe you met him?'

Rosie cast her mind back. 'Yes, I did. But only for a moment.'

'A moment too long, I bet. Anyway, he stood at her side the whole time with a smug smile on his lug. Every time Burger spoke, she glanced at him first as if to check that she was performing the way he wanted. I was shocked when she told me they were married. Two of the many things I know about Burger is, one, she isn't fickle in her love and two, she gave her heart to my Adam's brother Ryan and was planning on speaking with him about why he walked away from that precious gift before she was even going to consider a new romantic relationship with anyone else. I tell you, when I see Ryan again, he's going to regret it,' snarled Chips. 'Faith is not the type of girl to ignore her feelings or her promise that she'd wait for one guy and in the next breath go ahead and marry someone else.'

Chips stopped talking and blew her nose again.

'Burger's visit to me was brief. We only got to speak for five minutes before that prat Ashley grabbed her by the arm and told her it was time to leave. As he hustled her from the room, Burger gave me such a terrified look over her shoulder I almost leapt up and chased her down. That was the last time we spoke. I've called and called her. Texted. Emailed. Tried everything, but she never answers. I've left messages on her voicemail telling her about everything going on here and still nothing. It's like we've been ghosted, and she wouldn't do that, she loves Dad too much.'

With each word the tingling of Rosie's spider senses increased. 'What about Alex. When did he last see her?'

'I think it was the same day. Ashley organised for them all to meet for lunch in the hospital café. Dad said Burger didn't touch her food and was very quiet. She looked surprised when Ashley announced they were going away the next day - on a long honeymoon. Because of that he wanted dad to go into the office immediately that day and prepare new wills for them both.'

'What did Alex say to that?'

'Popsicle told Ashley that it wasn't possible to prepare the documents in that timeframe. The legal and banking worlds don't move that fast. Besides, Faith's financial affairs are quite complicated.'

'How so?' asked Rosie.

'Her parents left her a very large sum of money which, along with the insurance payout from their deaths, was all put into trust. Popsicle is her trustee. Dad said he told Ashley that all the investments would need to be audited by an independent body before the Will and EPA documents could be drawn up, witnessed and registered. After that his law firm would have to lodge a notice of advice along with a copy of Faith and Ashley's marriage certificate to all the financial groups dealing with her portfolio advising of her name change. Only after that, could the investment portfolio change of beneficiary forms be submitted and confirmed.'

'I bet that went down well,' murmured Rosie.

'Popsicle reckons Ashley's cheeks got redder and redder as he itemised the steps he intended to take before drawing up the new will and an enduring power of attorney. But the real icing on the cake, the one that really upset Ashley, was the strict caveats dad said Burger's parents had put on the trust fund – regardless of her marital status she is not allowed to change the beneficiary until after her twenty-fifth birthday.'

'That sounds like a lot of ho-ha.'

Chips gave a sad chortle. 'Oh yeah, most of it was bullshit. Popsicle was throwing up a heap of barriers on purpose. He wanted to have a private heart-to-heart with Burger before he did anything with her finances.'

'Do you know where your cousin is now?'

'Nope. As far as anyone knows, neither Burger nor Ashley have been seen in Perth for over twelve months. I went and checked out the townhouse in Albany again last week. I've been doing that fortnightly just in case. There's no sign she's been there. The first time I went, I ran into some guy who was feeding the cat. Scotty, I think he said his name was. I asked if he knew where Burger and Ashley were, but he said he hadn't heard from either of them. I thanked him for looking after Fleabag and bought her home with me.' Lucy sighed. 'Burger hasn't contacted the university about a leave of absence. Nor has she attended any classes. They've dropped her as a current student. There's been no sign of either of them at Ashley's parents place either. Popsicle has had someone watching the house. Isn't there some whizz-bang search you can do on the police computer to find her?'

'You know I can't, Chips. Faith married the guy and neither of them have broken the law, so I don't have due cause. My investigative powers are limited in that regard, but there are some options open to me. Text me his family details will you and I'll look into what I can later, but for now, Alex has to be our first priority. I want to speak with your father as soon as he wakes up.'

'Mobile phones aren't allowed in ICU. I'll call you the moment he's moved to a ward.'

'Do that, or if his condition changes. I'll get on a flight to Perth as soon as I can,' Rosie announced, as she mentally crammed together and prioritised a list of tasks she needed to deal with before that could happen. A sudden thought struck her. 'By the way, Chips, how did you know to ring Senior Sergeant George to pass on a message to me?'

'I rang the Police Commissioner at his home. He and Popsicle have worked together on some high-profile cases over the years, and cheat each other at golf every other week. I told the commissioner who I was and why I was trying to track you down. I begged him for help because your mobile kept going to message bank. After a little persuasive dialogue about the importance of family at a time like this, he relented and gave me the Senior Sergeant's number.'

Wow, young Lucy Chippens was going to make a fantastic lawyer if she could wheedle that sort of information out of the Commissioner of Police.

'Alright, Chips, call me if anything changes. I'll be on the next plane.'

'Thanks Aunt Rosie. I knew you'd sort this out.'

'Don't get your hopes up, young lady. There may be nothing I can do.' As Rosie disconnected, she swung around and tossed the blue folder Sergeant George had given her onto the table in front of a goggle-eyed Bayden.

'Are you leaving us, boss?'

'Only for a couple of days, Bayden. In the meantime, you'll be starting a new investigation for us. The Mount Ibour side of things is probably a dead end, but every detail still needs to be followed up.'

'I haven't heard of anything going on in the district, boss. Is this a cold case?'

'No, it's red hot, and will involve plenty of foot slogging around town on your part.' Rosie explained the passing of counterfeit notes at the pub. 'You'll need to take a photocopy of the notes and visit every business in town.'

Mark groaned.

Rosie grinned at the thought of his size nine's paining him as he tromped up and down the hot streets of Mount Ibour in pursuit of information.

# 18 |

## Chapter Eighteen

Rosie squeezed her way through the boisterous crowd gathered at the Bottomless Keg. Six bartenders were being kept on the hop by revellers demanding refills for jugs of cold, frothy beer as celebration of the town's cricket win kicked into top gear. Rosie cast a glance over the staff faces, but none of them bore any resemblance to the description she had of Jackson Michaels.

She circled a group of high-spirited people who were laughing and joking with each other about the cricket. Along with some good-natured jostling they were basically a harmless bunch out for a good time. She paused on her circuit of the room to stare at a man who wore a pristine white tee-shirt with the words 'Frothy' stencilled across the front in bright red ink. He was perched on bar stool with his chin hanging low to his chest. Rosie placed two fingers on the side of his neck to check for a pulse. He snorted, smacked his lips together and began to snore. Rosie shook her head. As predicted by Noel, the owner of the Bottomless Keg was out for the count.

She took another gander around the room, but her quarry remained elusive. Rosie decided to try the bar's office. Spinning on her heel she ran smack into a solid wall of muscle. Two strong arms wrapped themselves around her and a deep, baritone voice rumbled sexily in her ear.

'We have to stop meeting this way, detective. People will begin to talk.'

Rosie stared up into a pair of pewter-grey eyes. The lids were crinkled at the corners with laughter lines as was the rest of the handsome face beaming down at her. Rosie flashed her teeth in an unrestrained grin.

'Hello, Bull' she yelled, over the ear-splitting hubbub of the bar room at the tall, handsome, grazier of Rivers Run Cattle Station, Charlie Morgan. 'I'm surprised to see you out partying. I didn't think this sort of hullabaloo would be your cup of tea.'

'I'm chaperoning,' said Bull, cocking a thumb towards a tall lad with a head of black corkscrew curls who was dressed in a set of grass-stained cricket whites. The young man was the spitting image of the man standing before her. 'Eli, hit a ton not-out, in the match today.'

Even as they glanced over, Eli was encompassed by a group of his team mates and handed a large glass of coke. His mates held their own drinks aloft and let out a roaring nonsensical chant of, 'Scull...scull...scull.' Eli complied with the request in six large gulps and was hoisted onto his friend's shoulders and cheered.

'Team's celebrating,' said Bull, with an amused grin. 'I'm just here to make sure they remember that he's not quite eighteen yet and nobody is to slip any alcohol into his drink.'

'Is that really, Eli?' exclaimed Rosie, staring at Charlie's handsome and lanky son. 'Good god, Bull! What the hell have you been feeding him? He's even taller than you are. What is he now? Six-four?'

Charlie Morgan's face glowed with paternal pride. 'Six-five and still growing. I put it down to hard work, good living and the fact that Rivers Run has the best beef in the world. It'll do it to you every time.' He stared down at the diminutive detective and added, 'It's about time you headed out our way for another visit, Rosie. You need feeding up on some good beef. See if we can't add a few centimetres to your own stature.'

'There's nothing wrong with my stature. I'm the perfect height for bringing down the Mount Ibour riff-raff.'

'So I hear,' Charlie grinned. 'Still, it's been ages and we'd love to see you. How's Sunday for lunch?'

'I'd really love to, but unfortunately, I've got a bit on my plate right now. Can I take a rain check?'

'Sure. You're welcome at Rivers Run anytime, you know that.'

'I do. Thanks.' Rosie returned his affectionate smile with a heartfelt one of her own. Her insides glowed with warm fondness of friendship for the man and his family. 'How's married life treating you?'

Charlie's face lit up. His smile almost blinded her. 'Fantastic.'

'I hope you're taking good care of our girl.'

Charlie looked appalled that Rosie could suggest he'd do otherwise. 'How could I not! Kelsey and Eli are the best things in my world.' He beetled his brow and a small vee formed over the bridge of his nose. 'I'm glad I ran into you just now, Rosie. Can you spare a minute? Kelsey's got something important she wants to discuss with you?'

'Only if it's a quick word. I'm actually trying to find the pub's manager, Jackson Michaels. You haven't seen him by any chance, have you?'

'Sure...two birds, one stone. They're both in the office,' said Charlie, nodding towards a closed door behind the bar. 'Ahh...Rosie,' he paused for a moment as if hesitant to speak. 'There's something else I think you need to be aware of.'

Rosie folded her arms and waited. Charlie gave a chin lift towards a group of men who weren't caught up in the frivolity going on in the bar room. Instead, they stood in a frowning circle and were listening attentively to a squat, bald man, dressed in black jeans and a plaid shirt, who seemed to be holding court. The sleeves of his shirt were rolled above his elbows and showed off his thick, hairy forearms as he waved his fist in the air as if to punctuate each word that spouted from his lips.

Rosie lifted her chin. 'What's that about?'

'There's a rumour doing the rounds that you've arrested Mort Patterson,' said Charlie.

Rosie chewed her lip, stared up at Charlie and realised she wasn't about to blab anything secret. The arrest was already on the news.

She gave a sharp nod. 'Yeah,' she said, wrinkling her nose in distaste. 'Kiddie porn.'

'Well, that man over there, holding court, is Zack Shandon. I overheard him spruiking earlier today. He's working hard to stir up some of the locals. I think he wants them to bust into the police station and castrate our once-respected church warden.' Charlie's face hardened. 'I understand the sentiment but you know what happens when guys like Shandon and his type take the law into their own hands. Someone innocent always gets hurt.'

Rosie reached over and patted Charlie's forearm. 'Thanks Bull. Why don't you go collect Eli, and wait for me in the office? I'll sort Shandon and his crew out.'

Charlie frowned. 'Do you want some back up?'

'Nah. I've got this.' She gave him a wink and hit speed dial on her mobile.

As Rosie sidled towards the vigilante group she yelled into the phone, 'Bayden, get your butt inside, now! We have a situation brewing.'

* * *

'It'll be easy,' growled Shandon. 'The town is just ripe for trouble. The cops will be stretched thin tonight keeping a lid on everything. It's a golden opportunity for us to take care of business undetected.'

'So, what's the plan?' asked a short, thin man whose hand shook so badly his beer slopped over the lip of the glass clutched in his fist.

'Well, Shaky, all you and Wazza have to do is start a punch up. With all these people here full of soup the pub'll blow like a powder keg. The cops will fall over themselves rushing to put a stop to the ruckus before it spills out into the streets.'

'What about you, guys? What will you be doin'?'

'While you keep our local constabulary busy, the rest of us'll slip into the pokey and pay our holier-than-thou church warden a little visit. There won't be anyone around to stop us,' said Shandon with a complacent smirk on his lips.

Most of the men in the circle around him murmured their approval. Shaky and Wazza, both shook their heads.

'But we might get arrested,' whined Shaky, clattering his glass against his teeth as he tried to take a sip.

'I agree with Shaky...it's definitely not a good plan, Zack my man. I mean just look at him. He's all skin and bones.' Wazza held up a chubby fingered fist and rocked back on his heels. The rubber thongs on his feet, squashed to resemble flat planks from the weight they bore, gave a squeaky sigh. 'He'd break in half if one of these bad boys connected.'

Rosie ran her glance over the sag of belly fat that hung low over the front of his oversized cargo shorts and rolled her eyes. It was amazing the high opinion Wazza had about himself. It was more likely that if he tried to do any physical activity he'd keel over from exhaustion or have a heart attack. Judging by the look in Zack Sheldon's eyes he also held the same view.

Wazza clicked his finger and thumb. 'I know, why don't we start a fire in the toilets...'

He didn't get any further voicing the dangerous idea. Shandon interrupted him.

'Stop showing your startling intelligence, Wazza. We ain't starting no fire. You're not actually going to hit each other. Just get yourself into a clench and start a wrestling match while shouting a few swear words at each other. That's all. Just make sure you bump into lots of bystanders. That'll be enough to set off a brawl. And then you two,' he pointed his forefinger first at Shaky then at Wazza, 'can slink out the back, leaving the cops with a problem on their hands. I've seen it done in the movies, works every time.'

Rosie glanced up at Mark who'd woven through the crowd like a will-o-wisp and fetched up at her side in time to hear Shandon's comment.

'Follow my lead,' she yelled at him and stomped over to stand right behind Shandon. Seeming to ignore the group she faced away from the rabblerouser and checked her watch. It was 7.30 p.m. In a loud voice Rosie shouted at her partner. 'Did you get the prisoner transport from Broome to collect Patterson like I asked, Bayden?'

With amusement bright in his eyes, Mark replied, 'Sure did, boss. They left about ten minutes ago saying they're going to take a meal break at the Kelly Creek roadhouse because of how busy it is in town tonight.'

Rosie winked at him and cocked her head to listen to the reaction their comments caused.

Wazza, not the brightest crayon in the box, yelled, 'Hey, Zack, did ya hear that? The bastards gone.' The other men in the group began to grumble.

'Shut up, you fools,' said Shandon, waving his hands to indicate they should tamp down their comments. 'This is even better for us. Shaky, you and the others, go get your vehicles. Let's go for a little drive out on the highway.'

Rosie watched in satisfaction as they left the bar.

'Bayden, get on the phone to the Senior Sergeant. Warn him there's a lynch mob heading out to the highway chasing a fictitious prisoner transport van. A spot of random breath testing should take care of them for the night.' Mark chuckled in amusement as he pulled his mobile from his breast pocket. 'And then get yourself back to the station and book me two seats on the next plane to Broome. Have a couple of uniforms meet us at Broome airport. Don't take any guff from the airlines that the flight is full – bump a couple of someone's if you have to. I'm getting Patterson out of town tonight; before any more trouble rears its ugly head. Get him ready, I'll be back at the station in half an hour to collect him.'

* * *

Rosie strode into the room used by the publican and his staff as an office. Seated behind a large, scarred, steel-framed table was Kelsey Morgan. She held a magnifying glass in her right hand and was pouring over a bank note.

'See Jackson,' she said, to a dainty, middle aged man who stood to the right of her chair. 'These twenty-dollar notes have the same serial number as the hundred that you found on Friday.'

Jackson Michaels manoeuvred the fingers on his left hand and gently removed the magnifying glass from Kelsey's grasp. He began to examine the bank note. With a soft click Rosie closed the door behind her. The roar of the bar crowd changed to a dull background drone. She nodded her head to a smiling Eli, who was perched next to his father on a tartan covered two-seater couch opposite the desk.

Kelsey glanced up and gave Rosie a delighted to see you smile that settled on her lips as well as around her bright emerald eyes. She struggled out of a creaky, swivel chair and raced across the room, only giving Rosie a moment to notice the changes that had taken place in her friend since they'd last seen each other.

Kelsey enveloped Rosie in a tight hug. 'Rosie,' she cried. 'It's so good to see you.'

Rosie savoured the warm embrace for a moment before taking a step back. She glanced down at Kelsey's rounded belly and grinned. 'A mini-me, Kelsey – that's awesome! Congrats girl.' She cupped her friend's cheek before casting a snappish glance at Charlie Morgan. 'Bull, why didn't you say something?'

'Because, Kelsey wanted to surprise you.'

Charlie rose to his full height and wandered over to stand behind his wife. He slipped a loving arm around her waist and allowed his fingers to cradle her belly. His face was aglow with love, pride and excitement. Rosie cocked a glance at Eli and was satisfied with the look of unadulterated happiness on the young man's face.

'Is this why you wanted to see me, Kelsey?' asked Rosie, pointing to the obvious baby bump.

'Yes and no. Jackson and I have come across some more counterfeit notes in today's bar takings,' said Kelsey, pointing to the only person in the room Rosie didn't know.

The detective held out a hand and introduced herself, 'Detective Rosie Bloom.'

A delicate, warm hand with only two fingers, settled softly in her grip. 'Hello detective. I'm Jackson Michaels or J-five if you prefer. I see you already know my bookkeeper, Kelsey.' There was a slight lisp and a strong New England twang to his words.

'Sure do. The Morgan's and I are old friends. What have you got for me,' asked Rosie, slipping seamlessly into her detective persona.

'Well, so far this weekend, we've come across six suspect notes,' said Kelsey. She settled back into the chair she'd previously occupied and moved the desk lamp so that Rosie had a clear view of money laid out on the surface in front of her.

'And they are very hard to distinguish from the real thing,' said Jackson. 'I'm not at all surprised the notes slipped past my staff and made their way into the till. I was being cautious after yesterday's initial discovery and asked Kelsey to do an audit of the notes from today's takings. Lucky for us she had the foresight to note down the serial numbers from the other banknotes or they might have slipped by.'

Rosie kept her face blank, not wanting to embarrass her friend. It wasn't common knowledge outside of Kelsey's close-knit family circle that she possessed a photographic memory. The memorizing of a few serial numbers was chicken feed to what she could really do with that huge brain of hers.

Sitting forward in his seat, Eli asked, 'Apart from the serial number, how else can you tell if money is fake?'

Kelsey's emerald eyes sparkled. 'Good question, Champ. Genuine notes are made of plastic, so they'll bounce back into shape if you scrunch them up. And, see this clear window?' Eli's glance followed to where Kelsey's neatly manicured little finger hovered over a wavy plastic strip that ran through the note. 'Well, that section should be a part of the banknote, not an addition.' She flicked her gaze up at Rosie, 'And for your information, these are part of the note.' She resumed the lesson, 'Another security feature, Champ, is that you shouldn't be able to scratch this white image embedded in the strip. These notes have all the correct features, the Australian Coat of Arms and the seven-point star when you hold it up to the light. The only give away that these aren't genuine are the slight size difference and a repeated number sequence. I'd say, detective, what you have here are washed bank notes.'

Rosie pursed her lips. 'Hmmm...'

Jackson's gaze flicked between the two women's faces. 'Washed?' he asked.

'If you're careful, and methodical,' said Rosie, 'it's possible to bleach the colour from a lower value note, say a five or ten dollar and transform it into a higher denomination. Whoever has done this has done a really professional job of changing fives to twenties and tens to fifties and hundreds. The colouring of the ink they used is correct, as are the security features...but, whoever used these notes made a big mistake. They should have made sure they didn't use two notes with the same serial number in the same transaction.'

Rosie studied each of the banknotes on the table without touching them.

Kelsey drew a clear A4 plastic sleeve from a drawer and handed it to her. 'It's possible our counterfeiter is not the person passing the actual notes, but an accomplice,' she said. 'What do you think, Rosie?'

Rosie didn't reply to Kelsey's query. Instead, she delved into the pocket of her vest for a pair of nitrile gloves. She pulled them on before carefully slipping each note into the safety of the plastic sleeve. Rosie tucked the evidence under the latch of the clipboard she carried. She'd get Bayden to send them to the crime lab for finger-printing but didn't hold out much hope for any useable prints. The money had passed through too many hands before being discovered.

'Tell me about the security monitoring system you have here, Mr Michaels.'

'Call me J-five, detective. Mr Michaels reminds me of my father, and he wasn't a nice man.' Rosie stared at him in silence. J-five sighed at her non-response and said, 'When I first started here there was no security to speak of, so I had a sixteen channel, NVR system installed. There are cameras mounted above the bar, around the beer garden and overlooking the car park.' Jackson minced over to a wall mounted cupboard and unlocked the door. Inside was a CCTV recorder connected to a laptop. He popped an SD card out from a slot in the laptop and held it up. 'I upload the previous 24-hours of footage to the cloud every morning and use it to check for any pilfering or sleight of hand at the till by the staff. It's amazing what employees think they can get away with.'

'I'll take a copy of this weekend's footage if you don't mind.'

'I thought you might, so I made this for you, detective.' Jackson held out the 2 terabyte digital SD card to her. 'I hope you find what you're searching for.'

'Well, it's a long shot, Mr. Michaels, but one we cannot ignore.'

Jackson scowled at Rosie's persistent use of his full name. 'Is that all, detective? I need to get back to work. I have a very busy pub to run.'

Rosie flicked a glance to the face of her watch to check the time. She needed to bolt if she was going to take care of everything on her to-do list before escorting Patterson from town. 'I want you both to come into the police station and make a statement.'

'What tonight?'

'No, Mr Michaels, Monday morning will be fine. Ask for Constable Bayden.'

Kelsey smiled at the mention of Rosie's partner. 'How is Mark? I'm surprised he's not here tonight,' she said.

'He's busy, organising the breath testing and arrest of a couple of troublemakers,' said Rosie. She flicked a wink in Charlie's direction. He must have caught her meaning because he grinned like a naughty schoolboy. 'Sorry I can't stay and chat. I'm on a tight schedule.'

She snatched the SD card from Jackson's fingertips, 'Thanks for the info, Mr Michaels.'

# 19

## Chapter Nineteen

After handing a subdued and very frightened Mort Patterson over to the two police officers who had arrived late to collect the prisoner, Rosie discovered she'd missed the last flight to Perth. Grumpy as hell at being delayed in her attempt to get to the injured Alex, she stalked into the relative quiet of the Broome Airport club lounge. Settling into an armchair, she put her feet up on the seat opposite and sank low in into the hard cushioning, intent on a power nap.

The phone discussion she'd had with Lucy about Faith began a slow whirl through her mind. It picked up pace. With a deep sigh, because sleep eluded her, Rosie straightened in the chair and grabbed her backpack. She pulled out her laptop and set it up on her knees. Firing it up she logged onto the airport's free WIFI and started to troll through Faith's social media sites. The Facebook, Twitter and Tik Tok sites hadn't been updated since the day Chips had been carted off to hospital, but her photo gallery was illuminating. Right up until July, Faith had appeared to be a happy healthy girl, whose life had become even more exciting with the advent of a new man in her life. Rosie studied a beautiful photo of her with a handsome soldier in full military dress. It was captioned, *protector of my heart*.

The pair looked relaxed, happy and deeply in love. After that there were only two more photos. One was of the man Rosie remembered meeting briefly at the hospital. He was jogging around an oval and had been framed in the shot by Faith's bare shins and the toes of the trainers on her feet. Posted underneath were the words – *Watch this space...getting fit with my bud, Ashley.*

The final photo she came across worried Rosie. Ashley commanded all Faith's attention by cupping her chin in a tight grip. He held her with a gaze that screamed possessiveness. The caption read – *Wedding Day.* The happy healthy Faith of earlier was gone. In this last photo her cheeks were sunken and hollow. She'd gone from a shapely size 12 to a bony size that bordered on an anorexic look. While all Rosie's worries might easily be explained away by the photo being taken at the wrong moment, what really concerned her was the look in Faith's eyes. They were filled with disillusionment and unhappiness.

Rosie dug out her mobile, ignored the fact that it was well after midnight, and called her missing niece's number. The call went straight to a recorded message advising that the recipient's voicemail was full. Rosie hung up and texted two capitalised words. CALL ME!

To keep track of the steps she'd taken, Rosie created a spreadsheet log to which she added the names of a few people to interview and the questions she wanted answered. With a curse Rosie realized she wouldn't have Bayden to do any legwork on this one, mainly because it was personal. Combined with the case she was investigating and the lack of information, Rosie knew the progress in the hunt for Faith would be slow, but she was reasonably confident that in the end she would track her niece down. What she would find – well, that was another matter.

Opening a new spreadsheet on her computer, Rosie entered and reviewed the information Kelsey and Jackson Michaels had given her about the counterfeit notes. Being a suspicious soul and not prone to take anyone or anything at face value, Rosie shot off an email to Mark requesting that he carry out a detailed background check on the pub manager, all the bar staff who had been working that week as well as the Bottomless Keg's owners Frothy and his rotund wife, Fizz. She knew he'd be surprised by her last request but, even in small towns, criminals hid behind bohemian nicknames and the "just one of the gang" façades they created for themselves in a community.

With a tired sigh Rosie eased her stiff neck, slammed the laptop's lid shut and settled back in the armchair. This time she had no problem going to sleep.

20

# Chapter Twenty

Ryan surfaced from the black to a loud ringing in his head. Gritting his teeth, he sucked in a long, deep breath that filled his lungs with dust. He coughed and had to ride a wave of agonising pain that started in his right leg. Slowly the throbbing waned from excruciating torment to a more manageable level, allowing his brain to function.

*Where the hell am I?*

A memory surfaced.

Afghanistan!

That's right, Afghanistan. The Taliban have invaded Kandahar and we are part of *International Combined Effort*. The mission is to guard Kabul airport and assist in the evacuation of foreign troops. No, that's not right. That's just the cover story. Knowledge slowly surfaced to the forefront of his mind. Ryan and his team had another mission. A clandestine one. His gut suddenly clenched.

*His team! Where are they? What's happened to them?*

'Captain Lamb...Captain Lamb...open your eyes, damn you.' A muffled, strongly accented American voice penetrated the roaring in his ears.

By strength of will Ryan forced his eyelids open. A blurry face hovered over him.

'Stay with me, Captain. A medivac team is on the way. We'll soon have you out of here.' He blinked as a woman with a red and white cross on her battle helmet came into focus. Out of where? Why was she blathering on about a medical evacuation team? The American medic waved a drug ampoule in front of his face and yelled, 'Are you allergic to morphine?'

He moved to see why he'd need the drug and a searing pain burned up his right leg. It dragged an agonized scream from his lips. 'Fuck...No. N...n...not allergic.'

A sharp prick preceded the drug hitting his blood stream. It bought a small amount of relief to his pain riddled body.

'What happened?' he asked through gritted teeth. 'Where am I?'

'On the Persian coast. Ten clicks south of Bandar Abbas.'

'Iran? Why the fuck am I in Iran?'

'The answer to that is above my pay grade, buddy. All I know is that we had orders to evacuate you and your team. At 0500 you broke radio silence to advise you were coming in hot and we were to take evasive action. We did our best to get to you but an RPG-7 caught you first.'

'How bad?'

'FUBAR, buddy. You're lucky to be still with us.'

'My mates, Seadog and Rowdy. Did they make it?'

'Don't know their names but the two guys who were with you are still in one piece. Knocked around some, but alive.' Sawyer, according to the name printed on her dusty fatigues, gently brushed some rubble away from his beard. 'Hang in there, Captain. We'll have you out of here in no time.'

'What's wrong with me?' asked Ryan, not ready to think about what misjudgement he'd made that had resulted in injury to the brave men he'd been working with.

Sawyer made full eye contact. She grasped Ryan's left hand and squeezed. 'Your right leg's a mess, buddy. I've staunched the worst of the bleeding, but there are bone fragments protruding from the wound. Don't try and move or you'll make things worse.'

Ryan returned the grip on his hand then felt his focus begin to slip as the morphine did its job. He drifted away in a sea of muted pain and confusion.

Clarity returned when his saviour bent close to his ear and said, 'Your ride's here, Captain.'

A babble of voices was accompanied by a lot of jostling as hands roughly moved him onto a stretcher. The screaming pain resurfaced, and he struggled to hold back the cries that echo around in his head.

'What's this, fucking amateur hour?' snarled the familiar voice of Rowdy. 'Will you guys' ease the fuck up. Can't you see your hurting him?'

The handling gentled. Through tear filled eyes Ryan glanced to his left and caught a blurry sight of big strong Rowdy, with his arm slung around Seadog's shoulder. He was using him as a prop. Both men were watching the handling of Ryan with grim expressions on their faces. Rowdy was shirtless and had a wad of bandaging wrapped around his torso. He could only be described as a walking wounded. Seadog's left arm was in a sling. His left cheek a mass of blood encrusted welts. Ryan was pleased he hadn't been lied to and they were both alive.

'You blokes all right?' he managed to croak.

'Yeah, Captain,' said Seadog. 'You bloody saved us with that exceptional tackle. Unfortunately for you, you copped the brunt of the explosion. Hang in there will ya, Shanks. Me and Rowdy want to buy you a truckload of beer when we get home.'

Ryan lifted a thumb. Through the dried blood, dirt and grime plastered all over Seadog's face his teeth dazzled with a blinding white smile.

# Chapter Twenty-One

Days of black merged to ones of pain-filled misty grey, before the black returned.

Time slid by.

Ryan knew he'd been moved more than once. Muted voices told him of travel and care. The drugs the voices supplied fogged his brain so much that interaction was impossible.

Suddenly a day came that was different from the others. Ryan slowly surfaced from the well of black, hovered in the grey and was pulled towards a lighter warmer shade, full of smells and sounds. An annoying monotone beep pierced his muddled world. He floated to the surface and stepped into a bright light to get away from the penetrating monotonous sound. The noise followed him and was joined by other sensations. A cold sharp scent of medicine and bleach. He made out a loud hiss. A tight band clamped around his upper arm then relaxed. Ryan tried to swallow. His mouth was dryer than the desert he'd been living in and his lips were stuck to scummy teeth. His tongue was like a fat useless lump of wood in his mouth. To top it off there was a burning itch below his right knee that he was unable to reach to scratch. At least the itch was more bearable than the agonising pain he'd suffered previously.

Someone spoke. A woman. In English. Australian accent. The woman mentioned the welfare of someone named, Alex.

A groan rumbled to life in his chest and escaped through his dry, chapped lips There was a movement at his side. Something cool touched his forehead – it felt nice.

A shrill alarm sounded. Startled, his eyes shot open.

## Chapter Twenty-Two

Rosie stared down at the man in the hospital bed. Longish dark hair curled around his ears and melded with a thick, scruffy beard that covered the lower region of his face. Along with a multitude of fading scrapes and bruises over his nose and neck, he had other more substantial injuries that needed time and care to heal. She ran her gaze across his muscular bare chest and ribs that spoke of the hard existence he'd been living in recent times. A muscle above the patient's eyes began to throb and tic. The rest of his body followed suit and twitched. Pain lines took up residence and joined the creases already living on his face, as he slowly surfaced from the drug induced blackness of unconsciousness.

When he groaned Rosie laid a cool hand on his forehead. 'Easy.'

The IV bag chose that moment to run dry and emitted a loud alarm.

Topaz eyes shot open and blinked rapidly. 'What the fuck...' cried the patient, flicking his glance around the hospital room. 'Where am I?'

The eyes widened and panic seemed to set in.

'Fuck…incoming…take cover!' he yelled and began to thrash around the bed as if trying to bury himself deep into the mattress.

Rosie acted fast. She pressed the emergency call button for the medical staff and lay across his chest, clamping his flailing limbs in a tight band.

'Calm down, Soldier,' she ordered. 'Lie still. You're safe. You're in hospital.' Rosie kept her thumb clamped on the emergency button.

'You're not military,' the soldier screamed. Panting he fought hard against her grip.

'No, I'm police. Lie still. You're safe.'

His movements slowed. 'We don't have any Aussie cops in the middle east. Is this all a trick to make me talk or are you a prisoner too?'

Rosie braced herself, not bothering to repeat herself, because she'd felt his muscles tense and knew he was going to try and throw her. The patient half lifted them both from the mattress before pain kicked in. He screamed and collapsed against the pillow.

'Calm down, Soldier,' she repeated, again and again. 'You're safe. Do you hear me, you are safe.'

A memory must have surfaced. 'I'm not in Afghanistan anymore, am I?'

'No, you're not. Talk to me. Tell me what you remember,' said Rosie, in an attempt to distract him from thoughts of fighting her.

The pain line on his face eased a little.

'I've been assigned to the ICE task force. The Taliban, they've taken over. Our mission is to provide security detail at Kabul airport and assist in the evacuations.'

Rosie's bullshit meter went into overdrive. She knew that all the coalition troops and civilians had been pulled out of Afghanistan in August 2021. 'What is ICE?' asked Rosie, hoping to learn more.

'International Combined Effort. We're a peace keeping force...provide protection from Islamic State...' His words came in gasps. Eventually they petered out and he began to groan.

Rosie spat out another question, hoping to keep his mind from the pain she could see raking his battered body. 'Do you remember your name?'

'Lamb...Ryan Lamb...Captain.' His gaze wandered over the monitors, along the blue curtaining that partitioned him from the occupant in the next bed and settled on her face. 'Where am I? Who did you say you were?' he asked.

'I am Detective Rosie Bloom, Western Australian Police Force. You're home, Ryan. You're in Fiona Stanley Hospital. A US military medical team took care of you after the explosion; did what they could for you and aided in the evacuation of you back to Australia.'

'Explosion,' muttered Ryan. 'What explosion...Oh, fuck... the American medic who found me...Sawyer, that was her name, she said there was an RPG.' He began to struggle against her grip again and in the process bumped his right leg on the side railing of the bed.

He let out a blood curdling scream and the bandage wrapped around what was left of his leg became stained with fresh blood.

Rosie reached up and gently stroked his cheek. 'Easy, Ryan...easy, lad. Just focus on me.' They locked stares. 'Now, deep breaths,' she commanded. 'In...one, two, three...now out, two, three. That's right. And again. Good, keep going, pain reliefs on its way.' Even as the words left her lips a nurse scurried to the bedside carrying a hypodermic and a full IV bag. She stabbed a needle into the line that fed into Ryan's wrist. Within moments the medication hit his blood stream and the lines on his face began to ease.

'How bad was the airport bombing?' he slurred.

Rosie waited for the nurse to check his vitals and leave before answering.

'You and I both know that you weren't hurt by the suicide bomber at Hamid Karzai airport, Ryan. That happened well over eighteen months ago. Your story doesn't wash.' Ryan's eyes widened. 'Your secrets safe with me. Whatever your mission was, I believe the end result is that it went FUBAR for you and your team mates. Judging by the look of you, we're lucky to still have you with us.'

'And my team?'

'Sorry, Ryan. I don't know. The army bloke, who was here earlier, wouldn't tell me.'

'What army bloke. What was his name?'

'Major Steel.' Ryan sighed and seemed to relax at the mention of the Major's name. 'Said he'd be back tomorrow to debrief and update you.'

Ryan took a long, jagged breath. 'They're good friends, Seadog and Rowdy. I hope they survived.'

Rosie thought he'd drifted off to sleep and was about to step away from the bed when Ryan suddenly opened his eyes again.

'What's wrong with me?'

Rosie locked her gaze to his and grasped his left hand in a firm grip. His fingers squeezed back. 'There is no permanent damage to your arms and chest. The shrapnel wounds are healing well, but you will bear quite a few scars for the rest of your life.'

'That's not all, is it? None of that explains the pain in my leg,' he said. 'Don't hold back – tell me the worst.'

'Your right leg and foot were a mess. The Doctors couldn't repair them. They had to amputate, just below the knee.'

'So, I'm useless to everyone now.' Ryan's eyes seemed to glaze over as the drugs started to take him back into oblivion.

'No mate, you're not useless. In fact, I need you to help me save Faith.'

'I love a girl named Faith. And she loved me,' Ryan slurred, 'But I fucked that one up badly as well.'

His hand went slack as he sank back into unconsciousness.

'I bloody hope you love her,' grunted Rosie, 'because she's going to need the *protector of her heart*.'

## Chapter Twenty-Three

Another long, tiring day standing watch in the cold, sterile, hospital room had left Rosie feeling confined and useless. Upon learning that Alex and Captain Ryan Lamb were both patients in the same hospital, Rosie had demanded the staff billet the men together in a private room. She'd been relentless in her request. Her opening gambit that they were family and deserved to be together was met with a mild, 'We'll see what we can do.'

Undeterred, Rosie pulled out the big guns – telling all and sundry that Ryan was a soldier who had sacrificed so much for his country and deserved the best. This hit a nerve with the medical staff. After that nothing was too much trouble. Now she had nothing to do but watch and wait for the men to recover. Showing patience wasn't her style, she needed to be out running down leads and bringing the criminal element of society to heel, and being hamstrung like this frayed her temper.

Rosie studied the soldier in the left bed. An infection had developed in his leg wound. Ryan had been put under heavy sedation while powerful antibiotics were intravenously pumped into his system. After a week the medication was finally bearing results.

Ryan's leg was now showing signs of healing. The good news of the day from his surgeon - they were going to begin easing him off the cocktail of drugs that had kept him fully sedated up to this point.

She flicked a glance right. In the bed lay a very thin, elderly looking, Alex, who, an hour earlier, had been returned from the operating theatre where the magical fingers of a cardio surgeon had implanted a pacemaker to control his slow and erratic heart rate. Alex was still sleeping off his own brew of drugs. Rosie checked the machines he was hooked up to and noted that the insertion of the pacemaker was already showing good results. The monitor at Alex's bedside counted a steady pulse of 60 bpm instead of the twenty and thirty-five it had been wavering between. His cheeks were now a warmer colour as well, so different from the terrible grey they'd been ever since the assault. As neither man showed any signs of waking up any time soon, Rosie began to pace back and forth with short sharp steps while staring at her mobile phone messages. There was one from Bayden containing the backgrounds checks she'd asked him to pull together for her. Intent, she scanned every word but nothing untoward stood out. Cranky at the lack of traction she was getting in the counterfeit case her knee jerk reaction was to send her partner a spate of text demands for more information.

*'Bayden, what have you found on the pub's security footage?'*

*'Bayden, ask Kelsey Morgan if there's anything to worry about in the Bottomless Keg's accounts.'*

*'Bayden, what happened when Patterson fronted the magistrate?'*

Almost immediately her phone buzzed. Mark's texts were as long-winded as his social chit-chat.

*Boss, hi, how you doing. Hope your B-I-L is on the mend. Nothing on the security footage has stood out, so far. As it is a slow, time-consuming task, SS George is pushing me to be more productive on other policing stuff, so I have to review the footage in my spare time. Will keep at it, I promise. I'll text you the moment I find something.*

*My feet are swollen and sore from trudging up and down the streets talking with the town's business owners. So far no one else has picked up on any counterfeit notes when doing their receipts and banking. I left a photocopy of the serial numbers with each business owner I spoke with and told them to keep a wary eye out.*

*I've called K.M. – there's nothing wrong with the accounts, and she'd know.*

*Would you believe it, Patterson made bail. Not a flight risk, the magistrate said. And before you ask - no sign of him at his house or around town. I think he's done a bunk.*

*When will you be coming back? Mark.*

Rosie grunted at the last question and glanced over the top of her glasses at her niece who dozed in a chair level with her father's elbow and made the decision to stay longer.

*'Bayden, not sure on return. B-I-L still unconscious. Working on getting us some help.'*

Rosie flicked her glasses off and resumed her pacing. She was frustrated at the time it was taking Alex to emerge from the twilight he'd dwelt in for over a week. She needed to know what he'd been up to and had got nothing out of him so far. On the few occasions he'd been awake he'd been mostly incoherent. As if hearing her thoughts, Alex gave a soft groan and lifted a hand to the bandage on the side of his scalp as if it pained him. Rosie rushed to her brothers-in-law's side.

'Alex...its Rosie,' she said, cupping his pale, warm cheek with her cool palm. 'Lie still and listen. The surgeon has inserted a pacemaker into your chest and it's working well but don't try and sit up without help. A couple of your ribs are broken and need time to heal.'

'That explains the sore chest but not the pounding in my head,' grumbled the man in the bed.

Rosie's heart soared. Progress. Alex seemed to be coherent and aware.

'Drugs and concussion, my boy, drugs and concussion. I think it's about time you changed your lifestyle.

'Concussion?'

'From the boot you tried to stop with your thick skull.'

'Ho ho!' he mumbled. 'The silver dingos cracked a joke.'

Rosie grunted but let the name slip past.

'Why are you here, anyway? Shouldn't you be off playing super-woman?' Alex gave her an owlish look as he blinked against the bright overhead light. Suddenly panic set it. 'It's Lucy, isn't it? Is she okay? Her operation didn't go wrong, did it?' Alex spat out the series of questions without waiting for a reply. Rosie saw the confusion in his eyes clear. 'No, that's not right, she's not sick anymore is she. That was last year.'

'Easy there, tiger,' said Rosie, settling her butt on the bed beside his elbow and running her fingertips gently down his cheek. 'Lucy is fine. That girl's a tower of strength. She does you credit. Look to your left. See, she's asleep in the chair next to you. It's been a tough couple of days as she watched over you both.'

'Both...what do you mean, both? Is it Faith, is she here? Is she all right?' he asked, his voice rising.

'Calm down before you bust open your stiches. No, it's not Faith,' whispered Rosie, momentarily leaning her forehead against his. 'I'm afraid our precious girl is still missing. But I'm going to fix that as soon as I've sorted you out.'

'Oh, my girls...' he moaned. Rosie was stunned to see a tear roll down his cheek. 'Rosie, you have to protect them for me. I opened a can of worms and I'm scared the girls will be hurt in the fall out.'

Chips awoke. She hopped to her feet and rushed to Alex's side.

'Popsicle, darling, I'm here,' she said, buzzing her father's thin, pale cheek with gentle, soft lips. 'Please, don't upset yourself. The doctors say it's normal to be a little confused after the trauma to your head.'

'Lucy, are you really here?'

'Yes, Daddy. I'm here.'

'Where's Adam. He should be here to look after you. He promised me he would. Is everything, okay? He didn't crash his plane, did he? Is that why we are at the hospital?'

'No. Adam is just fine. He had to go to the base and report in with his commanding officer. He'll be back to see you again tonight. We're here because you were attacked coming home from work. Don't you remember?'

Alex stared at her. Confusion clouded his eyes. His gaze drifted towards the next bed. 'Who's in the bed next to me?'

'It's Adam's brother...Ryan.'

'Ryan! The soldier? But isn't he the bloke who...but she loves him...she's married and gone...'

Lucy nodded.

'I'm going to punch his lights out. He left our precious girl to fall into the clutches of that brute...'

'You'll do no such thing,' said Rosie, with a lopsided grin. 'Ryan's a trained commando and even as injured as he is he could take you apart with his little finger. Besides he's going to help me retrieve Faith and return her home to us - so play nice.'

Alex stared at his daughter and Rosie noted the hope that shone in both their eyes. She prayed she wasn't about to disappoint them.

## Chapter Twenty-Four

'Detective Graves?'

A trim, middle-aged blonde, dressed in a loose, button-down white cotton blouse over tailored black trousers and flat soled black boots that zipped up at the side, stood next to a desk stacked neatly with files and an assortment of stationery within easy reach of busy hands. She looked up from a file she was reading and stared myopically over the top of her glasses at Rosie.

'Yeah, I'm Graves, who are you?'

'Detective Bloom, Regional Crime Force...'

'RCF...you're a bit off your patch, aren't you, detective?' She stared at Rosie, her face devoid of any of the thoughts or emotions ticking over in her brain. 'Bloom did you say?'

Rosie gave a small chin lift to indicate that the detective had heard her name correctly.

'Detective Graves, I understand you're in charge of the investigation into the attack on Alex Chippens.'

Anne Graves gave a slow nod. 'Now why in the world would the Silver Dingo be interested in a simple assault case?'

Rosie decided her first task was to get this detective onside. 'Call me, Rosie. Alex Chippens, is my brother-in-law.'

'Oh, that explains the Police Commissioner's interest as well. The victim being a relation of the Silver Dingo.'

'More like the Commissioner and Alex are lifelong friends who spend most Sunday's wangling twenty cent pieces out of each other while pretending to play honest golf,' said Rosie, with a roll of her eyes.

Detective Graves grinned and seemed to relax. She turned, took a seat in a black swivel chair. She pointed to the visitor's seat set at an angle on the left of her desk.

'Take a pew and tell me how I can help you, Rosie?'

'I'm not here to tread on your toes or interfere in your case, detective, but what can you tell me about Alex's assault?'

'Call me, Anne.' Detective Graves slid forward an A4 ring folder.

'Cast your peeps over this.' Rosie lifted her brows at the meagre contents in file. 'At this point I'm happy for all the help I can get. We've not got much to go on because, Mr Chippens, hasn't been able to give us a statement as yet and there were no witnesses to his assault. As for evidence,' Anne shrugged and checked the dial of the slim watch on her wrist. 'I'm still waiting for the fingerprint analysis on the wallet to come back from the lab. They've had a backlog, but I've been promised a report by three this afternoon. Won't help if our offender isn't in the system of course, but I did get an interesting lead from the City of Perth CCTV city cam footage.' Anne flicked a neatly manicured finger towards the folder in Rosie's hand. 'Check out page three.'

Rosie flipped to the indicated page and studied a blurred, grainy and badly pixelated photo grab of a hooded man. 'What or who am I looking at, Anne?' she asked.

'That bloke was walking a short distance behind Mr Chippens just a few moments before he was attacked.'

'Any ideas who he is?'

Anne shook her head. 'Nope, not a clue. But...' she smirked, 'the tech lab boys did a bang-up job splicing together a nice little video taken from the shop and street cams in the area. They're now working on getting me a clearer picture of his face.' Anne stroked her forefinger under her chin and sighed. 'If we can catch up with him, he'll have some explaining to do. But I don't like my chances.'

'Anything else?'

'Tomorrow, I'll release the video in a public appeal – we need help to identify him. Here,' the detective fiddled with the computer mouse to open a file on her desktop. She spun the screen around so Rosie could get a clear view. 'Take a gander. See if you've ever crossed paths.'

Video footage began to play. Rosie balanced her half-moon reading glasses onto the tip of her nose and leant closer to the screen to study the recording as it played out. She easily recognised the neat and familiar figure dressed in a charcoal business suit with a hard-covered attaché case in his left hand.

'That's Alex,' said Rosie, tapping the screen that showed her brother-in-law busily working on his mobile phone as he strolled away from the doors of a high-rise office building instead of paying attention to the environment around him. 'What's that building?'

'That's Central Park Tower,' said Anne. 'I believe he has an office there.'

Rosie nodded but didn't take her eyes from Alex as he wandered down St Georges Terrace still oblivious to his surroundings.

She shook her head. 'I'm going to have a serious discussion with him about paying more attention to his surroundings,' she murmured.

Detective Graves snorted. 'Good luck with that. See it all the time, especially in the young ones.'

The recording changed to a different street. The footpath and road were empty.

'Williams Street,' murmured Anne.

Moments later Alex rounded the corner. Fifteen seconds later so did a very thin individual wearing dark track pants and an oversized matching jacket with the hood scrunched into a heap at the back of his neck. Greasy-black hair had been pulled into a top knot high on the back of his head. His feet were encased in elastic-sided, steel-cap work boots. His hand was up so they couldn't get a clear look at his face. As both men strode towards Elizabeth Quay, the man following Alex yanked his hood up to cover his hair, tugging it down, so it concealed his features. He shoved his hands deep into his jacket pockets and increased his pace. Oblivious, Alex strolled into the park that fronted Elizabeth Quay. Hoody followed. The video ended.

'That's it, I'm afraid. The next camera in the series had been vandalized. The one after that was located at the ferry terminal. There was no footage of either man.'

'Who found Alex?'

'An officer on patrol. Mr Chippens was found in the camera black spot. This guy,' Anne, scrolled the file back and pausing it on the image of the man tailing Alex just before he pulled his hood up, 'wasn't picked up again on any other footage.'

'So, hoody must have had some mode of transport nearby,' said Rosie. She tapped her fingernail against her front teeth as she studied the blurry patch of tufted hair growing below his wedge of cheese shaped nose that was caught in the moment before his hood concealed his face totally. 'Is that all you managed to get from the security cams?'

The detective's top lip hooked up into a pleased smile. 'So glad you asked. When we backtrack in time to street footage taken earlier that evening,' said Anne, 'guess who we found lurking in the doorway of the Heritage Wine Bar on St Georges Terrace. And yes, before you ask, he did go in and buy drinks. No, he didn't use a credit card. The barman remembers him though, thought him a very odd duck. Not only because he was dressed in clothing more suited to the gym than a night out at a swanky restaurant bar, but because he spent most of his time standing at the front window staring out in the street while gulping down glasses of bourbon. Double shots, to be precise, that he paid for with one hundred-dollar notes. And now Detective Bloom, I have a very interesting side fact for you. That week-end three counterfeit one-hundred-dollar notes were found in the takings of the Heritage Wine Bar. As you can understand, The Serious Crime Squad, is extremely interested in having a word or two with this individual,' said Anne, tapping the image on the screen.

Rosie's spidey senses began to tingle. 'You and me both, Detective Graves. I thought it was strange that SCS was handling a simple mugging. Now, do you want to know what I'm currently working on in my neck of the woods?'

Anne cocked an eyebrow. Rosie gave her a summary of her latest case. When she was finished a slack-jawed Detective Graves took a long moment before she was able to form the words of her response.

'Wow, that's some co-incidence. I can only see our association as being very beneficial to both our cases.'

Rosie gave Anne a feral smile.

'You and me both.'

Rosie gave a mental fist pump. Finally, she was getting some traction.

'Do me a favour Anne. Compress the video for me and email it through to my partner, Constable Bayden, Mount Ibour police station. I'd like to see if he can spot hoody on any of the footage we took from the Bottomless Keg.' Rosie leant forward and wrote down Mark's email address on the back of one of her business cards before handing it to the detective. 'My mobile and contact details.'

'What are the chances that this guy is in your backyard?' asked Anne, her fingers racing across her computer keyboard.

'The possibility is there...whether he's still around or has moved on to greener pastures is the question. Or there may be a crew of spenders doing the rounds, but it can't hurt to look. Besides, I can't have Bayden getting his size nine's too cosy under his desk while I'm away,' she grinned. 'He'll have to slog the hot streets again showing this photo to all the local businesses in an attempt to trace our man.'

Detective Graves chuckled. 'I do the same with my subordinates. It teaches them to be thorough and makes them better officers.'

Rosie sat back and tucked her glasses away in her pocket. 'One more thing. Do you have some spare time? Alex is conscious and ready to give a statement about what he can remember.'

Anne shot to her feet and grabbed the black jacket hanging on the back of her chair. 'Absolutely. Let me just grab a lackey.'

# Chapter Twenty-Five

The hospital room bulged at the seams when Rosie, Anne Graves and her partner Peter Fenton joined Chips and her blond, RAAF pilot at Alex's bedside.

A nurse followed them in, scowling. 'Hospital policy – two visitors only.'

Rosie held up her badge. The nurse gave everyone a suspicious look. 'Mask up,' she growled and scuttled from the room.

Chips turned away from her father with a look of despair on her face. She spotted her aunt and rushed over. Rosie was enveloped in a sweet spicy cloud of jasmine as Chips flung her arms around her neck.

'Aunty Rosie,' she cried, her usual calm demeanour missing. 'Can't you talk some sense into these guys? Dad and Ryan are planning to leave the hospital today. They want to start a hunt for Burger.'

Anne crooked an eyebrow. 'Can't you just Uber for a burger?'

Chips flicked the detective a puzzled frown, let out a sob and buried her face into Rosie's shoulder.

'She's talking about my other niece, Faith,' Rosie explained to her companion while she stroked the back of her niece's dark cropped head. 'This one is known as Chips.'

Anne rubbed the back of her hand over her honey tinted lips to hide a smile. 'Oh, I see.'

Rosie began to wonder how hard a hit her reputation in the force as a hardnosed investigator was about to take by letting the two city detectives see her as an aunt instead of the hardened copper she was. She gave a mental shrug and decided to go with the flow.

Tears glistened on Chips's cheeks when she lifted her head from Rosie's neck and began to rant. 'They can't leave! Popsicle only had surgery yesterday and was unconscious for a week before that. His brain's still not working properly and his ribs are still paining him. As for Shanks! Grrrr...the bloody man is impossible. The fact that he's just been through hell and back and needs some time to heal doesn't seem to penetrate his thick skull.'

'Shanks?' asked Anne, not bothering to hide her smirk of amusement this time.

Rosie pointed to Ryan. 'Captain Lamb,' she said and noticed his face was flushed as he restlessly tugged at the sleeve of the Flight Lieutenant's uniform, trying to get his attention.

'Has your family got some sort of food fetish?' murmured Anne, her eyes sparkling with suppressed laughter.

Rosie ignored Anne's joke and unhooked the stranglehold her niece had around her neck. 'Dry those tears and listen up, Chips. Ryan will always put others and his mission first. That's one of the traits that make a good commando. And from what I've heard, Ryan is...was...an exceptional commando.'

'Commando, my ass,' snarled her niece. 'Just because one of the hospital staff said Ryan's leg is now on the mend, he's taken that to mean it's all systems go. Bloody hell, Aunt Rosie, he's as weak as a kitten!'

'To be expected.'

'I know that, you know that and lucky for us so do the nurse staff. They refused to discharge him this morning. But the idiot is now planning to hook it anyway.' Lucy turned and glared at the RAAF officer who had a goofy grin on his face. 'And Adam's no bloody help - he's even offered to drive the getaway wheelchair. All that did was get Shanks snarking over how he's not going to be restricted to a bloody wheelchair. Soldiers don't get pushed around like toddlers in prams, I think is how he phrased it. Minus the swear words of course.'

Ryan seemed to finally succeed in catching his brothers attention. 'Chappie,' he snarled, 'get me pair of damn crutches.'

Shoving the bedding away from his lower limbs he revealed a pair of blue cotton boxer shorts, strong well-toned thighs and his bandaged stump. The sheet and IV line tangled. Ryan waved his arm around in frustration, unsuccessfully trying to dislodge the material. Chips hurried over to his side, pushed Adam aside and with gentle hands straightened Ryan out.

'If I was talking to Ryan,' said Chips, pushing her face close to his, 'which I'm not, because I'm still angry with the stupid bugger for leaving Burger without a word of explanation...' Ryan dropped his eyes and looked shamefaced, '...but if I was talking to him, I'd say something like, Shanks that's the morphine making you think you're invincible. Without it you'd be in a whole world of pain.'

Ryan blinked at her owlishly, gave a sheepish grin and promptly fell asleep.

Lucy gave a sigh of relief. 'He keeps doing that.'

'It's the drugs. How much longer before they totally wean him?' asked Rosie.

'The doctor said at least a week, maybe two.'

'And when can he go home?'

'Not for a couple of months. When his stump...Oh, I hate that word...when his leg has fully healed, he's got rehab and still has to be fitted with a prosthetic limb. Until then they want him to build up his body strength.' Lucy pointed to the blond RAAF pilot with bright, sparkling eyes, who had slipped a loving arm around her waist. 'This is Adam by the way...bloody troublemaker. I don't know what I see in him.' Adam lifted a hand by way of a greeting and drew Lucy closer, cradling her against his chest. She snuggled in. 'As for Popsicle, he's just as bloody hopeless. I caught him trying to sneak out to the office this morning. For God's sake, Aunt Rosie do something will you.'

Rosie roared with laughter. Ryan awoke with a start and everyone in the room stared at her.

'Heel boys,' she ordered. 'We've got a lot of ground work to cover before you can charge off into the wild blue yonder to play hero.'

A snort beside her reminded Rosie why they were here.

'Alex,' she said, pointing to her companions. 'I'd like you to meet Detective's Anne Graves and Peter Fenton from the Serious Crime Squad. Detectives, this is my recalcitrant brother-in-law, Alex Chippens. His daughter, Lucy, her soon to be husband, Flight Lieutenant Adam Best-Lamb.' Chips cheeks pinked at the mention of Adam becoming her husband, but Rosie was ruthless in her pursuit to ensure nothing further should get in the way of solving the problems before her. 'I think you two should get married while I'm still in Perth. It'll save me breaking away from the investigation to make another trip to the city.'

'Aunt Rosie...we're going to wait until you find, Burger.'

'Is she missing?' asked Anne.

Rosie shrugged. 'We'll see. Alright, enough of this you lot. Alex, Detective Graves needs to speak with you.'

Alex gave the visitors a bashful look and pulled the sheet high up on his chest to hide the fact he was wearing his PJ's. He gave his hair a hand brush to comb it neatly into place. Rosie was amused that with everything going on in his life, Alex's greatest concern of the moment was his appearance in front of the police.

'Alex, I want you to fully co-operate. Tell the detective and me, everything you remember. Then the three of us will have a serious discussion about what you've been working on.'

Alex gave Rosie a bland innocent stare that didn't fool her one bit.

She hardened her voice, 'It's important. You must tell us everything. I think it's all related.'

Alex flicked a glance towards his daughter. Rosie took the hint.

'Chips, you need a break. You're worn out. Scoot for a while will you. Go find your Zen or something.'

'Oh, but...' protested Lucy.

'Do it,' she commanded, before lowering her voice and whispering, 'You know how protective Alex is of you. He'll speak more openly to us if you're not in the room. Now off you go and take that handsome pilot of yours with you. While you're gone, get us all some coffee will you.'

Adam took Chips by the hand and drew her towards the door. 'Come on, Lucy. I think everyone would enjoy a chocolate chip muffin with their coffee. I know I would. I also want to check out the lay of the land – I need to put operation Tennille into effect.'

The door hissed closed and the noise level in the room settled into the relative peace allowed by the beeps and dings of the patient monitoring equipment.

Detective Graves flicked Rosie a puzzled glance. 'What is Operation Tennille?' she asked.

Rosie shrugged her shoulders. 'No idea.'

# Chapter Twenty-Six

'Do you recognise this man?' Detective Graves positioned herself to the right of Alex's hospital bed to hand him a copy of a grainy photograph.

Alex scrunched his eyebrows as he studied the snapshot. 'It's not a good photo is it...a bit blurry.' After another moment of thought he shook his head. 'No, from what I can see this bloke doesn't ring any bells. Who is he?'

Ryan, cranked his neck to peer around the monitor keeping a check on his vital signs in an attempt to get a clear look.

'A good question, Mr Chippens. Tell me what you can remember about the evening you were attacked.'

'I don't recall much at all really. Only a few disjointed images come to mind.'

'Like?' prompted Detective Graves.

'Well, I remember working late - on something private. It must have been close to eleven o'clock in the evening when I left the office. The street was quiet. I decided to check some information online using my phone as I strolled down to the ferry.'

Anne Graves nodded. 'That gels with the security footage.'

'That's about it really,' said Alex. 'I don't remember reaching Elizabeth Quay. I was reading my screen, everything after that is blank. The street seemed quiet...oh, I said that already, didn't I.' Detective Graves nodded. 'Sorry. Since the thump on my head my memory has more holes in it than a wedge of Swiss cheese.'

Uncomfortable and not able to hear everything clearly, Ryan leant forward to grab Rosie's hand. He gave it a tug. 'Help me sit up, will ya, detective,' he said. 'I'm getting a kink in my neck trying to peer around all this damn equipment.'

Without a word she dropped the side barrier on his bed and tucked a hand under his armpit. He clamped his hand on her upper arm for leverage and tugged himself into a sitting position. With her aid he managed to swivel both his legs around, so they hung over the edge of the bed. When she settled next to him on the mattress she gave him a smile. The way her lip curled back reminded him of something. He dwelt on the memory for a moment and from the back of his mind a conversation with Burger surfaced. She'd once told him the media loved to call her detective aunt The Silver Dingo. He now saw why.

Suddenly the world began to spin. Ryan grabbed at the edge of the mattress for balance and closed his eyes, willing away the nausea that swirled low in his guts. The last thing he wanted to do was heave.

'All right?' murmured Rosie in his ear.

'Yeah. I'm just waiting for the room to stop doing a sideways tilt.'

'Just breathe' she said, and patted his hand.

The whirling in his head slowly ceased. Ryan cracked open an eye and sighed in relief when everything stood still. 'I like you, detective. You don't fuss at a man.'

'Not my style, Captain. Besides I need you up and mobile. We have a mission, you and I. How soon do you think can you be ready?'

Surprised, Ryan's other eye snapped open. 'As soon as you need me to be. The physio's going to set me an exercise program. I can do that anywhere. But I won't be combat ready for at least a month. I'll need my prosthetic limb for that.'

'Fit will do fine...for now. And, I have the perfect place for you to work on the combat ready while you do some other stuff for me – if you agree of course.'

'Sure. Anything. Will it help find, Burger?'

'We'll see.' Rosie stroked the back of his hand again. He found the gesture soothing. 'Now listen closely to what Alex has to say, because somehow, his attack is connected with a case I'm working on.'

Ryan glanced across at Detective Graves. She was a nice-looking woman with a trim figure and well-dressed in that middle-aged, professional sort of way. Her neatly manicured fingers were fiddling with her phone.

'Alright, I've recorded all that, Mr Chippens,' she said. 'I'll get Fenton to write up your statement and bring it back this afternoon for you to sign.'

Alex sighed and seemed to deflate back into his pillows. He looked exhausted.

Rosie stirred and leant forward, a bright gleam in her eyes. 'Alright, Alex,' she said. 'Now tell us what it is, that you've been poking around in. And don't lie to me, you know I have a very sensitive...' She tapped the side of her nose with the tip of her forefinger.

Alex's brows beetled together, and he began to fuss with his bedcovers as though they needed it.

'Alex! Stop trying to avoid the conversation.' A pink blush started at the collar of Alex's pyjama shirt and crept rapidly up his neck until his whole face was flushed. The beseeching look he gave Rosie was ignored. As though giving up Alex sighed and began to speak.

'Do you remember,' he muttered, 'the day Lucy was rushed to hospital with appendicitis?'

Rosie nodded. 'Yeah, I was in Perth to give evidence in court. I came to the hospital to see you.' In an aside to Ryan, she muttered. 'That's the day Faith got married.'

'Don't remind me,' Ryan growled. The fact that Burger was now married hurt like blazes.

'When Faith arrived at the hospital she had a bloke in tow. He introduced himself to me as her husband and she didn't look happy about it,' said Alex. 'Yeah, I know we were all upset about Lucy being ill, but my eyes still worked.' Alex stared at the wall opposite as though deep in thought.

Rosie gave him a prompt. 'Alex.'

'What? Sorry...where was I...Oh, that's right, Faith. What I really noticed was the new husband manhandled her. He kept a tight grip on her arm - held her in place at his side and whenever he moved, he'd grab her wrist and drag her along with him. Whenever we got close, Faith and I, he'd intervene like a jealous child.'

'Bastard!' A hot surge of anger sprang to life in Ryan's chest. It stole away his ability to see and hear as his mind filled with the thought that Burger was being mistreated. Why would anyone hurt someone so precious? 'I've never understood people who insisted on imposing their will over others, bending and reshaping them to suit their own ideals. Makes me want to lash out and punch the husband real hard.' Ryan was almost overwhelmed by a strong urge to get up and pace. Or do something to get rid of the red-hot anger that now clouded his mind. He stared down at his leg. The sight of the missing limb and reality of his situation jolted him. He clenched his fists until the knuckles turned white and his arms trembled.

'Breathe and focus,' came the command from beside him. 'Remember, anger clouds the senses.'

Taking Rosie's words to heart he clamped his jaw tight, took a long, steadying breath. It worked. Slowly the flash of rage dissipated and full use of his senses returned. The conversation going on around him began to penetrate.

'I dropped the ball,' said Alex. 'My attention at that moment was focused solely on Lucy and what was going on in the operating theatre.'

'Understandable,' said Rosie, releasing her supportive grip on Ryan's now relaxed fist, giving it a firm pat.

Alex rubbed the heel of his hand across his forehead, massaging the creases that had excavated deep furrows on his brow. 'The following day, Faith didn't show up at the hospital like we'd arranged. Concerned, I messaged her. She didn't answer. It scared me.'

Alex's attention drifted away again.

'Stay focussed, Alex,' snapped Rosie.

Alex jumped. 'Sorry, it's my brain. It zones out on me.' He took a deep breath. 'Anyway, I was really worried something had happened to Faith. Later that day the husband rang me. He apologised they'd not made it to the hospital to see how Lucy was doing, but Faith was sick in bed with a raging headache. Migraine he called it. He expected her to be better the next day and organised to meet me at the hospital cafeteria because he had some things about Faith's future he wanted to discuss with me. When I arrived at the hospital the next morning, they were already in visiting with Lucy. It was only a short visit, five minutes at most.'

Alex's restless hands smoothed the already neat sheet across his chest with flat palms. 'That's when the alarm bells really went off,' he murmured. 'Not only did Faith not look like Faith – she was dressed in a designer dress, high heels, thick makeup - but she gave me no greeting. No joyous hug, no jokes about us eloping together. The poor girl barely looked at me. Her head hung down like she was ashamed. Throughout the whole meeting she never spoke one word that wasn't coached. The new husband hogged most of the conversation. He made all sorts of demands concerning Faith's finances. She just sat staring at her lap. Every now and then he'd squeeze her arm and she'd nod. It broke my heart. I had to come up with some creative legal mumbo jumbo to stall until I could get her alone to find out what was really going on.'

Rosie nodded. 'Chips mentioned you had.'

'The husband wasn't a happy man when they got up to leave, I can tell you. I took a shot at getting her alone by inviting Faith to have dinner with me - just the two of us. I'm positive she was about to say yes, but he stepped in and put a stop to it with some cock and bull story about it being his mother's birthday and that they were going to take a scenic helicopter flight. It was to be a special gift from Faith. One she'd organised. Now I know that was a lie. Ever since her parent's death, Faith avoids flying.'

'But that doesn't make sense,' said Rosie. 'Susannah and Lee didn't die in a plane crash; they died as a result of terrorists.'

'Yeah, I know, but to Faith, flying means travel, and travel means going overseas, where bad things happen.'

'No wonder Burger was so relieved when I told her I thought my time overseas in the Middle East was finished,' said Ryan. 'She didn't know I was being sent for another stint. I got ordered back to base before I had a chance to speak with her.'

Alex stared at Ryan. 'Is that why you left Albany so abruptly?'

'Yes and no. I did go to find her - to explain and say goodbye, but someone had different ideas.' Ryan sighed as everyone stared at him. 'I was sent a photograph, purporting to have come from Faith. She was wrapped in some bloke's arms...they were enjoying what looked to be a very sultry kiss. The text message indicated she loved him. I felt played and it made me angry. I'd already gone through a nasty break up with my fiancé after she did the dirty on me and my knee jerk reaction was to up and leave. I was halfway to Afghanistan by the time I'd cooled down enough to come to my senses. The photo hadn't even come from her phone. I wanted to call her, apologise for being an idiot by not giving her a chance to explain, but there was a total communications blackout on the mission.'

Alex rolled his head sideway on his pillow and with watery eyes stared at Ryan. 'This bloke in the photo, what did he look like? Was he tall, broad across the shoulders with dark hair, dimples and very expensively dressed.'

'Don't know about the dimples...but yeah to the rest.'

'Ashley!' snarled Alex.

Ryan flicked a glance at Rosie in an unspoken question. 'The husband,' she responded. 'Anyway, let's not get side-tracked. We'll discuss this photo and why you were shunted out of the picture later. For now, Alex, I want to hear the rest of your story.'

The man in the other bed rolled his eyes. Ryan smothered a grin. Rosie was relentless in her pursuit for answers.

'After the encounter in the hospital, I made it my mission to find out all I could about my new nephew-in-law. I hired a Private Investigator to do a background check on him and his family.'

Alex suddenly clammed up. He stared at Rosie. She rolled her hand encouraging him to go on, but he seemed hesitant. Finally on a sigh he spilled the beans. 'The mother's a supposed lush. She spends more time in a rehab clinic drying out than she does in the home. Ashley himself is, quote, *"a businessman."* He runs a company called Bearcub Enterprises. Their core objective is to absorb cash businesses into their portfolio whether the owners are in the market or not. After the takeover these enterprises suddenly make huge profits. The PI found out that along with his father, Ashley is listed as a board member of six shell companies. The main one in use at the moment is called Nimble Investments.'

'That name sounds familiar, don't recall why,' said Ryan. 'Why does he need all those companies?'

'Money laundering,' mouthed Rosie and rolled her hand for Alex to keep talking.

'My investigator tells me Ashley has a reputation as a ruthless operator. There's also a cousin, who acts as his henchman. Together they carry out some questionable business aided by some very seedy characters. In this underworld he goes by a nickname...'

Rosie's head shot up. 'What name?' she snarled.

'Cub. I believe you're aware of the father.'

Rosie leapt to her feet exclaiming, 'Cub... as in, the son of Bear?'

Alex nodded and began to chew his bottom lip.

Ill contained fury poured from every pore of Rosie's being. Ryan's eyes widened in surprise as he watched her stomp back and forth across the length of the room in what seemed a random loop.

'What's up?' asked Detective Grave. 'Why does the mention of these Bear and Cub characters upset you so much?'

Rosie didn't reply. She began to mutter. 'Dammit...I knew he reminded me of someone...the husband...that day, at the hospital when I met him.' She glared at Alex and growled. 'I put the feeling aside. There were more important things going on – like Lucy's operation and you, Alex, looking so grey and ill. Harping on about how you'd failed as a parent because one was sick and the other had snuck off and gotten married. Then there was the court case I'd been testifying at – I was worried that the evidence and confession wasn't enough to get a conviction and it was important that I did. All those issues pushed that old case to the farthest part of my mind.'

'Case? What case?' asked Detective Graves.

Ryan watched Rosie make another circuit of the room. Curiosity got the better of him. 'Who is the Bear?'

Rosie mumbled, 'The cub might be a bigger version of his father, but I bet the apple doesn't fall far from the tree.' She looked up. 'In his hey-day Robert Watson was well-known by the criminal underbelly as The Bear. He once ran a syndicate that controlled a large slice of the city's organised crime.'

'Still does,' stated Alex. 'According to my investigator, now-a-days he's one of the main players behind the regional drug trade as well. Along with many other questionable enterprises too numerous to mention. My PI also told me that if you wanted to disappear, especially from the roving eye of the police, Bear is the man to see.'

'Robert Bear Watson. Yes, he's a well-known scumbag, but why does the mention of his name upset you so much, Rosie?' asked Detective Grave.

Rosie stopped pacing and blurted out, 'He's the man who had my husband killed.'

A stunned silence hung over the room.

The door burst open, causing everyone to jump. Chips, carrying a cardboard tray full of takeaway cups, sauntered in. Adam dashed in after her with a large blanket covered lump in his arms. As soon as they were in the room, Chips slammed the door closed and leant against it giggling. Adam carefully deposited the bundle onto the floor. A black nose appeared, the blanket shook and was flung aside allowing a beautiful German Shepherd dog to scrambled to its feet. The tension in the room broke.

Ryan opened his arms. 'Tennille,' he cried.

The dog took one look, her body quivered in glee. She let out a happy yelp and leapt. She hit Ryan smack in the middle of his chest. He closed his arms around his girl and together they fell in a tangled heap on the bedcovers. Tennille smothered his face in doggy kisses.

Ryan roared with laughter, the first joyful sound he'd made in a long time.

'I'd say operation Tennille was a complete success,' smirked Chips, plonking the tray of coffees down on her father's bedside table. She picked up the photo abandoned there. 'What's this about?'

Ryan pulled himself erect. Tennille with a happy pant settled close to his side and nestled her head into his lap.

Detective Fenton's phone rang.

'That, Lucy, is a photograph of the man we suspect was following your father just before he was attacked,' said Detective Grave.

The paper in Lucy's hand began to shake.

'Do you recognise him?' asked Rosie.

Before Chips could reply Fenton gave a fist pump. 'Yes,' he cried. 'We just got a match on the fingerprints, Boss.'

'I know exactly who the man in the photo is,' said Lucy.

## Chapter Twenty-Seven

TWELVE MONTHS EARLIER.

Ashley draped his right arm across my shoulder and took a firm grip of my upper arm. We were seated in the cafeteria of RPH. The table was littered with untouched coffee cups and a plate of tasty treats. Sitting across from me, with a furrow of worry lines across his face, was Uncle Alex. I cast a pleading glance his way. Ashley caught the look and squeezed his fingers as a reminder to stick to the script he'd laid out for me that morning or my family would suffer. I was so ashamed of the mess I'd gotten us all in, I lowered my gaze.

'Here Faith, have a piece of cake,' said my uncle, pushing the treat nearer to my cup.

I shook my head. Fear churned in my belly. In a brutal fashion, as he'd pounded himself into me that morning, with his version of lovemaking, Ashley had informed me exactly how he would punish my family if I disobeyed him in any way. To the rhythm off his belt connecting with my back, I was given instructions on how to behave, what I could and could not say and when I would be allowed to speak. If I broke any of his rules, I would never see my family again. If I discussed our marriage or our personal life, I would never see my family again. And, if I made any sort of fuss – well elderly men fell down stairs all the time.

'Now, Alex,' said Ashley, his tone, friendly and jovial. 'I can call you Alex, can't I? Unk, just doesn't sound right to me?'

'No, Unk wouldn't be right coming from your lips, Ashley. That is a private term of affection that solely belongs to Faith.'

I held back a gasp. My uncle's attitude was ice cold. Had he guessed something was wrong? I flicked a quick glance up at his face. It was shuttered. Ashley didn't like being put in his place. A pink flush stained his throat at the insinuation that we had a special relationship that he wasn't a part of. I bit my lip. I didn't want Ashley antagonised; he might just hurt Unk out of spite.

'Well...Alex,' Ashley said, belabouring my uncle's name in a mocking drawl, indicating he wasn't going to be intimidated. 'We need to discuss Faith's finances. Now that she and I are married, she wants me to relieve you of the burden of looking after her. I'm sure it's just a matter of signing a few documents – you can organise that can't you?' Uncle Alex raised one eyebrow but remained silent. 'Then there is the matter of her Will and an enduring power of attorney,' Ashley ploughed on, not concerned with building any sort of friendly relationship with my uncle, but only in having his demands met. 'As we're leaving on our honeymoon tomorrow and will be travelling extensively for an extended period of time, she wants to get those documents drawn up and signed today. Isn't that right, Sunflower?'

He tightened his grip over a welt on my shoulder and squeezed. Somehow, I kept the pain from showing on my face. 'Yes.'

'Get everything ready. We'll come by your office at five tonight.'

I felt Uncle Alex's gaze boring into the top of my head. I glanced up, read a question in his eyes. Ashley's fingers dug in. I pressed my lips together and nodded. Uncle Alex's gaze left my face. He flicked an ice-cold glance over the fingers clamped on my shoulder.

'I'm sorry young man,' he said. 'The legal world grinds away on a slower treadmill than you're used to. What you ask cannot be done. Not by tonight or indeed in any haste. Faith's finances are diverse and complicated. They are also tied to her trust fund. Before we can draw up any paperwork, an audit must be carried out by an independent auditor. Only after that can I legally draw up a new Will and enduring power of attorney. After Faith signs the EPA documents they must be sent to the courts for registration, along with a *name change advice* notice. For that I need a copy of your marriage certificate. Have you got that?'

'The celebrant said it would take six to eight weeks,' growled Ashley, 'before we received our registered copy.'

'Well, there you go then. I can't move forward without it. I will need certified copies for all the financial groups who are dealing with Faith's portfolio. Ten should do it. Change of beneficiary can't go ahead until that is done.'

An angry stain coloured Ashley's face. His hand, which was now clamped around the back of my neck, shook with suppressed rage at having his demands thwarted.

'I may be Faith's trustee and guardian,' continued Uncle Alex, in a calm and reasonable tone, 'but I cannot sign over her finances or their management, to you or anyone else. Her parents placed a very restrictive covenant on the trust.' In the same non-confrontational tone, Uncle Alex continued to set barriers in Ashley's way. 'Beyond reasonable living costs and education fees, the bulk of Faith's trust will not be available or even transferrable until she reaches the age of twenty-five, regardless of her marital status. She's not allowed to change the beneficiary of the trust or her trustee until then.'

I looked deep into the back of my uncle's eyes. I knew his darling face very well. He was up to something. I'd never heard about the covenant before. As far as I was aware Uncle Alex had always openly and honestly discussed every detail of my finances with me. He always went to great pains to include me in any decisions that affected my life. On more than one occasion he'd told me that if I would prefer someone with more experience to manage my money I only had to say so. I never felt the need because all our property investments had proved to be sound. As a result, my trust had grown nicely and there was a tidy sum waiting for me to claim whenever I chose to.

'How long will all that take?' snarled Ashley.

'Oh, at least six months, maybe even twelve. An audit can be a long, drawn-out process.' Uncle Alex held up a finger, to keep Ashley's comments in check while he finished. 'A necessary evil, I'm afraid.'

'That's bullshit.' Ashley's cheeks blazed red as he battled to keep his temper under control. The fingers on my neck squeezed hard. It was a battle not to react. 'We can go to court. Have the restriction overturned.'

'Oh sure.' A small tic of mirth twitched at the corner of Uncle Alex's eye. 'You could probably get a hearing schedule in the next two or three years. But, no matter what, the audit must be done. The lawyers will insist. Do you think it would be financially viable for you, Ashley? I mean to say, legal fees and court costs alone, could eat up a large sum of your personal money.' Uncle Alex shrugged, 'but maybe you can afford it. Tell you what; I'll give you the name of a couple of reputable legal firms. Why don't you see if they are willing to take you on as a client? I'd offer to do it myself but as I'm Faith's guardian and trustee, it would be a conflict of interest.'

'I don't need your recommendations. I have my own lawyers.' Ashley rose abruptly, grabbed my wrist and dragged me to my feet.

'Just start the paperwork for the Will, Alex.' There again was the emphasis on my uncle's first name. He flicked a business card across the table. 'Here's my email address. Let me know when everything is ready.'

Uncle Alex rose slowly to his feet. He looked weary. 'Faith darling, would you meet me for dinner tonight? Just the two of us? You don't mind, do you, Ashley? It has been a long time since I've had a chance to spend any time with my girl. Besides, there are personal family things I'd like to discuss with her. Things that you would find extremely boring. And if, as you say, you're going away on your honeymoon tomorrow, I won't get another chance any time soon.'

Uncle Alex had just gone off script. Here was the perfect opportunity for me to ask for help. I opened my mouth but before I could speak, Ashley butted in, 'Sorry, Alex, she can't. Today's my mother's birthday. Faith, the beautiful soul she is, has kindly arranged to take us all on a helicopter flight to view the city lights. Mum is really looking forward to the treat. Isn't that so, Sunflower?' He twisted the hand that gripped my wrist, and I could feel my bones crunch. I quickly nodded and the pressure eased. 'We would ask you to join us, Alex, but there's only room for four. Another time perhaps...when we get back from our honeymoon.'

Uncle Alex nodded, leant forward and kissed my cheek. 'I love you. Don't ever forget that,' he whispered.

His words nearly broke my heart.

* * *

There was no sign of MC when Ashley pulled his Jaguar into his parent's drive. He hooked his hand around the back of my neck and frogmarched me to our room. I stood in the corner of the room to wait as he bundled our luggage together.

'Come on,' he said, jerking his head.

Ashley shepherded me out the front door. The Jag was gone. In its place stood a brand spanking new Jeep Grand Cherokee. He threw our bags into the rear of the four-wheel drive.

'Get in,' he ordered.

Before I even got my seatbelt clipped he'd leapt behind the steering wheel and planted his foot on the accelerator. The Jeep peeled away from the house as though the demons of hell were chasing us.

'Drink.' He shoved a black, insulated water bottle into my hand. I hesitated. He raised a bunched fist. 'Drink it, now.'

I took a large gulp from the bottle. The water had an odd taste. Within minutes my eyes grew heavy. I began to nod.

'Where are we going?' I asked, from uncooperative, numbs lips.

'To our new home.' Anger fizzed in his voice. His face was still stained red from the encounter with my uncle.

'What about your parents, aren't we going to say goodbye.'

'I already have. Now be quiet,' he snapped. I clamped my mouth shut.

Within moments I drifted off to sleep. Every now and then, I would surface back to a fuzzy consciousness. When Ashley noticed, he would press another drugged drink onto me. Time passed. Eventually, a slap and bang against the side of the vehicle dragged me back to almost full awareness. Judging by the stiffness of my neck, the throb of my head and the nausea in my empty belly, I had been out to it for days. I cracked open gritty, light sensitive eyes to squint through my half-opened lashes at the world streaming past the window. We were speeding along a rough dirt trail. A red sunset cast a glorious hew over a clump of banksia shrubs that brushed long silver-leaf branches along the jeep's paintwork as we sped past. I rock left and right in my seat whenever the vehicle skidded around another shrub. Suddenly, we left the thick growth of native shrub and sped up a steep sand dune. The flora around us changed to coastal wind grass, spiky leaf spinifex and yellow-flowering clumps of ground cover. In the distance the ocean came into view and sparkled like fiery diamonds in the waning sunset. I glanced ahead and spotted an unpainted, fibro cabin, with a crooked, wooden veranda tacked along one side, a lean-to on the end. It had one window. A metal shutter, propped open by an iron bar, hung drunkenly over it. Next to the shack grew a beautiful bloodwood tree. Its majestic canopy shaded the rust riddled roof. I flicked a quick glance to an enormous metal-clad workshop to the right of the cabin. It looked new. Hanging off its side was an awning that acted as a garage over a sun damaged, cobweb covered caravan with deflated tyres. The tiny van didn't seem big enough to house a full-length bed.

I slid a sideways glance at Ashley as he skidded the SUV to a halt in front of the shack. He turned in his seat with an enormous smile on his face.

'Welcome home, Sunflower.'

# Chapter Twenty-Eight

Ashley's face was flushed with excitement. He dragged me from my seat. With a firm grip on my wrist he tugged me along a short sandy track away from the buildings. We halted at the edge of a sheer drop. A path, wide enough for one person to traverse, zigzagged down the slope and ended on a pristine creamy-orange sandy beach. The deserted shoreline ran on for kilometres each way before ending at the jagged outcrops of storm carved granite and brick red bedrock which curved out into the ocean before curling back to form a crescent. The vast expanse of water in the inlet was only broken by one small, atoll that was within wading distance of the shore. Loud seabirds, clustered on its bare, rocky surface, heralded their presence.

Like a proud parent, Ashley, gestured in a wide arc at the vast expanse of natural beauty. 'This is all ours. We will jog the entire length of this beach every morning.'

He turned and indicated to a spot near the shack where it seemed someone had attempted to mark out a garden bed. 'A perfect spot for the veggie patch. Let me know what you need. I'll get you the supplies.'

His hand tightened on mine and once again I was pulled along in his wake. This time towards the rust-tainted door of the shack. He flung open the door.

'Come and meet my cousin.'

My unwilling feet halted inside the door. I took one breath and gagged. The hot airless room reeked. There were unwashed dishes spread over every surface of the combination kitchen, dining, lounge area. They were joined by the debris of beer cans and upended empty bottles of Jim Beam. Flies and maggots feasted on rancid food that overflowed from a rubbish bin beside the stove. What I could see of the floor, hadn't seen a broom or mop in years.

A thin man was seated at a four person Formica table in the centre of all this squalor. His back was turned to us. All I could see of him was the tattoo of a snake that ran up his spine and disappeared beneath a long braid of greasy, black hair.

'Rattler,' said Ashley, seeming to ignore the mess. 'Come meet the wife.'

Rattler rose, in bare feet and shorts, turned and smiled.

'I believe we already know each other.'

Horror waged a fierce battle in my breast.

'Surprise!' said the rat faced weasel who'd haunted my time at UWA. That was until Ashley had come along and put a stop to it. Or so I had thought.

I stared up at my husband, then at his cousin, Russ Johnson. Fear and loathing filled me as realisation crashed in. Everything that had happened to lead me here had all been part of a plan. I turned to run. A rock-hard arm clamped around my waist like a band of steel. My feet were lifted from the floor. I kicked out, hard. Heard a grunt and a curse.

'Fucking bitch.'

RFW's hand snaked out and grabbed my flailing foot. There was a click that weighed my leg down. Startled, I glanced down to see what was going on. A shackle, attached to a length of chain and secured to a bolt in the floor, was clamped around my ankle.

I freaked. 'Let me go, you bastards,' I screamed.

Whirling my arms in a wild spiral. I aimed to land a punch on Russ, but missed. Altering my trajectory, I had a go at my husband whose arms were viciously clamped around my waist. I made contact. He let me drop like a sack of potatoes. I landed with a breath snatching thud on the floor. The jar of the impact vibrated up through my wrists and knees. Biting back the shuddering pain, I rolled slowly to my feet and hissed at the men.

'Fuck Cub, you need to teach her some manners,' snarled RFW.

Ashley's hand swung back. He slapped my face with an open palm - hard. My feet lifted. I flew across the room and tumbled into a heap amongst the disgusting rubbish flowing from the bin. Shell-shocked, I lay amongst the filth and cradled my stinging face with both hands. I bit back on the howl of pain trying to escape my lips. Ashley grabbed a handful of my hair and hauled me to my feet. He shoved his face close to mine.

'Stop blubbering. You will wear that,' he snarled, pointing down at the shackle on my ankle, 'until you learn to show respect and be a proper wife.' He shoved me away. 'Now get to work. I want this floor so clean I could eat from it.'

He turned to his cousin. 'Come on, Rattler. Let's you and me go build a bonfire on the beach. Bring the Beam with you.'

Russ smirked down at me. He made a show of rubbing the obvious bulge in the crotch of his shorts. 'Welcome home, darling.'

# 29

## Chapter Twenty-Nine

TWELVE MONTHS LATER

'Got everything?' asked Chappie.

'Crutches, check. My girl, check.' Ryan dropped his hand over the back of the seat to stroke Tennille's silky ear. 'Now it's time to go find my heart.'

Adam buffed him on the shoulder. 'Well, let's get this show on the road. Aunt Rosie – sorry, that's Lucy talking - Rosie said she'd meet us at the airstrip at the other end. You right for now?'

'Yo, bro.'

With a cheeky grin, Chappie hopped out of the pilot's seat of the Lancair Mako to wander around outside, doing pre-flight checks. Ryan settled into the co-pilot's position and studied with interest the multitude of dials and switches on the dash. He had no idea what half of them were for. He would get his brother to walk him through the various uses on the long flight. It would keep his mind occupied and off the stress he carried around about Burger.

Ryan was more grateful to his awesome brother than he could express. Unasked, Chappie had wangled a couple of days of leave from the air force and borrowed a plane from a friend, all to ferry

Ryan on this trip. Having the luxury of a private plane meant Ryan didn't have to run the gauntlet of stares and veiled comments by the airport public about his leg. Something he was still coming to terms with. More important to Ryan was the fact, Tennille, was free to loll on the back seat instead of being caged in a cold, noisy cargo hold of a commercial aircraft.

Ryan picked up the flight map to study their destination. They were following Rosie's instructions - well her orders really - and were about to fly to an isolated airstrip in the Kimberley. Ryan didn't understand why she had demanded he come to her stomping ground, but she had. He shrugged. Well, if it got him closer to finding Burger who was he to argue.

He'd kept busy over the last few weeks, filling his days with doctors' appointments, ADF rehabilitation clinic visits and physical therapy. Ryan had worked hard at the physio. To bolster what he learned and prepare for the introduction of a prosthetic limb into his life, he put in extra work at a local gym. Ryan and the orthopae-dic appliance guru at Interface Orthotics had discussed in depth the various prosthetics available, what was achievable and what would suit his new lifestyle - whatever that was going to be! He'd asked a ton of questions, done a lot of internet research. Finally, he'd settled on a robotic carbon fibre leg fitted with a silicone cup to house his stump. He'd decided to supplement this choice with a second pros-thetic. A blade. That nifty device would give him the flexibility to run on most surfaces. He felt he had most life contingencies covered with his choices, now it was just a waiting game as both limbs had to be designed and built to his specs.

In between all the medical stuff, Ryan's commanding officer had organised for him to attend a series of counselling sessions. Ryan hated the thought of having to share his inner turmoil and had argued against going. Major Steel sorted his objections out in three words.

'It's an order!'

Ryan obeyed the command. While he had hated the idea, he'd dragged himself along to the sessions anyway. He was surprised to learn that most of the turmoil he currently experienced was grief. With understanding came the chore of working through the grief process to achieve acceptance. One of the first steps he'd taken was to undergo a detailed debrief with Major Steel and his aide about the circumstances that had led to his injury. The outcome of that session, his sacrifice had been well worth it. Both his buddies had made it home in one piece.

When he asked the Major about the status of the men, Ryan had been informed, 'Physically both Baxter and Stone are fine, Captain Lamb, but a clandestine operation like the one you were involved with, can mess with a person's mind. It's caused by the stress of living on the knife edge for so long. So, keep up your own counselling sessions. They'll help.'

'Yes, Sir.'

'I understand you're going away for some much-needed R&R. While you do that, I want you to make some life decisions about your future.' Ryan had stared at him, knowing there was going to be a punch line. 'Unfortunately, military life is no longer an option for you.'

Well duh! Even a halfwit could have worked that out. Ryan bit back the words. He was still a soldier and the man before him was his commanding officer. He deserved to be treated with respect. 'Yes sir. I had already come to that conclusion.'

'Good man. In a few months you'll have to front the medical board. After that it will just be a matter of completing some paperwork. Thank you for your service, Captain Lamb. Dismissed.'

And with a final salute his thirteen years of service were over. Not even a how can we help you transition into your new life. Ryan wondered if Seadog and Rowdy had also been so summarily dismissed. Surprisingly, Ryan wasn't that upset for himself, mainly because he already had a life plan, but he was concerned for his friends.

He settled back into his seat and tugged out his mobile.

'Ho ho ho and a bottle of rum, it be Captain Shanks me hearty.'

'Hi ya, Seadog, how's it hanging man?'

'Medical board just snatched my career.'

'Fuck...no. What about Rowdy?'

'Him too. You, Shanks?'

'It's SNAFU, buddy. Paperwork's on the Major's desk.'

'Bummer. Well at least the surf's up dude.'

'Yeah, I hear ya,' said Ryan, pleased that at least Seadog had an outlet to occupy his time while he came to terms with the rapid changes about to hit his life. 'Listen, I've got a small job on and need some of that tactfully acquired gear you've got secreted away.'

'How'd you know about that?'

'I didn't come down in the last shower, bud.'

A grin tugged at his lips as he listened to Seadog's bark of laughter.

'Text me what you need, Shanks. I'll check out the golf bag. Do you need a hand with your job?'

'Not at this stage, but I'll let you know if the situation changes.'

'Cool. We're here if you need us, man,' said Seadog, before disconnecting.

Heartened by Seadog's breezy but sincere offer of help, Ryan plucked up the courage to bring up the photo of the woman he loved. Lovely, happy go lucky, Faith. Her face shone with the joy she had for life as she snuggled in tight against his chest. He ran a loving finger over her face and made a promise.

'If you're not disgusted by me, and can forgive me for my stupidity, Cutie, I'm going to spend the rest of my life keeping that radiance glowing bright.'

Adam leapt into the cockpit and startled Ryan from his musings. 'All right, Shanks?'

'Yeah, bro. Let's rock and roll, mate.'

\* \* \*

The aircraft touched down with a gentle bump. As they taxied to the end of the runway Ryan was still in awe at the spectacular landscape they had flown over. Whoever had described the remote Kimberley as rugged and barren had been wrong.

'Did you see that gorge and those waterfalls, Chappie? Weren't they just glorious? It's been a long time since I've seen that much water in one place.' Ryan grinned. An unusual warmth of happiness settled low in his gut. 'I wonder if anyone would mind if I kicked back with a can of beer and cast a line into that magnificent river we spotted. What was its name?'

'According to the map - Annie River. Sounds like an awesome plan mate, but fishing in the Kimberley man, you want to be careful. I reckon the river's full of croc's. You don't want to go feeding another limb to one of those beasties.'

The smile fell from Ryan's lips.

'Awe, shit, Shanks. How bloody insensitive can I be. You know I was kidding, right bro?'

From the rear seat, Tennille stuck her muzzle forward and rested her chin on Ryan's shoulder. She whined. Ryan flicked a glance between the two of them and snorted with suppressed laughter.

'Don't worry about it, Chappie. It's better when you don't pussy-foot around and pretend like nothing's happened.'

Chappie dropped a light punch on Ryan's upper arm. 'That's awesome dude, because you know I don't have a filter for my mouth.'

Ryan grinned as he glanced out of the cockpit windscreen. A white four-wheel drive was heading their way. It zoomed over tussocks of straw-coloured grass that surrounded the bitumen tarmac and kicked up a red dust trail behind.

'Looks like we've got a welcoming party,' said Chappie, taxiing the plane over to where a young man alighted from the driver's seat.

Ryan cast a curious glance over the face shaded by a well-worn Akubra. A riot of black curls fought to escape the hat. The eyes were protected by a pair of wrap-around sunnies, but the cheeks and chin, exposed to the sun, were deeply tanned. The youth stood at least 6' 6". His dusty moleskin trousers carried the stains of a rugged workday and his long slim legs ended at a pair of riding boots worn down slightly at the heels. He lifted a laconic hand to brush away a swarm of flies in a gesture of calm casualness and smiled.

Ryan reached for the ceiling to stretch his spine. He let out a long sigh of relief, it had been a long flight.

'Thanks man,' he said to his brother, not having to explain his gratitude for the trouble Adam had gone to on his behalf.

Chappie nodded. 'All part of the service. Wait here, while I go get your pegs from the luggage compartment.' He unbuckled his seat belt and flung open the door. Ryan was hit with a blast of scorching air.

He glanced down at his stump. It was neatly encased in beige stocking to protect the almost healed wound. His gaze flicked to the pair of loose-fitting shorts he wore and swore. Even though the outside temperature was in the high thirties, he should have worn jeans. He'd forgotten there would be people around to notice his leg.

'Suck it up soldier,' he growled, as the plane rocked slightly from his brother opening and closing cargo hatches.

Tennille climbed into the pilot's seat and panted in Ryan's face. 'Are you ready for a break girl?' he asked, stroking her silky ears.

Tennille gave a soft 'Woof,' and slurped her tongue around her muzzle.

Ryan shoved open his door. Tennille flew across his lap with a joyful yelp. She immediately began sniffing everything in sight. Chappie appeared in the open doorway, held out the crutches. He stood back, slid his hand into his pockets, to give Ryan space to manoeuvre himself from his seat.

The young man leaning against the vehicle straightened to his full height and ambled over.

'G'day. Welcome to Rivers Run. I'm Eli Morgan.' He held out a hand. Without even a flicker of pity he waited patiently for Ryan to adjust his crutches so he could shake hands.

'Ryan Lamb – call me Shanks. This is my brother, Chappie.'

'And the dog?'

'Tennille. She's not a problem, is she? If so, I'll just leave...'

'No, it's cool. Station's full of creatures of all descriptions. It's what we do.'

Tennille came charging towards them. She wiggled in delight when Eli bent down to give her a thorough scratch from head to tail.

'Rosie said to expect a visit from her tonight. She's really stirred things up around here with her hush, hush money hunt mission. The Brains Trust has already started work on tracking down bank accounts and some such. It's made Dad happy, as it's keeping our desert nymph off her feet. Doctor's orders...'

'Desert Nymph? Brains Trust?' The raft of names confused Ryan. He brushed away a fly that found his ear interesting and gave Eli a puzzled look.

'Sorry, that's Kelsey, my mum. Well step mum really. But, she's great. She's very, very pregnant and is supposed to stay off her pins. My dad, Bull - you'll meet him when we get to the homestead, and I saved her from the Tanami desert a couple years back. Dad would have met your plane today but as you know its tourist season. He and Uncle Jimmy had a fishing trip to host - more an excuse to catch some fresh barramundi for dinner if you ask me. Hey, you might like to cast a line in yourself. Anytime, just say the word. I love to fish.' Ryan's eyes widened with the rush of unstructured conversation pouring from the lad's mouth. Eli took a deep breath, and thankfully paused. 'Sorry, I'm told I sometimes talk too much.'

'You think?' Ryan held up his hand in apology. 'Sorry, Eli that was rude. I've just gotten out of hospital and my tolerance level is at an all-time low. Before that I was overseas for a long time where social niceties took a back seat. To top it off, Rosie asked me to come here to help her out with something, but didn't explain what. I know absolutely nothing about Rivers Run, the people or even what she wants from me. Maybe you'd like to help out with that.'

A smile that could have lit up a city block bloomed to life on Eli's sun-darkened face. 'Typical of our sneaky silver dingo. Okay, let's get your stuff loaded into the car and on the drive to the homestead, I'll tell you a little about the place. If I begin to waffle or go off track, just tell me to put a sock in it. No offense will be taken.'

Chappie sprawled like a wet rag along the back seat of the vehicle. He allowed his head to loll back against the headrest and closed his eyes. Tennille leapt in beside him and slurped her tongue along his cheek. He cracked open an eye and glared at her.

Ryan grinned. 'Was it a long flight, old man?'

'You know the air force motto, Shanks. Never miss an opportunity,' was Chappie's sleepy response.

Ryan snorted in amusement. He turned his attention to their driver. 'So, tell me about yourself, Eli?'

'Be careful what you ask for...I'll give you the short version...promise.' With a flash of teeth, Eli gunned the engine and headed across the open paddock at a breakneck pace. 'Amongst other things I'm a grazier, stockman, horse wrangler, manager, tour guide, and saviour of desert nymphs.'

'Wow...I bet there's a story or two there.'

'Sure is, but we don't have time for any of that right now. One day you should get Rosie to tell you about her *Well of Bones* investigation. For now, we'll start with basics. The Morgan family have been custodians of Rivers Run for over 100 years. Our land extends from just south of Mount Ibour, across the Northern Territory border and out into the Tanami Desert.'

'That's a fair whack of land.'

'Well over a million acres. And even though Rivers Run beef is one of the best meat products available on the market, drought and other economic factors have taught us not to put all our eggs in one basket. We run a variety of livestock – sheep, pig and a few goats. We also breed the best stock horses in the Kimberley. In the eastern paddocks there's a thriving orchard that my grandmother established. Rivers Run markets its own brand of jams and preserves.' Eli pointed to a distant mountain range. 'Over that escarpment is Zentra Hill. A diamond mining company has leased the mineral rights. Good luck for us. It provided enough funds to build Rivers Run Caravan and Cabin Tourist Park.

So, as well being in primary industry we've branched out into tourism and very popular we are too. During the dry season we provide our visitors with horse-riding treks to some of our beauty spots, fishing excursions and for those interested in experiencing the way of life on a cattle station, there's a display of stock skills.

We are especially popular with artists and photographers because of the diverse flora and fauna... sorry, now I sound like an advertising campaign.'

'Busy life. The four of you don't run the whole shebang on your own, do you?'

'Pfft...no, man. We employ about twenty hospitality staff plus a dozen stock hands. I'll bring you up to speed on the immediate family, as you probably won't meet the others anyway. There's Dad. His name is Charlie Morgan, but everyone calls him, Bull. Then there's my gorgeous step mum Kelsey. Mac – that's Uncle Jimmy, is the station's foreman. He was born here and is Dad's best friend. His wife, Naomi, is our camp manager and the best cook in Australia, if not the world. Then there's Aunt GG and my cousin Bren. She's Dad's sister. He's her son. You won't meet her. She's away overseas at some tourism conference. Cuz is here, though. He was apprenticed to a chef in the city but that went belly up when the country went into lockdown for that COVID 19 pandemic and all those city businesses closed. Naomi's taken him under her wing and between the two of them you'll never eat better in your life.' Eli rubbed his lean flat belly and gave a contented sigh.

From the back seat a sleepy voice murmured, 'Sounds very much like a family affair.'

'Oh yeah...Rivers Run is all about family. Just ask the Silver Dingo.'

'Aunt Rosie - you call her Silver Dingo?' said Chappie, cracking open his eyes with a look of disbelief.

'Not to her face. Not brave enough,' chortled Eli. 'You her nephew?'

Unchecked laughter rolled from Ryan's chest. 'He will be as soon as he can pin Lucy down on a wedding date.'

Adam sat forward and gave him a light buff on the shoulder. 'Well smart arse. I predict something similar for you in the future.'

The smile left Ryan's face. 'She's married remember. And probably won't want me,' Ryan added under his breath.

Eli gave them a puzzled look as he halted the vehicle in front of a large two-story granite homestead. He pointed along a stone path leading through a lush garden to a screen door. 'We always use the kitchen entrance as it's the heart of our home. Come on in, get yourselves settled.' He lifted his nose and sniffed. 'Awesome, Bren's cooking.'

Ryan's stomach rumbled at the tantalising smells wafting from an open window. It caught him by surprise. He hadn't really been hungry or even interested in food since his injury. Maybe it had something to do with how the hospital food may have been hot when it left the kitchen, but by the time it arrived on his bedside table it had usually congealed to a pile of cold unappetising tasteless mush.

Eli bolted from his seat. Ryan looked around with interest as he slowly emerged from the vehicle. Across the open area from where they'd parked, a small mob of cattle lolled around in a stockyard that was bordered by a row of transportable buildings. Eli pointed and began turning a slow circle as he recited, 'Cool rooms, stables, stock hand dining and activity hall, stockyards and station's offices, heavy vehicle garage and married quarters. Go five hundred metres along that walkway and you'll find the orchard and the stock hand's sleeping quarters.' He turned towards the house and gestured up, 'From the homestead's upstairs balcony, which runs around the entire second storey, you get fantastic views of everything including Annie River.'

Ryan stared. 'Where's the cabin and caravan park?'

Eli pointed south. 'Go back to the main highway. A few kilometres down the road is Rocky Watering Hole. We built the park there. Access is from Zentra Hill Road. We have a full-time manager living onsite to keep the business separate from home life.'

'Smart. But shouldn't you be taking us there?'

Eli grinned and headed towards the screen door. 'Nope.'

Ryan hesitated, shrugged and followed. Taking his time, he negotiated the step up to the slate tiled veranda. Tennille stood at the kitchen door wagging her tail, unsure if she would be welcome inside. A very pregnant strawberry-blonde woman with magnificent emerald-green eyes stepped out onto the porch and bent to pat her.

'In you go, beautiful,' she said to Tennille, holding open the screen door. 'My boy, Banjo will show you where the water bowl is.' With a polite yip, Tennille went through the complicated sniffing ritual of greeting an unusual striped cattle dog. Both animals wagged their tales, decided they were friends and trotted happily into the house. The woman placed a hand on the arch of her back as if it pained her.

Eli smooched her on the cheek. 'Shouldn't you have those feet up?'

'Stop fussing, Champ. You're as bad as your father. I promise you I've been sitting all morning.'

'Only because you've had your head buried in the computer following some interesting lead.' She blushed and turned away from his cheeky grin.

Eli winked at Ryan and disappeared through the door.

'Hi and welcome. I'm Kelsey.'

Ryan shuffled his crutch and held out his hand. She grasped it softly and he noticed a line of jagged silver scars along the length of her arm.

Adam leant around Ryan, 'Hi I'm, Chappie, and this is Shanks. Thanks for opening your home to us.'

She smiled kindly at Ryan. His stomach clenched. Here it comes, he thought, the sympathy and pity he didn't want. 'You are both very welcome. Rosie helped save me from some very bad people and to come to terms with some of the darkest days of my life. Any friend of hers is welcome.' Her words took him by surprise. 'Well, don't just stand there littering my doormat, come on in. The kettles on and Bren's made you some vanilla slices.'

'And they're delicious,' mumbled Eli, his mouth crammed full of food.

\* \* \*

Ryan sank back on the comfortable bed with Tennille snuggled in close to his side. His muscles and butt ached like a bitch. If he thought the people at Rivers Run were going to mollycoddle him because of his injury, he was greatly mistaken. After plying him with coffee and the best vanilla slice he'd ever eaten, Eli had dragged Ryan down to the stables. Adam followed along grinning like a cheshire cat.

'This is Roundup,' said Eli. Ryan stared at the saddled monstrosity of a grey horse with strong, sturdy legs. 'And this is my horse, Rainbow.' He stroked the muzzle of a coal black beauty in a loving gesture. 'Come on, Shanks, time to mount up and go check out the new calves in home paddock.'

Ryan stared to where his lower leg had once been.

'Not a problem,' exclaimed Eli. 'I've bolted a riding boot to the stirrup of your saddle. A bit of a makeshift job I'm afraid, but should work a treat.' And before he could protest Eli had tossed Ryan up into Roundup's saddle.

Chappie, the crafty devil, grinned and backed away. 'You're on your own, Shanks,' he stated. 'I need to go file the flight plan for my return trip tomorrow. Then the very talented Bren is going to show me where I can cast a fishing line.'

'Bastard.'

Chappie's laughter could still be heard as he beat a hasty retreat into the house.

'Right,' said Eli ignoring the interaction. 'I'll just shorten this stirrup strap. Bingo! There you go, Shanks, now you can slide your leg into the top of the boot and use it for balance.'

Eli was right. The improvised riding device did work a treat. And after Ryan gained some confidence, he enjoyed a fantastic ride in the open air. But oh boy! His unfit body sure protested now. He felt like he had as a new army recruit after his first PT session. Ryan had a lot of work to do to get back to fighting strength.

He was just drifting off to sleep when there was a gentle tap on his bedroom door.

'Yeah?' he called.

'Shanks,' Kelsey's soft voice floated through the wooden door. 'Dinner's ready.'

'On my way.'

Ryan forced his protesting body erect, heaved himself onto his crutches and made his way into the connecting bathroom to stare at the pain med's the doctor had prescribed for him. It would be easy to use a handful of them to get over this hump. He stared at his image in the mirror for a heartbeat. The whites of his eyes were sallow. Lines had etched grooves and crows' feet around the edges of his eyelids. The skin that peaked out from under his thick dark beard was pallid. Taking the meds was not the way back to health. With a growl he tossed the medicine bottle into the rubbish bin and stuck his head under the cold tap.

'Time to re-connect with the world,' he muttered as he opened the bedroom door.

A tantalising aroma filtered down the hallway. His stomach let out a long growl. Crutches bumped softly over exquisite Persian carpet as he followed his nose to the sound of happy laughter and clanking plates. Ryan hopped in to the country style kitchen that housed a double-sized cook top and oven, an enormous two door fridge and an eight-seater dining table. The window over the sink had been flung open and a soft, bush scent drifted in on the breeze. It was homely and inviting. Something he desperately missed.

'This looks awesome, Bull. We don't get fed like this by the air force,' said Chappie, drooling over a large platter of freshly baked bread rolls.

An older version of Eli tugged an enormous tray of baked fish from the oven. He turned, spotted Ryan loitering in the doorway and smiled. 'Hi, you must be Shanks. I'm Bull Morgan...hope you like barramundi.'

The kitchen door blasted opened. Detective Rosie Bloom blew in loaded down with laptops, boxes and demands.

'Eli, take this lot for me, will you. Hey there, Bull. I'm seconding your office and your wife.' She flicked an intense glance his way. 'Ah, Shanks, good, just the man...I've got some security footage I want you to start on...'

'Hello, Rosie. Good to see you too,' said Bull, without batting an eyelid. 'Dinners ready. Bren, set another place at the table, will you, buddy. Eli, store Rosie's gear in the lounge where the counterfeit crusaders can set up their base of operations.' He gave Rosie a meaningful look. 'The office chair is not good for Kelsey and the baby.'

Like a co-ordinated dance the lads sprang into action. Ryan watched with amusement as Rosie was divested of her burdens, guided to a seat beside Chappie and the table set around her, all before she had time to protest. Bull pointed to a chair on her right, 'Take a load off, Shanks.' He then raised his voice. 'Dinner's ready.'

Eli charged back into the room like a Melbourne Cup winner crossing the finish line. He dove into a chair. 'Awesome. I could eat a whole barra on my own I'm so hungry.'

'And when couldn't you?' laughed Rosie. She eyed him up and down. 'I swear you've grown another metre since I saw you last. How tall are you now?'

'6' 6" these days.' He held a white socked foot out for her to admire. 'Size fifteens. Gotta get me boots made by special order these days.'

'Eli, Rosie doesn't want your enormous clod hoppers in her dinner plate,' said Kelsey, as she waddled into the room.

Bull leapt forward, pulled out a chair and helped his wife ease into her seat. The love that radiated between them filled the room. Ryan felt a stab of yearning. This is what he had wanted for him and Faith.

'Okay, start,' said Bull.

Eli grabbed a plate and loaded it with roast vegetables and a great chunk of fish. He shoved it towards Ryan. 'Eat,' he commanded.

Ryan flicked a glance at all the food, then over to his brother. Bren was handing him a similarly loaded plate. Bull passed a third plate to a smiling Rosie. Ryan took a small forkful and was in heaven. The meal was marvellous. He ate more than he'd eaten in a long time.

The family were warm, friendly and inclusive. The chatter around the table drifted from the day-to-day activities of station life and preparations for the upcoming wet season to the Red Earth Festival being held in the nearby town of Mount Ibour the following weekend.

Rosie eased back in her chair, gave a discrete belch. 'Great tucker, as usual. Thanks. Can I talk business now, Bull?'

Charlie Morgan grinned. 'Nope. Coffee first.' In an aside to Ryan, his host said in a loud stage whisper, 'She's a brilliant detective, but has terrible people skills, especially when she's focussed on a case. So, we're training her.'

Ryan held back a snort of laughter. Not so Chappie. His soon to be aunt glared at him and said, 'Quiet you, or I'll put you to work too.'

'Sorry, no can do, Aunt Rosie,' said Chappie, smirking at the blush that rose to her cheeks by his ready adoption of her. 'I'm flying out in the morning and have flight planning to do. Besides I won't be back until army here,' he pointed to Ryan who watched the interaction with ill-concealed amusement, 'has whipped himself into shape.'

'I've been giving some thought to how we can help you with that' said Bull, filling Ryan's mug with coffee from a glass carafe. 'I know Eli took you riding today, Shanks. How'd that go for you?'

The earthy aroma of freshly poured caffeine tickled his nose. Ryan took a tentative sip from his mug. He hummed in delight as the flavoursome rich taste danced across his tongue. 'Delicious,' he sighed. Easing back in contentment he answered Bull's question. 'Once I got my balance worked out, it was great. I'd love to do more of the same.'

'Excellent. This week is round up time for the yearlings. We sure could use some extra help. Also, Kelsey my love, I know you're going stir crazy stuck here in the house. I thought we could set up our day camp at Bunyip Billabong and you could come along.' He flicked a gentle smile in his wife's direction before turning to the white-blond lad across the table. 'Bren you can run the BBQ and keep an eye on our expectant mum while I muster.'

'Oh, Charlie, I could swim and paint,' breathed Kelsey in delight.

Bull grinned, 'We all can...swim that is. The cool water will be excellent for your legs, my love. And Rosie, before you protest, your crack team of investigators can work on your tasks in the evenings. Okay?'

Ryan leant back and smiled, pleased he was about to have some useful activities to work with. 'Swimming would be great for me, too. And the freedom of being on horseback.' He sighed in delight at the normality of it all.

'Good, excellent, sorted. Okay Rosie, while the boys clean up the kitchen, you can take your crew through to the living room and discuss business.'

# Chapter Thirty

Ryan hit pause on the video. Taking his time he thoroughly examined each face on the laptop screen. Zero was his current enthusiasm rate for the tedious and boring frame-by-frame search he was doing of security footage. Rosie had given him the task saying it was important, so he plodded on. Not spotting the target, he took a moment to settle back in the soft leather of the armchair and rub at his tired eyes with the heel of his hands. A deep sigh escaped. Deciding he needed a break from the screen he stared up at the matt white ceiling and began to reflect on the current state of affairs. They didn't seem to have made much progress over the last couple of weeks. It crossed his mind that police work involved a lot of mindless plodding in the quest for hard evidence. Once something was found everything stopped while the technical people did their thing. And for what? What had they really achieved? Every step forward had led to a brick wall that they had to find a way around. First, the crime lab had made a match to the fingerprints lifted from Alex's empty wallet. Next, they had matched the same prints to one of the counterfeit notes spent at a Perth wine bar. But when forensics had finally gotten around to processing the fake money from the

Bottomless Keg, they'd come up with nothing useful. According to their fingerprint guru, the notes were a smear of confusion from being handled by too many hands.

Then there was the CCTV footage taken on the night Alex was attacked. The man following Alex had been identified as Russell 'Rattler' Johnson. It seemed Johnson had quite a rap sheet stemming from his youth. Most related to drug offences. Then he'd gone to work for the Watson family and seemed to have cleaned up his act - on paper anyway. He'd only been questioned once in recent times. Some poor sod had received a vicious beating, which had left him in a coma in hospital. As there had been no witnesses to the incident, or none that were willing to come forward and give evidence, no charges were laid. Eerily the injuries the victim bore wore a marked resemblance to those suffered by Alex. Ryan shook his head. While they might have a name to go with the fingerprints and could tie Johnson to the wallet and counterfeit notes, they had no proof he'd actually attacked Alex. Rosie had said a good lawyer was likely to argue that Alex had fallen and Johnson had just taken advantage to rob the man as he lay injured on the ground. Combined with the stories Chips had related to Ryan about how Johnson had stalked Burger at the university, Ryan decided that the vicious sod needed taking down.

Rosie's counterpart, Detective Graves, had sent uniforms on a search of Johnson's frequent hangouts, to invite him into the police station for a chat, but it turned out Johnson was an elusive soul. He hadn't been seen in any of his usual haunts for well over twelve months. Hence Ryan's current boring task. Rosie had him reviewing months of security footage gathered from businesses around Mount Ibour in the hope they could spot the bloke. Ryan wasn't holding his breath. The tediousness of the task, made him restless and frustrated. He couldn't see how this helped to find Faith.

Ryan flexed tight muscles in the back of his neck, hooked his fingers together and reached for the ceiling to ease away the tension. It felt better than good. Days in the saddle, rounding up cattle, strength building swimming sessions and eating tons of Bren's excellent cooking had all but dispelled the havoc his injuries had created. Both his physical and mental strength had improved thanks to the good people of Rivers Run.

Ryan lowered his gaze to settle on the woman propped up against a pile of pillows on the brown leather couch across the room from him. He couldn't suppress a smile. Kelsey had been a restful and interesting companion whenever he'd taken a break from the arduous roundup work Bull had assigned him. She was smart, articulate on a large range of subjects and her artwork was fabulous. Under her talented fingers the verve and beauty of the Kimberley sprang to life on the canvas, leaving the beholder with a sense of actually being present in the moment.

Ryan let his gaze drift over her legs and was pleased to see the cool waters of Bunyip Billabong had done their job. The swelling in them had visibly reduced. And she was doing the right thing by having them propped up on the couch while her nose was buried in a laptop. From what he could gather she was delving deep into the complicated world of finance and money laundering. Suddenly, a piece of financial information, that may or may not be relevant, floated to the forefront of his mind. He decided to share.

'Kelsey, my father owned a cash business in Albany. After he sold the café, the buyer used an intermediary to try and pressure him into selling our home as well. I found the offer and acceptance paperwork torn up on the table when I returned home. I have often wondered if that was some form of money laundering scam that the buyer was involved in. I have some info...' Ryan picked up his mobile to scroll through the texts he'd received from Burger about her snoopy investigation but Kelsey's words forestalled him.

'The intermediary for the purchase of the Beach and Rock was a man named Brian Zelinski. He then went on to manage it. Born March 4, 1972 to poor circumstances. His mother worked as a cleaner at the local school to earn enough money to put food on the table. His unemployed father spent the food money, plus anything else he could get hold of, on gambling and drink. Life until the father's death in 1980 was hell for them both.

After graduating top of his class in high school, Zelenski received a scholarship to study at UWA, where he excelled in accounting and business studies. At the age of 22, he graduated with a master's degree and proceeded to set up an accounting consultancy business in the city.' Kelsey cocked an eyebrow at Ryan. 'I'm still trying to track down where he secured enough funds to remodel himself as the affluent business man he appeared to his clients as, because almost immediately upon leaving university he dressed in designer suits, spent big, wined and dined with some very affluent people in the best restaurants and dated a high-profile very rich socialite. I suspect some creative accounting on his part to systematically syphon funds from the girlfriend's family accounts.

Once he'd established himself, Zelenski had his clientele introduce him to other lucrative cash business owners. Along the way he made contact with and gathered together a portfolio of questionable underworld entities. He became well-known as the font of knowledge for how to secrete money away to avoid paying taxes. On June 12, 1995 one of his clients, who didn't heed his advice, was arrested for tax evasion and money laundering. Zelinski was investigated but had covered his trail so well nothing against him could be proven. All charges were dropped, but as a result of the investigation most of his clients, fearing being caught up in the fallout, deserted him.'

Ryan listened in fascination as Kelsey reeled off facts, figures and dates from memory about all of the players and the amounts involved.

'To all intents and purposes, it looked like Zelenski's career was over, but that little hiccup secured him an introduction to Robert Watson. The Bear, as he is known in various underworld circles, recruited Zelenski to be his bookkeeper and financial advisor for a string of café's he owned. Brian Zelenski kept his head down and worked hard. It paid off for him because he rapidly moved up the organisation ranks until he had control of most of the finances. He then put in place a complicated but effective laundering operation. Had I been the taxation auditor for those books they would never have got away with what they have. One of the recommendations I'll make to Rosie is to secure a warrant so I can investigate the current auditor for graft and corruption.' She gave Ryan a wide smile and rubbed her hands together as though she relished the idea. 'Anyhoo, that's a whole other ball game. Now where was I...oh, yeah! 2020.'

Ryan suspected Kelsey hadn't lost her train of thought because she seemed to have a brain that whizzed through and recalled information like a computer.

'Bear Watson moved Zelenski from Perth to Albany. Put him in charge of a chain of businesses that Bearcub Enterprises already owned. He gave instruction for Zelenski to expand their portfolio in the district. Which he did. Over time the new ventures weren't as profitable as Bear expected. His son, Cub, became so concerned he went to Albany to investigate. So as to not raise Zelinski's suspicions of why he was really there, Cub spent time negotiating a contract with the Huntsmen Motorcycle Club to act as distributors for their burgeoning counterfeiting and drug operation. He also set about reviewing the books of each business they owned and put in place new procedures.'

Ryan raised his eyebrows. 'You know that how?'

'I've been following the Watson/Huntsman money trails. Bearcub Enterprises, Sasha Holdings, W&W Services are only some of a large portfolio of shell companies used by the Watson family to filter their dirty money overseas. Nimble Investments, another of their off-shore accounts, is used to bring the washed funds back into the country. It was Nimble Investments that bought the Beach and Rock Café on January 1, 2022, for $450,000 and made three unsuccessful offers for the Lamb home...Oh, but you already know that. Sorry.'

'Don't be sorry. I'm amazed you can memorise all that?' said Ryan.

A tinge of pink coloured Kelsey's cheeks.

'Don't be embarrassed. I think it's absolutely splendid.'

Kelsey wriggled in her seat. She stared at Ryan like she was ready to burst.

'Is there more?' he asked.

'There sure is, and it's dynamite.' She grinned. 'When I dug around the peripheral of Brian Zelinski's personal finances, I discovered he'd been making regular transfers to a Bermudan bank account. So, I took a closer look. Turns out Bear Watson's concerns were justified. Brian Zelenski was fleecing the Watson's and had managed to secrete away a large sum. Ten million in fact.'

'NO! Holy sh...underpants batman!' Ryan caught the profanity behind his teeth before it slipped out. He knew Bull didn't allow coarse language around his family. Ryan was totally on board with that. 'But why transfer the money to Bermuda?'

'It's a notorious tax haven. The Bermudan government doesn't impose tax on any corporate income, dividends, interest or royalties. Legally run corporate giants like Google and Nike are just some of the legitimate businesses who take advantage of the soft business laws by keeping their bank accounts there as well. In my past life I've tracked down a lot of embezzled funds to that country and found ways to siphon it back to where it belonged.'

Ryan stared at the angelic looking Kelsey in absolute amazement. She must have read the question in his eyes because she quirked an eyebrow at him. 'Don't look so surprised. I was a forensic accountant, auditor and special investigator for a firm that works in tandem with the Australian Federal Police, Interpol, Europol Criminal Asset Bureau and the FBI. And even if I say so myself, I was an exceptional forensic accountant, auditor and special investigator, before...' she waved her palm around the beautiful room.

'Do you miss it?'

'The hunt maybe, but not the being stalked by criminals or the extremely lonely life I led. Undercover work is hard.'

'Don't I know it,' muttered Ryan. Kelsey didn't so much as lift an eyebrow to question him about his last mission. Ryan appreciated the restraint. There were some things he just couldn't talk about. 'So is Zelenski still fleecing the Watson family?'

'Not anymore, three months ago, and two days before your girl's uncle was attacked, he fell down a flight of stairs in his home. Broke his neck and died.'

Ryan nearly choked. 'Just like my dad!' he managed to strangle out between clenched lips.

Kelsey eyes pooled in tears. 'Oh Shanks, I'm so sorry...'

'I've come to terms with his death, but it seems like an awful big coincidence that they both died the same way. What were the coroner's findings? Did they rule Zelinski an accident like my dad?'

'Coroners verdict is still pending. What makes me suspect this probably wasn't an accident is that on the same day he died Brian Zelinski's Bermuda bank account was drained of all its funds. I followed the money transfer...don't ask,' she said, lifting an elegant forefinger to halt the question on his lips, 'Just believe me when I say I have my ways. Anyway, the money took a circuitous route around the globe, bouncing in and out of accounts, until it eventually settled into the waiting arms of Nimble Investments.'

'Bloody hell!'

'Indeed.'

'Sorry, didn't mean to swear,' murmured Ryan. He gazed intently at the surveillance footage taken at a local nursery while he mulled over everything Kelsey had just told him. 'Burger, sorry that's Rosie's niece, Faith Bergman, I mean Faith Watson.' It hurt him to say it. Kelsey nodded, gave a gentle, understanding smile but didn't interrupt. 'She once told me that Brian would receive satchels of cash, late at night, at the café. They were delivered via a courier service called Dash Deliveries.'

'Those satchels contained skimmings from the tills of Albany's nightclubs and pubs. I understand Bearcub Enterprises own quite a few of them,' said Rosie, stalking into the room. 'Also, some of it was business protection money collected by Huntsmen enforcers, on Zelinski and Watson's orders.'

'Hello Rosie, nice to see you again.' Kelsey smiled in welcome, not showing any surprise that the detective sailed into her lounge room unannounced. 'Are you staying for dinner?'

'As I've been reliably informed by the Morgan menfolk, on more than one occasion, the best steaks in the world come from Rivers Run. The answer is, of course I'm staying for dinner. I've already put my order in with Bren.' Rosie shoved away Ryan's socked foot that was propped up on the coffee table. She settled her butt in its place. Hands on knee she stared at Kelsey. 'Because of your excellent work with the Dash Deliveries manifests, we've traced the collection route for some of the money. I've emailed Detective Graves. She's sending undercover officers to Albany to sniff around. Their job is to follow the main players and identify who they are shaking down. When she has a handle on everything, they'll execute search warrants and make arrests.' She cocked her chin to look over her shoulder at Ryan. 'Shanks, my lad, we're running out of time. Once word gets out about the takedown, Bear Watson is going to bolt...if he hasn't already.'

'What do you mean?' asked Ryan.

'Well, unfortunately for us, Alex's private investigator got careless. He was spotted. Now he's lost track of Bear. Which is a bugger because I planned to get him to lead us to his son...and Faith.'

'So will finding this Johnson bloke be of help?'

'It's an avenue. The cousins are very close almost joined at the hip. Around the time Cub disappeared, so did Johnson. Apart from that one time in June, when we caught Rattler on camera, no one has seen him. I wouldn't be surprised if they were in hiding together.'

Ryan spun his laptop around to show her an image on the laptop screen. 'I've found this.'

Rosie leant forward and studied the screen. Russ Johnson stood in line at a cash register hugging a large, potted fruit tree in his arms.

'What an odd thing for him to buy,' she murmured.

'Yeah, check out the scowl on his face. He sure doesn't look happy about it, does he?'

'It screams of domesticity,' said Kelsey, flicking a quick glance over the image.

'Where was this footage taken?' asked Rosie.

Ryan checked the file. 'Green Fingers Nursery.'

'They're on Kapok Street, in town,' said Kelsey. 'New owners took over middle of last year. I do their taxes for them.'

Ryan checked the file date and his heart gave an excited thump. 'Rosie, this footage is only two days old!'

Rosie folded her arms across her chest. Her eyes glazed as she stared up at the ceiling. 'Hmmm...so Rattler Johnson was in Mount Ibour two days ago, buying plants,' she murmured. 'I'll get Bayden to check their takings for anything amiss. You never know...'

A freshly showered Bull strolled into the room bringing with him a waft of lavender and something wild and spicy. Kelsey closed her eyes and drew a deep breath in through her nose. A smile lit her face.

'How's the investigation going?' Bull asked as he ambled over to the couch to move the cushions so he could settle in behind his wife. She snuggled back against his large chest and rebalanced the laptop on the top of her rounded belly. It jumped. Bull laughed and placed his giant mitt gently on the lower portion of Kelsey's stomach so it cupped the baby bump. 'Hello wife...hello daughter.'

The laptop jumped again. Bull gave a goofy grin. Rosie rolled her eyes.

'God save me from besotted men,' she said, but Ryan noticed the softness around her eyes and lips as she watched the loving couple. She took a sudden breath and, in complete contrast to the look, she began to spit out orders. 'Kelsey, do some of your whizz bang magic will you. See if the Watson's or anyone associated with them, have a finger in any local pies.'

'Sure.'

'Shanks, check the rest of the security footage for that day. Main Street, shopping centre and pub. Let's see if he went anywhere else.'

Ryan nodded. His mobile chirped. He scowled at the screen, annoyed at the interruption, just as things were starting to get interesting. He pushed the annoyance aside when he saw the caller was his brother.

'G'day, Chappie. How are the skies, bro?'

'Blue and smooth, Shanks, blue and smooth,' was the laughing reply. 'Listen up old chap. A rather large, oblong shaped box arrived for you this morning. Marked orthopaedics.'

Butterflies of excitement kicked into gear low in Ryan's gut.

'You bewdy,' he exclaimed. 'It has to be my blade. The robotic limbs not supposed to be ready for at least three months. Can you...'

'Already done. It went by overnight courier. You should get it in the morning.'

'Awesome, thanks buddy.'

'And one of your mates, Sea doggy, is it?'

'Seadog. What about him?'

'He called by the airbase, gave me a bag of gear for you.'

'About time.'

'Come on, spill, what's in the backpack?'

'Some stuff from his golf bag to help me find Burger,' chuckled Ryan.

'Ah, I see.'

'I bet you do,' laughed Ryan. 'Did you send it?'

'Is the Pope catholic? I taped it to the prosthetic box for you. How long before you find our girl? I want to get married.'

'Working on it, bro. Talk soon.'

'Roger wilco.'

Ryan grinned. Chappie always lifted his spirits.

'Good news?' asked Bull.

'Sure is. I'll soon be mobile. My prosthetic blade is on its way. Chappie reckons it'll be here in the morning,' said Ryan, flashing him a smile. 'Now Rosie, tell me, what are we going to do about finding this Johnson bloke?'

'Now that we have some evidence he's in the district, Senior Sergeant George can get uniforms to keep a sharper eye out. Bayden and I will do the rounds of the real estate offices to see if anyone has rented a place to him or Cub...'

'Charlie, what do you know about a place called Brahman Crossing?' interrupted Kelsey, glancing over her shoulder at her husband.

'It's an old cattle station. The property line skirts the national wildlife park and runs right up the Eastern Arm of Cambridge Gulf. It was owned and run into the ground by a bloke called Bob Middleton. He died about ten years ago.' Bull rocked his hand from side to side indicating the time frame was a rough guess. 'After his death, the family put the property on the market as they lived in Asia and weren't interested in coming back to run a floundering business. Parks and Wildlife made some murmurs about absorbing the land into the national park but the property was snaffled up before they could raise the funds from the federal government. The new owners sold off what was left of the cattle and declared the land would be kept as a nature reserve. About two years later the homestead and outbuildings were leased to a business conglomerate intent on establishing a wellness centre. Rumour has it that Red Earth Wellness is a very exclusive, incredibly expensive place but I've never heard of anyone who has been there. I don't know what they do for staff - not anyone local that's for sure.'

'Why do you want to know about Brahman Crossing?' asked Rosie. She stood and leant on the back of the couch so she could stare down at Kelsey's laptop screen.

'Because Red Earth Wellness were only granted a ten-year lease for Brahman Crossing homestead and that lease becomes due in ten months. There have been a number of attempts to buy the property but they were all rejected which is a good thing, because when I dug a little deeper into the business structure of Red Earth Wellness, I discovered they are a subsidiary of Nimble Investments.'

'No...' drawled Rosie, leaning closer to the computer screen.

Excitement fluttered to life in Ryan's breast. 'And this property, it's nearby you say, Bull?'

Charlie nodded, 'Northwest of Mount Ibour.'

Ryan stared up at Rosie, with a glimmer of hope in his chest. 'How about I reconnoitre the place? See who's hanging around the homestead.'

Rosie's remained silent. Sick of reviewing security footage and with a desperate need to be more physical in the investigation, Ryan shuffled forward in his seat and pushed his talents forward. 'Come on, Rosie...this is the kind of stuff I'm good at.'

Rosie didn't blink. 'No, we can't. Police need probable cause before they can poke around. Nimble Investment holding a lease on a property is circumstantial at best,' she murmured.

'I'm not police,' stated Ryan. 'What's to stop me?'

'Don't even think about it buddy,' growled Rosie, her blue eyes going ice cold.

'But that Rattler bloke could be there, and so could Cub.'

'No, I need untainted evidence.'

'The case isn't as important as finding Faith.'

'No, it's not!' snapped Rosie. 'But we have to do this by the book.'

Bull cleared his throat. 'Rosie, I'm sure Shanks could do this without jeopardising anything or anyone. Besides, shouldn't finding your niece be our first priority?'

'Yes, it is, but I still need a bloody good reason to go poking around out at Brahman Crossing. A photo of a man carrying a plant doesn't give me that.'

'No, but the property paperwork might,' breathed Kelsey.

Rosie's head snapped around. 'Why do you say that?'

'When I dug deeper into the ownership of Brahman Crossing, I discovered the title is held by The Faith Bergman Trust.'

Ryan's shoulders straightened. He opened his mouth to announce, whether the stubborn detective liked it or not, he was going out to Brahman Crossing to take a look. From the corner of his eye, he caught the slight shake of Bull's head in his direction. Ryan clamped his lips shut.

Rosie straightened to her full short stature, 'Cancel my dinner. I need to go chase up these leads.' She stalked from the room with her phone plastered to her ear. 'Bayden, get down to Green Fingers Nursery...'

With the help of his crutches, Ryan rose, 'Bull, Kelsey, when my stuff arrives tomorrow I'll be heading off. Thank you for your hospitality.'

'Hang on a sec,' said Bull, carefully moving Kelsey aside and struggling to his full height. 'If you plan to go sightseeing in the national park you'll need an appropriate vehicle, maybe a camera and some fishing gear. Let's head on up to the vehicle shed. I'll show you what I can lend you.'

'Are you sure? Rosie is going to be furious when she finds out where I've gone. I don't mind for myself but I don't want to cause you guys any grief?'

'What's she got to be angry about? I'm lending you a buggy so you could take a look around the district and at the national park.'

'You do know I'm going to Brahman.'

'Of course we do,' said Bull, flicking a glance towards Kelsey who nodded her agreement. 'And we consider finding your girl is more important than any paperwork. So does Rosie, it just that she's constrained by the legalities of her job. But you can bet your boots she'll move heaven and earth and use even the flimsiest excuse to get a warrant for Brahman Crossing. Now tell me what other equipment you're going to need to supplement what you've already got coming?'

They fell into a discussion about what Bull could provide as they wandered out of the house and up to the vehicle shed.

# Chapter Thirty-One

After following the GPS co-ordinates to a spot close to where the Brahman Crossing homestead was located, Ryan manoeuvred the off-road dune buggy into a clump of brush situated at the bottom of a shrubby slope. Tennille leapt from the passenger seat and waited patiently for him to balance himself on his prosthetic blade. A few leafy branches tossed over the vehicle ensured it was hidden from prying eyes. Before him a faint animal trail led the way up a small ironstone dotted hillock. With Tennille by his side, Ryan took his time to scramble along the loose, stony earthen track. Learning to walk on the new limb was a challenge. His brain didn't want to trust the device and he found himself continually staring down at the position he placed the blade each time he moved, trying to judge whether it was safe enough to trust his weight to it. A day's practise was all he'd allowed himself before the urge to head out and reconnoitre Brahman Crossing overtook him. He knew he was going to be in deep shit with Rosie - but she'd just have to suck it up. Doing something physical towards finding Faith was more important to him than abiding by stifling police protocol.

When he reached the peak of the hillock, Ryan lowered himself to his belly and crawled to the edge of the ridge. Below was an expansive valley, one third of which was covered in a lake. A magnificent waterfall thrummed as it cascaded down from the bordering iron-banded cliffs, feeding in fresh water. A magnificent rainbow rose from the plumes of spray, splashed up and arched elegantly over the wildlife teeming along the billabong's surface and shore. An imposing kangaroo buck, his chest muscles rippling with strength, stood guard over a court of does and joeys as they grazed on a lush stretch of grassland that spread beyond the trees near the shore. Lorikeets and rosellas chattered noisily as they flashed their colourful feathers and swooped amongst the branches of giant bloodwood, flowering wattle and river gums. It was a glorious sight. Ryan could envision himself swimming in those waters, carefree and happy with Faith at his side. He shook his head. He couldn't get ahead of himself. Who was to say she would come here with him or that she even wanted to see him?

Ryan forced his daydream back into its box and focussed his attention back to the task at hand by hauling out a pair of binoculars from his backpack. About a kilometre south of where he lay, he spotted a two-storey brick and stone building. It had a satellite dish and solar panels on its roof.

'Must be the homestead,' he murmured.

He studied the structure. It couldn't possibly be the exclusive wellness centre, Bull, had spoken of, because, although the building had good bones, it was in a depressing state of disrepair. Dry leaves dangled from dust laden spider webs under blocked and sagging gutters. The soffit had developed dark mildew stains. The roof needed replacing. What was left of the solar panels were cracked and covered in scale. The house surrounds told a similar tale. Flower beds were overgrown and choked with weeds. Pathways poorly maintained, some areas showed wide cracks where gushing water had washed its foundations away. Trees and branches, felled by some forgotten storm, rotted in place. Ryan shook his head. What a shame. With some care and attention, the homestead and garden could be a handsome and arresting sight.

Desperate to catch some sign of movement in the house, he focussed the binoculars onto the windows. The paint flaked shutters were closed. He flicked a glance at the front door. The presence of a hasp and staple secured by a large padlock meant the house was probably unoccupied. Ryan's heart sank as a stream of sour acid did a swirl through his gut. Faith wasn't here. He'd been so sure. With a curse he rolled onto his back and stared up at the cloudless sky. Tennille whined and used her muzzle to give him a nudge. Her action jolted Ryan back from a descent into the dark, unproductive thoughts that often hovered on the edge of his mind. His therapist had called it PTSD. Ryan just called it a pain in the arse.

'I'm okay girl. I'm just reassessing.' He rolled back onto his belly and dragging his thoughts away from the dark. 'Don't worry, we'll find her.'

Tennille ran her raspy tongue up his cheek. With a smile Ryan gave her a scruff between the ears before lifting the field glasses once again. This time he scanned the valley.

'Let's see what else we've got other than mature trees, flocks of skylarking birds, fat and contented kangaroo. Well, looky here, Tennille, we have more trees. Sorry, can't see any humans yet, girl.' A slight movement among the bloodwoods caught his attention and his grip on the binoculars tightened. 'Hang on a sec...' he breathed, and almost jumped out of his skin when a mob of emus, their long, thin legs elongated like ballerinas dancing across a stage, charged out from the shady tree belt and swerved, at full canter, towards the fresh water.

'Fuck! Sorry, Tennille, bloody false alarm.' He rubbed a clenched fist along the centre of his chest where a shaft of disappointment prodded him. 'We can't expect to find our quarry in the first five minutes, can we? Just be patient, Ryan,' he told himself.

Cranking his neck Ryan began a search further up the valley. As he turned the binoculars north, he discovered his view was blocked by the large boulder that currently threw shade over them both. Ryan stared at it. The large chunk of ironstone hung out over the side of the ridge. Rolling along the ground, he manoeuvred his way around a clump of spiky spinifex to the base of the rock. Melding himself against the stone's surface he slowly rose to his feet and carefully crawled up the boulder. The pattern of his camouflage clothing, combined with the rocks mottled colouring, effectively made him seem like part of the environment. Ryan peered north and caught the gleam of sunlight striking something bright and metallic. Ignoring the sear of heat from the sun-baked rock as it seeped through the heavy cotton twill of his shirt and pants he trained his glasses onto the reflection.

He gave a wry chuckle.

Beyond the belt of trees, the emu mob had just evacuated, was a row of stone walled cottages.

'Now what have we got here?'

From his position Ryan couldn't get a clear view of the buildings. The canopy of the bloodwoods hampered his view. Sliding back to the base of the boulder he leaned down to give Tennille a firm pat on the ribs. 'Come on, Girl, it's time to take a hike north. I want to see if we can get a better look at those buildings.'

Still wary of the prosthetic, Ryan took most of the descent down the slippery slope on his butt. The last thing he needed was to take a tumble on the loose gravel and break something. Not only would it piss him off it would give Rosie a whole arsenal of ammunition to throw at him for disobeying her.

'One in the eye for you Silver Dingo,' he muttered, when he made it to the bottom of the slope without incident.

Standing, hands on hips with a grin of satisfaction on his face, Ryan surveyed the area he intended to traverse. He estimated he'd need to trek about a kilometre to take up residence on the cone shaped hillock jutting out of the red earth between two pointed slopes. With a click of his tongue for Tennille to follow, he set out slowly to hike to the base of the new ridge. After a few uneven steps Ryan began to trust himself and push his prosthetic. He increased his speed and strode out with more confidence. He found that the more he relied on the blade to do what it was designed to do the more his own self-belief and confidence grew. By the time he slid into position at the base of another ironstone boulder on the cone shaped hillock he felt confident he was getting the hang of the capabilities of the blade.

Peering through the field glasses Ryan found he had an excellent view of a row of six squat stone cottages. Each one had corrugated colourbond roofing, solar power panels, and a view to die for. This was also the point where the excess water in the billabong over-flowed. It trickled down a sheer face of a flat sheeted granite cliff, into a rocky waterway that flowed about fifty meters below. Ryan imagined the gentle burble of this waterfall could quickly change to a deafening roar when the heavy seasonal rains came. He was impressed to see how each of the cottages had been designed and built to take advantage of the breathtaking view by having its ve-randa cantilevered out over the edge of the cliff so it projected out into space.

Reflected sunshine dazzled Ryan's eyes as it gleamed from some-thing metallic on the far side of the second cottage. He focussed the field glasses on the spot and could just make out a portion of a car's headlight and the chrome of a vehicle's front grille.

With a satisfied grunt he traced the length of the cottage's veranda with the binoculars. He noted the outdoor furniture was tatty, but serviceable. Lounging chairs had been spread untidily around the glass, outdoor table as if recently abandoned. An open bottle of wine still had chill beads running down its length. Satisfied by the promising signs that the cottage was currently occupied, Ryan scanned further along the patio's length and came across an ashtray on the floor next to a hot tub. He lifted his gaze and adrenalin surged. Along with the steam rising from the hot water there was a thick cloud of smoke. A stocky arm lay along the edge of the tub with a cigar clamped between ringed fingers. The arm moved, took something from the other hand and reached over the side of the tub to put a glass of wine down on the floor. When the head of wet, dark hair was lifted, Ryan was able to study the facial features of the middle-aged man wallowing in the hot water.

'Bloody hell,' he murmured, when he recognised the face from the vast array of photo's Rosie had taken great delight in shoving under his nose over the last couple of weeks. 'I've only gone and found Detective Bloom's much reviled and elusive Bear Watson. Boy Scout points for us, Tennille,' he grinned. 'We've just gathered another piece of information that supports her justification for that bloody search warrant she's on about.'

Tennille, lying on the ground beside him lifted her head and gave him a red-eyed stare before resettling her head back onto her paws and letting out a soft snort.

Ryan rolled his eyes. 'Glad you're interested,' he chuckled. Tennille ignored him and began to snore.

Ryan shook his head and went back to watching the man wallow in the tub. Half an hour later the patio glass door was flung open and a bald, heavily tattooed man dressed in a black polo shirt stepped out onto the deck. He spoke, tapped his wristwatch and held up a towel. Bear rose from the watery depths of the tub. Stark naked he alighted onto the deck and stood with his hands on his hips, letting the water drip from his bare skin, as he displayed himself to the world with a self-satisfied smile. He spoke and pointed to the scenery. Baldy looked at his watch. Bear clenched the cigar between his teeth, took the towel from his companion's hand and rubbed it vigorously over his wet hair. Tattoo man spoke again and Bear flicked the remnants of his cigar over the wooden railing. It arced out into the void before taking the long plunge to the river below. Bear nonchalantly patted his minder's upper arm as they strolled into the cottage.

Ryan yanked a notebook from his backpack and wrote down a detailed description of the companion as he waited for further events to develop. It wasn't a long wait. In less than half an hour both men stepped out of the sliding door. Bear was now dressed in bone coloured, tailored slacks with a short sleeved, button down, linen shirt that had been immaculately pressed. They headed down the side steps of the building, towards the car. A minute later the blue four-wheel drive pulled away.

'Come on Tennille,' said Ryan, scuttling down the slope. 'Let's see where they're going.' At a fast clip the man and dog raced to where they'd hidden the dune buggy.

# 32

## Chapter Thirty-Two

With a prayer, I crawled around on my hands and knees and gave the wax on the ugly brown linoleum a final buff. Hopefully this time the shine would pass my husband's critical inspection. I sat back on my heels to ease the ache in my back. Ashley chose that precise moment to storm in through the door. He didn't bother to wipe his feet. I stared at the clumps of soil and dried grass he'd trekked with frustration. Quickly I lowered my head. It would only take a wrong look and Ashley would give me another black eye to match the one I already sported.

'Stop slacking off, woman,' he growled. 'Get into the kitchen. I want you to cook a decent roast lunch. My dad's on his way.'

I flicked him a surprised glance but Ashley didn't notice. He'd spun on his heel and was staring at the dirty trail his boots had left.

'For god's sake, Faith, look at this mess. Can't you do anything right? Do you enjoy the back of my hand or something?'

'No, Ashley,' I squeaked, cowering into a small heap on the floor to make myself less of a target. I had worked hard to convince him he'd broken my spirit in the hope he would keep his hands to himself. 'I'm sorry. I'll do better. I promise.'

'Fix it. NOW!' he yelled. 'And make sure lunch is better than the usual bloody muck you serve up.'

The knot in my chest tightened. I knew his words were meaning-less because everything I served, he ate with gusto, but the constant criticism was like water dripping on a stone. It had worn away at my self-worth so badly that I was unsure if anything I did was right. I chewed on my bottom lip and silently crawled past his booted foot. With the soft cloth in my hand, I scooped the dirt into a mound. Every moment I expected him to lash out at me. For once he kept his hands and feet to himself. With a grunt he stalked back out into the yard. I let out a grateful sigh. It was a relief he hadn't felt the urge to teach me a lesson.

I rose to my feet and carefully disposed of the dirt in the dust-bin by the stove. Every item of cleaning gear I'd used was returned to its regimented place in the cupboard under the sink. I double checked its neatness. A noise in the yard drew my attention. From the kitchen window I spotted Ashley, by the bloodwood tree-stump on the far side of the yard, digging a hole with a flat bladed spade.

What the hell?

Ashley considered all activity in the garden my responsibility. He wouldn't willingly be digging a hole for any of the potted fruit trees I still had to plant. Curious, I took a couple of steps backwards so I wouldn't be seen peering out and watched as he flung sandy loam in all directions. My nosiness was quickly rewarded. After a few more stabs with the spade there came a solid thunk. Ashley stopped digging, bent to scoop away a few handfuls of earth away and eased up a large, rectangular, plastic tub. He tucked the box under his arm and headed to the workshop. This was where he and Russ spent most of their days. I had no idea what they did in their hidey-hole, I didn't really care, so long as they weren't bingeing on alcohol. Even better, it was time I was left in peace. A lone tear rolled down my cheek. With a jerk I brushed it away, angry at myself. I couldn't afford to fall down the pity hole. If I did it would break me. I lashed out with my foot and slammed the cupboard door shut. The chain attached to the shackle around my ankle rattled. I stared down at it and wondered if it would be safe to try and pick the lock? I had to be careful – any scratch marks or signs that I'd attempted to unlock the mechanism would result in severe retribution from my husband. Bugger it, I would give it a go. I checked out the window to see if the coast was clear. The height of the sun indicated it was late morning. With a start I recalled Ashley's orders about lunch. If I didn't get a move on with the meal it wouldn't be ready on time and the result, for me, would be painful. I let out a curse. I would have to try later.

I raced over to open the noisy rattle trap of a refrigerator that daily threatened to give up the ghost and die. Yanking open the freezer door, I delved amongst the small collection of frozen packages until I came across a leg of lamb. This I dropped it into a bowl of hot water to defrost while I set about peeling the carrots I'd picked from the vegetable patch earlier. The soothing routine freed my mind to mull over today's turn of events - Robert Watson's visit. It was a huge surprise. By my reckoning, and the change of seasons, we'd been living in the secluded shack for well over twelve months. During all that time neither of Ashley's parents had visited. Not that I was surprised by his mother's absence. From the snippets of conversation, I'd overheard from Ashley's evening chats on the phone with his father, I'd worked out that Sasha Watson spent a lot of time at a so-called health resort. I suspect health resort was a euphemism for a rehabilitation clinic. At no time had there been any indication Robert planned to travel to our neck of the woods. My imagination went into overdrive. It spat out a range of bizarre ideas and scenarios that cascaded over each other in an attempt to come up with a reason for the visit. Sanity finally prevailed. Robert probably just missed his son.

The roast sizzled in the oven; the veggies prepped. It was time to make a dessert. It would be expected. I ignored the chugging hiss of the fridge when I opened the door to scan the shelves for an idea of what to make. My roving glance fell on a bowl of cooked rice left over from the previous night's curry dinner. Perfect! I'd throw together a spiced apple rice custard. The pudding could be slipped into the oven to cook as soon as meat came out.

Satisfied my food preps were complete I headed into the bedroom to change out of the scruffy house dress I had on. I stared in disgust at the two designer frocks that hung on a peg on the back of the door. Ashley had bought them. Neither dress was to my taste but whenever he was in the mood, he would insist I wear them. I hated those times because they always ended the same – with me being brutalised. With a sigh I opened my bedside drawer to pull out fresh underwear and stared at the meagre contents contained within. There was a faded olive housedress, similar to the grey one I currently wore, a pair of running shorts, a plain grey tee shirt along with some serviceable underwear. I had no other possessions except for one pair of scruffy running shoes that Ashley kept locked away. On the day we'd arrived at the shack, Ashley and Russ had lugged all my gear, including phone, laptop, family photos and clothing down to the beach where they'd stacked them on top of an unlit bonfire. When all was ready, Ashley had dragged me down to the beach and forced me to watch Russ pour petrol over everything.

'Say goodbye to your old life,' he'd smirked, as he added a lighted match.

I watched as all my connections and mementos with the past were destroyed in a ball of fierce flames and acrid smoke. This was Ashley's first lesson, designed to teach me he was my master. Since that day, my life had been reduced to caring for and feeding two bru-tal men, a beach run once a day and the nurturing of a productive vegetable garden. The last two activities were done under Ashley's strict supervision. The rest of the time I was kept barefooted and chained in the shack. Ashley kept my shoes locked in a small safe, along with the satellite phone, shackle and cars keys. Every aspect of my life was controlled by him. I was even told if and when I could eat or sleep. Any amount of affection I had ever felt for the man had long since died.

As much as I didn't want to wear it, I selected Ashley's favourite dress to put on. It was powder-blue with a flared skirt. I dragged a hair brush through my thick tress before twisting it into a neat bun at the nape of my neck. Nervous energy fizzed through my veins as I pondered the risk of asking Robert Watson to mail a letter for me. I ran my finger along the chipboard at the back of my bedside cabinet to find the loose piece of veneer and fished out a makeshift envelope I'd hidden there. It had been crafted from a food box and was sealed with a flour paste. I stared at the address I'd scratched on its face with a fire blackened stick.

*For the urgent attention of Detective R Bloom, Western Australian Police Headquarters, Perth, Western Australia.*

Inside, on a piece of charred paper I'd managed to salvage from the incinerator, I'd written in small, cramped letters - *Aunt Rosie, please help me. I'm being held captive. We are living in a shack some-where on the north western coast. We are about three hours from the nearest town, Faith.*

It wasn't much in the way of information. In the past year I'd only ever been away from the shack once. That had been a few months ago. Russ had been away at the time. Our food supplies were low and to Ashley's horror he'd run out of Jim Beam. While I lay blindfolded on the back seat of the car, he'd driven us to a town so we could shop. Before I been allowed to exit the vehicle Ashley had threatened that if I looked at anyone or spoke without his permission, the lives of my uncle and cousin would be forfeited. I obeyed, of course. I couldn't risk their lives. I did try to take furtive notes about my surroundings while in town, but the place was quiet and all I really saw was supermarket shelves and a few parked cars. The lady at the checkout made some joke to Ashley about the cricket match that was on and if it hadn't been for us, it would not have been worth opening that day.

After our return to the shack the idea of preparing a letter to my aunt came to mind. When we went to town again, I might be able to leave the envelope on a shelf in the supermarket and hope someone would pick it up and mail it for me. It was a long shot. I had no idea where my Aunt Rosie was stationed, only that it was somewhere in the north of Western Australia. It did cross my mind that there might be nothing she could do as I had foolishly married Ashley, but I had to try. After I secretly crafted the message, I'd waited on tenterhooks for a chance to put my plan into action. I was gutted when the very next week RFW had returned from wherever he'd slunk off too and resumed the shopping duties.

With shaky fingers I slipped the envelope inside my bra and re-adjusted my clothing. Accompanied by my constant companion, the chain around my ankle, I manoeuvred my way from bedroom to the bathroom. There I set out clean towels, double checked that the plastic shower cubical, sink and toilet all sparkled with cleanliness and there was nothing for Ashley to berate me for. Satisfied, I hurried back to the kitchen. As I pulled on a fresh apron I glanced through the window. A cloud of dust was being kicked up by an approaching vehicle. To the west I spotted a second, smaller puff that resembled the beginnings of a willy-willy, but it died almost immediately.

I fastened my gaze on the sky-blue SUV. It skidded to a halt in front of the shack. Almost immediately a tall, muscular man, dressed in black trousers and a black, short sleeved polo shirt, emerged from behind the wheel. His bald scalp reflected the bright sunlight and made the tattoo of a spider's web that covered the back of his head appear realistic. With a rapid step the big guy skimmed the front of the vehicle to open the offside passenger door. Robert Watson, looking cool and unruffled slid from the comfort of the air-conditioned cab into the noonday heat. He waved away a swarm of friendly flies, placed his hands into the small of his back and stretched. At that moment the metal door of the workshop flew open with a clang. Ashley, wearing his baseball cap turned backwards on his head and a wide smile on his lips, hot-footed towards the vehicle in a long, loping stride. As he fetched up in front of his father, Robert, a short, solid man that barely came to the level of his son's chest, reached up and with an open hand, smacked Ashley across the face. The slap echoed across the yard with a resounding crack. I clasped a hand over my mouth to muffle the gasp of shock that escaped my lips. The last thing I wanted was to bring attention to myself. In trepidation I waited for my husband's temper to explode. To my astonishment he stood cradling his reddened cheek with the palm of his hand and stared down at his feet like a naughty schoolboy.

The loud volume of Robert's angry words had no trouble reaching my ears. 'How could you let that useless fucking cousin of yours jeopardize our whole operation?'

I couldn't catch Ashley's murmured response, but of his father words, I had no problems.

'He's only gone and spent unsanctioned, faulty funds at a wine bar in the city.'

Ashley's head snapped up. 'When?'

'June. When he was in Perth doing a job for me.' Robert's cheeks glowed red from suppressed anger. 'The notes weren't clean, Cub. Now we've got people poking around, asking questions.'

This time I heard Ashley's response clearly. 'What people? What job?'

Robert gave Ashley a measured stare. Something shifted in his eyes. He chose to answer only the first question. 'There was a guy asking questions at the gym.'

'What sort of questions? Who was he?'

'No idea.'

Ashley shook his head, 'Well there's nothing at the gym that can be traced back to us. I put a squeaky-clean manager in place before I left for Albany. We were going to give it another year before we started redistributing from there again. Remember?'

'Yeah, I remember. I'm not losing my marbles just yet.' Robert folded his arms across his chest. 'It was probably that damn private investigator the lawyer hired. He's been asking around the traps about you and your whereabouts.'

'Well, it doesn't matter, Dad. I'm safe here. No one knows about this place, not even the mugs we've had stashed up at the homestead. The gym is clean. There's nothing going on there that can be linked back to us.'

'Not so! The bloody drug squad jacks raided it two days ago,' growled Robert. 'I bet this is all because of bloody Russ. Why my sister didn't have him aborted is beyond me.'

'What's Rattler got to do with the gym?'

'He dealt fucking wolfies from the fucking locker room. He left a stash of the bloody stuff in a hidey hole. Stupid, fuckwit! Bastard cop dogs found it. I knew I should have gotten someone else to do the job...he can't help himself...has to branch out on his own all the fucking time. Fucking...'

Ashley raised his voice and interrupted Robert's rant. 'What job?'
'Not relevant...'

'Of course it's relevant,' snarled Ashley. 'I can't help you if you continually leave me out of the loop. Now tell me,' he commanded.

The men glared at each other. Suddenly Robert capitulated. 'Zelenski. I got Rattler to take care of the bastard.'

'Fuck, dad. You can't just knock someone off and expect there to be no repercussions.'

Purple veins swelled in Robert's neck. 'Yeah, well, it had to be done, Cub. He was shafting me...us.' He gave Ashley a sideways glance and confessed, 'I got Rattler to warn the lawyer off at the same time.'

'You did what? Fuck, Dad!' shouted Ashley. He began to pace back and forth. His feet kicked up dust as he muttered a series of fucks at the top of his voice. Suddenly he stopped mid-pace, turned to his father and with a snarl spat out, 'You might as well have painted a target on us.'

'Well blame, Rattler. It's his egotistical stupidity that created this mess. None of this would have been traceable back to us, if it wasn't for him. That's why I've come for a holiday at the homestead. To think about a course of action while things cool down.' Robert studied his son. 'You do realise we might have to sacrifice him. I can't have the cops poking their noses into our family business.'

Ashley glared at Robert, and the father seemed to back down. 'He's made the crew uneasy, Cub. The Huntsmen's sergeant-at-arms has been spouting threats about pulling out of our deal. He's also very curious to know what happened to one of his mules, a bloke called Slugger.' Ashley's head jerked up. His attention wandered away from his father to a new patch of growth on one of the sand dunes. His lips folded but he remained silent.

'I can't give him an answer because I don't know,' added his father. 'And that Scotsman you left in charge is angry at the mess Rattler left behind for him to clean up. He did his best to make Zelinski's death look like an accident. He did a good job but is not happy.'

'And the money that Zelinski nicked? What about that?'

Robert gave a smug grin. 'I got it back.'

'How?'

'You know Crispin Caspian's bookkeeper, Ayham Chandra?' Ashley nodded. 'Well, he found it and syphoned it back into our off-shore accounts,' said Bear Watson, rubbing his hands together in delight.

Ashley scowled. 'So, Caspian now knows where we keep our money. I don't like it, Dad. He's a slippery toad, always trying to insert himself into our business dealings. As for Rattler...,' Ashley lowered his voice and muttered something I didn't catch.

Robert's reply was curt and clear. 'I know he's family, but I may have to make an example of him. Where is the little prick anyway? Spider here wants to have a word.'

Ashley nodded towards the shed. They ambled off in that direction with Robert still grouching about the ruckus Russ had caused.

I stepped away from the window, my heart banging hard in my chest.

*Bloody hell!*

The letter in my bra began to burn a brand against my skin. I definitely couldn't ask Robert for help. Not only was he aware of goings on but he was also a main player. I momentarily considered asking the bodyguard, Spider for help.

*Don't be dense, Faith. A henchman isn't going to risk life or limb for the battered wife of his boss's son.*

Letting out a growl of frustration, I made sure my tether didn't tangle on the furniture as I scurried into the bedroom and shoved the letter back into the hidey-hole. I would just have to wait for another opportunity.

To avoid being in the firing line from any fall-out from the disciplining Ashley's father had handed out to him, I raced around the dining table laying out the best dinnerware and making the table look as elegant as possible. I ignored the grumpy huff of protest from the fridge as I scanned its shelves to ensure there was plenty of cold wine and beer. Slamming the door, I slung open the overhead cupboard and pushed the unopened bottle of liquor to the back, out of sight. If Ashley started on the spirits, there'd be no holding back his fury at his father's treatment towards him in public. He would take it out on me.

An hour later, I removed the roast from the oven, set the meat to rest and slipped the pudding in to bake. As I straightened my back, I heard the crunch of approaching footsteps, accompanied by laughter.

Well, that was a good sign.

For the umpteenth time I flicked a quick glance around the room to check it was spotless. I glanced through the kitchen window. Ashley and Robert, closely followed by Spider, were making their way towards the shack. That the men all seemed to be on friendly terms was important to me because it would help influence Ashley's mood when his father finally left. There was no sign of Russ, but that didn't concern me. I hated him more than my husband and the less time I spent in his presence the better.

Pleased I had timed the meal well, I was standing the way Ashley demanded, with eyes downcast and hands clasped at my waist, when my father-in-law and husband entered the room. Robert strode towards me, grabbed my chin painfully between his thumb and forefinger and lifted my bruised face towards the light. Eyes blazing, he scowled at what he saw. My heart stuttered. Was I about to receive the help I so desperately needed?

'Cub my boy, how many times have I told you son? Never the face. It spoils the view.' Robert gave me a sour grin and stalked over to take a seat at the head of the table. With a flourish Robert took a swig from the glass of beer his son handed him and let out a loud belch. 'Ahhhh, now that really hits the spot.'

My hopes died in my breast and added another layer of ice around my heart. I stared at him in disbelief for a heartbeat before flicking a glance at the muscle-bound Spider who hovered behind his boss's chair. I caught a flash of emotion on his face. It was so fleeting I almost missed it. It looked like sympathy. A shaft of emotion swelled in my breast. I sucked back the tears that welled in my eyes, turned my back on the men and set about carving the roast with clamped lips and a cold heart. There would be no help for me.

One of the meals I quietly placed on the table remained untouched, the chair at the table vacant. Russ never showed up to eat.

\* \* \*

My father-in-law belched in contentment as he pushed aside his empty dessert bowl. He reached up and clamped a firm hand onto Ashley's upper arm.

'Righto Cub, I've come up with a plan. The boat arrived yesterday to collect our last lot of tenants. I'm going to take Rattler off your hands for a few days. I need him to pack up and clean out the workshop, crate up our laundry gear and prepare it for shipment to the new location I've got in mind. There's a newbie due in at the homestead soon. Rattler can get a cottage ready for him. I was going to borrow your wife for that but recalcitrant nephews need to be punished for stupidity. This can be Rattler's penance.'

He jerked his head at his henchman. 'Load the car, Spider.'

Spider rose from his seat. As he made his way towards the door he gave me a nod. 'Thank you for the delicious meal, Mrs Watson.'

Wow, manners and gratitude – not a common commodity around here.

Ashley's voice cut into my thoughts. 'Who's the newbie, Dad? Someone I know?' he asked as he refilled his father's beer glass.

'Nah, don't think so. Name's Mort Patterson. Not our usual type but I did promise to help him, as a favour to Caspian. Patterson's a smooth customer with a million-dollar smile. I don't like him myself, and wouldn't trust him as far as I could spit, but money's money. He's paid up-front for resettlement into a new life in Thailand. That's all that counts as far as I'm concerned.'

'Bloody Caspian, he'll milk us dry it we don't watch him...'

The abrupt wave of Robert's hand cut him off. Ashley glanced my way, probably to see if I'd noticed. I kept my hands busy and my eyes lowered to give the impression I wasn't paying any attention to them. He must have been convinced because, from the corner of my eye, I saw Ashley give his father a slight nod.

'When does Patterson arrive?' he asked.

'Not exactly sure. Bingles will airlift him in by chopper, probably late Friday or Saturday. It all depends on how many scenic flight bookings he's got on his books. Now listen up Cub, now we are alone, there's something else I want to discuss with you. I need you to finish checking this last batch of notes, close up all our open jobs and get some new ID's made for this Patterson bloke. I want to get shot of him as quickly as possible. Have it all finished by the time I pull out next Sunday.'

'Shit, Dad. That's a ton of work. With you taking Rattler away, I'll have to do it by myself. It'll be a real push...' Robert stopped Ashley's protest with a chopping motion of his hand.

'You've got missy here,' he snarled, poking a forefinger in my direction. 'About time she started to pull her weight. She's not doing much else, is she?' Ashley shook his head. 'Right then. I'll send Rattler back to you when I've finished with him. He might have Patterson with him. Keep the slime ball here and away from me until I leave. I don't want him connecting my face with the hideout.'

'And what about me and my face? I'd don't want anyone connecting me with this place either, you know.'

'You're fine, Cub. Patterson doesn't know you from a bar of soap, but me and him...we had a face to face in Broome when I took his money. As I only took him on as a favour to Caspian, I had to pretend to be a lowly grunt working for the middle-man to gauge his mettle.'

Ashley frowned. 'Bloody Caspian again...'

'Can it will ya. Just stash the bloke out back for a day or two will you. And tell bloody Rattler to keep his fucking mouth shut.'

'Just how much longer am I going to be stuck in this god-forsaken place, Dad?' growled my husband. 'I'm going fucking stir crazy here. I hate it, being out of touch with you and the business. Errors are creeping in. Smarmy wanna-be's like Caspian are starting to get a foothold on our turf. I don't like it and I can't fix things from here.'

Robert reached up and patted Ashley's cheek. 'Once we get shot of Patterson, I think we'd all enjoy a change of scenery. How about Queensland for you and me? Does the Gold Coast tickle your fancy?'

Ashley's dimples erupted as his face broke into a huge grin of delight. 'Fuck yeah. It's about time I got to enjoy some decent entertainment and nightlife again. I really miss going to the track, and my weekly poker game.'

'Not to mention,' Robert said, with a sleazy grin. 'Monica and the stable of gorgeous girls she's got waiting for us at Scarlet's. I bet she's missed you.'

Ashley stared at me across the room. 'Yeah, it's been far too long. She at least knows how to please a man.'

I kept my face blank and didn't react to the verbal chastisement because I'd be happy if I was never required to please him ever again.

'Come on, Cub,' said Robert, let's go admire this beach of yours while Spider loads up the car.' Father and son kicked back their chairs and headed for the door. As he passed me, Robert cocked his head in my direction. 'She signed that paperwork yet?' he asked. 'We've got less than a year left on the lease you know.'

His words startled me. I almost dropped the stack of dirty plates I was carrying to the sink. What paperwork?

'I know, but her uncle's got the finances too well tied up. And a forged lease won't work.'

A glow of appreciation ignited in my breast. Good on Uncle Alex.

'We could replace her with a ringer. Someone more compliant...' said Robert, scratching the cleft in his chin with his thumb as if giving the idea some thought.

Fear tightened its grip around my heart.

'No,' snapped Ashley.

His bark caught Robert by surprise and his feet stopped moving as he stared intently up at his son, 'You haven't gone and fallen for her, have you?'

Bear's comment showed me that Robert didn't have any understanding of his son's true nature. Ashley was a ruthless obsessive. He would allow nothing and no one to come between him and the object of his obsession - me. Ashley was also cunning. He knew just how to handle his father and how to keep what he wanted.

'Nah, Dad, nothing like that. It's just that I've put so much time and effort into training her to do things just how I like them. You enjoyed your lunch, didn't you?'

Bear nodded. 'She certainly knows how to cook, that's for sure.'

'And her uncle can't negate the lease if he can't find her to sign the paperwork. So in a way, the property is effectively ours. Her money will still be there in a couple of years when she turns 25. We can look at it then, okay?' Robert scrutinised the blank look on Ashley's face. 'Besides we've got too much work on hand in finishing this job and starting the next. You'll need me to focus my attention on breathing new life into the Queensland branch...right? I also want to divert the funds from Nimble Investments and start afresh with some new shell companies and off-shore accounts. Ones that Caspian and his book keeper don't know about.' Bear Watson ran a hand over his dark, thinning hair and massaged the back of his neck as he listened to Ashley's reasoning. 'It would be a waste of valuable time having to start from scratch on the home front when I need to focus on protecting and developing new businesses. I think you're right that I should leave it for now, Dad. The family business is more important.'

Robert reached forward and placed his stubby fingers on Ashley's forearm. The gold and diamond signet ring on his little finger caught the light and a prism of colour flashed on the ceiling.

'I totally agree, Cub. We need to fly under the radar for a spell, especially after what happened with the lawyer. Something else Russ messed up.' Robert sighed. 'I don't know why you're even worrying about it. Besides we might find a better property in Queensland. Think you can put up with her for now? Its only eighteen months before she's of age and we can get shot of the legal constraints on the trust.'

'Sure. I sometimes take on too much all at once. It's good you can keep me grounded.' Ashley patted the hand his father had rested on his upper arm. 'Hey, do you want me to send someone to work in the private investigator's office to keep an eye on things?'

They strolled from the room, their voices fading. I missed the rest of the conversation, which was a bugger. I was desperate to know who this private investigator was and why whatever they were doing was so interesting to the Watson men. Maybe they had some other schmuck lined up to deceive.

I slammed down the dirty pot in my hand. Forget it, Faith. You've got bigger problems - like the fact that Robert has just told your husband to get rid of you and even though Ashley seemed to have diverted his father's attention from the idea for the moment, I wouldn't put it past Robert to go behind his son's back and deal with me on the quiet.

My time was running out. I needed to find a way to escape and soon.

## Chapter Thirty-Three

Ryan kept the dune buggy off-road and trailed the plume of dust being kicked up by the SUV. He kept the buggy's speed down, to ensure there was no evidence he was around. Cresting a small rise, Ryan slowed to an idle. The SUV was heading straight for a hodgepodge of buildings grouped together to resemble a beachside settlement. He spun the steering wheel to head away and misjudged the pressure of his blade on the accelerator. The buggy tail whipped and skidded on the loose gravel. It sent up a small dust cloud. Ryan cursed. He took off at speed and beat a hasty retreat north. A few minutes later he spotted a small rocky outcrop with a cluster of brush growing at its base.

'What do reckon, girl? A good spot to hide the buggy while we headed back on foot for a look-see?'

'Ruff',' replied Tennille. Ryan grinned as he ran the buggy deep into the clump of shrubs. The dog was good company. She didn't argue with any of his decisions.

He alighted from his seat and set about concealing the buggy with fallen branches. He then set about brushing away all traces of the wheel marks that led to the spot. Ryan took a step back and ran an experienced eye over the area. Satisfied the vehicle was concealed enough to fool the casual glance of anyone wandering by, he pulled on the backpack.

'Come on girl.'

They set off at a steady pace. Crouching low they negotiated the undulating sand dunes, stubby salt bush and wind grass and made their way back to the cluster of buildings. When they were close Ryan used a hand to signal Tennille to halt. He took a knee and eyed the area for cover. A Bauhinia shrub growing near the peak of a small dune seemed adequate. Man and dog belly-crawled to take refuge under the dense branches. Once settled Ryan took out his binoculars to scan the area. He needed a safe approach route, one that would give cover so he could get a look in the windows of the shack and maybe listen in to what was going on inside.

Ryan quickly realised his current position wasn't ideal for long term surveillance but good enough to show him that except for coastal ground cover and tufts of wild grass there was only one large tree in the whole area and that was useless as cover. It grew too close the rickety veranda. The out-buildings were surrounded by a large expanse of open space. There was nothing to use as cover. Ryan swore. Any attempt to get close in daylight could prove detrimental to both his and Tennille's health.

He slid out from under the shrub. 'Keep low Tennille,' he whispered. 'We need to loop around to the south-west to check for a better spot.'

Ryan rolled over the crest of the dune to find himself perched above a glorious turquoise ocean. The expanse of water was nestled in the arms of a crescent bay and had an exquisite orange-cream sand beach. A gentle swell slapped against a treeless pile of granite about a hundred meters from the shore. Ryan ran his field glasses over the islet's surface. It was littered with washed up kelp, nesting gulls and bird excrement.

'I wonder if this is part of the marine sanctuary Bull mentioned?' murmured Ryan.

He spotted a depression, large enough to conceal both of them while allowing an unhampered view of the buildings.

Ryan reached over and laid a gentle hand on Tennille's head. 'Come on girl, let's you and me take a quiet swim,' he whispered.

After stowing the equipment he'd need for surveillance into a waterproof bag, Ryan repacked all the electronic tracking gear, radios and phone into the back pack. He jogged back to where he'd hidden the buggy to bury the bag under a pile of stones. With his gear safely stowed, Ryan headed further downwind from the settlement.

Crawling into position on a dune he checked up and down the beach to ensure it was clear in both directions. A final glance at the general area of the shack satisfied him all was quiet. On his belly he slithered silently along the sand and into the surf. He swam in a straight line out to sea with Tennille by his side. They made a slow, wide arc, to approach the islet from the rear. The height of the rookery concealed them from the shore. At the rear of the atoll the rocks were staggered to form a climbable, uneven staircase. Ryan hooked his arm under Tennille's hind legs and gave her a boost up out of the water before climbing out himself.

'Stay,' he ordered. 'I want to investigated.'

Careful not to disturb the brooding birds he crawled over warm rocks, rancid kelp and acrid bird waste to the dip in the rocks. He checked the view. It was perfect for his needs. Settling comfortably onto his belly Ryan splayed his prosthetic, taking care to avoid the jagged granite shards that poked up around him. The last thing he needed was to damage the blade. To make room for Tennille he gently moved a couple of nests then gave a soft whistle. Tennille crawled over on her belly and snuggled in to his side.

She whined when a gull screamed its protest at the loss of the favoured nook. Ryan scuffed the top of her head.

'Never mind girl. I don't think we'll be here long. There can't be much to hold the interest of our crime lord this far from civilisation.' He flicked an appreciative glance around the large, deserted bay. 'Me, on the other hand, I could happily spend my days here. It's a beautiful spot, girl. Looks like there'd be good fishing and the water was lovely and warm for our swim.'

Tennille gave a sneeze, nestled her head on her paws and closed her eyes, uninterested in the scenery.

A blazing sun soon baked her fur and his clothes dry. To blend in, Ryan reached around, gathered together handfuls of kelp and covered their bodies. He nestled low and trained the binoculars to study the large steel building located nearest to the beach. It had an air conditioning unit fitted in one wall, a row of solar panels and a satellite dish on the roof. Unlike the shack, the workshop style building seemed to be a reasonably new addition and was in excellent condition.

'Someone lives here, Tennille. That well-tended vegetable garden screams of long-term care.' His dog cracked open an eyelid and gave him a red, myopic glare. Ryan grinned at Tennille's version of a stinky eye at having her sleep disturbed. 'I can't see the Bear, but we're definitely in the right place. That's his SUV parked next to the flashy Jeep Grand Cherokee. I wonder who he's visiting?'

Ryan made a note of the number plate of both vehicles. He'd ask Rosie to do a licence check. That would be after she'd finished tanning the leather from his hide for slipping his leash and coming to investigate. He chuckled to himself. He was positive she'd be very creative in her use of language.

K.A. HUDSON

He lifted the binoculars. A full scan of the area showed him all was quiet. He took the opportunity to unzip his waterproof pack, pull out the tripod and connect the field glasses to them. In the long term it would be easier on the shoulders than staying propped up on his elbows. Ryan took a slug from his water bottle and considered the antics of the birds nesting around them as he waited for some activity on the cliff above. While one bird remained huddled over her clutch of eggs the other escaped the ammonia and rotten fish scented nursery to dive and hunt in the pristine waters of the bay. He noticed some of the nests were occupied by newly hatched chicks. They were loud with their demands for food. He glanced up. Gull's glided and hovered overhead. Some landed, others took flight. The whole atoll was noisy, smelly and full of busy life. Ryan loved it.

He reached up to scratch his bearded chin. 'I wonder what the hell Robert Watson is doing out here?' he murmured. 'From everything I've heard about the man, this is as far from his comfort zone as you can get.'

Suddenly the smile left his face. Maybe he shouldn't have followed the SUV. He could have taken the opportunity to search the cottages and homestead. There might have been some information amongst Bear's possessions about the whereabouts of Ashley and Faith. Ryan's gut soured. Had he made a mistake? Should he go now? Indecision took hold. He squirmed. The rocks dug into his chest and hips. He had trouble zoning out. Normally Ryan had infinite patience during a stakeout and found it easy to ignore the discomforts. Since his injury and learning all was not well in Burger's world, all that inner calmness had deserted him. He was desperate to find her, frustrated at the length of time it was taking and anxious about what would happen when he did. That was his ultimate worry. Was she going to reject him? The bang of a car door dragged his attention away from his internal musings and the black pit that hovered around the periphery of his mind. He looked into the binoculars and observed the tattooed bodyguard open the rear of the SUV, spread a tarp then wander into the large workshop. He was only out of sight for a minute. When he reappeared, he was carrying an inert figure slung over his shoulder.

Bloody hell, was that a dead body?

A movement to the left caught Ryan's eye. He moved the glasses and his heart began to bang hard against his ribcage. Standing talking with Bear was Cub Watson.

# 34

## Chapter Thirty-Four

While I scrubbed the lunch dishes, I kept a covert eye on the activity in the yard. Spider's arm muscles bulged as he lugged three large plastic tubs from the workshop to the SUV. Pineapple-yellow and off-green showed through the opaque sides of the boxes. The tubs were full of money.

'Bloody hell,' I gasped under my breath. 'Where did all that cash come from?'

Spider stowed the tubs onto the rear seat of the vehicle and slammed the door shut. He wandered around to the rear of the vehicle and flung open the cargo doors. He took his time to spread a piece of canvas over the floor before he headed back to the workshop. Moments later he reappeared. This time the bloodied body of Russ was slung over his shoulder. With his legs wide apart, Spider staggered to maintain balance under the weight, as he made his way to the car. He heaved his shoulder and the inert body fell into the cargo bay. Russ didn't move. Was he dead? I didn't really care, except it would cause a problem with my husband.

I cast a quick glance in Ashley's direction. He seemed unconcerned as he circled the garden beds with his father. His face was devoid of any emotion as he listened to whatever Robert said. When their meandering bought them level with the vehicle Ashley stopped and opened the front passenger's door. He put out a hand to assist his father into the passenger's seat. Their voices carried as they chatted. I quieted my actions to listen.

'Dad, I'm going to set up a temporary shell company and move all that money today. I promise I'll get all that other stuff finished as well. Don't take on any more work. Not until I'm back in the saddle. In the meantime, see what real estate you like on the Gold Coast. I'll join you next month.'

Robert gave his son a tender kiss on the cheek and patted him on the shoulder.

'Whatever you say, Cub, you're the boss.'

Ashley gave a nod of farewell to Spider and watched the SUV roar away. My husband stood in the cloud of red dust with a speculative look on his face. The family dynamic and power base seemed to have shifted in that short tour of the property. I wondered what that was about.

Ashley turned towards the shack. I pulled away from the window so I wouldn't be caught staring and busied myself with the last of the luncheon debris. I wondered what sort of mood I would have to deal with when Ashley came inside. Probably bad. The only positive I could see from Robert's visit today was that we'd gotten rid of the troublemaking Russ.

# 35

## Chapter Thirty-Five

I hung the tea towel over the oven door handle to dry. The door burst open. Ashley blasted inside with power and purpose emanating from every pore of his body. Terrified, I straightened, bowed my head, desperate not to attract his attention. He strode over to where I stood. My heart stalled. I gripped my hands tightly together and waited for the slap. Instead, he reached down and undid my shackle.

'Come with me,' Ashley ordered. 'We've got a ton of work to get through before I can get out of this place.'

He took a firm grip on my upper arm and yanked me through the doorway. I stumbled along, using the sides of my feet to walk on in an attempt to avoid the spiky double-gee's that grew in abundance all over the path. One three-pronged thorn pierced my foot.

I yelped. 'Can you slow down, please, Ashley. The prickles are running wild at the moment. Without my shoes I have to very careful where I put my feet.'

Eyes dark and hard, glared down at my curled-up toes. He let go of my arm. I bent to pull the painful thorn from my foot. Ashley cursed. I decided to try and sweeten him up. Maybe I could win a concession, like my shoes, which I was going to need if I was to escape. I stood up and cupped his cheek with the palm of my hand. 'Please darling, could I have my trainers to wear. Things will go much faster if I can at least walk around safely and not have to worry about the nasties.'

Ashley's mercurial mood did an about face. The darkness left his eyes. He gave me the boyish grin that had once endeared him to me. I lifted the corner of my mouth and gave him a tentative smile in return. It was as if I'd flicked a switch on in him. He pulled me into his arms and covered my mouth with searing hot lips. I fought hard to not stiffen in disgust. My mind did a quick assessment on how to quash his ardour before he decided a brutal romp around the bedroom was desirable. I gently ended the kiss and reached up to stroke his cheek in a loving gesture and set about distracting him. 'Do we have time? Didn't Robert say it was imperative that you to finish this job before Sunday?'

The heat left Ashley's eyes and suspicion flared in its place. 'You heard that did you?'

He studied my face. I maintained direct eye contact and thought innocent thoughts so nothing would show on my features.

'Dammit to hell and back, Faith' he snarled, and just like a recalcitrant schoolboy he kicked at a weed growing in the red earth with the toe of his five-hundred-dollar trainers. A cloud of dust sprayed up in the air, blowing back on the breeze and covered us both in dirt. 'Why does our marriage have to be this way? Why can't it by like it was when we first met? Just the two of us living alone together, happy and so much in love, no outside world butting in and getting in our way.'

Ashley was delusional. I didn't remember our relationship ever being like that. An idea sparked to life deep inside me. Maybe I could make some headway here. Manipulate him into taking a course of action that I might be able to take advantage of.

'It can be that way. You're an intelligent and capable man, Ashley. You don't really need to be doing your father's or your cousin's bidding. Why don't we get into the car right now and drive away. There's a whole world out there for us to enjoy. Can't you see it? I can. There I am dressed in an exquisite gown hanging off the arm of the sexist man alive. We could go to all the exciting places you miss, live life to the fullest, while enjoying each other. And when you tire of the high life, we can lock out the outside world and retire to the peace and tranquillity of our own luxurious home. There you can watch sports on your big screen TV as you exercise to your heart's content in our personal gym, followed by a long hot sauna and a sensuous massage.' I wiggled my eyebrows to add emphasis to my words.

Ashley stared, hunger alive in his eyes. I held my breath and continued to gently stroke his face. I prayed the seed I'd planted would bear fruit. If we left here, went somewhere where there were people, I might be able to free myself from this torturous life.

Suddenly, the shutters slammed down in his eyes. They went dark and blank. 'Stay here. I'll go get your shoes,' he growled. A shaft of disappointment stabbed me in the chest. I'd failed.

I followed my husband's progress as he stomped towards the shack. It struck me that with its open metal shutter sagging drunkenly over the window, the place resembled a Cyclops with a sleepy eye. I automatically checked the glass was clean. Ashley flung open the door. It banged hard against the outside wall and knocked the shutter prop away. It fell. The glass rattled. I bit my lip and prayed he hadn't broken the pane, because that would mean I'd have to live with the shutter locked in place in stuffy darkness until the men could be bothered to buy a new one to replace it. Knowing my husband, he wouldn't rush, because as long as it didn't affect his comfort, he wouldn't consider it important.

The soft sea breeze lifted a loose strand of hair from my face. I took the small moment of freedom from Ashley's company to draw in a deep breath of fresh air while I listened to the steady thrum of the ocean as it tumbled onto the sand. A purple crowned fairy wren caught my attention with its chatter. The cheeky devil wagged its tail as it danced along the vegetable garden fence. I let my gaze wander along the neat rows of mature plants, some of them fruiting, others flowering. An orange ringed butterfly flitted amongst fat, slow-moving bees as they drifted amid the foliage seeking sweet pollen. A glimmer of warmth touched my soul. If it wasn't for my present circumstances, this could be a wonderful place to live. Not the shack itself or the people in it, but the area. Being untouched and tranquil, warm and peaceful, a damaged soul with a broken heart could be slowly restored by such serenity and beauty.

*Oh Ryan, wherever you are, I hope you are safe and happy.*

I lifted up my face, closed my eyes against a pool of tears and delved around in my mind for an image of his topaz eyes. They memory was hard to find. I'd locked it away so deep I'd nearly lost all recall.

Goosebumps ran up my arms. A tingle touched the back of my neck. My eyes shot open. It was the sensation I got when Russ covertly ogled me. Except this current feeling didn't make my skin crawl. There was no impression of malice or lust. Puzzled, I turned to study the landscape behind me. Tussocks of curly spinifex, wind grass and salt toughened coastal shrubs dotted undulating sand dunes. Shrubs swayed with the rhythm of the soft sea breeze. Nothing seemed out of place. I glanced up into the branches of the bloodwood tree shading the shack. Perched high in the thick canopy was a crow. It ruffled its glossy black plumage, gave a depressed caw and cocked its head to stare arrogantly down at me through the white irises of its eyes as if saying, 'what are you looking at?' The bird seemed unconcerned by its surroundings so I took it to mean there was nothing amiss near the shack. I turned and stared across the small white caps that sparkled in the afternoon sun, hoping to see a boat but the turquoise sea was empty of human activity. Gutted, I lost hope and lowered my gaze. It drifted over the bird rookery. A flash caught my eye.

* * *

Through the binoculars Ryan drank in the sight of the woman he loved, as she held her face up to the sun. She was so slender now that when she'd first emerged from the shack, he'd been unsure if it was really was Burger, but that action, the one where she worshipped the sun put paid to that moment of doubt. Ryan rubbed the heel of his hand over his aching heart. Chips had been wrong in thinking that Faith needed their help. The loving gesture as she'd cupped Cub's face with the palms of her hand along with the kiss she'd bestowed on him had screamed of love and affection. He had no doubt she was right where she wanted to be. With the man she loved. His heart ached as he dragged his gaze away from the sight. Heart-broken he rolled onto his back to stare at the cloudless sky. A searing pain of loss marched a parade inside his chest. Burger didn't love him. She loved her husband. It was over. He'd chosen to walk away. Now he had to suffer the results of his action. Serve him right.

Ryan decided it was time to leave. He wasn't going to stick around and help destroy Burger's happiness. He loved her too much for that.

'It looks like we're not needed here, Tennille,' he choked out. 'Time to wash our hands of this whole bringing down the Watson crime family quest thing. Let's go check in with Rosie, return the buggy to Bull and then you and me girl, we're going to get the hell out of dodge. How's a walk around Australia sound?'

Tennille snuggled in beside him, licked his cheek and whined. Ryan reached over and gave her ear a gentle tug. 'No. Ok. Well, we'll think of something to do.' Tennille whined again. 'I know you love her. We both do. But as you can see, we're not needed here.'

Grief formed a huge lump in his throat. Moisture welled in his eyes. God, even losing part of his leg hadn't hurt this much. He brushed at his eyes with the back of his hand.

'Get a grip, Lamb. It's over. Just accept it and move on.'

He sucked in a deep breath and rolled back onto his belly. He reached out to remove the screw that secured the field glasses onto the tripod. Blinded by tears he misjudged the distance and knocked over the stand. They tilted. The lenses caught a shaft of waning afternoon sunshine. Light flared.

'Fuck!' He slapped a palm over the glass but was too late to stop the tell-tale flash. Ryan froze, hardly daring to breathe. 'You stupid, bloody, halfwit grunt. What are you, a recruit?'

Inch by inch he moved to peek around the large rock he was hunkered behind to check if the married couple on the headland had noticed.

Faith stared right at him.

* * *

The flash was gone as fast as it appeared. My heart leapt. I stared intently at the islet. As far as I knew there was nothing on the bird nursery to reflect sunlight. Something had also disturbed a large portion of the bird population because they'd taken to the sky en masse and hovered overhead, screeching in protest. I held my breath and waited, but whatever had caused the ruckus must have gone because the gulls slowly glided back to their rooks. I studied the layout of the granite mound. Each nook and cranny was filled with twiggy nests, noisy chicks and busy parents. Except for the great strands of kelp that had been washed up, the atoll was almost bare of vegetation. I noticed some of the seaweed had moved since the previous day but wind and waves might account for that. To my naked eye there didn't seem to be anything else out of place. I took a step forward hoping to get a better look but at that moment Ashley emerged from the confines of the shack. He saw me staring seaward and grabbed me fiercely by the wrist.

'What's the matter?' he asked, giving my skin a painful twist. 'What are you looking at?'

'Nothing.'

I shifted my focus to the sparkling caps of waves so he wouldn't suspect there might be something of interest nearby. His grip tightened. I winced at the pain.

'Please, you're hurting me. There is nothing wrong, I promise. I was just watching a sea eagle,' I blurted out. I had no intention of alerting him to the fact there might be someone around. I'd be locked away. I wasn't about to let that happen. Given an opportunity, I was going to make a break for freedom. My husband's hot gaze bore into me, distrust and disbelief written all over his face. As if on cue, a white-bellied bird of prey let out a piercing scream. The sea eagle hurled itself into the surf like an arrow seeking a bullseye. I pointed and watched in awe as it lifted elegantly from the water's depths with a fish clutched in its sharp talons. 'See. Isn't it the most amazing thing you've ever seen?'

Ashley grunted, let go and shoved my shoes at me. 'You and your bloody nature. Come on, we don't have time for this. There's too much bloody work to be done.'

* * *

Ryan very slowly lowered the glasses. Huddled behind the rock he propped his back against its rough surface and rapidly packed his gear. He had to leave before Faith sent the Cub to investigate. About to shove the field glasses away he gave in to the strong urge to take a final look at the woman he loved. This time her husband stood at her side. He had a firm grip on her arm. Ryan didn't like the look of pain on her face. Suddenly he noticed Faith had a black eye.

'The bastard!' he snarled through clenched teeth.

Faith pointed in his direction but skyward. Ryan cast a quick glance up. A sea eagle on the hunt cut through the air, like an arrow to a target. It shot into the water and neatly plucked up an impressive sized fish. Relieved he didn't seem to be the subject of the couple's attention, Ryan flicked his glance back to the headland. Cub stalked toward the workshop. Faith trailed behind with a look of pure hatred on her face.

\* \* \*

'Check each bank note, and be thorough,' Ashley instructed as he shoved a magnifying lamp in front of my face. I stared through the glass at the tip of the pencil he used to point with. 'In this plastic sleeve is the authentic note. Your first job is to check each of the one-hundred-dollar bills in this box against the original. Pay particular attention that none of the colour has smeared. All the images must align. Make sure the serial number is printed twice, once in brown ink and once in green ink – here and here.' He dropped a piece of paper next to my hand. 'This is the list of serial numbers for this batch. When you've finished this lot, you can move onto the fifties.'

I stared in amazement at what must have been at least ten thousand, one-hundred-dollar bills stacked in front of me. There were more in a box at my feet.

I began to blab before I could stop myself. 'Wow I thought money couldn't be successfully forged. Didn't you once tell me the government has in place all sorts of security features?' I ran the note between my fingertips. 'These are awesome. Feel real.'

Ashley flashed me a superior smirk. 'That's because they are real, Sunflower. This particular note used to be worth ten dollars. I devised a state-of-the-art laundry process where we wash the colour from fives and tens so none of the security features are compromised. The notes are reprinted at a higher denomination. Clever hey?'

'I'll say. I didn't know that was even possible.' I was stunned. Surely it can't be that easy to fake Australian currency.

I straightened my back and took a moment to check out the workshop. The place screamed man cave. It held all the comforts I'd been denied. An air conditioner, wall-mounted, flat-screen TV with state-of-the-art sound system, cushioned recliners. The walls were covered with autographed sporting memorabilia and oversized bookshelves, jam-packed with movies and music discs. I shuffled into a more comfortable position on the cushioned stool I was perched on at the spacious work table to enjoy the blast of chilled air coming from the air-conditioning unit. I could feel my husband's gaze bore into the side of my face so I shifted my attention back to him and gave him a sweet, innocent smile. His eyes filled with hunger and desire. I tamped down the wattage of the beam to reduce the chance of him descending down the rabbit hole of licentious thoughts.

I held up one of the counterfeit notes. 'Does the washing and printing take place here in the workshop?'

'Nah. The printing press is at our homestead.'

'Homestead? Where's that?'

'About forty kilometres east of here.' Ashley indicated to a vague direction inland.

'Do you own this homestead?'

'No, we lease it. And all the land that runs from here at the beach to the edge of a town called Mount Ibour. You ever heard of it?'

My heart leapt, the name was familiar, but I couldn't think why. Here was something I could add to the letter for Aunt Rosie.

I shook my head. 'No, I don't think so. What part of the state are we in exactly?'

'The Kimberley. This property is called Brahman Crossing.' Ego and the urge to brag got the better of Ashley's common sense. 'Have you ever been here before?'

My heart stuttered. Here was another name that played a note in my songbook. I just wished I could recall the tune. 'No, Ashley. Should I have?'

He almost keeled over in laughter. Puzzled by his amusement I patiently waited for him to answered my question. Finally, Ashley brushed a tear from the corner of his eye. There was something about our whole conversation which kept him amused as he continued to leak information.

'No...not especially,' he chuckled. 'You'd like the homestead, Faith. The house is big, lots of garden space. Needs repairs though. There's lots of birds and butterflies. Actually, creatures of all types because of a fresh water billabong. All that nature is too countrified for my taste. I'd rather city night life.'

Excitement fizzed around my gut. The knowledge was useful. We were on a property in the Kimberley near a place called Mount Ibour. I kept my face blank as I fished for more.

'So why did you and your father choose a remote cattle station? It must be a real hassle to look after all the stock as well as run your laundry. I mean how do you stop the employees from poking their nose into your business?'

Ashley roared with laughter. 'We don't run a cattle station, you ninny,' he choked out. 'The locals all think Brahman Crossing is some sort of a wellness centre. You know, a retreat for people recovering from serious illness.'

'And it's not?'

'Well, sort of. We do run a retreat, but it's for anyone needing to maintain a low profile, especially from the law. We then smuggle them out of the country and give them a new life abroad. It costs them big bucks for the privilege, of course. As a bonus to us, we get our guests to work the laundry while they wait for resettlement. It was a sweet gig but we have to chuck it in for a while.'

'Oh, why's that?'

Ashley began to set up a laptop on the bench opposite me. I thought the well of information coming from him might have dried up but just as I replaced the banknote, I was checking, under the magnifying glass he spoke. 'Russ made some mistakes in Perth last June. He's drawn unwanted attention our way. That's why Dad took him away – so he could read him the riot act. He'll be back in a few days. In the meantime, I have to come up with a new scheme that will keep him busy and out of sight. Maybe then he'll stay out of trouble.'

Not wanting to sour Ashley's mood with discussions about Russ, I steered the conversation away. 'Wow, I can't believe you've been running a holiday camp for criminals. That's really smart, Ashley.'

His dimple appeared. 'I told you when we first met that I was a very smart businessman.' He moved to the far end of the desk and spread a handful of Australian passports under a second magnifying light. 'Now, enough chit-chat from you my girl, we've got a lot of work to get through.'

\* \* \*

I heaved a sigh of relief as I placed the final fifty dollar note into a plastic tub and clipped the lid in place. I pulled my shoulders back and arched my back. My neck was knotted and tight. I rotated it a few times to loosen it up. I'd spent the entire night and most of the morning hunched over the table diligently scrutinising a huge sum of counterfeit money.

'I've finished the fifties, Ashley. There were sixty notes with faults.' I indicated to a cardboard box at my feet marked rejects.

Ashley's brows rose. 'Thank you, Sunflower. I must say you're much faster and way more accurate than Rattler.'

'I aim to please, my darling.' I gave him a slight smile, but felt dirty inside. All night I'd prostituted myself using sweet words, terms of endearment and small gestures of affection to keep his mercurial mood from going dark again. It had worked. He was totally relaxed. I was relieved because it was almost time for me to move on to phase two of a plan I had devised. Tonight, I was going to make a bid for freedom.

* * *

Ryan's ears ached from the constant squawk of the seabirds congregated on Gull Disco - his name for the bird poop-encrusted granite knoll they all shared. The layer of dried seaweed hadn't protected either of them from the slop of bird droppings constantly being discharged by their avian neighbours as they went about their normal life. Tennille's gorgeous coat was matted and white. She had long ago stopped enjoying the stakeout and now lay with her head buried under the backpack trying to hide. Ryan felt sorry for her. Maybe he should have left her at Rivers Run in the care of Kelsey and Bull.

He was bored. There'd been no movement at the beach settlement for well over twelve hours, not since Faith had been dragged into the workshop. Ryan wondered what the hell they were up to. For the umpteenth time he considered taking the opportunity to sneak into the shack for a squizz. Temptation convinced him.

'Come on, Tennille, lets move.' His dog's head shot up. She eagerly rose to all fours, stretched her butt to the sky in a graceful bow and yawned. Ryan sympathised. He too needed a break. 'Let's go to the buggy, take a meal break. I suppose I better give Rosie a call as well. She'll be going ballistic by now. After that, while you watch our gear, I think I'll take my chances and have a scout around the cabin.'

Ryan shuffled to his left knee. He was about to throw the seaweed aside when the workshop door suddenly flew open. Cub stepped out into the noon day heat. He reached for the sky in a long drawn out stretch and yawned so loud Ryan caught the sound of it. A weary looking Faith trailed along in his wake. Cub spoke to her and pointed to the shack. She hurried away in that direction. Meanwhile Cub disappeared back inside the workshop only to remerge a moment later clutching a folding chair in his fist. He set it up in the shade of the workshop, so it overlooked the bay. He slumped into the seat and stared at the islet.

'Shit.' Ryan placed a gentle hand on his dog's head. 'Down, Tennille. The bastard is looking right at us.' At Ryan's sharp tone Tennille dropped to her belly and nestled close against his side as though offering comfort. 'It's okay, girl. We can't swim away unseen at the moment so I guess we're stuck in the disco for a while longer.' Ryan stroked the fur between Tennille's ears until she relaxed.

With careful movements Ryan resettled onto his belly. He watched the man on top of the cliff loll about in the chair as he gazed at the calm ocean. Cub gave no indication he'd noticed anything out of the ordinary. It was a full ten minutes later before Faith returned. In her hands she carried a large bowl and a mug. She held them out towards her husband with a sweet smile. Cub reached up, grabbed her forearm and yanked her to her knees. Ryan could see her battle to stop the drink from spilling. Cub spoke, removed the cup from her hand and took a large gulp. Faith crawled to a spot close to his chair and settled on the ground next to him. He snatched the bowl from her. Ryan ground his teeth in fury as Faith was made to sit with her head bowed while Cub ate. When he'd finished, he dropped the bowl into her lap and murmured something. She looked up and mouthed a thank you. Cub twisted his hand in the long plait that hung down her back and pulled her hard against his leg, effectively making her immobile. He closed his eyes and seemed to go to sleep.

Ryan studied Faith. His anger raged deep. There was a circle of black around her eye. Her cheeks were sunken and her body gaunt. There was no sign of the joyous laughter that had once lived on her face.

* * *

Ashley was tired. While I'd prepared him some lunch he'd had another mood swing. Now he was in full bully mode. I held out his green tea. He jerked me to the ground. I battled hard no to spill the cup or bowl. He would punish me if I did. I knew no amount of affectionate handling was going to appease him so I remained silent and held out his drink to him. Ashley snatched it from my hand and took a large gulp.

'Lunch,' he demanded, gesturing for me to hand him the bowl. He ate most of the green salad I'd prepared and his mood suddenly shifted.

'You did a good job on those bank notes, Sunshine. You can eat what's left.' He shoved his almost empty bowl at me.

'Thank you, Ashley. Did you have enough yourself?'

'It'll do for now. I'm tired. I'm taking a nap. I want you to stay exactly where you are. I can't rest properly if you're not right by my side.'

'I won't go anywhere. I promise.'

He gave me a blank stare. I don't know what he read in my face but suddenly he reached down and twisted my hair around his hand. With a tight grip he pulled me hard against his leg.

'Just to make sure.'

I sat in the awkward position and slowly ate the few remaining lettuce leaves he'd left in the bowl. As nourishment it wasn't much, but every little bit would help to fuel my engine. As I ate, I kept myself entertained by watching a brindled tern go about its busy nesting work on the rookery and waited for the telltale signs that my husband was deep asleep. Suddenly Ashley gave a sleepy snort. The fingers wrapped around my hair relaxed a tad. I reached up and gently drew some of my plait from his fist. Not too much because he would notice and then there would be an altercation. The painful pull on my neck eased. I sighed in relief and settled into a more comfortable position. I'd use this time to rest and plan. After licking the bowl clean, I set it on the ground beside me. My eyes drifted shut. In the twilight of sleep, I mapped out the things I would need to do to escape.

# Chapter Thirty-Six

I stretched out my calf muscles. Ashley had awoken from his afternoon nap stiff and grumpy. I suggested we work the kinks out with a little exercise. I didn't want to sound too enthusiastic because his first reaction would be to do the opposite. It worked. Ashley announced we would take a run along the beach. Satisfied, I continued with my gentle manipulation.

'I read somewhere once that Australian commandos are some of the fittest people in the world. Did you know it's been reported that it only takes those guys thirteen minutes to run two point five kilometres on dry sand. That's a pretty fast clip, don't you think?'

Any challenge to the male ego, especially my husband's, can't go uncontested. He rose to the bait like a river trout to a fly.

'Pftt...two-point-five in thirteen,' Ashley snorted. 'That's kid's play. Those army grunts are a bunch of mediocre sissies. I could easily do that time.'

'Really? What do you reckon you could achieve at full pace?'

Ashley gave me a thoughtful look as he stretched out his quads. 'Time me,' he said, handing me the fitness tracker from his wrist. 'I'll do the length of the beach to show you how good I really am.'

I smiled and laid on a bit more charm. 'Oh, I'd like that. I love watching your body move when you run. It's so...' I felt sick inside as I hugged myself as though delighted by the image.

Ashley stuck out his chest and preened. 'Tonight, you can show me just how much you like my body.' He pulled my long plait away from my shoulder with a jerk and began to nuzzle at my neck.

I forced out a giggle. All the while my skin crawled from his touch. I held back a shudder against the loathing weaving its icy tentacles around the lump in my chest. To get away from him I took a slow, careful step back and started to make a fuss about the size of his bicep muscle.

'Look at that. You've certainly worked hard to get the right build and muscle tone. I bet you can put in a much better time than any old soldier. But before you go tearing up the beach, we should warm you up properly. How about a slow jog to the end of the beach. Then I'll keep time while you do a solid sprint.'

Ashley flashed me a dazzling smile. 'Come on, beautiful,' he said, with a sharp slap to my butt. 'Let's rock.'

Showing off, he took off along the sand at a fast clip. Satisfaction swelled in my breast. Playing up to his ego seemed to work a real treat. I followed a careful pace behind. For my own well-being I always made sure to never run faster than my husband or have him realise how much reserve I held in my tank. I kept that little gem well hidden. After a year of jogging long distances every day and spending the rest of my time doing hard physical work, I knew I could run a lot further and faster than he ever could. Now-a-days Ashley was all flash and brag. The consumption of vast quantities of the booze he and Russ indulged in daily had made a significant mark on him.

As I strode out, the sensation of being watched returned. I slowed down a tad and scanned the sand dunes to my right. They seemed empty. A quick glance over the gentle swell in the bay revealed no sign of a boat. I gave the bird sanctuary a thoughtful stare but could see nothing untoward. I gave up searching. Whoever it was obviously had no intention of making contact. I increased my pace, to narrow the gap between Ashley and myself before he growled at me for being too slow. In my mind I ran through my plan. If all went well today, by midnight I'd either be long gone from this place or dead.

Either option suited me just fine.

* * *

Ryan focussed the binoculars on Faith as she strode out on the sand following in Cub's wake. He enjoyed watching her run. She moved with the economy and elegance of a good long-distance runner. Ryan was curious though. He could tell by the way she paced herself she was conserving energy by controlling her speed. To what end?

When the couple reached the eroded rock at the end of the bay they halted. Faith pulled out a watch, said something to her husband. He set up like he was on a starter block. After a nod from Faith he took off in a flat-out sprint. Throughout the course of the afternoon Faith seemed to time him through some sort of a harsh workout. To Ryan's trained eye he could see the man was being pushed to the point of exhaustion. He grinned. He might be able to take advantage. If the Cub zonked out, Ryan could gain access to the shack and speak with Faith.

* * *

For hours I ran Ashley ragged. I enjoyed setting him impossible targets, pandering to his self-image and applying a thick layer of awe. Anytime frustration threatened to rear its ugly head over a failure to achieve a goal, I'd fudge his next set of times to make him look good.

Ashley's showing off took a gruelling toll on his energy reserves. On the return journey to the shack, I made sure he kept face by slowing my own pace with a pretence at exhaustion. Ashley continued to show off but stumbled several times.

We entered the kitchen. Ashley ordered me to prepare him a steak dinner. He kicked off his shoes, left them in the middle of the room and staggered over to slump on the couch. With socked feet up on the coffee table his eyelids drooped. Without a word I set the table, pulled steak from the fridge and tossed together a salad. I kept my actions slow, quiet and soft to minimize the chances of making any sharp noises to disturb him.

While I waited for the skillet to heat on the stove I glanced over at my husband. To test the waters I asked, 'Ashley darling, would you like a drink with dinner? How about a glass of that red wine you like so much?'

My heart pounded loud in my ears as I waited for him to respond. There was no reaction from him. I tiptoed over to his side. His chin was nestled low on his chest. A soft snore escaped his lips. It was music to my ears. He was out to it.

Time to go.

Back in the kitchen I switched off the pan, grabbed the water filled plastic milk bottle I used for my potted herbs and on the balls of my feet crept towards the unlocked cabin door. Carefully I turned the knob. The door cracked open on its hinges. Fresh air of freedom lifted a tendril of hair from my face. I let out a deep-throated scream.

# 37

# Chapter Thirty-Seven

Russ stood on the doorstep with a stranger at his elbow.

'Hello faithful.' He grabbed the front of my shirt, tugged me against his chest. He plastered slobbery lips against mine, tried to thrust his wet tongue into my mouth. I shoved with all my might. Unprepared, Russ staggered back a couple of steps. I gagged as I slashed the back of my hand across my mouth to wipe away the drool he'd left behind.

A sleazy smirk appeared on his bruised face. 'Did ya miss me, darling?'

I grabbed the body of the door to slam it in his face but it was snatched away from my fingers. I backpedalled with a squeal of surprise. Ashley levelled a sawn-off shotgun over my shoulder at the two men on the doorstep.

'Geez, Cub,' said Russ, holding up a hand that was clutched around the neck of three bottles of Jim Beam. 'What sort of fucking welcome do you call this?'

Ashley tilted the nozzle of the gun slightly to the left so it was directed at his cousin's companion. 'Well, Rattler, as you never text or call what's a bloke to think?'

Russ's face split in a wide uneven-toothed grin. He waved the bottles of spirits in my husband's face. 'But I never come back empty-handed.'

Ashley chuckled. He flicked an eyebrow at the handsome dapper man who accompanied his cousin. 'Who the fuck are you?'

'Mort Patterson.'

'You're not due in for a couple more days.'

'I had Bingles fly him in early.'

'Why?'

'Because I hate staying in the same cabin as your father. He's no bloody fun. And that minder of his, Spider...spends all his time fussing around the old bloke like they're newlyweds or something. Always making sure he has everything he needs; baking little treats...fucking hell, it's embarrassing.' A malicious grin touched Russ's mouth. 'Speaking of food, has our little lady got our dinner ready yet? I'm starving.'

Ashley flicked a glance my way and the bully in him was back. 'Put two more steaks on the grill, woman,' he growled.

I turned away and made my way to the stove. I struggled to breathe against the lances of despair gouging painful slashes in my chest. I'd been so close. A few more minutes had been all I needed, but the untimely return of the detestable Russ had just ruined everything. Hot tears welled in my eyes but I refused to shed them.

'Come on in, Mort. Take a load off,' said Rattler, barging into the kitchen. He flung open a cupboard, grabbed a handful of glasses and began to dole out large slugs of the spirits. Within ten minutes, the men clustered around the dining table had almost emptied the first bottle of booze.

'Is the legendary Bear living nearby?' asked Mort, with a touch of awe. 'I would consider it a privilege if I could meet him.'

'You already have, mate, in Broome. It was him that you paid to make the arrangements for your resettlement overseas,' smirked Russ, unconcerned he'd just made the link that Bear Watson had desperately wanted to keep under wraps.

Mort's eyes widened with surprise.

Ashley glared across the table at his cousin and wiped the malicious smile from his face. 'Oh, by the way, cuz, the Bear wants you to go to Thailand with Mort.'

'What the fuck for?'

'We're packing up shop. He's got a new job for you - but he'll explain it to you.'

I absorbed the news with quiet satisfaction. I could only see positives in RFW leaving. When the steaks were seared on the outside and rare in the middle I served the meal. Ashley flicked me a glazed look. I guess the hard work he'd put in on the beach had lowered his tolerance level for the alcohol because he seemed totally befuddled. Unsure how it might affect his temperament I gave a tentative smile.

'The steak is just how you like it, Ashley. Will there be anything else?'

Before he could reply, Russ piped up, 'So Mort, why don't you tell Cub your tale of woe?' He snatched the steak from his plate with his fingers and ripped into the cooked flesh. The steaks juices ran down his chin. He wiped it away on the shoulder of his tee shirt, leaving a long greasy blood stain.

Ashley waved a finger at the hard backed chair positioned in the corner of the room. I obeyed his silent command, went over and sat on it. Through lowered lashes I checked out our guest. Mort Patterson had movie star good looks, soft soulful eyes and dazzling white teeth, that flashed whenever he was spoken to. In a gentile fashion he neatly propped his knife and fork against the rim of his plate, directed his pearly whites in Ashley's direction and gave a sad shake of his perfectly groomed head.

'The policing and justice system in this country has some serious flaws. The cops and judges make up their minds and condemn a man by deliberately misinterpreting facts.'

'Do tell,' said Russ. There was a malicious gleam in his eye as he tore away another mouthful from the steak and chewed with an open mouth.

'Not once was my explanation listened to without prejudice.'

'And that was?' Ashley slurred.

'One day, while I was surfing around on the internet, I found some web pages that contained photographs of children. I didn't really understand what I was looking at, but as a warden of the church I thought it was my duty to investigate. I joined up to the site, got a password and started to troll through the web pages and photos. I made a comment here and there, downloaded some content, all in an attempt to give the impression I was an active member of the site. I thought I could get some fellow member's details. I would then make a detailed report to someone in authority.'

His smarmy, slick excuse horrified and sickened me to the core.

'You're amongst friends here, Mort. Cub and I both know you're innocent,' smirked Russ. He exchanged an unreadable look with my husband who cocked a crooked smile of encouragement at the newcomer.

'We don't judge,' slurred Ashley.

'Well, that's a relief,' said Mort, taking a tiny sip of what must have been his fourth large glass of liquor. 'You can never tell how people are going to react when you discuss this kind of stuff.'

My gut soured with disgust. I tried not to squirm into my chair. We were harbouring a paedophile in our home. I hated it. Did Bear and Cub's lust for money have no boundaries?

Mort picked up his cutlery and cut a neat wedge of steak. He popped the sliver into his mouth and began to chew. 'This is a wonderful meal,' he said and flashed me an appreciative smile. 'You are an excellent cook.'

Mort's attention to me triggered Ashley. He shoved his chair away from the table. As he rose unsteadily to his feet he said, 'Come on, Mort. Let's go take a walk. I'll want to show you where you'll be staying from now on.'

Russ gave an excited grin. He snatched the bottle of Jim Beam from the table, lifted it and took a slug. He too swayed to his feet. 'Grouse idea, Cub.'

Mort cast a puzzled look around. He seemed confused by the sudden interruption to the meal. Without a word he rose from his seat and waited to be shown where to go. In a friendly gesture, Ashley slung an arm around Mort's shoulder. Together they tottered towards the door. Goosebumps rose on my arm. Ashley's sudden friendliness didn't sit right. I'd never seen him act this way to anyone. Not even his cousin. I was also confused. There was only the caravan outside and it was hardly habitable. Maybe the intention was for Mort to bunk down in the man cave.

At the door my husband turned and glared at me. 'Get this place cleaned up, Faith. Then wait on your chair for me. You and I have some unfinished business.'

My heart sank. I'd spent the last twenty-four hours building up my husband's expectations. Now he was ready to collect. My voice cracked when I whispered, 'Yes, Ashley.'

My hands shook badly as I cleared away the used plates. With a belly full of hard liquor Ashley would be brutal as he slated his lust. He always was. In desperation I filtered through a mountain of ideas to come up with one that would divert him. Only one idea really stood out - booze. After the exhausting workout he'd had today, could I get Ashley to drink himself into oblivion? It was worth a try. I hurried to the cupboard, pulled out a fresh bottle and put it on prominent display on the table. With any luck the inviting warm colour of the spirit would catch his eye and lure him away from all other thought.

Uncertain about the success of this plan I stood at the sink and mentally prepared myself while I completed all my chores. The dishes clattered badly from the tremble in my hands as I scrubbed them clean.

I was startled by a loud crack out in the yard.

* * *

Ryan made landfall. As he crawled onto the beach he heard the distinctive pop of gunfire. He glanced towards the shack, caught the flash and bang of two more shots. He dropped to his belly. Had he been made? Scanning the rise, he saw no sign of movement towards the beach.

Terror leapt to life in his breast. Was Faith alright? Had someone hurt her?

'Stay, Tennille. Hide. I'm going to take a look.' His dog raced to a nearby shrub and hid. Trusting her to do as she'd been trained, Ryan took advantage of the darkness to cover his approach as he raced up the track nearest the workshop. When he was level with the top he hunkered down and took a careful peek over the top. The sound of voices carried to him from the far side of the yard. He couldn't get a clear look as the vegetable garden interfered with his view. Ryan flicked a glanced toward the shack. A beam of dull, yellow light lit the window and traced a rectangular frame around the door. Suddenly, there was movement behind the glass. Burger peered out into the gloom. She had a puzzled expression on her face. Ryan's heart rate slowed to a more manageable pace. The temptation to slip into the building and speak with her gave him a shove. He hugged the wall and skirted around the workshop. He crawled across the open space to the vegetable patch. He rose to his knee and took a look. Two hops would see him over the garden fence and onto the veranda. He prepared himself. Suddenly, uneven footsteps crunched nearby.

'Shit,' he muttered, and rolled under a nearby shrub. He curled into a tight ball and froze. Two scruffy sandshoes stumbled to the bush where he hid. They halted.

'Where the fuck did you say, Cub?'

'Keep going, Rattler. It's next to the washing machine.'

'Can't see a fucking thing...'

'Well, switch the bloody light on, you stupid nong.'

'Oh, yeah!'

The shoes moved. A bright beam lit the yard. Ryan let out a silent curse. There was no way he could approach the building without being seen now. He glanced into the laundry area. Rattler's attention was focussed on his search. Ryan took the opportunity, slid out from under the bush and drifted away like a ghost, heading back to the beach.

\* \* \*

*Crack...crack, crack.*

Was that thunder? In puzzlement, I stared through the kitchen window at the sky waiting for it to light up. It didn't. The night remained dark and silent. Suddenly the yard light came on. Russ let out a loud curse as he crashed around in the laundry lean-to. I sighed. I bet he was leaving another big mess for me to clean up. As to what he was searching for - I'd given up a long time ago trying to understand half the things he and Ashley did.

I stepped away from the window and grabbed another glass to dry. I successfully managed to put away the dishes without breaking any. A major achievement considering my shaking hands. I set the clean cast iron pan to dry on the stovetop. Later I would season it with oil. With nothing left to do, I obeyed instructions and sat in my chair. I had to wait a long time and was actually nodding off to sleep when Ashley and Russ staggered back inside. Both men were covered in grime and sweat.

Russ was pepped up and talking. 'Man, that was awesome. It's like being on the side of the angels. Guess I won't be going away now.'

Ashley cast him a grim look. 'Shut your cakehole. Bear's not going to like it.'

'Awe, man. What can he say? He's been paid, so where's the harm. I reckon all you need is a drink...' Russ spotted the bottles on the table and rushed over to crack one open.

'It's not good for business,' snarled my husband, following him.

'So, who's gonna know?'

Curiosity got the better of me. I forgot my place and piped up, 'I heard a loud bang outside, Ashley. Is there a problem?'

I rose to my feet and moved towards him.

Russ, cocked an eyebrow at me as he handed Ashley a full glass. 'She's getting a bit nosy, isn't she. What if she blabs?'

Blab. What the hell was he on about? I had nothing to blab about. Besides, who the hell did I have to talk to anyway? I flicked a puzzled glance in his direction. I was caught totally unawares by the back of Ashley's hand. It smashed across my cheek with his full force behind it. I flew sideways. My ribs caught the corner of the table. The bottles and glasses rattled, almost toppled to the floor. I let out a loud screech as the air whistled from my lungs. I tumbled into a formless heap on the floor and lay there with my arms wrapped around my chest struggling to breath. As if coming from a vast distance, Ashley's hard voice penetrated my fog of pain.

'Mind your own business, Faith. Or you will become a permanent fixture out in the yard.'

I raised my eyes beseechingly. He ignored my huddled form,
snatched up a bottle and stalked over to his armchair. Russ looked
down at me with a malicious grin before joining him.

# Chapter Thirty-Eight

Salt laden air stung my split lip. From the windy crag above the beach, I watched Ashley stagger along the shoreline in a drunken shamble while waves of black misery killed off the last of my old self leaving me dead inside. Russ's early return had not only ruined the opportunity I'd so carefully crafted to escape but had also destroyed the tentative truce to Ashley's bullying. It would take a major miracle for me to get away now. Unfortunately, miracles and I weren't on speaking terms. I just had to accept that this was going to be my life until I died.

A warm breath touched my cheek. 'Enjoying the view, sweet 'n faithful?' Russ whispered close to my ear. He leant forward and applied slobbery lips to the curve of my neck. I stumbled back, horrified that I been so absorbed in my dark thoughts I'd allowed him sneak so close to me. Russ's hand snaked out and grabbed mine. He jerked it towards his groin. 'Wanna feel a real man?'

I reefed my hand away before I was made to touch him. My guts roiled with sour revulsion. I made no attempt to keep my contemptuous hatred of him from showing on my face.

'Back off you disgusting creep!' I yelled. 'I wouldn't want you if you were the last man on earth.'

'Tut tut, you mustn't talk like that. Everything is falling into place - it won't be long now. Soon you're gonna enjoy the taste of me.'

'Not going to happen. You might think you've an unassailable position of influence at Ashley's side but I bet he wouldn't like to know you're trying to poach on his territory.'

'He wouldn't believe you, even if you had the guts to tell him, Faithful. He trusts me.'

'Shall we test that theory when he comes back? It will only take one little smile from me in your direction and Ashley will explode. I'd hate to be in your boots then.'

The rat face weasel knew I was right. Ashley's angry jealousy was legendary in our household. Kinship wouldn't be enough to save Russ if my husband caught him touching me.

The yellowish green bruises on his face, Bear Watson's reminder to do as he was told, contorted into weird shapes as a look of frustration bent his features out of shape.

In a harsh tone he announced, 'They're dead you know.'

Confused by the sudden change of subject, I unwittingly took the bait. 'Who's dead?'

'Saintly Uncle Alex and that snooty-nosed cousin of yours. Ashley ordered me to do it while I was away last June.'

The world seemed to halt on its axis. Deep in my chest my heart gave a painful clench like hot knife had cleaved it in two. My knees wobbled.

*Dead! How could my precious family be dead? Ashley had promised me they wouldn't be harmed.*

With effort the world came back into focus. I caught a look of malicious enjoyment deep in Russ's eyes. I had no intention of giving him any more satisfaction or enjoyment from the pain he'd just inflicted on me. I folded my lips, turned and made my legs move.

Russ stepped into my path. 'You don't you believe me, do you, little Faithful? Think I'm not capable.' He yanked a mobile phone from his trouser pocket and shoved it under my nose. 'Take a look.'

Involuntarily, I glanced down. A photo was on the screen. It was the sickening image of a bloody, beaten man sprawled on the ground. I took a closer look. Through the bruising, swelling and blood splatter I recognised the darling features of my Uncle Alex.

'I have more. Wanna see?'

'I've got work to do,' I said, pushing the phone away before he could flash up any more graphic photos.

I brushed past his outthrust arm, ignored the rawness of my ribs and sprinted across the yard. The last thing in this world I wanted or needed to see was images of my family's dead bodies. My mind was a shattered mess; broken to such an extent I didn't want to live anymore. Everyone I'd ever loved was now lost to me. I was all alone in the world. As for Ashley, the bastard, had lied to me. He'd vowed that no harm would ever come to Chip's and Unk, as long as I stayed with him. Well, fuck him. He didn't have that threat to hold over me anymore. Nothing and I mean nothing, was going to hold me back. I was going to get out of here, even if it cost me my life.

Footsteps pounded on the turf behind me. Russ grabbed my wrist, swung me around and tugged me hard against his chest.

'Ashley made me do it you know. You know how he likes to hurt you. He said he would cut off your ears if I didn't do as he ordered.' He cupped my face with damp palms. In a low voice he said, 'You're so beautiful. I couldn't take that risk. I'd never treat you the way he does, Faithful. I'd care for you like a queen if you'd let me.'

Revolted, I jerked away. If I'd learnt anything in this life it was not to believe any of the corruption that spouted from Russ's mouth.

He was a vicious creature who got off on inflicting pain and fear. Well, two could play that game.

Letting all the hatred I felt for him fill me, I snarled, 'Don't you ever touch me again. If you do, I'll feed you to Ashley.'

I stalked to the outdoor laundry, ran a sink full of water and took my time to hand wash the soil marks from the pile of clothes in the tub. My ribs throbbed as I dragged the basket of wet washing to the clothesline. I couldn't stop the hiss of pain every time I reached up to peg out a shirt. Under my breath I let loose a litany of curses for my husband's dark, volatile temper and the ready use he'd made of the back of his hand. I added Russ to the mix. Had it only been twelve hours since his return to the shack? In that time, he'd effectively destroyed the small element of peace I'd managed to establish. Ashley had been so much better without his cousin around, but unfortunately the bastard knew how to strum my husband's chords and set fire to his insecurities. I'd noticed Russ had been especially busy since returning from the yard the previous evening. I began to wonder if the walloping Bear had meted out to him or the threat to send him away had triggered in him a bout of spiteful revenge because he seemed to have embarked upon a game that involved establishing a wedge between father and son. At breakfast he been filling Ashley's head with all sorts of crap about how father bears underappreciated their cubs. He also obliquely referred to the fact that Bear's love of money seemed to have overridden any sense of decency, and that it was a good thing they'd done what they'd done so they weren't tarred with the same brush. I couldn't work out what he'd meant by that statement but it had had an effect on Ashley. His mood had visibly darkened over the hours of being spoon fed the vile, ill-concealed spite. In a foul mood he'd stormed away to take a run on the beach.

As I pegged out the last item of clothing the sensation of being watched returned. I flicked a quick glance over my shoulder, to check if rat face was about to make another play for me. He stood at the far end of the yard staring at a pile of freshly churned earth with a self-satisfied grin on his face. The impression wasn't coming from his direction. It also didn't have the same creepy vibe I got when I knew he was watching me. Maybe it was our guest, Mort Patterson. I glanced toward the caravan. The spider's web was still across the door. Mort can't have bedded down in the workshop. It was pad-locked. Actually, now I came to think about it, I didn't recall seeing him again after he'd headed off for a stroll with Ashley last night. Where was he?

*'Why the hell are you wasting your time worrying about it, Faith?' I growled to myself. 'There's a more important subject that needs your attention.'*

With a snap of my fingers, I jettisoned all the useless speculation going on in my head and zeroed in what was most important – my escape. I cast a glance at the sky. The wet season seemed to be over. The searing heat of the dry hadn't quite kicked into high gear yet so the daytime temperatures were at their best if I was to slog through the bush on foot.

I needed to harvest some veg from the garden so I had food to eat. I could carry it and some water in plastic milk bottles. With a half-formed plan in mind, I returned the empty clothes basket to its hook on the wall above the laundry sink, opened the cupboard and grabbed my gardening toolkit. Accompanied by the squawk of seagulls as they glided on the sea breeze high above me and the caw of the grumpy crow that liked to perch in the tree next to the shack, I wandered around the thriving vegetable patch. The garden was the only solace that existed in my life. With my hands in the warm earth, my head in the fresh air and my heart filled with the love of nature around me, it was like a balm to my damaged soul.

Selecting a small weeding fork, I knelt among the row of beetroot seedlings. Being mindful of my injured ribs I routed out a stray weed. Sunshine kissed my shoulders and warmed a tiny portion of my soul as I eased my way along the beds weeding, until I came to the mature tomato bushes. I snuck a guilty look around to make sure I wasn't being watched, which was silly because I did this every day and no one knew I had any other purpose for the food other than for the men's dinner. I picked a good pile of blushing red, vitamin rich tomatoes and set them in a heap next to the garden gate. So as not to raise suspicion about the amount of fruit I'd harvested, I would cook a stuffed tomato bake for dinner and turn the rest into ketchup. The sauce could easily be stored in the plastic bottle and would be a ready source of food for me when I was on the run.

As I worked the garden, I let my mind drift over the current state of affairs. In his arrogance I think Ashley still believed the fairy tale I'd woven around us - I'd finally submitted to his rule and loved him. My hard-won concessions - being allowed to wear shoes and not being shackled – were still in force. I wish I had the combination to the safe where Ashley kept the car keys and the satellite phone.

*Well, if wishes were horses, Faith, you could fly out of here on the back of a winged stallion.*

I shook my head at the tangent my thoughts were heading. I reeled them back. I'd have to manage my escape on foot. Ashley and Russ would give chase, there was no doubt, because Ashley was a ruthless obsessive. He would hunt for me to the ends of the earth and if caught his punishment would be brutal. I would have to put some time and distance between us to have any chance of disappearing. Could I drug their evening meal? I'd need some sort of knockout drops. Russ probably still had some of the Rohypnol I'd heard him bragging about using, but there was no way I was going into his bedroom to search. That was an activity fraught with too much danger.

A bee lazily buzzed past my ear on its way to feast on the flowering grevillea that grew alongside the potted herbs and broke my train of thought. I sat back on my heels and stared at the sparkling ocean. A boat would be the perfect solution to all my problems. If I got away, maybe I would buy one. Chips and I could sail somewhere far, far away. My throat tightened. A tear slowly rolled down my cheek. I couldn't do that. My wonderful cousin was dead. A sob swelled in my breast. It threatened to break free. If I let it out, I would break. I clamped my trembling lips and viciously thrust the garden fork hard into the soil to take my grief out on a stubborn weed. Pain seared along my ribs. With a moan I grabbed my ribcage and rocked in place, riding out the agony.

The screech of an unoiled car door being opened dragged me away from my inner turmoil. I flicked a glance over my shoulder. Russ unloaded a plant pot from the rear of the clapped-out vehicle he'd returned in the previous evening. With his arms clutched around the plant he kicked the stubborn door shut.

'I see your pussy whipped hubbies bought you another fruit tree,' he growled, staggering over. He dropped the pot on top of the pile of tomatoes I'd just picked.

'Watch what you're doing,' I cried, angry at the loss. 'Those were for dinner.'

He snorted. 'Bloody salad, no thanks. You are going to cook me a big, juicy steak.'

Ready to throw caution to the wind I opened my mouth to tell him to shove it. I was saved from the indiscretion by Ashley, who chose that moment to pound up the garden path. His shirt was soaked with perspiration, his face flushed. A river of sweat had plastered his hair to his scalp. He looked grey and ill.

Ashley checked his smart watch, grunted and glared at his cousin who was still had an inane grin directed at me.

'What's going on?' he snarled.

Russ picked up the plant. 'Just asking if there was anywhere special your wife wanted your gift planted.' Faced with Ashley's obvious bad mood, all traces of the smile disappeared from Russ's face and the cockiness left him. 'I'll put it over near the stump and you can tell her where you want it later, mate.'

I focussed all my attention on Ashley and didn't acknowledge Russ's presence in any way. With care I tried to appease the jealous monster lurking in my husband's eyes.

'Thank you, for the lemon tree, Ashley. It was a very thoughtful gift.' He grunted and continued to glare. 'You weren't gone very long. Wasn't the beach to your liking?'

'No,' he growled.

I held my breath and waited. Ashley vaulted over the fence, bumped Russ aside and squatted down in front of me. His breathing was laboured, and reeked of stale alcohol. With harsh hands he brushed the hair away from my sweaty cheek, cupped my face with his palms and squeezed. 'I missed having you at my side.'

My face hurt. I could see suspicion dancing in the background of his actions. 'I missed our time together too,' I said, hoping to divert the path I could see his mind was travelling. I tried to select my next word with care. It was never good if there was a perceived criticism. 'I'm sorry I couldn't manage a jog today but my ribs...'

Even though his tone was contrite and consolatory, the grip he had on my face remained painfully tight. From the corner of my eye, I saw Russ dump the tree near the pile of freshly churned earth and slink towards the shack.

'You're so clumsy, Sunflower. You must be more careful.'

So, Ashley wasn't so repentant he was about to admit my injury was his fault. He tugged me towards him, captured my lips in a demanding kiss that tasted stale and sour. I gave the minimum response that I knew I could get away with. He jerked me harder against his perspiration-soaked body, reached under my legs and lifted me up into his arms. I groaned as pain flared along my rib cage. I knew there would be no escape from what was coming so I closed my mind as Ashley carried me to our bedroom and kicked the door shut. In his haste he tore my dress away before tumbling me to the bed. I kept silent, closed my eyes and pretended enjoyment while I waited for him to finish, grateful that this time he hadn't felt the need to flog me with his belt. Over time I had learnt to shut down and not think about these moments.

When Ashley was sated, he rolled away and began to snore. Careful not to disturb the sleeping monster, I slipped from the bed and gathered together my torn clothes. That's when I heard a snigger. I spun around.

Ashley hadn't moved. I scrutinized his face. He was sound asleep. The window was closed and the curtain drawn. I flicked a glance at the bedroom door. It was ajar. The hairs on the back of my neck rose and my stomach knotted. Russ had been watching us.

* * *

Late in the afternoon the men were sprawled in the lounge chairs they'd pulled out onto the veranda and were hitting the bottle hard.

'Stay where I can see you,' Ashley ordered as I pottered from the vegetable patch to the laundry and back. Russ murmured something to my husband and pointed to the far end of the yard. 'And plant that damn tree before it dies.'

The potted lemon stood next to a pile of churned earth. I couldn't believe Russ had willingly dug the hole for me. There had to be a catch. I assessed both men warily but they'd gone back to their conversation and seemed to be ignoring my activities. I shrugged, filled a bucket to the brim with water and carried it over. As I bent forward to empty the pail into the freshly dug hole, I caught a glimpse of what was at the bottom. The horrified scream of terror didn't stay locked inside my head. It erupted from my throat in a deafening roar almost drowning out the vicious laughter coming from my husband and his cousin as they watched me stumble back. I took one look at them and threw up the contents of my stomach.

# Chapter Thirty-Nine

Ashley dead-locked the door and stuffed the key into the front pocket of his trousers. Russ cracked open a new bottle of Jim Beam. He poured out two large slugs for them. In his haste to get to the booze, Ashley, neglected to reattach the shackle to my ankle. I sat as quiet as a mouse in my hard-backed corner chair mending my torn dress and did nothing to draw attention to myself. I felt ill. The rancid sourness in my gut was being churned up by the butter-flies of fear that were trapped there. Images of the lifeless eyes and marble white face of Mort Patterson scrolled over and over in my mind, like a music track stuck on repeat. There was no doubt I lived with depraved men but I never considered they were capable of cold-blooded murder in their obsessive pursuit of whatever they wanted.

My eyes filled. My vision blurred. I had to blink away the tears before I stabbed myself with the needle. I took a deep breath and decided as soon as the men were asleep, I was going to break out of the shack somehow and run.

'Bottoms up,' said Russ, raising his glass in a toast.

Ashley copied the salute and tossed his drink back in one large gulp. Russ took a tentative sip from his own glass and immediately refilled my husband's.

'Sorry, wasn't ready. Let's try that again. One, two, three, scull.'

Suddenly Russ and Ashley were competing in a shot drinking competition. Through lowered eyelashes I watched. It didn't take long for me to realise that the sneaky bastard Russ only pretended to knock back his share of the spirits. For every slug he poured for Ashley, he only took a small sip of his own. Before it was noticed he quickly refilled the glasses. Apprehension gnawed at my gut as I watched the contents of the bottle sink rapidly down my husband's throat.

What the hell was rat-face up to?

Russ cracked a new bottle and poured. He held out the glass to Ashley but his chin had sagged to his chest. Russ reached over and shook him by the shoulder.

'Hey there Cuz, not flaking out on me, are ya?'

Ashley snorted but didn't rouse. A satisfied smirk touched Russ's mouth. He heaved himself up from the soft armchair and swayed in place. His watery red-eyed gaze roamed in an unfocused fashion around the room. When his glance fell on me it halted.

'There you are...well, well, well, my sssweet little Faithful. Guess it'sss just you and me.' Russ stared down, cupped his hand over his groin and gave it a wiggle. 'Let'sss have us some fun.'

He lurched in my direction as if his legs were made of rubber. Though he was drunk as a lord, had trouble stringing his words together, and couldn't navigate a straight line, there was absolutely no doubt he was still capable of hurting me badly. Terrified by the thought of him touching me, I let my sewing drop to the floor and scrambled to my feet. I'd suffered months of abuse at the hands of my husband, there was no way I was going to let Russ add to that nightmare.

'Ashley, help,' I yelled.

My husband, undisturbed by my cry, let out a loud snore as Russ lurched in my direction. I spun my chair around and shoved it into his path. He stumbled but his flailing hand caught hold of the back of the sofa to stop himself falling flat on his face. He sneered, pulled himself erect and staggered towards me undeterred.

'Now, now, Faith, don't be shy. You know you want me.'

My heart began to pound. I swept a desperate glance around the room seeking a way to evade him. Both the door and window shutter were locked. The key tucked in Ashley's pocket. I backed away and considered locking myself in the bathroom, but the door was paper thin. One determined kick against the flimsy panel and it would splinter. Then I'd be in real trouble because I'd be cornered in a room with nowhere to go.

A thought flickered to life.

*Arm yourself, Faith.*

I shot a glance into the kitchen. My knives were locked away but the cast-iron skillet on top of the stove was a possibility. It had a heavy base, hefty enough to make Russ see stars if I landed a good blow. I just had to get to it. I ducked around the table, reached out. My fingers brushed the pan handle. I was jerked away by two strong, wiry arms around my chest.

Russ dragged me back against his body and ran his tongue up the side of my neck.

'You taste so good...' he crooned, taking another lick of my skin.

Sickened by his touch and the foul stench that radiated from his sour, sweaty body, I kicked back with the heel of my running shoe, aiming for his shin. I missed. Russ tightened his steely grip around my chest and squeezed. I struggled to draw breath.

'Let me go,' I gasped.

'Shhh, my sssweet little Faithful. We don't want to disturb the sleeping cub, now do we?' he slurred in my ear. 'You don't know how long I've waited for you. Much too long. Did you enjoy the gift I planted out in the garden for you? Ssspecial wasn't it.'

The image of Mort Patterson's dead face stirred up the bile in my gut again. I gulped against the burn in my throat.

'He'sss not the only one out there. I'll take you for a tour later.'

Horrified and sickened at the thought I writhed, like an eel in a fisherman's cooking pot, trying to break his hold. Russ tightened his hold, the world started to go black. Before I passed out, I made a last-ditch effort by craning my neck until his jaw was within reach of my teeth. I latched on; bit hard. He howled and let go. Able to breath, I greedily sucked in a large breath. Quick as a whippet Russ grabbed the back of my head.

'Bitch,' he snarled.

He slammed me face down onto the table. My cheekbones crunched. Russ used his full body weight to pin me down. With the palm of his hand, he ground my face hard against the laminated table top. Hot pain shot across my face. I screamed.

'That's enough foreplay for now. Time to open up, little girl.' He shoved a knee between my legs. Fighting off the fog of agony I locked my ankles around each other to stop him getting his other knee in to spread my legs.

'You're mine, do you hear?' he growled in my ear. 'Not that snivelling Huntsman, Slugger - mine. I made that bastard suffer for demanding a kiss from *my girl*. He cried like a baby when I made him dig his own grave.' He thumped the table near my nose with his fist. 'As for soldier boy - so gullible. He was no match for me. I've got a special place all for him.'

Soldier boy! Who was he talking about? Not Ryan! Had he done something to that beautiful man? Russ rambled on in my ear, about things he'd done to others while his fingers fumbled their way inside my clothing.

'Cub shouldn't have taken you away from me. I think I'll punish him for it later. You were always supposed to be mine. I told you so in the letters I left on your car. Remember. Why didn't you listen? Why did you have to let Cub take you?'

Silence followed his drunken ramble. I continued to resist all attempts to allow access to my body, by keeping my legs locked and pressing myself to the table. Suddenly the hand inside my dress stopped moving and Russ became a dead weight. Had the alcohol finally taken its toll. I shifted my numb hands. I unlocked my ankles. Russ roused. His probing fingers found the elastic on my knickers. He yanked hard, they tore and pooled on the floor around my feet. Fear, disgust, loathing melded with the degradation that already tainted my soul. I had to get away. This rape would be the end of me. To give me strength I tapped into all my emotional turmoil, lay my palms flat on the table, braced my feet and surged upwards. Caught unawares, Russ stumbled backwards across the room. He came to a crashing halt against the kitchen cabinet. Breath exploded from his lungs. I shot a look over my shoulder and watched in satisfaction as his knees buckled and he slumped to the floor.

'What the fuck is going on,' yelled Ashley, rising from his chair. He wove an unsteady path across the room towards us. He blinked owlishly down at Russ who was lying slumped in an untidy heap against the cupboard.

'She wanted it,' Russ slurred. 'She was positively begging me to service her, Cub. I was fighting her off, mate. Honest.'

The skin in Ashley's cheeks marbleized to grey-white. His eyes changed to the colour of midnight. Terror surged through me.

'He's a liar. He...Russ...he got you drunk on purpose, so he could rape me.' I screamed, attempting to penetrate the hot lava of anger that consumed him.

Ashley lashed out. The force of his open hand across my face lifted me off the floor. I flew across the room and collided with the front of the stove. Breath bolted from my lungs in a long, howling gasp. Winded, I could feel my lips move as I desperately tried to suck in oxygen, to no avail. The room began to dim. Suddenly and with a noisy rush, my ability to breathe returned. I gulped in a loud wheezing breath. Hurriedly, I pulled myself upright and drank in the sensation of air filling my lungs. I stared up at my husband and was petrified by the cold fury on his face as he stalked towards me. His lips moved, but every sound in the room was muffled by a reverberating buzz in my ears. My tongue tasted blood. Ashley raised his fist. With a sob I waited for death to claim me.

Russ stumbled to his feet with a look of absolute delight on his face. My hearing returned in time to catch his gleeful snigger. Ashley's fist stopped mid-flight. He swung around to grab his cousin by the throat. Russ's eyes bulged, like two overripe gooseberries, as they threatened to explode from their sockets. He fumbled with useless fingers at Ashley's wrist trying to make him loosen his grip.

'Cub, mate, it's me, Russ. Your best bud,' he choked out. 'Let go will ya.'

Ashley started. He let go. A look of relief cut across Russ's face. Ashley's shoulders sagged and his stance relaxed.

'That's better, Cuz. No harm no foul. We agreed when we started this, that we were going to share. Remember?'

Ashley went stock still. The black filled his eyes again, this time eliminating all traces of any colour they possessed. In an even, measured tone, he said, 'the money, yes, but not Faith. Never, Faith. *She's mine.*'

Ashley's knuckles took on the appearance of being cast from ivory as he reapplied his finger to Russ's throat. He lifted his feet off the floor. Russ thrashed his limbs around in a frantic dance that resembled an uncoordinated puppet on a string. I watched in horror as his eyes bulged and reddened with blood.

'Ashley,' I whispered. 'You're killing him.'

Ashley's expressionless face stared down at me until Russ's body stilled. I pointed. Ashley raised his eyes to study his handiwork. He slowly unclamped his fingers and let his cousin drop to the floor. Russ landed with a resounding thump and didn't move. I stared at the motionless heap for a heartbeat before flicking my glance back up to Ashley. I couldn't hold back the sob of dread that escaped when he locked his emotionless gaze onto mine and I read their meaning.

He reached down and unbuckled his trouser belt. 'So, my darling wife, you need servicing do you.'

To brace myself against the brutality to come, I reached around behind me. My hand fell on something long, thin and solid. I wrapped my fingers around it and surged to my feet. Without hesitation I swung my arm with all the power I could muster. The flat bottom of the skillet in my hand landed with an ominous crunch against the side of my husband's face. Ashley's head snapped right. Awareness left his eyes. His knees buckled. In slow motion he joined his cousin on the floor. I let the skillet drop as though it burnt my skin and stared in shock at what I had done.

*Run, Faith. Ashley's going to kill you when he wakes up.*

Without hesitation, I shoved my hand into the depths of his pocket. With shaking fingers, I yanked out the key and sprinted for the door. I fumbled with the lock. The key slipped and I almost dropped it.

With a panicked breath I cried out, 'Come on, you stupid thing, open.' The key slid home and I flung the door wide. The taste of freedom touched my face. Frazzled, unprepared by the suddenness and violence of events, I hesitated.

'Faith, if you want to live you have to go,' I growled. 'Remember the plan. Use the beach. Follow the coastline. Run on the hard sand, close to the waterline. The tide will wash away your footprints. Get a move on.'

Released from indecision, I sprinted toward the beach.

* * *

After enjoying a good break away from the constant squawk of the bird sanctuary, Ryan thought long and deep about the next step he'd need to take. Last night had been a close call. He'd almost been caught attempting to sneak into the shack. It had been a foolish plan; one he'd spent the day admonishing himself for. Judging by the way the husband treated Faith his being caught talking to her could have had severe consequences for her. He had to be more careful, for her sake.

Tonight offered a better opportunity for him to infiltrate the enemy camp undetected anyway. Both men had been binge drinking all day. Ryan was positive they'd either be passed out or so drunk that a herd of elephant could tromp through the shack unnoticed. Still, it wouldn't pay to be careless. He'd do a reconnaissance at 2 a.m. If the coast was clear, he'd go in and try to make contact with Faith. It was important to ask her what she wanted to do. Until then he and Tennille would wait out the hours of darkness bedded down on Gull Disco. Less chance of being accidently stumbled over by drunken feet that way.

Ryan waded away from the beach. With silent strokes he swam into deep water. Tennille, paddled at his side. The swell began to roughen. It splashed their faces. He stopped and trod water. He needed to check if rough weather was brewing. He didn't want to get marooned and not be able to return to the beach tonight. Ryan stared up at a sky ablaze with bright, gleaming stars. A sapphire blue nebula splashed dusty colour across the expanse from horizon to horizon. There were no storm clouds but the breeze was quickening.

Tennille swam a circle around him and whined.

'Just checking the weather girl,' he muttered.

She whined again and looked toward the beach. Ryan turned and caught the sound of frantic breathing and desperate footsteps racing along the sand.

* * *

I sprinted down the sandy track that led to the beach. Ignoring my burning face, aching ribs and the raft of other injuries that plagued me, I pelted along the wet sand, driven by panicked desperation. I headed in the opposite direction to the one we usually took when we jogged, hoping that by taking a different route it would throw Ashley off the scent long enough for me to get some distance between us. I pounded along the sand, close to the water's edge. I reached the granite outcrop that curved out into deep water and formed one side of the bay. I stared in horror at the swell that crashed high on its stony cliff. My plan to swim around wasn't going to be possible. The water was too rough for me in my condition. I'd have to climb the rough rocks instead.

Dragging in a deep breath, I gritted my teeth against the pain that was my body and began a slow crawl over sharp, slippery rocks that could easily tear my flesh from my bones. With persistence I gained some height, was halfway to the apex when my foot slipped on a piece of moss. My knee thumped hard onto a flat rock. The jar of it shot through my entire body like I had been slammed against the table again.

*Shit, you have to be careful, Faith. You can't run with a broken leg.*

A splash behind me made me twist around in terror. I stared into the eerie moonlight searching for movement on the sand. I couldn't spot anything, but that didn't mean Ashley wasn't there. My heart picked up its pounding pace and I began to sweat. Frightened beyond measure I renewed my efforts to conquer the cliff before Ashley came charging down the beach to claim me.

I crawled the rest of the way to the top. Reversing the procedure, I managed an uncomfortable backwards slither down the other side. When my feet made flat ground I collapsed to my knees, relieved. In awe I stared at the stretch of coastline in front of me. From what I could see it was uninhabited and extended in a straight line for a long, long way. I staggered to my feet. In blind panic I started to run. My ribs kicked up a protest, my lungs heaved as they chased air. I stumbled. Fell flat on my face.

*You stupid girl. Pull yourself together. You know you have to pace yourself.*

I pulled myself up. In a concerted effort to rein in the terror driving me, I set off with a slow count in my head. I repeated the numbers over and over again until they played an upbeat tune. I matched my steps so they harmonized with the music in my head. As I ran, I became one with the rhythm. I pushed on, listened to the beat and zoned out to everything else around me.

I must have run for hours. It came as a complete surprise when the first light of a golden dawn washed over the white caps and chased the shadows up the surrounding dunes. With the return of awareness, I felt my strength waiver and my body began to scream out its need for something to drink. Stupid me, in my rush to get away, I'd left the water bottle behind. Fatigue reared its ugly head.

I glance up ahead to where a weathered vertical wall of bedrock presented me with another challenging climb. Maybe I could take a break before I attempted it. I took a swift peek over my shoulder. A speck in the far distance moved relentlessly in my direction.

*Awe shit! Ashley.*

I picked up my pace. At the base of the cliff, I scrambled up a granite boulder, that at some time in the past had been dislodged from the rock face, to make use of a foothold higher up. As I shoved my foot in the slot, I noticed my shoes were showing the signs of the hard life they'd had. Where I'd repaired them with fishing line, the previous week, the stiches had started to tear. I prayed they'd see me through this final challenge.

Taking care, I scaled the wall. The climb wasn't as difficult as it looked, which in my exhausted condition was a bonus. It took five minutes to reach the summit. In my haste to scurry over the top I didn't notice a mat of slimy algae coating the rock underfoot. My shoe slid. My foot shot out from under me and I lost my balance. I stuck out my left hand to stop myself face-planting into a rock pool. A sharp wedge of granite, hidden under a tuft of kelp, grazed the flesh along my forearm and peeled back a large flap of skin. Blood coursed down the back of my hand, dripping from my fingers onto the rocks. An ocean spray, thrown up by the waves as they pounded against the cliff, washed over me. I bit back a scream at the sting of salt in the open wound. Hopelessness made a grab at me, as pain and exhaustion threatened to overwhelm me. I just wanted to lay down and give up the fight.

*Do you want to get caught?*

I shook my head at the voice in my head.

*Then move.*

I sat up and ripped a strip from the hem of my tattered dress. Snatching my bottom lip between my teeth against the agony, I pushed the flap of skin back into place. Sweat was pouring off me by the time I'd wound the makeshift dressing tight and tied it in place.

I scrubbed the tears from face, rolled to my knees with my arm cradled against my chest and stared back at the speck still moving relentlessly in my direction.

'I'm not going back,' I yelled in defiance at the distant figure. 'I'll die first.'

Without exposing myself to the skyline, I crawled over the slippery rocks. When I came to the other side, I discovered it was a sandy slope. I took the descent butt first and landed with a soft thud onto another beach. I rose to my feet and stared. My heart lurched. Nestled between two sand dunes was a beach shack. Its flaking paintwork that had been bleached by a forever hot sun from azure blue to mottled off-white was the best sight in the world.

'Help,' I yelled leaping to my feet and sprinting full pelt along the sand. I couldn't take my eyes from the building. I was terrified it was a mirage. 'Please, someone...I need help.

The shutter on the window was down. The steel door padlocked. My heart plummeted. Even though my actions were futile, I leaped onto the veranda anyway and pounded on the closed shutter. The sound echoed inside and spoke volumes to the place being empty.

Crippling disappointment swamped me. I stumbled from the porch, fell to my knees and pounded the warm sand with clenched fists. Had all my effort been in vain? Had I escaped hell, come so far, for nothing. A rib shaking sob caught me by surprise.

*Don't give in, Faith. The devil is just behind and heading this way.*

I couldn't let him arrive in triumph to reclaim me.

Surely, where there was one building there would others. I stood up. The muscles in my legs twitched in protest. I swallowed and realised that thirst also had her tight grip on my throat. My arm stung like a bitch.

'Bad luck. Time to move.' I croaked. I took a step and cramp bit hard in my calf muscle.

'Fuck,' I screamed, and tumbled onto my side.

With two hands I grabbed my limb and thrashed around in the sand. I banged hard against the porch framework. A section of board dislodged. I slid into a hole. Ignoring my predicament, I rubbed a fist over the cramp trying to work it out. The pain eased. I lay with my tear-filled eyes closed and waiting until I could straighten my leg. My muscle relaxed. With a sigh of relief, I opened my eyes and stared around. I lay under the porch.

I carefully rolled onto my stomach, scooped out a few handfuls of sand until my reaching hands met with fresh air. Curious, I slid my head and shoulders through the short tunnel to take a gander. Deep underneath the porch was a small, cool, hollow. Dappled light filtered down from between the floorboards. There was enough room for a woman of my size to burrow in and hide. An idea formed. Happy, I wriggled out butt first to find some camouflage. I limped to the back of the shack and took a peek around. Vehicles had once formed a makeshift track but there were no recent tyre tracks. The road was almost fully overgrown. Well, that was a bugger. Guess I'll just have to continue on foot to find help.

With a shrug, I staggered between a couple of salt bushes and a tuft of sword grass, searching. I found a young sapling with a tenuous grip on the soil. I grabbed hold of the stem and gave it a good yank. It uprooted easily enough. With my foot I tamped down the ground to cover up the unearthing. With bush in hand, I staggered back to the beach and set about making a new set of footprints to disguise where I had actually gone after which I ran to the door of the shack again before heading off down the beach as if I'd discovered the place unoccupied and had continued on. Stepping backwards in my new tracks I returned to the porch. With the shrub, I eliminated all traces of myself as I crawled into the burrow. I pulled the young sapling in after me until it blocked the entire entrance and planted its roots deep into the sand, hoping that from the outside it would look like the plant had grown there over time. In the cool dappled light, I crawled to the far side of the burrow, dug a hole and curled up into a tiny ball. Using handfuls of sand, I covered most of my body.

It was so cosy in the quiet tomb exhaustion overtook me.

\* \* \*

A snuffle jerked me awake. An animal was sniffing the porch.

'Whatcha' got girl?' asked a deep, husky male voice.

My heart leapt into overdrive. There was someone here. A shiver ran down my spine. I held my breath, unsure whether to be excited or terrified. Odd footsteps echoed above my head. The padlock on the door rattled. Who was it on the porch? It wasn't Ashley. That hadn't been his voice. I craned my neck to get a look through one of the knotholes in the wood above my head. It was covered with the tread of a shoe. Exhaustion, thirst and injury had taken their toll but I still questioned the risk of calling out for help. Surely anyone seeing the state I was in wouldn't disbelieve my need for aid? I hesitated because Ashley hadn't been that far behind me on the beach. He was sure to have a convincing story to tell when he arrived to claim me back.

*Do I take the risk?*

Deciding yes, I opened my mouth. The man spoke. 'The building's padlocked. So, she couldn't get inside. Let's take a gander around the back.'

I slapped a hand over my mouth. Whoever it was knew about me and was searching.

Nails scratched on the floorboards, accompanied by a loud snuffle.

'Woof.' The dog scratched at the knothole I'd been looking through.

*Awe shit, it could bloody smell me.*

I took shallow breaths and prayed the man couldn't interpret what his dog was trying to tell him.

'Hmm, yeah, I see it, girl. Looks like blood. There was some up on the rocks too.'

He left the porch and strode out onto the beach. I looked down at my half-buried arm and gave a silent curse. Wet, bloody sand clung to the makeshift bandage. There were large blood droplets leading from my sapling to where I lay.

*Careless, Faith.*

A tear slid down my cheek. My heart quavered in fear. Danger was close. I burrowed even deeper into the sand in an attempt to disguise my scent from the dog. Above me the click of animal claws left the porch as the dog followed the man onto the beach. They didn't go far because I could hear the dog racing around on the sand barking in joy like it was playing some sort of game. I was just beginning to relax when a large handful of sand landed around my sapling.

*What the hell?*

The padlock above me rattled.

'Come on, you bastard of a thing.' The door groaned as it was swung open.

Uneven footsteps hurried inside the shack. Cupboards banged. Something heavy was dragged across the floor. Dust trickled onto my face when some object thumped onto the porch and was unfurled. Suddenly my burrow became darker and the noises above me muffled, but there was no mistaking the distinct groan of protest as the shutter was thrown open. Something thumped into place on the porch and I heard the distinctive creak as someone dropped into a chair. The dog gave a sharp bark that rapidly turned into a deep chesty growl.

'Shhh, not a sound,' said the man. 'We're about to have company.'

The dog ceased her warning.

Puzzled, confused and tense, I found it hard to breathe. The advice to the dog had been good, so I took it onboard and concentrated on remaining in a quiet calm zone while I waited for the next series of events to unfold. With slow breaths I listened to the rhythmic thrum of the ocean as it lapped the shore. Dust mites danced in beams of muted light around me. The air tasted of the tang of cool sand, salty sea and spicy sandalwood floorboards. Suddenly above me the man began to sing. My burrow filled with the most wonderful music.

*The first time ever I saw your face,*
*I thought the sun rose in your eyes,*
*And I thought the moon and the stars were the gift you gave...*

He had a magnificent baritone voice that touched a chord deep inside me, one filled with exquisite topaz eyes. The black cloud of melancholy, always present in my life, dissipated when a glimmer of love from deep in my soul was released. Silent tears slid down my cheeks as the music wove its magic, soothing the ache my heart always held for what I had lost. I closed my eyes to drift in the beauty of the melody.

My private concert was abruptly interrupted when a vehicle roared up to the shack.

The dog barked.

'It's all right, girl. I was expecting him.'

The dog fell silent.

The chair above me creaked once.

\* \* \*

Ryan stopped singing and tried to look relaxed in his seat on the porch of the old ranger's cabin, but in fact his muscles were coiled. He was ready for action. He kept one hand on the pistol hidden between the chair and his leg. In the other he held a dog-eared novel he'd found on the table inside. To all intents and purposes, he presented the image of a man relaxing in the fresh air outside his cabin. An SUV bounced over a nearby sand dune onto the beach and skidded to a halt about twenty meters from the porch. The driver's door swung open and a wild-eyed Russ Johnson emerged from its confines. His face and throat were a riot of bruises. The whites of his eyes bloodshot. He seemed jumpy as he flicked a nervous glance around before settling the restless gaze on Ryan.

'Hey man, nice place you got here.'

Ryan went for casual nonchalance. 'G'day mate...help you with something?'

Russ's red eyes studied Ryan for a long moment. 'Do I know you?' he asked.

Rosie had insisted Ryan not shave off his scruffy beard or trim his long unruly hair. "Less chance you'll be recognised," she'd said. He hoped that was true.

'Doubt it. Not unless you're into marine biology.'

'What are you, the park ranger?'

Ryan nodded. 'What do you need?'

'I'm looking for a woman, blonde, twenty-three, about yay high?' said Russ, thrusting a hand out to indicate a height of about five feet.

'Who isn't? This scares 'em off,' said Ryan, casually stretching out his right leg.

Russ ogled the prosthetic limb. He gave a snort of laughter. 'Bit crippled for this sort of gig aren't ya? What happened?'

'Shark.'

'My name's Russ by the way. You are?'

Ryan could tell his visitor was putting on the casual attitude but he wasn't really pulling it off because he was as twitchy as hell. Ryan carefully flicked off the safety on the gun. He didn't give his name, instead asked a question of his own. 'Who's this blonde bird you're looking for?'

'Name of Faith, she's my cousin's wife. The poor kids mentally unstable from the drugs she's addicted to. Whenever she can't get a fix, she goes off the deep end. Of late she's had all sorts of delusions running through her dipsy brain. Reckons she's being held captive or some such nonsense. Last night, out of the blue, she took to her husband with a skillet and belted him around the head. I tried to stop her.'

'Is that how you got all those marks on your face and throat?'

'Yeah.' Russ pushed a probing finger at the dark blue marks on his neck and winced. 'I don't understand why my cousin didn't have her committed, cause she's dangerous the way she is.'

'Well, I wouldn't like to run into a nut job like that. How's the husband?'

'Let's just say she's a widow now.'

'Shit man. You call the cops?'

'Nah, not had a chance yet. I need to track her down first. Can't have her out in the world. She might hurt someone. Once I find her, I'll take her into the hospital so they can sedate her, then the cops can deal with her after that. You sure you ain't seen anybody?'

'You're the first person I've spoken to in days. Where did you say she went missing from?'

'Brahman Crossing beach.'

'When?'

'Late last night.'

'What type of vehicle she driving.'

'She's not – she's on foot.'

'Well, shit man, Brahman Crossing is at least twenty clicks down the coast from here. It would be a marathon effort to reach here on foot, especially in the dark. I reckon you're looking in the wrong place. It's much more likely she's sleeping it off under a tree near the house or has returned to her own bed by now.'

Russ grunted. He shoved his hands deep into his trouser pockets, turned a wide circle to study the confusion of dog prints and scuff marks in the churned-up sand where Tennille had been racing around chasing a tennis ball. Tennille didn't like the visitor moving around. She rose to her feet and came to stand at Ryan's side, her unblinking stare on Russ. Ryan dropped the book he was holding into his lap and placed his free hand on her head.

'Steady girl,' he murmured.

'Nice dog, you got there...ahh. Sorry, I didn't catch your name?' Russ moved a step closer to the porch. Tennille gave a fearsome display of her teeth and her chest rumbled with a deep, chesty growl.

'You better back off - the dog's antisocial. She doesn't like people. Me neither. That's why we live alone out here.'

'I'll get out of your hair then. I just need to take a gander inside, to make sure she's not here.'

Russ lifted a finger and pointed towards the door of the shack. At the same time, he withdrew his other hand from the pocket of his trousers and allowed it to drift around to the arch of his back. Ryan, positive the man had a gun snugly tucked in the waistband of his pants, wasn't distracted by the manoeuvre. He rose to his feet and pointed his own weapon at Russ's chest.

'Keep your hands where I can see them,' Ryan snarled.

Russ froze.

'Fuck man. Lighten up will ya'. I just wanted to make sure she hadn't snuck in while you were busy down on the beach.'

Ryan stepped away from the porch and flicked his chin towards the door. 'Knock yourself out. There's no one inside.'

'Alright keep your hair on,' said Russ, trying to sound gruff. The tremor in his voice gave him away.

Keeping a wary eye on the gun in Ryan's hand he stepped onto the porch and stuck his head inside the doorway. Ryan knew that all he would see would be the stage he'd set. A sleeping bag unfurled on the mattress with a man's rumpled shirt strewn across it. His back-pack lying on its side beside the bed. Tennille's water bowl on the floor next to the free-standing, chipped-enamel stove and the sink he had dressed with an upside-down coffee mug and bread plate, giving the impression they were draining after their last use.

'Satisfied, I'm alone?' growled Ryan.

Russ nodded.

'Good, now you can take your problems and piss off. I don't need the grief.'

\* \* \*

Tremors of fear danced up and down my spine at the sound of Russ's croaky voice. Evidently Ashley's crushing grip to the throat hadn't quite killed his cousin off, but it certainly sounded like he had a sore throat from the experience. And if he was out looking for me then the men must have made up.

*Pity!*

Facing this new dilemma, I wondered how I was going to con-tinue to evade Ashley, the weasel, as well as the man and his dog. To avoid the tenants of the shack I'd have to wait until the dead of night, when the man and dog slept, before I crawled out and got on the move again. As Russ was focussing on the beaches, I couldn't afford the chance my footprints being spotted before the tide washed them away. It was time to leave the shoreline and head inland. I wasn't looking forward to coping with the bush at night. And there was still Ashley. Where the hell was he? He hadn't been that far behind.

I took a slow, deep breath and tuned into the bizarre tale Russ was weaving about my mental health. Did he really think his story would hold water?

'Well, I wouldn't like to run into to a nut job like that,' the man above me said. 'How's the husband?'

'Let's just say she's a widow now.'

*I'd killed Ashley!*

Something fundamental inside me broke. I was now a murderer. Just like the men I despised. It didn't matter that it had never been my intention to kill Ashley. I had, and that was wrong. Not a religious person in any way, shape or form, I closed my eyes and prayed for my soul.

'Good, now you can take your problems and piss off. I don't need the grief.' The brutal tone jerked me back into the here and now.

He'd believed every word he'd been told and was very angry I'd bought trouble to his door. I definitely had to avoid this man.

Dust rained down on my face as feet thumped on the boards above my head.

Russ said, 'If she shows up on your doorstep, don't believe a word she says. Remember she's delusional. Just contact me at Brahman Crossing. I'll fetch her and get her the help she needs.'

The vehicle fired up and roared away. Silence settled around me. Suddenly the shrub near me shook. A bottle of water rolled into the burrow. A protein bar followed.

'I think, Burger, it'll be safer for you to stay right where you are for now. That Johnson character may not be the sharpest tool in the shed but I wouldn't put it past him to double back on foot to spy on us for a while. I'm going to sit right above you and read. Boredom and the heat of the day should drive him away fairly soon. I'll know when he leaves. We'll head off then ourselves and get you some help. My dune buggy is a reasonable walk from here. Do you think you can make it? Or I can go by myself to fetch it and come back for you.'

My bottom lip wobbled. It was the use of my nickname that was my undoing. Something deep inside me unravelled. A torrent of tears rolled unchecked down my cheeks. I gulped back a sob and took a punt that he was a man of his word and would help me.

'No, I can walk. Please don't leave me,' I breathed out.

'I won't, I promise. While I bore our spy you drink the water, eat the food and rest.'

## Chapter Forty

'Burger, it's time to wake up.'

A gentle tap against my cheek dragged me from a deep sleep. I blinked open my eyes and let out a startled squeak at the sight of a cloud of dark curly hair floating in front of my face. My brain kicked into gear as I realised the vision was a bearded face, attached to a head and neck that was shoved through the hole I'd made to get under the porch. In the gloom I couldn't make out any of the man's features, other than an unruly mop of dark hair, but his presence seemed familiar and safe.

'Sorry to disturb you, but it's time for you to come out of your hidey-hole. We have to get moving. It's going to take until sunset to get to the place where I stashed the phone. I need to call Aunt Rosie.'

'Aunt Rosie?' I stared at him in bemusement.

'Bloody Chappie, he's got me calling her Aunt Rosie now.'

My heart began to hammer hard in my chest.

It couldn't be.

'Ryan?' I breathed. 'Is that you?'

A soft hand brushed my cheek. 'Hello, Cutie.'

Amazed at the turn of events, I crawled towards daylight, towards the man I'd loved with my whole heart. How was it possible that Ryan was here? I had to be dreaming. Maybe I really was delusional. He flashed me a smile. My heart nearly exploded in excitement. Then reality kicked in. I can't have Ryan see me like this, knowing I was not only soiled goods but also a murderer. Tears filled my eyes. In that moment I hated the universe. It just didn't deal fairly.

I shot out of the hole and staggered to my feet. I was nearly up-ended when I was met by a furry bundle of joy with a happy face and a lolling tongue.

'Tennille,' I cried.

Falling to my knees, I wrapped my arms around her neck. She whined softly in my ear. With wet eyes I lifted my glance to meet Ryan's. He watched with his face twisted in a look of apprehension. Why was he worried?

'How is it you are both here?' I asked, allowing my gaze to run across his face and down his body searching for the old and familiar. A chill ran through me when I saw pink puckered skin on his arms. 'Oh Ryan, you've been hurt?' I cried, rushing to my feet to trace my fingers along the scars.

'Do I disgust you?' he asked.

Puzzled I stared deep into the eyes I'd dreamt about for so long.

'No. Why should you?'

'Not even this?' He held out his leg. I looked down. His right leg was missing below the knee. My gut contorted with a grief over his loss.

'No, why should you disgust me? Am I heartbroken you've been hurt? Yes, most definitely. But you don't disgust me. On the contrary, you're the one who should be revolted.'

He reached forward and gently grasped my battered fingertips. 'Never, Burger. Why do you say that?'

'Oh, Ryan, I've made such a mess of everything since you left me.'

'And for leaving the way I did, I apologise. I was tricked into believing something about you that wasn't true. Before I had a chance to discover what was really going on and talk to you about it, I found myself on assignment overseas with no way of contacting you.' His eyes scanned my face. 'Will you forgive me, Burger. Let me make it up to you. I don't care how long it takes but when you're ready can we still make a life together?'

'Of course, I forgive you.' The tears I'd held back for so long began to glide down my cheeks. With a sob, I faced the reality of the situation and gave up my last chance at happiness. 'As for the rest, I'm sorry, Ryan but it can't happen.'

He stepped back as if I'd slapped him. 'I do disgust you.'

I tightened my grip on his fingers. 'No, you misunderstand me. I couldn't ask that of you. I'm soiled goods. My life is a mess. I...I...I've killed. I'm a murderer. Didn't you hear, R...R...Russ, I...I...I killed my husband.' A gut-wrenching sob exploded from my lips.

Ryan pulled me hard against his chest.

'You loved him very much, didn't you?' he murmured.

'No, Ryan. I never loved him. I was tricked into marriage by Ashley. You're the only one I love. It's always been you.'

Ryan's chest against my cheek shuddered as if he had trouble breathing. 'And I love you, Faith. More than you could ever know.' He dusted sand from my jaw with the ball of his thumb. 'Let's go find the Silver Dingo and get her to sort this mess out.'

* * *

With a heavy heart I followed Ryan as we made our way back along the shoreline. We jogged for over two hours, retracing my staggering steps of the night before. My brain and fatigued muscles screamed in protest.

*No, not that way. I can't go back to the shack.*

The terrified objection hovered in the back of my throat, but remained unspoken. I'd learnt the hard way not to question others. I pushed on, gave all that was asked of me as I put one foot in front of the other. I glanced down at my throbbing arm. Ryan had treated my wound by smearing it with an antibiotic cream and applying a field dressing. The pristine bandaging was now stained with fresh blood. I touched it gently and my arm burned as though on fire. With my luck it was most probably infected. A shiver ran down my spine.

'Not far now,' Ryan said, glancing back over his shoulder. 'Are you alright?'

I nodded, too tired to waste the last of my energy on an answer. He reached back, took me by the hand to guide me up a track to the top of a sand dune. As we crested the top, my knees wobbled. My legs decided they'd had enough and gave out. I landed on my butt.

I stared up in surprise. Ryan reached for me. I cringed, waiting for the slap.

'Sorry, I'll do better...I promise,' I cried, holding up a compliant hand.

Ryan stopped dead, a look of shock on his face. Slowly he squatted down in front of me and with gentle palms cupped my cheeks. 'You don't have to do better, Faith. I know of no other person in the whole world who could have stood up to and survived what you have been through. You are the bravest, strongest, most awesome person I've ever met. I'm proud of you, sweetheart. Try to remember I'm not the brute you were married to, or his cousin. I don't want to change you, make you into something you don't want to be. If you need to rest, want to eat or drink, go to the toilet, it's okay to speak up. If you're angry, frustrated, sad or frightened, it's alright to yell, argue, cry and scream. Though if you could keep the loud noises at a minimum until were out of here, I would appreciate it. If I do something you don't like, say so. And above all if you don't want to do something, tell me. Together we'll sort it out.' Tennille trotted to my side, whined and licked the back of my hand.

I reached up and stroked her head. Trusting that what Ryan had said was true, I took a punt. 'Ryan, I don't think I can go on.'

He smiled and handed me a water bottle. 'Then we'll take a break.'

Even though my throat screamed out for the moisture, I sniffed the contents of the water bottle with suspicion. Ryan raised an eyebrow.

'Sorry...Ashley has...had a tendency to drug my drink.'

Without a word Ryan gently removed the bottle from my hand took a large gulp before handing it back to me. He ran a soft hand over the top of my head before settling in the sand beside me. I took a long slow sip and revelled as the tepid water slid easily down my throat. It was like mana from heaven. I flicked a glance at the man at my side. He looked so different from when we'd last seen each other. His shorn crop was now long and wild. His handsome sun-browned face was hidden behind a curly bush of beard but the eyes were the same. Warm like treacle. I wanted to spend a lifetime drowning in them. He caught me staring and smiled.

Embarrassed, I pointed to a small device clutched in his hand. 'What's that?'

He held it out for me to see. 'A GPS, it's homing in on the buggy,' he said. 'Not far to go now. Can you go on? If not, I'll carry you.'

'I'll be fine.' I tried to clamber to my feet but my muscles refused to work. I stared down at my traitorous legs. Without a word Ryan stood and lifted me into his arms. He dropped a light kiss on my temple. 'Come on, Tennille. Last leg, girl.'

To my amazement he began to jog along a faint animal trail, not seeming to notice the weight of me. The ride was smooth. I hooked my arms around his neck, gave in to temptation and nestled my face into his neck. I drew in a deep breath to forge a memory of his scent that I could carry with me for the rest of my life behind bars. My mind drifted away.

I was startled when Ryan said, 'We're here.'

I lifted my head and stared around. I couldn't see anything except a rocky knoll with a bush encrusted overhang.

'Where's...'

Ryan grinned as he lowered my feet to the ground. He pointed through some brush at a small cave that was unnoticeable unless you looked for it. Parked inside I could just make out the shape of a vehicle.

'Is that for us?'

'Sure is.' Ryan moved some rocks and delved into the churned soil. He gave a yank and unearthed a backpack. 'Just a precaution in case the buggy was found,' he said. He opened the bag and pulled out a phone.

'Wait here a mo.' He jerked his chin to the top of the slope. 'I need to go up for a signal.'

I watched Ryan climb. He was as nimble as a mountain goat. When he got to the top of the ridge, he pulled out the phone and checked the screen. He grinned down at me and gave a thumbs up.

\* \* \*

Ryan switched on the mobile and was hit with a rush of messages. Two from Seadog, the rest from Rosie. The detective hadn't pulled any punches with her first.

'*Get your ass back pronto before you ruin the investigation.*'

The second had been sent two days later and the tone had altered.

*'I'm worried. Are you safe?'*

Ryan hit speed dial. On the second ring Rosie answered.

'You better be back at Rivers Run, soldier boy. If not, I'll kick your butt so hard your nose will bleed.'

You had to love the feisty detective's way with words. Ryan chuckled and decided to take the wind out of her sails.

'I've got her,' he interrupted.

'Faith? You've found her? Is she alright?'

'Watson and Johnson did a real number on her. Mentally she's splintered but not smashed. Physically she's battered but not irreversibly dented. On the verge of exhaustion, but managing to hang on by a thread. She's one tough cookie.' Ryan heard Rosie's sigh of relief and hated that he was about to destroy her newfound peace. 'But there is a problem. You need to get yourself out to Brahman Crossing. Not the homestead. Though there is an animal of interest hibernating in one of the cottages there.'

'A Bear?'

'Yeah, and he's unaware of our interest if you want to surprise him.'

'I need probable cause.'

'Well, here's an anonymous tip for you. Go to a shack at Brahman beach. That's where Watson and Johnson were keeping Faith stashed - against her will, I might add. I'll send you the co-ordinates of the place. I suspect you're going to find Cub Watson in not too good a shape – he may even be dead.'

'Bloody hell...what did you do?'

'Not me, Rosie. Faith says she hit him with a skillet so she could escape. Go investigate.'

'Right. And what about you two?'

'I don't have enough fuel in the buggy to make it back to Bull Morgan's but enough to make it to Mount Ibour. Where do you want me to take Faith while you're out and about? She needs some-where quiet and safe. A motel?'

'No. Take her to the Mount Ibour police station. I'll warn them you're coming and get them to keep her out of sight.'

'Roger that. And Rosie...'

'What?'

'Keep your eyes peeled. That Johnson character is still in the mix and the bastard is armed.'

# Chapter Forty-One

'Bayden, collect the crime scene gear. I've had an anonymous tip about a suspicious death,' yelled Rosie. Mark's feet shot from their comfortable position hooked on the corner of the desk. He leapt to his feet. 'And break out the weapons. We might need them on this one.'

'Yes, boss,' he acknowledged, as he hurried from the room.

While her boots pounded along the corridor towards the Senior Sergeant's office, Rosie punched GPS co-ordinates into her phone. She stuck her head around the door and didn't give Noel a chance to say anything. 'Senior, just had a report of a suspicious death out at Brahman Crossing. I'm taking Bayden to investigate. Oh, and there's a man coming in - Captain Ryan Lamb. He'll have a girl with him – Faith Watson. I need you to make sure she's kept secure.'

Rosie shot back out the door and was off racing towards the car park before the station boss had time to ask any questions.

\* \* \*

Rosie signalled for Mark to kill the lights and engine. He did and allowed the vehicle to roll along the rough sandy track towards the beach shack. The entire place was in darkness. She stuck her head out of the window to listen and was met with the usual insect noises typical of the Australian Outback.

'Stop here.' Rosie double checked her Kevlar vest was secured snugly in place, switched on her body camera and slid her weapon from its holster. 'Watch yourself, Bayden. These are the type of people who shoot first and don't ask questions.'

'Right, Boss,' replied Mark, imitating her actions. He slipped from the police vehicle, closing the door with a gentle snick. Rosie followed. They squatted down in front of the grille to assess the area. A northern quoll, foraging for insects around the large tree stump in the yard, hissed. Rosie felt her partner jump.

'Easy, Bayden' she whispered. 'It's only the wildlife. Now, on my signal we make for the veranda. You go left of the door, I'll take the right.'

'Aren't we going to wait for armed response?'

'We're it, Bayden. Senior and Hewlett are manning the station. Fort and Joyce are on highway patrol and Green is away on leave. Nearest backup is six hours away in Broome. This can't wait. You good?'

Mark nodded.

'We go on three. One - two - go.'

Weapon drawn, held at the ready, Rosie crouch-ran to the porch. Bayden dogged her heels. She leapt right, slammed her back against the building. When her partner was safely in position, she held up her hand and did a finger countdown. On three she pounded on the door with a clenched fist.

'This is the police. Open the door and show yourself with your hands raised above your head.'

Silence. Even the cicadas had ceased their endless chirps.

Rosie thumped the door again. 'Mount Ibour police. Open up.'

Rosie gave her partner a chin lift. Bayden reached across and twisted the doorknob. The door swung open with a slow groan. Rosie took a deep breath and caught the distinctive coppery tang of blood. She cocked an ear. Except for the drone of blowflies, the inside of the shack was quiet.

'Torch, Bayden,' whispered Rosie.

Mark knelt and, without exposing himself to the gap in the doorway, rolled a lighted torch along the ground so its beam lit up the room.

Rosie risked a quick peek inside. The body of a large man lay in a pool of drying blood on the floor next to the table. The rest of the room seemed empty. She reached inside and flicked on the overhead light. A dull 60-watt globe came to life. A glance revealed a laminate table with four chairs, two comfortable looking recliners, a worn-out couch and a high-backed, hard chair that had been set in the corner of the room. On the far side of the combination kitchen lounge were three closed doors.

'We'll do a room by room, Bayden. Stay alert.'

They went through the same precautionary procedure to clear the shack. The first room was a basic but immaculately clean bathroom. The second a master bedroom with a neatly made double bed, two bedside tables without a speck of dust and a closet full of men's clothing.

Finger to lips, Rosie indicated Bayden should open the third door. It barely moved under his gentle touch. He had to shove hard against it to get it to open wide enough for them to gain entry. A quick glance in was enough to show the room was empty. Her nose wrinkled in distaste. The room reeked of stale sweat. Mark picked his booted feet carefully through a cesspool of dirty clothes, discarded shoes and empty beer and spirit bottles, to reach the wardrobe.

Rosie wondered if he would need a guide rope to find his way back out of the mess.

He flung open the cupboard door and let out a loud whistle.

'What?' she demanded, raising her weapon and pointing it into the open aperture where Bayden shone his torch.

'Look at this,' he said. She made her way to the closet and glanced over his shoulder. A photo gallery had been pasted at the back of the wardrobe. All the images were of the same woman. 'Looks as if all the photos were taken using a long-range lens. I'll make some inquiries see if we can identify her.'

'No need,' said Rosie. 'I know who it is.'

Mark glanced down at her with a cocked eyebrow.

'It's my niece - Faith.'

Thoughts rampaged as Rosie made her way back into the kitchen to stare down at the face of the badly beaten man.

'And this fellow is Ashley 'Cub' Watson.'

She reached down, placed two fingers on his neck to check for a pulse. His skin was cold. A fetid stench rose from his body.

'He's dead. Get on the radio and call it in. We need a forensic team out here pronto. And make sure they bag that skillet.'

* * *

In the pale rosy light of dawn Rosie paced up and down the yard sucking in fresh air as she waited for the forensic team to finish their preliminary investigation of the crime scene. Her gut was clenched tight because she was faced with the unenviable task of investigating her niece for the brutal killing of her husband. Rosie wondered what had driven Faith to such lengths. Angry, she spun on her heel. Her glance fell on a large padlock hanging open on the workshop door. They hadn't searched the building yet. Needing something to occupy her while forensics got on with things, Rosie drew her weapon.

'Bayden,' she said, 'Why do you suppose a workshop, located on an isolate patch of ground in the middle of nowhere, needs such a large padlock? I think you and I should go take a peek. Don't you?'

'Don't we need a warrant?'

'Bayden, Bayden, Bayden, have you learnt nothing over the last three years? If we suspect that a person has in their possession a "thing relevant to the offence", we can enter the premises without a warrant to look for that person. Now I do believe we are still trying to locate the offender of this crime and any possible murder weapon, don't you?'

Mark gave her a cheesy grin and drew his weapon. 'Yes, I believe we are, Boss.'

'Good. Come on let's go check it out.'

They stalked over. With due caution Rosie flung open the door. The building was empty. From the doorway she spotted something that really piqued her interest. On the surface of a sleek work table was an ID card printer and a stack of blank plastic cards. To the left of this, clipped to a stand and positioned under a large magnifying light, were two blue booklets that strongly resembled Australian Passports and in a plastic sleeve what looked like it contained a one hundred dollar note.

Rosie's lips split in a feral grin.

'Well, well, well, what have we here?'

Beside her Mark let out a long slow whistle. 'Counterfeit?'

'Won't know until we take a closer look. No...' she put out a hand to stop him from entering. 'We won't go in – I don't want to compromise the scene. Radio Senior Sergeant George, tell him we need a search warrant that not only covers the shack but also all out-buildings. Then we can rip this place apart.'

'What about major crimes? Won't they need to take over?

'No. As far as I'm concerned, murder takes precedent. I'll give Detective Graves a call after the search and update her on what we find.' Rosie glanced back over at the shack. 'How much longer will forensics be? I want access to the main building?'

'Another couple of hours yet, boss.

Rosie sighed. 'Right, well while we wait, we might as well head back to the station and have a chat with Faith. Maybe she knows where the cousin, Rattler Johnson, has gotten too. I want to have a long chat with that one – he's got a lot of explaining to do. I'm also not comfortable with him roaming unchecked around the neighbourhood. I want him where I can keep an eye on him - under lock and key.'

# 42

## Chapter Forty-Two

The ride in the dune buggy was an exhilarating experience. Ryan steered with confidence and precision. Tennille sat between us with her tongue flapping in the breeze as we zoomed at a breakneck pace along quiet dirt tracks and over small ridges. A sense of freedom threatened to overwhelm me. I wanted to yell and scream in delight. It had been so long since I'd experienced anything like it. At twilight, when Ryan slid the buggy onto a bitumen road, I saw evidence of civilisation.

'Not far now,' he said.

Gnawing fear replaced my exhilaration as the reality of my situation hit home. I forced a smile to my lips and nodded in response.

Ryan double checked his GPS doodad, turned the wheel to the right and planted his foot hard on the accelerator. Defying all the road rules, he drove at high speed along the blacktop. Within minutes we were zipping down a quiet street of a largish town. Ryan cut the buggy across a block, swerved into a driveway and skidded to a halt at the rear of a two-storey, glass and brick building. He clambered out. With a gentle hand helped me alight before slinging a protective arm around my waist. Keeping a vigilant lookout, he escorted me at a limping pace towards the recessed front doors. I glanced up at the wall above the door where a blue and white sign read, 'Mount Ibour Police Station'. My heart sped up. I had to clamp my jaw tight, to stop my teeth from rattling in fear. As the automatic sliding doors parted, a blast of cold air-conditioned air brushed my face. I couldn't hold back a shiver. The grip on my waist tightened. I drew comfort from Ryan's support and forced my shaky legs to carry me inside to face my future behind bars.

A young, fresh-faced officer was standing behind a large counter. He lifted an inquiring brow. 'Help you folks?'

'Captain Ryan Lamb. This is Faith Bergman.'

'Faith Watson,' I gently reminded him.

Ryan flicked a startled glance at my face. 'Sorry, Faith Watson. Detective Bloom told us to report in.'

'Yes, Sir. We were expecting you.' The constable interrupted Ryan's explanation and busily moved towards the self-locking door that gave access to the police station's work areas. 'If you could take a seat in the waiting area, Captain Lamb, I'll radio the Detective and let her know you've arrived. She'll want to speak with you when she gets back.' He settled a blank gaze onto me. 'Ma'am, I need you to come with me.'

'No,' snapped Ryan, 'She's not leaving my side.'

I placed a gentle hand on his chest. 'It's fine, Ryan. I was expecting this.' I stared up into his warm eyes, drinking them in for the final time. He opened his mouth, ready to argue. I placed my forefinger onto his lips to silence him. 'Thank you, for coming to find me, and for helping me. I don't think I could have made it without you.'

'You're a strong woman, Burger. You would have found a way.'

'Take care of yourself, Ryan.'

'I'll be here when you come out. I love you, Faith.'

Sadness filled my soul. It could never be. I knew what had to be done, but it still hurt.

'Ryan, I'm honoured you feel that way but we are two worlds apart. It's time for us to say goodbye.'

With an aching heart I turned and allowed the police officer to escort me through the door. The snick of the lock at my back had such finality to it that I had to stiffen my spine to complete the trek through the series of hallways that led into the lockup area. The constable wordlessly pointed to a bleak, vacant cell. I stepped inside and turned to face him. The door slammed shut in my face. I sucked in a shuddering breath full of stale musty air and turned to eye the cement pallet that was to be my bed for the foreseeable future. With a sigh I stumbled over and sagged into a defeated heap onto the thin, blue plastic mattress. Curling up into a tiny ball, I swallowed hard against the scorch of bile at the back of my throat and stared at the wall. My body ached. My arm throbbed. Images from the nightmare of my life pressed in. Not wanting to wallow, I rolled onto my back and let my gaze comb the cell walls. They were a dull boring grey. Misspelt obscenities, dates and ditties, none of which were entertaining, had been scratched into the plaster by previous tenants. In the corner of the cell the stainless-steel toilet bowl gave a watery burp as an air bubble escaped the pipes. I stretched and my earlier cramp threatened to come back. I flexed my toes to ease the muscle. The movement knocked the faded grey-wool blanket onto the floor. Ashley's training kicked in. I staggered upright, picked it up and refolded it into a neat rectangle before aligning it precisely with the foot of the bed. I let out a deep sigh, wondering what the universe was going to throw at me next. Surely, it couldn't be any worse than knowing my last chance to be with Ryan had been destroyed. Grief at the loss danced a powerful jig in my chest. Losing him the first time had been a bitter pill. This was worse. I was a murderer. We could never be together again. The knowledge that Ryan's memory of me would always be tainted by the fact that I was a killer broke my heart. Hot tears welled in my eyes. With a sob I fell onto the hard bed and cursed the day I'd forgotten to set my alarm.

## Chapter Forty-Three

Ignoring the rawness of his overworked stump, Ryan paced the waiting room. He was too riled up with anger and frustration to settle on one of the hard plastic chairs designed to make a person's visit to the police station's waiting area as uncomfortable as possible. Anxiety and antagonism fuelled the large bonfire in his chest. The police had taken Burger away from him. Locked her in a jail cell. It wasn't right. Fury boiled like hot lava in his chest. How could Rosie have allowed this to happen? Where the hell was she, anyway? She should be here, fixing this. Fuck, he was going to give her a piece of his mind. Ryan reefed his mobile from his pocket and dialled. His call went unanswered. With a curse he hung up and spotted the day-old text from Seadog. Needing a distraction, he opened it.

*Rowdy's gone AWOL.*

Shit! Could this day get any worse? Seadog answered his call on the second ring.

'Shanks, dude, thank God. Where the hell have you been?'

'On a mission. What's going on?'

'I can't get a hold of Rowdy. He's been much quieter than usual. His medical discharge hit him hard, I think. Now he's kind of lost.'

'When did you speak with him last?'

'Five days ago.'

Ryan ran his fingers through his scruffy mane. Seadog had every right to be concerned as the men usually checked in with each other every day. Ryan himself had texted but hadn't been in a position to call.

'Tell me about your last confab?'

'We had a beer at the pub just down the street from here. Rowdy wanted to know what was going on with you.'

'He actually said all that?'

Seadog chuckled. 'No, what he actually said was "Shanks?", and left me to interpret. So, I told him about the equipment I'd dug out of my golf bag for you. I asked him if he could think of anything else you might need. Rowdy shook his head, sculled his beer and gave me a farewell pat on the back. Since then - silence. I've been to all his haunts, but he's nowhere to be found, neither is his motorbike. I'm praying he's just gone for one of his long rides.'

'Let me try his mobile.'

'Good luck with that – he isn't picking up for me. How's things with you. You get everything sorted?'

'I found Faith. But now she's in jail.' Ryan filled his mate in on the events of the last week.

'Shit man – what can I do to help?'

'Not much any of us can do at the moment. Concentrate your efforts on finding Rowdy, that'll help me,' said Ryan.

'Righto.'

'Hang five will you while I try his number.' Ryan disconnected and immediately called his missing team mate. The phone was answered by Rowdy's message bank with a terse, 'Leave a message.'

So, he did. 'Rowdy. Seadog's not surfing and I'm hobbling around like a three-legged dog. Both of us are bereft you're not talking to us. What's going on, bud? Call me.'

Ryan hung up and stared blankly at the suicide helpline poster on the wall. Suicide amongst involuntarily discharged ADF personnel was a real threat and he wondered what dark thoughts were going through his friends mind now that his planned future had been snatched away. Rowdy, the quiet one of their group, wasn't alone fighting that battle. Surely, he knew that. Ryan understood the struggle his friend was having finding his place in civilian life. They all were. Seadog hid it better than most because he had channelled all his energy into surfing, but before long he too would hit crunch point. What the three of them needed was a new goal to move towards. The tingle of an idea came to life in the back of Ryan's mind. Before he could take it out and examine it his phone buzzed.

'Seadog, I said I'd call you back.'

'Shanks?'

Ryan's heart leapt. 'Rowdy. It's good to hear your voice, bud. You okay?'

'Fine. Where are you?'

'I'm in the waiting room of Mount Ibour police station at the moment. Why?'

There was no reply. Rowdy had hung up.

Ryan hit redial and his call went straight to message bank.

'Shit,' he muttered. He stared down at Tennille who watched him with patient eyes. He leant forward and ran a soft hand over her silky ears. 'Trials and tribulations, girl. Trials and tribulations.'

Tennille licked his fingers before settling her head onto her paws. Her eyes never left his face as he hit speed dial once again.

Seadog must have been hanging over the phone. 'Any luck, Shanks?' he asked anxiously before Ryan could speak.

'I've just had a five-word conversation with Rowdy.'

'As many as that?' Seadog's sigh of relief sounded loud and clear down the line. 'Thank the fuck! He's alive then?'

'Yeah, the same thought had crossed my mind...' Ryan looked up in surprise and paused. The doorway was filled by a well-muscled giant, clad in black leathers. The neatly barbered man, a motorcycle helmet tucked under one arm, strode into the room and thumped a beefy paw onto Ryan's shoulder.

'Ahh...Seadog...'

'What?'

'Call off the search party.' Ryan watched the giant settle into a seat and stare wordlessly around the room. 'The big man's just strolled in.'

# 44

## Chapter Forty-Four

I awoke to a raised angry voice outside my cell door.

'What the fuck were you thinking, Noel, locking her in a cell. I told you to keep her safe.'

'No, you didn't. You said there was a suspicious death. I was to keep her secure. I interpreted that to mean in a cell.' The man's growl was accompanied by the rattle of keys in the lock.

I pushed myself upright and shuffled over to the corner to stand with my head bowed just as I'd been taught. My heart pounded hard against my ribs. I was hot, my wrist and arm ached. The metal door squeaked as it open. I stared at my tattered shoes and waited. A soft, gentle finger lifted my chin. I stared in trepidation into a pair of ice-blue eyes. I don't know what they saw but I saw a cold fury burning in their depths and shuddered with dread.

\* \* \*

Rosie stared in shock at the tiny waif, who stood meekly in the corner of the cell with her head bowed. The girl's dress, faded and worn, was shredded around the hem and her shoes looked ready to fall apart. Rosie rushed forward to place a gentle finger under Faith's chin and tilted her face up to the light. Anger surged deep inside her at what she saw. Her niece's top lip was split and swollen, her face a riot of bruises and her underfed, thin limbs were covered in black marks, cuts and scrapes, some of them old, others very recent. But worst of all, the one that broke her heart, Faith's usually sparkling eyes were full of terror.

Spotting the filthy blood-encrusted bandage on her niece's arm she growled, 'Noel, get a doctor here, pronto. And make sure they send a woman.'

Noel glanced over Rosie's shoulder to stare at Faith. 'Shit, Constable Hewlett didn't tell me she was injured. I don't know what the academy is teaching these young ones.'

'I need a room,' snapped Rosie, chopping off his beef about the shortcomings of the latest batch of new constables assigned to the station. Faith began to tremble under her fingertips. Contrite at using the harsh tone and scaring her, Rosie mellowed her tone and addressed her niece. 'Faith, my darling girl, I'm here and you're safe. No one is going to hurt you ever again and when this dunderhead gets out of the way, you'll be out of this horrible cell.' She shoved Noel firmly to one side with her forearm and guided Faith out of the door.

'I'm not dreaming, am I? You're really here aren't you, Aunt Rosie?' Faith asked in a shaky whisper.

'Yes, Burger, it's me, and you're safe.'

The stiffness went out of Faith's spine and she slumped against her aunt's shoulder. Sobs wracked her poor frail body. Rosie wrapped her arms around her and cradled her close. She let Faith sob until her tears were spent.

'Use interview one,' murmured Noel, as he brushed past them. 'I'll send Hewlett in with a change of clothing and a camera. You know what has to be done.'

Rosie nodded. 'Yes, I do! And Noel, once the doctor arrives, no one is to disturb us.'

The senior sergeant nodded. 'You realise Bayden and I will have to conduct the interview.'

Rosie glared. 'I'm not leaving her.'

'I didn't expect you would.'

Rosie opened the door to the interview room. 'In here Faith.' She wordlessly watched her niece go and stand in the corner with her head bowed. What the hell had they done to her?

'I'm sorry to do this to you, Faith, but I will have to take all the clothes you're wearing, including your shoes, for forensic examination. And when the doctor gets here, we will have to examine you and take photographs of all your injuries.'

'Okay,' whispered Faith in a soft, sad voice.

\* \* \*

'Faith, this is Doctor Nails.' I cast a quick glance at my aunt then flicked a look at the woman standing tall at her side. She had beautiful russet hair that cascaded from a hairclip high on the back of her head and fell elegantly over one shoulder. Best of all, her eyes were warm. She gave me a sweet smile, full of compassion.

'Hello Faith. I'm Janelle Nails but you can call me Rusty.'

I gave her a tentative smile. Before I could be berated for breaking the rules I quickly lowered my gaze and stared at my tightly gripped hands.

'Faith, do I have your permission to make a sexual assault examination and to photograph your injuries before I treat your wounds? I promise to make my examination as non-intrusive as possible.'

The thought of anyone witnessing the scars of my degradation sickened me, but I was in the system now and had to do all that was asked of me. Besides it couldn't be any worse than what I'd live through. Could it?

'Yes,' I whispered. I hooked my bottom lip between my teeth and closed my eyes against what was to come.

I heard Aunty Rosie suck in her breath when I shed my dress for her.

'What are these,' she asked, tracing a soft finger along the welts and scars on my back.

'Ashley did them with his belt.'

The camera clicked. 'And the bruises at the top of your legs?'

'Russ...'

And so it went on. The examination took hours. Every mark was discussed, documented and photographed. Aunt Rosie and Dr Nails were very gentle but I still felt the violation I'd suffered as I relived every moment.

The doctor touched my cheek. 'Open your eyes, Faith?' I did. She held up a syringe. 'This is an antibiotic and tetanus shot. The other,' she added as she held up a second needle, 'contains lidocaine, which is a local anaesthetic.' She lifted my wrist and examined it. 'I don't like the feel of your wrist. You could have a fracture from the fall. After I've stitched your wound, I'll fit you with a temporary cast.'

Aunty Rosie wrapped a warm blanket around me while the doctor went to work cleaning and stitching.

'There you go young lady, that's the worst of it over. You can get dressed now.'

Aunt Rosie placed an entire outfit, with the price tags still attached, onto the table in front of me and helped me dress. I stared down at the garments in amazement. It had been so long since I'd worn anything new.

The doctor cocked her head at Rosie. They walked to the door talking.

'Be gentle, Detective. She's close to cracking. I'll swing by in the morning to check on her injuries.'

'Thanks Rusty. On your way out will you let Senior Sergeant George know we're finished here and are now ready for him.'

My heart constricted. It was time to face the music. As the doctor left, I couldn't stop myself, I wordlessly reached out and grabbed my aunt's hand to stop her going as well.

'It's all right Faith. I won't leave you. Why don't you take a seat.' Obediently I sat.

I jumped when the door swung open. A tall, friendly looking dark-haired police constable entered bearing a tray loaded with hot beverages and sandwiches. He smiled at me as he slid a plate of ham and cheese sandwiches on the table in front of me. The door swung open again and the middle-aged policeman with three stripes and a crown insignia on his shirt sleeve, entered. I leapt to my feet and bowed my head.

Aunt Rosie reached up and gently tugged on my hand. 'It's all right, Faith. You don't have to stand,' she said, patting the chair next to her. Uncertain, I sank onto the edge of the seat. Both men settled into the chairs across the table from us. After a quick look at them I dropped my gaze. In a soft voice Aunt Rosie said, 'Can you look at us, Faith?'

I did as she asked. 'Good girl.' Keeping the same gentle tone my aunt performed introductions. 'Faith, this is my partner, Constable Mark Bayden. You made have heard me speak about him. This is Senior Sergeant Noel George. They need to talk to you about everything that's happened. Do you feel up to it?'

I nodded.

Constable Bayden reached up to an overhead cabinet. He pushed a series of buttons before clearing his throat and stated the date and time. 'Mrs Watson, I need to inform you that this interview is being recorded in both audio and video format. The nature of our conversation is for you to assist us with our enquiries. No formal charges have been laid against you at this time. Do you understand the nature of this interview and agree to speak with us?'

I dropped my gaze, took a deep shuddering breath and nodded. Constable Bayden craned his neck trying to make eye contact with me. 'I'm sorry Mrs Watson. You will need to look up at the camera and speak your answers clearly.'

Under the table Aunt Rosie placed her hand softly on my knee and gave a supportive squeeze. I took heart from her presence.

'Yes. I agree,' I whispered, raising my head to stare at the wall behind his head.

'For the record, please identify yourself.'

'Faith...Faith Watson.'

'Mrs Watson, do you understand that you are here on a voluntary basis and are free to leave at any time?'

'Free,' I exclaimed. 'But how can I go free. I hit Ashley hard with the skillet. Rat-face said I killed him.'

Constable Bayden lifted an eyebrow. 'Rat-face? Who is Rat-face?'

'Rattler...Russell Johnson. He's Ashley's rat-faced cousin.'

'Was he present when you hit your husband?' asked Senior Sergeant George.

'Yes...you see...Rat face had a plan. He'd been plying Ashley with alcohol all day. When my husband finally passed out, he took the opportunity...to...to attack me.' I sucked in a gasping breath still sickened by the thought of his hands on me. I had to force the words out. 'He tried to rape me...to make me his...' I turned to my aunt. My chin quivered and my voice shook as I tried to make her understand how awful it had been. Unfortunately, it all came out in a jumble of words. 'He was the one who wrote all those scary anonymous letters when I lived in Albany, and he says he killed that man, Slugger for trying to kiss me, and buried the body in the dunes near the shack. Oh, Aunt Rosie, you have to help that other poor man, Mort Patterson.'

'Mort Patterson! Why does he need help?'

'They buried him where I was going to plant the fruit tree.' A sour burn rose in my throat at the image of his dead eyes. I folded my arms on the table, dropped my head onto them and began to sob. 'He wasn't a nice man but his poor family must be so worried.'

A soothing hand ran up and down my back.

'Bayden,' Aunt Rosie barked, 'you need to get the forensic team to do a sweep of that yard. See what they can find.'

I looked up. Relief swamped me.

'Right, Boss,' replied Constable Bayden. He jotted down a note in the file in front of him.

The Senior Sergeant held up a finger to my aunt. 'Detective Bloom, you are present in this interview as a support person to Mrs Watson only. Please hold back on the questions or I will ask you to leave.' I heard her teeth grind as she silently nodded.

The senior sergeant slid an upside-down photo in front of me. 'Mrs Watson, I need you to take a look at this. Tell me if you recognise the person in the photograph. I must warn you it is not a pleasant sight, so brace yourself.'

He turned the shot over. It showed the badly beaten face of a man. My gut knotted.

'Yesssss...that's my husband, Ashley Watson. Did I do that?'

'I don't know, you tell me. How many times did you strike Mr Watson with the skillet.'

I straightened my back and for the first time looked directly into his eyes. With tears streaming down my face, I choked out, 'Just once.'

'And is that all you did?'

'No...' I took a deep, shuddering breath and confessed, 'I...I...I stole the key for the door from his pocket and ran away.'

'And where was your husband.'

'He was crumpled on the kitchen floor.'

'How was he positioned?'

'On his side.'

'And Mr Johnson, where was he when you struck your husband?'

'Unconscious - on the floor next to Ashley, but I swear Ashley was breathing. And there was no blood.'

Noel gave me a blank look. 'Your husband was only knocked out, Mrs Watson, you didn't kill him.'

'Oh, I see. He's still alive then, and you're here to send me back.' I hung my head and whispered a frightened plea, 'I know he's my husband, but I don't really have to go back, do I?'

'No!' spat my aunt. 'Oh, precious girl, I would never allow anyone to send you back to that life. You're safe now, darling.'

'Are you sure I don't have to go back?'

'You don't have to go back,' said Noel. He reached across the table and applied a gentle pat to my clenched hands. 'No matter the outcome of this interview, you do not have to return to that life.'

Aunt Rosie leant towards me. 'Faith, can you tell us exactly what happened to make you use the skillet.'

In chronological order I recited all the events that made me take up the weapon against my husband.

When Aunt Rosie opened her mouth to ask another question the Senior Sergeant glared at her. She folded her lips and glared back at him. Silence sat heavy in the room. I caught an amused smile in the corner of Constable Bayden's mouth as he watched the byplay but when he noticed my gaze he straightened his features.

'Mrs Watson, are there any firearms kept in the house?' asked Senior Sergeant George.

I nodded. 'Yes. Ashley has a sawn-off hidden in the cushions of his chair. And Russ always carries a pistol. Anything else would be locked in the safe or in the workshop.'

'Who has access to these weapons?

'Russ and Ashley.'

'You?'

'No. I was kept chained up most of the time. I've only been into the workshop once, with Ashley, and that was to audit the banknotes while he did some work on the passports. Besides I don't know the combination. If I did, I would have taken the car keys to escape.'

'Your certain, we won't find your prints inside the safe?'

'I'm sure.'

'And the bank notes – where would we find them?'

'There are boxes buried in the yard. Ashley's father, Robert Watson, took away others.'

Aunt Rosie blurted out, 'Do you know where Robert Watson is?'

'Yes.'

Senior Sergeant George's phone dinged. He glanced down at the screen. 'I'm suspending this interview,' he announced. 'Detective Bloom, a word with you outside. Now.'

I stared, horrified, as he stalked out into the corridor. My aunt was in trouble.

* * *

Rosie glared at Noel George's retreating back. With grim determination she patted her niece on the shoulder. 'Bayden, pour Faith another cup of tea while I go speak with the Senior Sergeant.' Her temper was up by the time she made the corridor. 'What?' she snapped. 'I wasn't asking questions about the murder.'

Noel folded his arms and glared back at her. 'What part of observer don't you understand Detective Bloom. Shit Rosie, you could have ruined the case. But as usual you have that uncanny dingo luck on your side.'

Rosie cocked her eyebrow at him. 'That message was the forensics report. It seems that not only was the husband bludgeoned with the skillet at least a dozen times, a bullet was fired into his brain through the roof of his mouth. They found the exit wound when he was rolled over. The killer would have had blowback on them. You didn't see any sign of that when you took her clothes did you?'

Rosie shook her head.

'That poor woman no more killed her husband than you or I. I'm going to hand this case and the interview back to you, Rosie. Find out who else was at the shack and get the brute off my patch.'

'Yes, Noel,' grinned Rosie. 'It will be a pleasure!'

* * *

Wide-eyed I stared at my aunt. 'You're sure I didn't kill him.'

'Yes, Faith, I'm positive. Ashley was shot?'

'Then it must have been Russ. He was the only other person there.' A weight lifted. I straightened my shoulders. 'Ashley really is dead and I didn't kill him?'

'No, Faith, you didn't. Tell us more about your life in the shack. Specifically, what went on in the workshop, any visitors you may have had, conversations you overheard, even if they don't make sense to you.'

I gulped back the swell of excitement as freedom from my old life was dangled before me. I needed to reel back my expectations because if it was snatched away now, it would kill me. Besides, a man was dead. I concentrated on all that had happened and recited to her the events as they occurred, from the day of my arrival at the shack. I held nothing back as I detailed every sordid moment until my escape. Somewhere deep inside me I knew it was cathartic to get everything out into the open. At the end of my tale, Aunt Rosie's kind-faced partner had tears in his eyes. He poured me another cup of tea and urged me to drink. I managed a small sip.

'Is that it?' Aunt Rosie asked.

I nodded. 'I think so.'

Aunt Rosie surged to her feet and stretched her back. 'Thank you, Faith. Constable Bayden will write up a transcript of this interview for you to sign. Tomorrow will be fine.'

Constable Bayden reached up to switch off the recorders.

'Come on, Burger. There's a very anxious commando and his dog waiting to see you. They've been wearing the polish off the waiting room floor all night.'

Startled I gasped, 'Ryan is still here?'

'Of course he's still here. Where else would he be. That man loves you to his very core.'

A chunk of ice fell away from my heart. Aunt Rosie slung her arm around my waist and we began a slow walk along a corridor back towards the self-locking door by which I'd entered all those hours ago. 'And I'm sure you'd like to telephone Alex and Chip's. They're dying to speak with you.'

My legs stopped working. I stumbled. 'Unk and Chips...they...they're not dead?'

'Dead? No, Burger. Is that what you were told?'

With trembling hands, I grasped her fingers. 'Are you sure? Rat-face showed me a photo on his phone. It was awful. Uncle Alex was all beat up. There was blood everywhere. Rattler said he'd killed him. Chips too. All on Ashley's orders. But that can't be right because Robert Watson was the one who sent him to Perth. He wanted him to do a job for him. One that Ashley didn't know about.'

'Did he now? That's very interesting. I'd really like to get a hold of Mr Johnson and his phone. I also want a long, serious chat with

Robert Watson. Especially about leaving you in the situation you were in.' The ice blue in Aunt Rosie's eyes had turned to granite. It did my heart good to know she was on my side. 'For your information Burger, both Chips and Alex are both alive and well. Yes, Alex was attacked, but he has almost fully recovered. I think talking with you, knowing your safe, is the final dose of medicine he needs to finish that process.'

At that moment Ryan limped into the corridor followed by a giant of a man dressed in bike leathers. When he spotted me standing in the hall, he charged the door, busting the lock. He rushed forward with his arms held wide. He stopped in front of me and waited. I stared at the love shining in his eyes. I did an internal check and felt no fear. Without hesitation I stepped into his embrace and allowed his arm to envelope me.

'I'm free, Ryan. I didn't kill him,' I gasped, finding it hard to keep the joy from my voice. 'I'm not a monster.'

'I never thought you were, Cutie.'

'I do need to ask one more thing from you, Faith,' said my aunt. I studied the concerned look on her face.

'Ask?' I said, startled. No one had asked me to do anything in a long time. I was always told. 'You mean I have a choice?'

'Always.'

It felt weird. I gave her a hesitant smile. 'Ask away.'

'I would like you to come to the shack and show me where everything is buried.'

I bit my lip. Fear bounced up and down on a trampoline in my stomach. Ryan gently lifted my chin with his knuckle. He gave me a gentle smile.

'The decision is yours, Faith. We won't make you go. But just so you know, Rowdy,' he pointed to his companion, who gave me a dazzling white smile, 'and I will be there to protect you.' He cocked an eyebrow at Aunt Rosie. 'Not negotiable.'

'I didn't expect anything less,' said my aunt.

His words made me feel safe. Suddenly my fear dwindled, knowing I would always be protected. 'Okay, but can we do it soon, before I lose my nerve.'

'I don't think that will ever happen, darling girl, but yes, we'll leave in a few minutes.' Aunt Rosie held out her hand to Ryan's companion. 'Detective Bloom,' she said by way of introduction. 'You are?'

'Rowdy,' grumbled the giant.

'Soldier?' He nodded. 'Awesome. Speciality?'

'Tracking.'

'Outstanding, a good skill to have on tap around here.' She tossed a set of car keys at Ryan. 'The silver Kluger out back - you and the giant can follow my police vehicle.'

'I do know the way.'

'Yes, but now the site is an active crime scene. Protocol dictates you must be accompanied by a police officer, and we must follow protocol, Shanks, so as not to jeopardise any evidence.' She grinned her canine grin. 'Come on you lot, don't dawdle. I have a criminal enterprise to clean up and a murderer to find and arrest.' She lifted her voice and yelled at the top of her voice, 'Bayden, get your gear!'

Deep from the bowels of the police station came a muffled, 'Yes, Boss.'

\* \* \*

I pointed to the clear patch of sand near the old tree stump. 'Ashley buried some tubs there.'

The garden shovel resembled a matchstick in Rowdy's giant fist. He and Ryan set to work digging. Within moments something hard was struck.

Aunt Rosie tossed both men a pair of gloves. 'Okay boys, put these on and pull it out.'

By hand Ryan and Rowdy cleared away the last of the sand until they'd unearthed not two but three boxes. With no effort at all they easily hauled the plastic tubs from the hole.

The forensic team, who hovered in the background, swarmed over the find like a plague of locusts.

'Wow, we've got birth certificates, death certificates, passports...'

'Driver's licenses, cash...'

Aunt Rosie left them to it and wandered over to me. 'Okay Faith, show me where you were going to plant that tree?'

With reluctance I lead her to the section of yard I'd been slowly turning into an orchard. My forefinger shook when I lifted it to point to where the hole had been refilled. I took a step nearer and the world began to swirl. Aunt Rosie placed a restraining hand on my elbow and turned to Ryan.

'You and Faith have a lot to talk about – go take a walk on the beach.' He lifted his brow and she quietly added, 'She doesn't need to see this again.' Ryan nodded.

\* \* \*

Rosie waited until Faith and Ryan were out of sight before turning to her partner.

'Bayden, I want you to dig here, carefully. You're looking for a body. Take your time. When you find something let forensics know.' With a greenish tinge to his face, Mark set slowly to work clearing away soil.

'Rowdy,' said Rosie to the tall man with sea green eyes. 'You and I are going to take a walk. According to Faith there's at least one more body to find.' She watched him survey the dunes and realised the tell-tale lines of stress around his eyelids had disappeared since being given something useful to do.

'This way.' She'd been warned Rowdy was a man of very few words.

'What are we looking for?' she asked.

'Soil and vegetation changes. Depressions, cracks, new growth, disturbed plants. Anything older than three years will be almost impossible to detect.' Rowdy slowly roamed along the dunes. Every now and then he would squat and study the lay of the land. Rosie stuck with him and found the silence of his company peaceful.

It was at least an hour before Rowdy pointed to a slight divot in the side of a dune not far from the shack's existing garden area. 'Here. The area was dug up about twelve months ago.'

Rosie stuck a flag in the ground and looked up at him expectantly. He inclined his head away from their current position.

'Come with me.' He led her over two dunes. 'This plot of ground shows an increase in ruderal species and a reduction in stress tolerant ones.'

'Ruderal?'

'A ruderal species is a plant species that is first to colonize disturbed land. The disturbance may be natural – for example from a fire or an avalanche, or the consequences of human activities. Not much chance of an avalanche in these parts. There's no sign of a fire having gone through the bush in the last five years but animal or human activity can't be ruled out. This looks too big for animal.'

'Good man. Forensics can take it from here. Why don't you go join the others on the beach.' Rowdy gave her a long slow stare. The stress lines returned to the corners of his eyes. Rosie patted his arm.

'If you intend sticking around let me know. I could use someone with your skills.'

A smile lit up Rowdy's face. With a nod he strolled away.

# Chapter Forty-Five

Detective Bloom watched Shanks, Burger and Rowdy climb to the top of a small knoll. Ryan wanted to show his two companions what he considered the heart of Brahman Crossing – the homestead valley and discuss what Faith wanted to do with the property. Rosie understood that after her experiences her niece might have bad vibes about the place and want to sell but her advice had been to wait. Ryan's idea to renovate all the buildings was a good one. Not only would it add value to the property but the time and activity would give all three of them something fulfilling to do while they healed and found their place in life.

She took a deep breath. It was time to go confront a bear.

Bayden followed Ryan's detailed directions and drove them to the cabins. As they approached, she noted the outside of cabin two was quiet. A blue SUV was parked in the carport. She pointed. Bayden drew the police vehicle to a halt so it blocked the vehicle in. Rosie slid from the passenger's seat and double checked the number plate. It matched the one Shanks had asked her to check. She took a quick peak on the back seat and spotted a row of plastic tubs. Satisfaction swelled in her breast.

'Stay alert,' she murmured to the two police constables that accompanied them. Bayden took a step back to scan the area. She trusted him to cover her back.

Up close, Rosie noticed the woodwork around the building was beginning to weather and was in desperate need of sanding back and resealing. As she pounded on the door paint flaked from the eaves above. The door jerked open. A muscle-bound man, sporting a tattooed web across his bald scalp loomed over her. He wore a flour covered black apron. Rosie sniffed the delicious smell of baking that wafted out of the door.

'Very domestic,' she said, holding her badge aloft. 'Detective Rosie Bloom, Mount Ibour Police. This is Constables Bayden, Fort and Green.'

'Bloody, Jacks. What do you want?'

'And you are?'

'Spider O'Shaughnessy.'

'Well Mr O'Shaughnessy, I need to have a word with Robert Watson. Is he here?'

The muscle-bound neck bulged as O'Shaughnessy allowed it minimal movement to nod. 'And what about Mr Johnson?' The corner of his mouth tilted in a sneer as he nodded again.

'Excellent, saves me a search...no,' she said, when he opened his mouth, 'there's no need to announce us. Constable Fort, Constable Green, please escort Mr O'Shaughnessy out to the police vehicle to wait for us.'

'I need to get my baking from the oven,' growled Spider.

'Very well – Constables accompany Mr O'Shaughnessy to the kitchen. Keep him there.'

With a wave of his flour-coated beefy paw, Spider stepped aside to allow them passage inside. Rosie strolled into a combination kitchen, dining and lounge. It had been furnished like all holiday accommodation cabins around the world, with serviceable fittings and fixtures. These ones showed a great deal of wear and tear.

A buzzer on the oven sounded. 'I have to get that,' Spider said. With a jerk of his thumb, he indicated to a glass sliding door. 'You'll find Bear out on the deck.'

He dashed over to the oven and began pulling trays of mouth-watering pastries from the oven. On the bench sat two loaves of bread proving. Rosie grinned. So, not just the muscle, Spider O'Shaughnessy, it seemed, was a domestic goddess.

She stepped out onto the wooden deck. Bear Watson was leaning with his back propped against the deck rail. He had a cigar gripped between his forefinger and thumb. He took a puff and blew the smoke directly into the bruised face of a thin, rat-faced man who stood in front of him. Rosie recognised Russ Johnson from the video footage.

At first their presence wasn't noticed.

'I've had enough of this place. I want to get out of here?' whined Russ. 'I need money.'

'Shut it, will you, Rattler. Why the sudden rush. Has it got some-thing to do with your face? Because you certainly didn't look that bad when I saw you last. Did you have a fight with Cub?'

'No, I fell. Now how about some money?'

Mark's boot scraped on the door track. Bear must have caught the sound because he glanced their way. His shoulders straightened and his brows rose in surprise when he saw her.

A slow sneer crooked the corner of his mouth. 'Well, well, well,' he exclaimed. 'As I live and breathe, if it isn't the Silver Dingo her-self. I am honoured. Hello, Detective Bloom. It is detective these days, isn't it?'

Rosie nodded and kept the turmoil churning in her gut from showing on her face. It was hard being face to face with the man she suspected of ordering her husband's death and who also knew about the brutal treatment Faith had suffered and had done nothing to stop it, but she had a job to do. Her own feelings had to be put aside.

'Well, this is an unexpected surprise. What can I do for you, detective? Are you looking for sponsorship for the local blue light disco or perhaps for the women's shelter?'

'No, Mr Watson, though if it wasn't for people like you, we wouldn't need a women's shelter. At least there is now one less woman who requires their help.'

Bear's brows rose in an unspoken query but the smugness didn't leave his lips. 'I have no idea what you're talking about.'

'I believe you know my niece – Faith.'

'Ah yes, my very lovely daughter-in-law. If you're here to ask me where she and my recalcitrant son are at the moment, I can't oblige. All I know is they're still travelling and enjoying an extended honeymoon. The kids are so absorbed in each other they forget to call home and let me know where they are.'

Rattler, his red-eyes restless and hands twitchy began to sidle towards the door. 'I need to finish that crating, Bear...' Rosie flicked her chin towards him and Mark casually stepped into his path.

'Don't leave yet, Mr Johnson. We need to have a quiet word.'

Rosie kept a wary eye on Rattler as she delivered the news no parent wants to hear. 'No, Mr Watson I'm not here to ask about the whereabouts of your son or my niece. I'm sorry sir, it is my sad duty to inform you that your son, Ashley, is dead. At 11p.m. last night my partner and I discovered him murdered at the beachside shack where he's been living for the last twelve months.'

Bear's face paled. The cigar slid from his fingers. He reached out to grab the deck's handrail for support. The poorly maintained wooden rail creaked under his tight grip and flakes of wood fell to the ground.

His marble-white lips shook. 'A...a...are you sure it's my cub?' he asked.

'Yes, Mr Watson. I'm sure. I will need you to come to the morgue and make a formal identification, but I can tell you that it is definitely, Cub.'

'What did you jacks do?' he whispered.

'Not us, sir. He was already deceased when we found him and had been for some hours.'

Bear coughed to clear his throat, took a deep breath and asked with force. 'So how did he die?'

'Cause of death will have to be ascertained by an autopsy, but I can tell you he was badly bludgeoned with a skillet.'

Bear flicked a glance at Russ.

'That mole of a wife of his, it must have been her,' blurted out Rattler, wiping his sweaty hands down the front of his rust-stained tee-shirt. 'He was alright when I left yesterday.'

'You told me you hadn't been back to the shack. Not since you dropped off Patterson.'

'I haven't.'

Rosie stepped closer to Rattler. 'Is that a fact? Then explain to me how you knew Ashley was dead early this morning.'

'I didn't.'

'That won't wash. I have a witness who was staying at the Ranger's shack. He told me you were out searching for Faith early this morning and that you'd stated she'd killed her husband with a skillet.'

'Well, she did.'

'No, Mr Johnson. Mrs Watson did not kill her husband. You did!' said Rosie, pointing to the front of his tee. 'As those dried blood stains on your shirt will attest. You can't belt someone with a skillet a dozen times or more and then shoot them and not expect to get splashed. There will also be gunshot residue on your hand from when you placed your pistol in his mouth and pulled the trigger.'

'No, I didn't.' Russ began to back away. 'Bear I didn't. I would never hurt, Ashley. He was my best mate. What reason would I have?'

'You shot Ashley after he caught you trying to rape his wife.' Rosie held up a finger with a set of handcuffs dangling from it. 'Russell Johnson, I am arresting you for the murder of Ashley Watson. You are also wanted for questioning in regards to the murders of Samuel 'Slugger' Corvis and Morton Patterson. Charges relating to the passing of counterfeit Australian currency, assault and battery, and occasioning bodily harm to a Mr Alex Chippens in Perth in June this year will follow. Constable Bayden – read Mr Johnson his rights.'

'Russell Gordon Johnson, you have the right to remain silent...' Russ took two hurried steps back and whipped out a pistol from the small of his back. He waved it in Rosie's direction then at Bayden.

'Back off. Both of you. I'm not goin' nowhere,' snarled Russ. Rosie stilled and held her hands out with her palms upwards. 'Ashley deserved what he got. They all did. Faith should be mine. Cuz knew that, but took her anyway.'

Beside her Robert Watson took on the persona he was named for as he let out a grief-stricken roar. 'You bastard, you killed my precious cub.' He gave Rosie a hard shove aside and launched himself at Russ. She stumbled, lost her footing and fell hard against Bayden. Together they tumbled in a tangled heap amongst the outdoor chairs and cushions. As she fought to find her feet Rosie saw Bear lock one hand around his nephew's gun hand. His finger's whitened as he squeezed and twisted. The pistol dropped from

Russ's useless fingers, bounced on his foot and skidded across the floor. Russ grabbed the front of Bear's shirt and attempted a head butt. In retaliation Bear grabbed a handful of Russ's shirt and slammed him brutally against an upright post. The action stunned Russ long enough for Bear to grab him by the throat. Russ's red eyes bulged. A panicked look crossed his face. In a frantic attempt to free himself from the grip he threw a sideways punch which connected with Bear's ear. The older man lost balance but didn't ease his hold. Clenched together the men fell sideways and hit the deck railing. The force of the impact shattered the rotting wood. Bear gave a loud grunt and his fingers went slack. Russ took advantage and swung a clenched fist. In his haste he missed connecting with Bears chin, overbalanced and stepped out into open air.

Rosie made it to her feet and lurched forward. Hands outstretched she made a grab for Russ Johnson's flailing arm. Her fingers brushed skin, clamped and missed. With a blood-curdling scream Russ plummeted to the river below. Too late Rosie realised she had misjudged her step and was herself in danger of falling to her death. Arms windmilling, she attempted to pull herself back from the precipice. Gravity grabbed her and she felt herself tilting forward.

A strong arm clenched itself around her waist and yanked her back.

'Gotcha, Boss,' said Bayden, holding her tight against his chest.

'Thank you, Mark. That's not a dive I want to take in a hurry.'

She stared down to where she expected to see Russ's lifeless body floating face first in the water. He was gone. At her side Bear Watson gave a strange gurgle. Rosie flicked a glance at him. He was leaning awkwardly against the railing post. He gave a watery cough and a stream of blood trickled down his chin. She looked down. A splintered section of wood protruded from his stomach.

'Shit,' she exclaimed. 'Bayden, get on the radio. Get us some medical help. Now.' As Bayden turned to comply, she added, 'And get Shanks and Rowdy down here, pronto. I need their tracking skills to find Johnson.'

Mark charged towards the screen door. It flew open and Spider O'Shaughnessy almost knocked him over as he hastened out onto the deck.

He spotted Robert Watson and howled, 'Bear...'

As his beefy hands made a grab for the man, Rosie, stepped in the way to stop him. 'No, Spider. We can't move him. A piece of the wood has gone right through him. It is still attached to the pole. If we pull him off, he'll bleed to death before help arrives.'

Spider reached out and took hold of Bear's hand. With tears pooled in his eyes he stared at Rosie. 'What can I do to help?' he whispered.

'Do you have a saw? We could cut him away and then lower him to the floor. Make him more comfortable.'

Spider nodded. At that moment a shamefaced Constable Fort arrived.

'Sorry Detective, he got away from us.'

Rosie glared. 'We'll discuss this later. For now, go with Spider, help him find some tools. But first tell Green to get out here with the first aid kit.'

Fort nodded and hurried away.

Rosie took hold of Bear's abandoned hand with one of her own and offered some words of comfort. 'Hang in there, Robert, help is on the way.'

'It's too late for me,' he said, with a strangled gurgle. 'Did that little shit Russ really kill my cub?'

'Yes, Bear, he did. I'm so sorry. I know you really loved your son.'

'Yes, I did.' Robert's eyes roamed over her face. 'You loved Ian, didn't you?'

She nodded.

'There is something...'

Rosie's heart thumped hard in her chest. Was he finally going to tell her why he'd had her husband killed?

'Kids together...he was always kind...others not. Helped me out once when I really needed it,' he gasped. 'I swear Rosie, I had nothing to do with his death.'

'Well, who did? And why'd he have to die?' snapped Rosie.

'Ask ah..ah.ggggrey...grey...mmm...an.'

'Grey, grey what? Grey man, what grey man? Bear. Bear. Answer me, Bear.' There was no reply. Robert Watson had breathed his last.

'Shit,' snarled Rosie. Sometimes the universe sucked.

# 46

## Chapter Forty-Six

I leant against the police vehicle to watch Ryan and Rowdy, along with a contingent of police, head down a dirt track towards the stream below. Somewhere amongst the water-smoothed boulders and river-bank shrubs they hoped to find the body of Russ Johnson. If they did, then, for me, this whole nightmare could be over.

Constable Green left the shack escorting a weeping, Spider, to a police car. The handcuffs around Robert Watson's henchman's wrists look tiny in comparison to the man. As they stepped past me, I put out a consoling hand and let it rest on Spider's forearm for a moment. He gave me a fleeting smile of gratitude before he clambered into the vehicle. Green drove him away.

After the dust of their departure diminished, I made my way over to the top of the path so I could watch the activity below. Ryan and Rowdy were crouched down near the water's edge. They seemed to be discussing some marks on the ground. Suddenly the bush noises around me stilled to silence. A banksia shrub beside me rustled and a hand shot out from its leafy folds. My wrist was grabbed, twisted up and yanked. I swung around and came face-to-face with a gloating Russ Johnson. He leant in and leered.

'Hello, darlin'. You're coming with me.'

I screamed at the top of my lungs, 'No I'm not. Ryan, Aunt Rosie, help me! He's here...at the top of the path!'

Russ raised his hand. 'Quiet, bitch.'

My experiences of the last twelve months boiled over. I refused to go down that track again. I swung my plastered hand, as hard as I could, at his face. The hard casing connected with the bridge of his nose. The plaster split. Blood spurted everywhere. Russ fell to the ground screaming.

'My nose, you broke my fucking nose.'

'I'll break more than that if you ever come near me again.'

I took a hurried step back as footsteps pounded up the path with Ryan in the lead. He took everything in at a glance. He grinned and swooped me up into his loving arms.

'Way to go, Burger.'

Russ, hands clutched over his nose in an attempt to stem the flow of blood, rolled to his knees. His eyes zeroed in on me. He moved, ready to charge. Before he could, Aunt Rosie, dove onto him and ploughed him into the ground.

'Gotcha, you bastard,' she snarled as she roughly secured him with a set of handcuffs.

# 47

## Epilogue

Ryan's heart full of love, swelled as he glanced down at the woman at his side. Her newly re-plastered arm now hung in a sling. The bruises on her face and body had begun to fade but the ever-present fear in her eyes had been slower to retreat. At least her smile came more readily now. Together they were working on the fears and he looked forward to the day the sparkle returned to her eyes.

Today Faith had dressed in a simple floral silk dress. She had left her long caramel hair to hang loose around her shoulders and down her back. It fluttered in the warm breeze giving her a carefree look as she stood and watched the plane taxi along the air strip. He wrapped a gentle loving arm around her shoulder and for the thousandth time that morning checked in with her.

'All right, Cutie?'

Faith gave him her special smile.

'Yes, Ryan, I am. No nightmares last night. How about you?'

'No nightmares either. It helps that we have a plan for our future together.'

'Do you think my family understand our decision to stay here at Brahman Crossing while we do the place up? I don't feel like I belong in that old world, yet. Is it the same for you?'

'Yes, darling it is. And don't worry about your family. In fact, I know your Uncle Alex is looking forward to coming to stay so he can manage all those ill-gotten gains that you inherited from Ashley. He's dead keen to use the funds in a positive way.'

'It was very clever of Kelsey Morgan to find all that money.'

Ryan gave her an amused grin. 'Wasn't it just. And as Ashley hid it away under your maiden name it's not even subject to probate. It's yours free and clear - all ten million of it. Kelsey said there will be more, but it'll take time to trace it all.'

'No rush. When she finds it and it becomes available, we'll find positive ways to use the money. Maybe we can set up some sort of PTSD program, but that's all in the future. Tell me about your other friend?'

'Seadog. What do you want to know?'

'Do you think he minds dropping everything to come help us with all this work we've planned?'

Ryan laughed as the big man wandered over to join them. 'Rowdy. Tell Burger what Seadog did when you told him to get his butt and carpentry skills up here for the job.'

Rowdy gave an amused chuckle. 'Nearly overloaded the plane with handyman tools and equipment. Like there's no local hardware store nearby that we can pillage.'

Ryan was amazed at how much the prospect of renovating the Brahman homestead buildings and the promise to let him aid Rosie and the police with tracking work had bought Rowdy out of his silent shell.

'Much to Seadog's despair,' continued Rowdy, 'the Flight Lewie had to jettison a lot of his gear to fit in all Faith's cousins' luggage.'

'Flight Lewie? I'm confused. Who or what is a flight Lewie?' asked Faith.

'Chappie,' murmured Ryan. 'Flight Lewie is military slang for Flight Lieutenant.'

Faiths lips formed a cute circle. 'Oh, I see.'

Ryan resisted the urge to lean forward and kiss her. He didn't want to scare her. She wasn't yet ready for spontaneous displays of affection just yet.

'Alex complained to me on the phone last night that he'd been reduced to a small carry-on bag, because of all the stuff Chips has insisted on bringing with her. She claims it's all for you as a girl needs stuff.'

Faith rolled her eyes. 'She didn't have to. I don't need much. I've done without for a long time.'

'Let her have this, Faith. It's her way of showing you how much you mean to her. Besides I think she and Alex had a wonderful time shopping together for everything they think you need.'

'You talk a lot with my uncle, don't you?'

'During our stint in the hospital we became good friends. And, of course, the fact that we both love you so much also helps.' His cheeks heated under her intense stare. 'He's asked me to call him, Unk. Is that alright with you?'

A wide and carefree smile, the one he'd been waiting for, bloomed to life on Faith's face and a momentary sparkle lit her eyes. She lifted a hand and rubbed at her chest as if her heart was about to explode. 'Oh, yes,' she breathed. She gripped his hand and gave it a squeeze. 'Absolutely, YES.'

With a warm heart, Ryan, nodded to the now parked plane. Chips was in the cockpit madly waving at them.

'Ready?' he asked.

'Ready,' she replied.

The door to the plane opened. In a wave of love the Chippens family erupted and engulfed them both.

Born in New South Wales K.A. Hudson spent a major portion of her life working and travelling in rural Australia before settling in the beautiful, leafy suburb of Ellenbrook, where she spends her days writing intriguing mysteries.

Years living in remote areas has given her a wealth of experiences and insight into the unique Aussie character which she uses brilliantly to create wonderful, suspenseful and intriguing mysteries set in the alluring and breathtaking landscape of the Australian Outback.

In 2021 K.A. Hudson's debut novel, *Constant Fear; Strength Comes From Within*, was published. Set around the unique lifestyle of Melbourne and the W.A. goldfields of the 1970s it is an enthralling tale with a wonderfully authentic and likeable main character, whose plight grips our hearts and attention.

*Well of Bones; Revealing Hidden Secrets*, her much anticipated second novel, was released for publication in 2022 and introduced readers to the feisty and enduring Silver Dingo, Detective Rosie Bloom along with a raft of heart-warming characters who live and work on a remote cattle station in the Kimberley. In this captivating and fully charged tale a spate of local troubles morphs into something far more sinister.

The Silver Dingo returns in *Ruthless Obsession*. This time Detective Rosie Bloom will be faced with one of the biggest challenges of her policing career.

Constant Fear:
Strength Comes
From Within

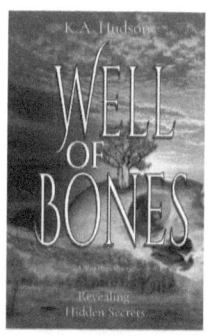

Well of Bones:
Revealing Hidden
Secrets